Almost the End of the World

Almost the End of the World

MIKE SCHLOSSBERG

An imprint of Roan & Weatherford Publishing Associates, LLC
Bentonville, Arkansas • Heber City, Utah
www.roanweatherford.com

Library of Congress Cataloging-in-Publication Data
Names: Schlossberg, Mike author.
Title: Almost the End of the World/Mike Schlossberg | The Perses Series#1
Description: First Edition | Bentonville: Mat Cat, 2026.
Identifiers: LCCN: 2025942891 | ISBN: 979-8-89299-069-1 (trade paperback) | ISBN: 979-8-89299-070-7 (eBook)
Subjects: BISAC: YOUNG ADULT FICTION/Loners & Outcasts YOUNG ADULT FICTION/Science Fiction/Apocalyptic & Post-Apocalyptic | YOUNG ADULT FICTION/Social Themes/Activism & Social Justice | LC record available at: https://lccn.loc.gov/2025942891

Mad Cat trade paperback edition June, 2026

Cover Design by Casey W. Cowan
Interior Design by Staci Troilo
Editing by Sabine Berlin, Laura Lauda & Ashlyn Carmichael

To my Dad:
I miss you so much.
But I will have good days.

To Cindy:
Your kindness lives on in your family.
You were just the greatest Mamat and MIL.

Chapter 1

A s a seventeen-year-old, I hadn't pondered my own death very often. Not until Perses, anyway.

Before then, on the rare occasion when my mind wandered toward my final moments and what lay beyond, I imagined myself as I hoped I would be—wrinkled, at peace, and surrounded by the people I had loved. The conclusion of a good life, a life well lived.

Apparently, instead, my death was going to come with my butt firmly lodged on my couch, a place where I had watched countless movies and played an unending parade of video games. It would come with my mom a few feet away, her hands clenching and unclenching. And we'd be watching CNN when we died, waiting for the impact of Perses.

The air outside was silent on this cold, January night. No trucks passed outside our rural home. No owls were in the air. No deer were leaping through my backyard. Even the bird feeder was bereft of other living things, though it was overflowing with food. It was as if the animals knew, somehow, and had all fled for greener pastures.

But there was nowhere to escape. That much had been made very clear to us over the past few months.

We all knew there was no hope, no matter what the President said. And, after all, hadn't we all been acting like it? The past sixteen weeks—sixteen weeks and five days if you want to be exact—had seen a nightmarish brigade of bad news. The riots and the banking collapse.

The hundreds and thousands of suicides every day, washing over us like a tide. The breakdown of law and order in large swaths of the country.

For the fifth time in the past few hours, I resisted the urge to stand up, shake my hands, and pace around my small living room. If this was the end of time, I didn't want my mom to die knowing just how scared I really was.

I'll say this—Mom went all out. She'd been squirreling away what little food we had left for a big, last meal feast. Baked ziti. Homemade ciabatta bread, my favorite, and homemade chocolate cookies that absolutely melted in your mouth.

When she'd taken out the plate of ketchup and put it in front of me, I had cracked and cried. That was from when I was a kid—when I excitedly made my own "peesa" from the "crust" she had baked. And through my tears, I'd ripped off a piece of bread, dipped it in the ketchup, and eaten it. She did the same, even if she couldn't make eye contact with me at that moment.

Looking at the kitchen, I whispered, "I don't have to wash them."

Mom's head turned slowly to me. Her eyes blinked with confusion. "What, Corey?"

Now, the remnants of dinner sat in the sink, and I glanced at the dishes. "I don't need to wash them."

Mom's gaze shifted from my face to the dishes, and her eyes closed for a moment. Then she blinked rapidly and looked back at the television.

Mom and I had chosen our usual seats to watch the end of the world, sitting on our well-worn couch. Mom would periodically glance at her phone, hooded eyes glancing surreptitiously at the glowing screen. We hadn't gotten good reception in the best of times, and now, as civilization fell apart, the notion of a text coming through was almost laughable. Even so, Mom stared, waiting for a call from Mack that we both knew probably wouldn't come.

We'd said goodbye earlier that morning, and Mack had held me up, gave me one of those bear hugs of his, and gruffly said, "Be good to her tonight." His face radiated pain like he was trying to cram a decade of love and memories into a moment.

"I will," I had said lamely, staring at a pair of brown eyes that looked ready to burst with everything left unsaid.

Mack, my father figure, and Mom's closest friend. I'd never see him again. There was almost no fuel left in his patrol car and the other three officers of the Robinette Police Department had called off, but Mack was out, on patrol. He'd be alone in the night when it came.

CNN was blaring on about the massive spike in religious services, how the Vatican City and Mecca and Jerusalem had overflow crowds so severe they were bursting at the seams. Like so much of the news lately, the shots were shaky and lacked their usual crispness. A username in the lower right-hand corner had appeared. *Courtesy of YouTube User SaintJimmy717*. I shifted. There hadn't been many camera shots taken by professionals lately. Most anchors, save for a few brave souls, had long since left to be with their families.

Abruptly, the camera cut back to the United States, revealing hospitals that were still astonishingly crowded. Death and illnesses didn't give a wit about anyone else's schedule—they came on their own when they were ready.

Somehow, the hospital CNN was covering was still fully staffed. And then an interview with a little girl, clutching a Kindle in a kiddie case like it was a teddy bear, revealed why. The doctors and nurses and technicians had brought their family to the hospital, so they could be together at the end of the world. There was an honor and a kindness at that moment that seemed incomprehensible. If the worldwide events of the past four months had been a cascade that sloped more and more violently downhill, this moment was a gentle glide into oblivion.

The corner of Mom's mouth was twisting upward like it did when she was about to launch into a rant. "You know this is the part where they veer into the compilation, right?"

I beat her to it. "Even at the end of the world, you gotta have a clip show."

Mom laughed. I'd miss that sound.

Would I? I had tried to keep myself busy for these past sixteen weeks and five days. It was the only way I could keep myself from thinking of the obvious. What came after Perses hit? But, now, as the Earth and its inhabitants lived their final hours, I couldn't help but feel the questions gnawing at the edge of my mind. I believed in God, more or less. Before all this, I always viewed Him or Her as some abstract concept that was beyond the understanding of our fragile little minds. Whatever the truth was, it would reveal itself when our time came. And besides, barring some tragic accident or genetic twist, I had time to consider my spiritual choices.

At least, that's what I had thought.

"Do you wish we didn't know?" I asked Mom.

"Hmm?" Mom was looking at the TV, which was now cycling through vigils around the world. Tokyo. Hong Kong. Even Beijing had released their normally strict controls against public rallies, and Tiananmen Square had never been so full. Wait, no, hadn't their government fallen last week? Were they on that list?

I brought my attention back to my question. "Do you wish that we didn't know the end of the world was coming? Do you wish this was just a normal night?"

Mom's brow furrowed and the creases on her cheeks deepened. In her silence, I stared at the television, which had now moved on to speculate about how large sections of the world had no idea. In the jungles of the Amazon, it was just another day. The Discovery Channel had sent a camera crew into one of those tribes to ask how they were handling the end of the world. The tribesmen had laughed it off. They had no concept of the world ending, no frame of reference to contemplate death on so large a scale.

"For me, no. For us, no. I'm glad we know what we know." Mom gestured at the TV. "But for everyone else, yeah. I wish they hadn't known."

I was about to ask what Mom meant, but I knew. We got to say goodbye. We had decided that, in the likely event that the Deflectors failed, we'd put our arms around each other and hold on. I had begun this world in my mom's arms, and I would exit it the same way.

But how many people would be denied that pain? How many thousands—millions?—had died in the riots and revolutions which had followed?

So many people hadn't been able to contemplate the end. So many had decided that waiting for Perses to hit wasn't an option, no matter what the Government said. I remember seeing some story about how the demand for painkillers was so pressing that the Government simply used its Martial Law Powers to stop their production. Of course, all that did was fuel a black market with demand so high that the feds changed their mind a week later.

And no one would be left to grieve. Bizarrely, I think that's what got me the most. We would all be dust and smoke, and no one would be left to mourn our collective lost future.

On TV, the smooth anchor was still talking, but for the first time all night, I actually felt like I needed to pay attention because the image had changed. The ten Deflectors were glowing, strategically placed up and down the East Coast of the United States, as per the instructions of the finest mathematicians in the world. They were squat little things, probably about a hundred feet high, hastily assembled on makeshift launchers that had been repositioned until the last moment. They looked like an awkward three-tiered cake, but with piping and vents jutting out in all directions. The ignitions were preparing for liftoff, with the ten glowing ships now thumbnail size in a grid. They took up the right half of the television, while some made-for-TV scientist prattled on the left side of the screen.

For all the doubt, every one of us who was still alive knew what was supposed to happen next. We'd paid attention, even as we tried not to, even as we tried to protect our final moments by shielding our hearts in cynicism. But it didn't matter because when hope fought cynicism, hope usually won.

So, we'd sat, listening to panels of experts on television and Twitter give us an overview of how the Deflectors were supposed to work. The

Deflector plan had been an international collaboration of every advanced nation in the world—well, except for Russia, which was still locked in some sort of civil war. Working at breakneck speeds, an effort that ultimately encompassed hundreds of thousands of people had built ten massive missiles. All ten would be shot up into space, and the nuclear-tipped missiles would impact Perses, and if the plan went right, they'd nudge the asteroid *just* wide, and life would go on. We could all get back to TikTok and Snapchat and whatever other inane pursuits distracted us before that freakishly warm day in September when all of our phones in Introduction to Psychology rang at the same time….

When Deflector One leaped into the sky, I wasn't thinking about the skeptics. I wasn't thinking of the countless scientists who had gone onto YouTube and Instagram, saying that the Deflector plan was a means of tranquilizing a panicked people, that it was the equivalent of shooting a gun at a cannonball and hoping that the bullet would alter the ball's trajectory. All I could think about was the thin chance that this would work. The most miniscule of possibilities that my life would not come to an abrupt end.

The still image of Deflector One was replaced by a cacophony of light and sound and thunder, and the image changed, tracking the squat ship as it arced into the night.

Mom and I usually sat on opposite ends of the couch. Not tonight, of course. Every life on this planet was about to be smothered, and neither of us planned to go without holding onto someone we loved. My fingers were clenched firmly in my mom's, and she returned her grip with an urgency that made me feel like a little boy again.

Deflector Two was next, and it jumped like a cartoon villain whose toes had touched lava.

The image repeated itself with Three, Four, and Five, the location of the Deflectors slowly traveling up the East Coast as each Deflector raced toward its date with eternity.

Deflector Six exploded on its launcher. Mom and I groaned and let go of each other's hands. The pressure which had been building in our small living room escaped, and I felt my hope seeping out of our poorly insulated walls.

I looked down. "That's it. That's all there is."

"Stop it, Corey. It can still work with nine. They said it."

I almost asked her the question I was thinking. What about with eight? Can it work with eight? Because you know that's not the only one which will blow up.

Two minutes later, Deflector Seven seemed to stutter on the launch pad, and I held my breath. But then there was another breath of fire, unleashed as if a dragon had poked its nose out of the engine and opened its meaty mouth to expose the flames inside. The Deflector took off like a bullet fired from a gun.

Eight and Nine launched without a hitch, and by the time Ten shot into the sky, I could feel the whole world holding its collective breath. Even CNN was silent, its seemingly ceaseless stream of narration finally falling victim to the tension of the moment.

From the northern tier of Maine, Ten blasted off, looking identical to Deflectors 1–5 and 7–9. Mom and I exhaled.

"And now, we wait," intoned CNN's Michael Gold. To my disbelief—I'd watched way too much CNN over the past few months—the screen was silent. Utterly silent and still. The blaring text at the bottom of the screen, *DEFLECTORS LAUNCH*, faded away, save for a small number in the lower right-hand corner of the screen which identified which launcher we were looking at.

Every ten seconds the image would change. Save for minuscule alterations in the angle of the Deflector we were staring at, the images were virtually identical. Nine Deflectors, racing to the stars. Nine Deflectors, Earth's salvation.

Somewhere, just off the site of the flaming wreckage of Deflector Six, I imagined a technician who had botched the launch. "What does that person feel like?" My voice had a dreamy quality to it, like I was listening to it from far away, disconnected from my body.

Mom knew what I meant, and when she spoke, her voice sounded like mine. "What about everyone who was hurt at that landing pad there? Is anyone taking care of them?"

My thoughts raced ahead. Is there really some random guy hiding in a closet, knowing they had been the one to make the mistake that would doom the planet? What did that weight feel like?

Oh, well. If that was the case, it was a pain that wouldn't last.

Abruptly, the screen changed, and blackness was the only visual. I let out a small scream—*The cable cuts out NOW?*—before realizing that the countdown clock was still running and the anchor was still talking. "The shot you see before you is a live view from the cone of Deflector One, just off of the nuclear missile sitting at its top."

"Jesus," Mom said.

"I didn't know they had that," I responded.

"I don't think anybody did." Mom shifted uncomfortably. "At least we'll know pretty quick if this thing worked or not."

"Everything I saw on TikTok said that no one really thought the Deflectors would make an impact," I said. "Too many variables and not enough time or technology to make it work."

"So did just about everyone on the Perses subreddit," Mom said. The countdown meter was at less than thirty seconds now. When it got to twenty, Mom added, "One way or another…." Her voice slid away, fading like a ghost in the night.

There was a flash of light and impact on the television, and then nothing else.

I screamed and leapt off of the couch. "Holy hell!" Chills shot down my arms, leaving me feeling like they were being scratched from the inside. "Did that just hit? Did the Deflector hit?"

The television cut to Gold, who had managed to keep his composure. "We can't be positive until we get confirmation—" Gold paused, and his head tilted just slightly to the left. "All right. Yes. Deflector One impacted on Perses."

I sat back down, suddenly out of breath, trying desperately to avoid climbing the ladder of hope that had been placed in front of me, even though I was already on the first rung. Every skeptic had said that the Deflector plan was insane. Every Deflector was supposed to sail harmlessly into space if they got off the ground at all. Well, they were one-tenth right on that front. But, the first Deflector had hit.

On CNN, the text returned, *DEFLECTOR ONE IMPACTS PERSES* and smaller text below that, *Eight Deflectors remain.*

Insanely, a split-screen cut to Times Square, where a crowd of nervous onlookers seemed to be writhing as one. A new countdown clock appeared. Deflector Two. Less than a minute until impact.

Deflector Two hit as well. A smidge of joy crept into Gold's voice.

By the time Deflector Five hit, Gold was standing in front of a massive graphic of the Earth, the egg-shaped Perses, and two lines. "We hadn't shown this graphic before, but here it is."

"Remember, if all four of the remaining Deflectors do impact Perses, that's not enough to confirm that we will avoid impact. While many scientists believe that it will do the job, it's not as if we've ever tested this before, and there are many doubters. So, we bring you this. A live feed, directly from NASA's own computing and satellite network." Gold gestured behind him, and the upper line glowed. "If the Deflector Mission has been a success, Perses will track along this line. If it hasn't…." Gold clasped his hands and placed them at his waist. "If it hasn't, Perses will track here. And we'll know."

The camera cut back to Deflector Seven, and when it impacted, I swear I was able to see rocks and sparks for a millisecond.

"Can you get anything on Twitter?" Mom asked, looking at her phone, still steadfastly refusing to call the service X. "I'm trying to see if there's anything coming out of NASA."

I took my phone out and quickly clicked away from the low battery warning. Twitter opened, and to my pleasant surprise, reloaded a slew of new content. No ads, for once.

I frantically read my timeline, clinging to the scraps of information like a starving child scrounging for bread. "NASA Observer says that he saw the Project Director run out of the room on a secure cell phone." *How does this guy know what a secure cell phone looks like?* "And that grey-haired woman from CBS reports that you could hear the control room scream with joy every time a Deflector hit."

"Speaking of, Eight impacted."

By the time I looked up, the camera had reset to Deflector Nine. "Two to go. And as for NASA Observer, come on. That's the kind of useless piece of information which could…." Mom started to laugh mirthlessly. "Well, I suppose that could throw the world into chaos, but that's silly, isn't it?"

Deflector Nine hit. One left. On the TV, Gold was silent again. And he was still silent, even in the immediate seconds after Ten made impact.

"This wasn't supposed to happen," I said, staring diligently at the television.

"No. Not at all." Mom leaned on her knees, her face somehow down-shifting to calm. I watched her, trying to read her inscrutable expression. How many times over the course of the past few months had we seen each other cry? As long as I'd live—if it was another two hours or eight decades—I'd never forget the way her face had shattered like broken glass when Mack dropped me off four months ago, my senior year at Augustus disappearing like smoke….

It had all been reduced to this. Humanity, linked in our impending demise, watching CNN or Fox or YouTube or Twitch, waiting for news on whether or not we'd see the sun again.

We were squinting at the TV now, trying to discern the slightest movement of the digital Perses on CNN's graphic. On our flat screen, it looked like it was the size of a quarter, and finally, I realized I couldn't see it properly from the couch. I leaned forward and looked at Mom. She nodded, and with me, we shuffled forward on our knees, approaching the television, our eyes now locked onto the particular arrangement of pixels that would determine whether or not we had a future.

We were halfway toward the television set when Perses ticked, ever so slightly, on the upward trajectory.

We stopped moving abruptly. Mom grabbed my wrist before I could take her hand.

"Come. On." The growl in Mom's voice had a quality in it I had never heard before—somewhere stuck between fear and desperation.

I was trying to talk, but the words were stuck in the back of my throat. I was not supposed to see Augustus again. Not hear my best friend Sid's stories about what his coach had done to abuse the team. Not supposed to be able to feel the grief of losing Josh earlier in the year, of knowing that our last day at Augustus would be our last day together. Not watch the twins Mo and Mika bounce off the walls, their goofy smiles radiating across campus. Not stare awkwardly at girls and wonder what I didn't know or feel the exquisite amalgamation of terror and joy when I threw my hat into the air at graduation, celebrating my entry to the real world. I was supposed to be part of a historical footnote, one of the billions of boys who had the misfortune of being born during the last days of Planet Earth....

No, there was no mistaking it. Perses had moved forward a few more ticks. It was absolutely moving on the upward track.

Mom let out a mixture of a laugh and a cry.

I didn't move. I absolutely, positively didn't move, scared to death that the slightest twitch of my fingers would reset the nightmare and I'd be back to staring at my own demise.

When Perses moved another couple of centimeters, I was finally able to choke out, "No way."

Mom was giggling and had brought her hands to her face. Tears were streaking down them. Mom's hand shot out, desperately clasping my shoulder. "Way."

Outside, dull booms filled the night sky over Robinette. I couldn't tell if they were gunshots or fireworks. Both. Probably both.

Michael Gold appeared in the bottom right of the screen. His trademark black glasses were off. His eyes were glistening. "We have yet to receive official confirmation—" In the background, there were whoops and wails as everyone in the studio behind Gold absolutely, positively lost their minds. "Quiet, quiet." There was no anger in Gold's voice. "We haven't received official confirmation from NASA, but multiple, highly placed sources within the federal government and NASA are telling CNN that the Deflector mission was a success, that Perses will skip past the top of the planet and miss us by roughly ten thousand miles, which is a hair in relative terms…."

The shot changed. Every human in Times Square was simultaneously jumping, hugging, and probably damn near exploding with joy.

In Beijing, the cultural divide between America and China had evaporated. The formerly silent crowds were now weeping in relief. I could see the individual people on their knees, clutching their chests with joy.

In Australia, fireworks above the Sydney Opera House. In Paris, the same, these above the Eiffel Tower. And on CNN, the text graphic blared, *WORLD SAVED—PERSES WILL MISS.*

The tears poured down my face, but my nerves were far, far too blasted for me to determine why. Was I crying for a future that had suddenly reappeared in front of me, as if the curtain which had been covering it had suddenly been pulled back? Was I crying for the dead, for all the troops who had died in the riots and all those who had ended their lives before Perses could take it?

Or was I crying for the simple reason that Mom and I would get to eat breakfast in the morning?

Mom squealed next to me as she stared at her phone. There were two notifications. *President to address nation momentarily* from Apple News and a text from Mack. Mom opened the text and laughed as she showed it to me.

Have the good stuff. See you tomorrow. Tell Corey I love him.

I laughed. Mack only said that from time to time. This seemed like a good time. I was also puzzled.

"The good stuff?"

Mom was already across the living room, thundering her way into the basement. I could hear her opening the freezer. When she trundled back up the stairs, she was holding a bottle of amber liquid and two glasses. She drew closer, and I laughed. Johnny Walker Blue. The glasses had ice in them, and with shaking hands, Mom poured the whisky into the tumbler she had thrust into my hands. A moment later her glass was filled too.

Mom took a deep breath, her expression even. "You get your future now, Corey. You get your future." And her face dissolved into a sea of tears and joy and exorcised pain.

On television, the scene had changed. The seal of the President of the United States had appeared, before dissolving to a shot of the President. *"My fellow Americans,"* the President began, his voice crisp and bright, his smile extending from ear to ear, those big, shiny teeth wide and bright. *"Our story has always been one of resilience. Tonight, that story goes into the next unexpected chapter."*

Mom and I clinked glasses, toasting wordlessly. I took one hell of a pull from the Johnny Walker Blue. It tasted like fire and life.

Chapter 2

Ow. Ow, ow, ow. God damnit, ow.

My head *really* hurt.

I finally opened my eyes, groaning. The sun was streaking in from high in my bedroom window, its golden rays catching me square in the face. I groaned and flung an arm over my eyes, dimly aware that the sun only shone that brightly when the afternoon had arrived.

My mind wandered, searching for the familiar, internalized sensation of grief and sadness and despair at the impending death of everything I had ever known and hadn't known… and my heart slipped away from that pain as if it had been covered in grease.

"Oh," I whispered, and a single tear ran down my cheek. I wanted to feel elated, but I just felt dust inside. I think the past few months—and really, few weeks, and then a few days—had just nuked my capacity to feel any emotion other than doom.

At that point, I smelled flour and sugar and butter. Mom actually *had* sugar and butter?

With a heave, I hauled myself out of bed, stumbled into my sweatpants, and threw on a tank top, trying to ignore the uncoordinated nature of my limbs, and particularly my left arm, which kept sliding into the space where my head was supposed to go. *See, this is why I don't drink. I feel like I've been hit in the head with a hammer.* Oh well. At least Mom would probably be as miserable as me.

Nope. By the time I remembered how sleeveless shirts worked, I was able to drag myself into the kitchen. Mom looked as bright and sunny as the weather outside. She had done her hair, the first time I'd seen her do that since she stopped going into work, put on a light coat of makeup, and was dancing around the kitchen, hopping from the skillet to the frying pan. "Good morning, Cor."

I stared at the food for a moment. It looked like bacon. But it didn't smell like bacon.

Sensing my confusion, a wry smile appeared on Mom's face. "Veggie bacon."

"Ahh. That explains the… yeah. Ahh."

"Shut up and enjoy your veggie bacon. It was all I could get, and it will help absorb the booze." Abruptly, she dropped her spatula in the bowl, the instrument clanking as it dropped, and I swore for a moment that my head was going to explode.

"Ahh. Loud," I groaned.

Mom snickered. "You really have been good at school if you are in that much pain."

I smiled wanly. "I actually listened to you. The drunks were never that fun. They spent so much time drinking their faces off that you couldn't figure out who they really were. That being said, right now, I wish I'd drunk a little more at Augustus. I suspect my head would hurt a little less."

"Well, this will help." Mom slid a plate of pancakes and bacon in front of me. My mouth began to water like a faucet that had been fully loosened.

"Oh, dear Lord, that looks good," I said. "Only thing missing—"
Plop. Mom placed a can of cherry filling in front of me, its top opened and dripping with goop.

"Pie filling definitely helps hangovers," Mom said. Despite my slowed reflexes, I figured out how to turn the can over and unload a third of the can on my pancakes. "Really?"

"Let me eat my cherry filling in peace."

With a smile, Mom sat down next to me, her plate filled with bacon, and brushed a loose strand of blonde hair out of her face.

"I'd kill for coffee right now," I said.

"Me too." Mom jammed a forkful of pancakes into her mouth, closed her eyes, and savored the taste. "Hey."

"Hmm?" There was pie filling all over my face. I suspect it looked like I had a red mustache.

"It's January fourth." Tears welled in Mom's eyes all over again. "Corey. It's January fourth. We were not supposed to see today."

I looked away. My eyes still hurt. I didn't want to cry again. I knew I would, later. But not now. Instead, I took Mom's hand and looked out the window, squinting, trying to see the Ford's house through our kitchen window.

"Wonder what they're up to now?"

Mom looked out the window and followed my gaze, wiping the tears from her eyes. "Nothing good. Last time I saw Jason he did not look like he was handling things well."

"Yeah. But who among us looked like they were doing okay?"

"That, my son, is a very good question."

"And speaking of, have you heard from Mack?" A slight ache was forming in my chest, the same ache I'd been fighting off ever since I'd been old enough to ask that question.

Mom was mid-bite, but she nodded. "Yes. We should see him later today when the State Police are able to make it in. Said the worst he had to deal with were naked drunks."

I shivered. "That… that does not sound good."

"It does not." Mom was laughing. "I'm just glad it wasn't worse."

Mom and I spent the next few hours on the couch, digesting. I realized that Mom was in a lot more pain than she let on, and she kept opening and closing her eyes as if caught between sleep and being awake. Obviously, neither of us had slept particularly well over the past few days.

We watched CNN, which seemed stuck in an epic mode of celebration. The anchors looked brighter and peppier than usual, almost as they had before the world's trajectory had taken such an ugly turn. The party at Times Square was still going, and the only thing which had shifted was the people, and everyone was jumping and dancing as if it was New Year's Eve. Religious leaders across the world were expressing thanks and gratitude toward God, discussing how our prayers had been answered and we had been spared the fire.

After twenty minutes, however, the tone of the news shifted, and Mom leaned forward. "Trouble."

"Yeah." CNN was cutting between shots of shootings and whole neighborhoods in flames. The images were a mash of human suffering—whole neighborhoods, city blocks, completely engulfed. Weeping families, clutching meager possessions.

And not a cop in sight.

I shifted uncomfortably. "Well, at least they aren't covering mass suicides anymore." Then I shook my head. "I'm glad I'm here." My mind traveled to the terror-filled nights that had led up to the events of yesterday. How the truck sounds outside our home had slowed to almost nothing, save for the occasional rumbling of military hardware. How gunshots had periodically filled our evenings, and then as Perses's impact got closer, our daytime. "I'm glad this is the only place I needed to be."

And then, the guilt. I had stayed at home, playing video games, donating blood twice, and waiting. Waiting for the end. I'd had that luxury… the luxury to be able to stay with my mom. To make sure she was safe.

Mom's eyes were closed, unaware of my most recent descent into the bowels of my mind. Her eyelids scrunched against her cheeks as if she was actively trying to block out the light.

On CNN, a monotone group in purple robes was chanting rhythmically, clutching fistfuls of flowers in one hand, pistols in the other. Behind them, flames roared demonically.

With a disgusted snap, Mom shut off the television, and the mobs in purple disappeared, taking their destructive flames with them. By now, the sun was threatening to dip below the tree line, and the first dull glimmers of the night were starting to shake their way through a shade. Mom stood, cracked her neck, and walked toward the door. "Let's get out of here. Go for a walk?"

"God, yes."

Mom waved her hand to the door, and I eagerly stomped into my shoes.

We walked a few blocks down the winding road which led into the heart of our small town, each lost in our own thoughts. The cold air was blistering, and I was grateful to be wearing the retro leather jacket which I had grabbed at a thrift store last year. It was at least thirty years old and still kept me warm. I flexed my fingers in my pockets. Balled them into fists. Marveled as we walked westward, toward the setting sun.

Mom, for her part, seemed to be in some sort of partial euphoria. There was a skip in her step. And I mean that literally—she actually took a child-like skip every few steps or so.

"Jeez, calm yourself, will you? It's not like they maintained this road under the best of circumstances." My voice trailed off, thinking of the flat tire my dad earned on this very road a decade ago.

Mom's mind must have gone there too, and I watched her fingers twitch reflexively. Then she forced a smile. "For all I know, it could have been that pothole there." She gestured toward a gaping hole in the middle of the street. "It's not like Robinette is known for its crack public works department."

Silence reigned as we both briefly fell into our own memories.

"If it wasn't that pothole, it would have been something else, Mom. Burnt toast. Spilled coffee. It was how he was made."

Mom's voice was steady when she spoke. "That day brought us Mack. It bought us freedom. It started us to where we are now." There was a pause as if Mom was struggling to put the words together—something I didn't usually see out of her. We walked on in silence for a moment, and I stared at the power lines that bracketed the streets, watching the birds, envying their ignorance. Then, Mom said, "Jim would never recognize you. Everything he had, you don't. We're very lucky, you and I."

"Luck feels strange sometimes."

"Sometimes, luck is just fear managed." Mom's voice retained a firmness that felt beyond me at that moment.

There were other things about that period that did not bear repeating, ground we had already trod a thousand times. I remembered Mom screaming at the insurance company. I remembered her weeping softly at night, the strain of the court appearances grinding on her. I remembered the flashbacks—the indentation on my forehead from where my dad's wedding ring had cut soft flesh, following by a blinding pain as my right temple hit the corner of the television stand. Scattered figments of my recollections from that period stumbled across words like "insurance" and "children's healthcare" and demands that I see that doctor in Philadelphia.

Mom sighed.

I looked at her. "What?"

"I miss the Beacon."

Oh. Our local diner. Somehow, they had remained open until a month ago, even accepting credit card payments long after most merchants had stopped. I thought about a chicken gyro and French fries and those insanely sour pickles you couldn't get anywhere else. In my mind's eye, I could see it. The thin parchment paper they used to keep the gyro from falling apart and turning your lap into a tzatziki-covered mess. The feel of the well-worn buttons on the diner's Pacman game, original from the 80s, and somehow still running.

"Yeah. I'd kill to eat there," I said. A slice of my childhood was gone forever.

Mom paused for a second, biting her lip thoughtfully. She brought her phone up to her ear. "We gotta eat, and the cupboard is a little bare. Let me try this."

I pondered the loss of the Beacon. How many childhood days? How many moments with friends? Hell, I'd taken Sid and Josh there over Christmas break last year. We closed the place down, laughing over gravy fries. Mr. Nostos practically had to carry us out.

The memories brought more blackness. I hadn't heard from Sid in days.

Mom's surprised voice brought me back. "Mack."

A minute later, the call ended. Mom turned to me and said, "All right, got him. He said he found a Wendy's that is open."

"That sounds amazing," I said. "And, surprising. They haven't been open all week."

"Apparently, some corporations were preparing for the world continuing, just in case," Mom said.

And Mr. Nostos couldn't. I wonder where he is now.

Mom must have read the look on my face. "Hopefully there's a place for Mister Nostos and his family in whatever comes next. Let's get back. I'm freezing."

《◇》

THE SUN HAD almost disappeared by the time we were back home. Mom turned on the news, but when it flashed to stories about the abrupt rise of abortions during the Perses Fall, she shut it off with an angry snap. "I can't. I just can't. Let's just sit here."

I almost took my phone out before deciding against it. Mom was right. No more news for a while. Instead, I closed my eyes, enjoying the companionable silence as Mom took a book off the shelf and began to read. She hadn't picked up a single book after Wikileaks, saying that the thought of having an expiration date on the amount of time she had to read was too tragic to comprehend.

I stared at her until my eyes grew blurry. When I opened them again, headlights were in the window.

"I was about to call him. I'm starving and we're out of bacon," Mom said.

"That's tragic."

"Quite. No one should ever be out of bacon. I can't wait until Giant opens again," Mom said.

Mack got out of his cop car, making the familiar and brief trek up our driveway and front stairs.

Mack was in his duty shirt, but it was almost as wrinkled as the paper bag that held our dinner, which, by the way, smelled ridiculously awesome. Mack had a gray mane that was usually parted off to the side, but today, his hair spiked in random spots, like his hat had been on for too long.

Mom kissed Mack a greeting on the cheek, and I caught her eyes welling up. Mack closed his eyes for a moment before holding Mom at arm's length.

"Have you been home yet?" Mom asked.

"Too quickly, but yes. Jill is fine, sends her love, and told me to give you explicit instructions. 'Tell Cara I better not see her tonight.'"

Mom laughed. "Busy night for her?"

"Oddly, no," Mack said. "According to the missus, the patient load dropped since yesterday. No one wants to die at a hospital when the world isn't ending." Mack released Mom and looked at me. "Little Man."

"Bigger Man." I nodded once. And then my eyes broke open like a window shattered, and I folded myself into his arms. Mack wrapped his around me, and even though I was adult-sized, and he in his mid-fifties, he lifted me off my toes.

When Mack released me, his eyes were sparkling, and he slapped my shoulder hard. "How about that, huh?" The words were weighted, as if they could encompass everything we were feeling and thinking at that unlikely moment.

"How about it," I echoed. Then I grabbed the Wendy's bag out of his hand. "Yoink."

Mom, who still had quicker reflexes than me, snapped the bag out of my fingers before I even realized what had happened. Without a word, she dug into the bag and handed Mack his food, a grilled chicken sandwich, and baked potato. I vaguely remember Mack had been trying to eat healthier before Perses had nearly ended the world.

We moved to the dining room, and Mom went to get drinks.

"I can't stay for long," Mack called after Mom. "We're still waiting on more staties to arrive."

"You get any of your guys back?" Mom asked.

"One of them, yeah. Frank. I can't find the other two yet." Mack stared holes into the wall behind me.

"That's better than nothing," I said. Mack was digging into his sandwich with gusto. I could tell it was missing some of the usual fixings. Honestly, Mack was probably just happy that it had meat and a bun.

"It is," he said. "I'm relieved we haven't had any real problems yet. Even our usual hot spots are relatively quiet."

I tapped my phone. "Doesn't seem like most of the rest of the world is handling it that way."

Mack nodded thoughtfully as he chewed. "Yeah." He picked up a piece of chicken that had dropped onto the table, adding it to the baked potato, and popping the adlibbed sandwich into his mouth.

"Gross," I said.

Mack shrugged. "May it be the worst thing you see in the next few weeks, Little Man."

"What's the worst you've seen out there?" Mom asked, sitting down and handing Mack a glass of water.

Mack gestured his head to the side as I jammed a fistful of fries in my mouth. God. I always liked French fries, but they tasted much, much better than usual. The salt levels were perfect. The fries had been fried to perfection, crispy on the outside, hot enough that they burned my mouth once I took an oily bite. "It hasn't been as bad as I was worried. Not yet, anyway."

"Any reason for that?" Mom asked.

Mack paused, considering his words carefully, deliberately. It was a trait I always appreciated about him. Maybe it was from his time in the police force, or his time in the military, but he always thought about what he said. Every word had meaning and purpose. "I suspect that the rural nature of Robinette is helping. Isolated people are less troublesome in difficult situations. But that isolation often leads to problems in and of itself."

I started to ask Mack what he meant by that when he abruptly changed the subject. "I was communicating with some of the rest of the folks in the state today. Sounds like there was no real trouble in Northampton. Augustus is just fine."

"Good to know," Mom said, nodding approvingly. "It was in a nicer part of town."

I stared from Mom to Mack. What was this? "It was," I said, warily.

Mom and Mack exchanged glances, and it clicked.

"Oh, you've got to be kidding me!" I pushed my food away from me. "You want me to go back to school? Now? Really?" The words were out of my mouth before I realized what I had said.

The corner of Mack's lip trailed upward, like the kid whose hand had been caught in the cookie jar. I'd seen that look before. When I wanted to go swimming in the old quarry and Mack told me about the accident that had happened in the southern part of the state, with the two dead kids. Or when I became friendly with B.J. Barry in elementary school and Mack let it slip that Mom shouldn't let me hang out at B.J.'s house, thanks to his dad, who was under suspicion for many, many crimes.

"This is our first dinner since the apocalypse was supposed to happen. Can you not bring in the heavy guns before trying to make sure I go back to boarding school?"

"We're almost at twenty-four hours," Mom protested meekly.

"There's no way the school opens anyway. Not for a while."

Mom opened her mouth to protest again, but Mack spoke first. "I wouldn't be so sure about that, Little Man."

Oh? I looked at Mack. He had placed the food neatly down in front of him. He continued, "I know this caught a lot of people by surprise, the Deflectors working, but not everybody. We haven't thought about this in a while, but the world will spin on." When I stared at Mack, my head tilted to the side like a confused puppy, Mack rubbed his thumb against his pointer and middle fingers. "Money, kid. Money. The world is still in a state of euphoria and shock, but at some point, the stuff that keeps the world going is going to need to start moving again. It's going to take some time, yeah. But the world will go on, and the sooner we can all get back to running like we're supposed to, the better."

"I don't know, Mack."

"I do," Mack said. "Watch. They'll open that school and all the others around it as soon as they can get enough teachers to march through the doors. I guarantee it."

Mack's words startled me with their certainty, adding to the burning sensation in my chest. I shook my head. "Uh-uh. No way." My eyes began widening as if they were out of my own control.

"Why?" Mom asked gently.

"Because I will not leave you here, now." It was a quick answer. Too quick. Without even realizing it, I had my hands clutching the dining room table, digging my fingers into the laminate surface, the smoothness yielding to the sharpness of my fingernails. "School won't be what it was."

I knew that second statement was true. I knew kids were gone and never coming back, and I thought of Josh and what he'd probably endured in his final hours. Josh wasn't the only dead one. There were others. So many others.

Mom reached over and took my hand. "Corey. I don't want you to stare at these walls while the world restarts. We're not there yet, but we will be. I want to get back to work. I actually miss it. TikTok. Instagram. Facebook. Corey, I miss Facebook. No one misses Facebook."

I laughed, but it was a hollow sound, and both Mom and Mack couldn't have missed the terror in my eyes.

"Corey, we don't have to make a decision now. We just think it's something you should keep in mind," said Mack.

"That's all, Cor," said Mom. "We can talk more about it later."

I nodded tightly, but my head was ablaze. Mack was right. The world would restart, and time would begin to flow again.

I just wasn't sure what was out there.

There were so many people who I'd never see at school again. So many red blazers that would never be worn, so many kids whose parents had moved into palatial survival bunkers or who had died trying to get into one. How many would really be back at the school? What would remain of a place that I had come to love?

Chapter 3

I DIDN'T HEAR the key enter the lock of my front door, but I did hear when Mack entered. "Little Man!"

I was so absorbed in Call of Duty that I dropped my controller. "Jesus Christ, Mack." I moved my headset to ignore the streams of inappropriately combined expletives pouring from the mouth of the twelve-year-old who was on my team. It was then that I realized that Mack was holding… oh, God. Was that what I thought it was?

It was. And that explained why Mack was smiling so broadly. "Come on. Get in."

"Come on, Mack, I'm a little old for this, aren't I?"

"Nope," Mack tossed the old police uniform at me. It landed over my head, blocking my view of the game. I assume that resulted in more four-letter words that ended with "stick," but I couldn't tell, as the throw had knocked my headset off. I sighed.

"Fine, fine, but this isn't still gonna fit me. I haven't worn it in years."

"Let's get some fresh air. Not as if there are a bunch of people traveling the country roads."

"Do I have to go outside?" I threw a measure of whining into my voice, hoping it would cover up the seriousness that my words conveyed.

No dice. Mack waved his hands and eyed me. "Little Man. Has the police car ever failed you?"

I rolled my eyes. Mack was in peak Dad-mode. "No, Bigger Man." The first time I had been in Mack's car, I was a concussion victim and had spent the drive to the hospital lolling in and out of consciousness, my whaling mother screaming at me to stay with her. Frightened by the experience, a younger me cringed every time I saw a police car. So, Mack came up with an idea—exposure therapy. He'd made a whole show of it. Brought me down to the police station, thrown me in a deputy uniform, and gotten the entire force to "deputize" me.

I think Mack's superiors expected a drive around the block and a trip to the Dairy Queen. Imagine their surprise when we came back an hour later... and then didn't get out of the car for another ten minutes because I was nestled in Mack's lap, playing with various switches and buttons and turning the lights and sirens on and off. I remember feeling simultaneously in awe of the machinery in front of me and utterly terrified that the moment would abruptly change... that I'd be dragged out of the car by angry officers. That the moment of peace, of joy, of protection, would be ripped out of my hands.

That first trip was just the start, and we'd spent many nights on patrol together. I'd never answered a call with him, though my instructions before any ride-along were the same. If there is a call, stay in the car. Don't move.

On these trips, we just drove through our sleepy town. We talked about Mom. About girls. About life.

So, I walked off to my bedroom, changed, and said goodbye to Mom. The next thing I knew, I was in Mack's patrol car, the cold night air tickling my face as Mack cracked the window. Mack accelerated down Wellington Road, gaining speed as he rounded the bend.

"Thanks. I think I needed this," I said.

"No one should be cooped up in their house too long," Mack easily slid his hands over the steering wheel.

"Agreed." I looked north, toward the direction of town. "How's it been?"

To my surprise, Mack's face crinkled, but just for a moment. "Fine." He refused to meet my eyes. "All right. Maybe not so fine."

"What's up?"

"Just a bit more tension than usual."

I realized by the twang that captured his voice when he said "tension" that his accent was back. Mack was from outside Atlanta, and his accent only sneaked into his voice when his mind went elsewhere.

I gestured toward town. "You mean the drunks?"

Mack waved his hand. "That's nothing out of the ordinary. Nah. We've had two domestic violence cases in the past week. One the day after Perses missed."

"Is that different than usual?"

Mack nodded slowly. "It is."

Now I was confused. "That's terrible and all, Mack, but why does that have your face twisted and your Georgia back?"

Mack ignored my gentle dig. "Little Man. Do you know what makes domestic violence spike?"

"No idea."

"It increases when men are unemployed. During recessions. During times of crisis." Mack's twang was deepening. "My point, Corey, is that it's a canary in a coal mine. Yeah, there are more drunks. But men are hitting women more. And as if that isn't terrible enough itself, it's a sign of something deeper."

I shivered, trying to cover just how sick I felt. The truth was that I could see it because I'd lived it. I could picture an emotionally broken woman, cowering in front of a man in a beer-stained t-shirt, a flat-screen television blaring in the background....

I could feel the bottom drop out of my stomach, and it wasn't just the pothole. I stared out the window at the starry night. The stars shone brighter in the cloudless sky than I remember seeing them before Perses. In some places, their reflection was so bright that they shimmered off the layer of ice that blanketed the ground.

We chatted more about the town and what Mack had seen the past week—the arrests and the quiet. Three of the four men on the force were back, and the state police had now started working regularly, providing aid as needed. That was a welcome relief to Mack. I could see the tension easing off his face as he spoke about having the extra help. Our town didn't have a ton of people—probably no more than a few thousand—but it was large and rural and empty. That meant an awful lot of ground to cover.

"Mom seems to be doing good," Mack said.

"She is. I think she's itching to get back to work though."

"They call her yet?"

"Yeah, her boss did the other day." Mom worked at a marketing agency in Scranton, the closest big city, probably about forty-five minutes away. "He said he's going to bring her back as soon as possible, but there's no work yet."

"That's better than nothing. Better than what a lot of folks out here have, as best I can gather. Seems like it's going to take an awfully long time before the economy really restarts."

"Government's going to have to step in," I mumbled. The truth was that I was worried about money. We'd been dirt-poor after my dad's arrest, but Mom had taken classes at night and had gotten a decent job. We'd never been rich, but we'd always been okay. I know Mom had dug into her savings to get us to the end of the world… and figured she hadn't budgeted much for an afterward that probably would never happen.

I chuckled without smiling. "Seems like no one is in the mood for memes yet, and that's a shame. I loved being able to tell my friends at school what on the internet was going to be popular before they knew."

"Speaking of school—"

"Mack. Please."

"We have to, Corey." Mack's voice was firm.

My hands leaped out of my lap like they had been shocked. "Mack, come on." I looked at him, trying to read his face in between the blurs of light that were thrown off the periodic streetlight. "You know what's happening out there. I don't want to go back."

"Don't you miss it?"

"Desperately. More than I've ever missed anything in my life."

The next thing Mack was going to ask was obvious. Why didn't I want to go back? "Bigger Man… it's not gonna be Augustus anymore."

"You are correct about that, Little Man. I wish I could argue otherwise."

I gestured outside. "You been to Giant yet?"

"No, I have not. I've only driven through the parking lot. It's surprisingly empty."

"I went with Mom the other day. Mack, people kept their heads down and barreled forward. The place was cleared out in an hour."

"Brave new world, Little Man. People forgot how to live."

"There won't be Friday lunches with the teachers. There won't be Saturday events. There won't be evening check-ins or those God-awful dances that Sid and I used to run from. There won't be pep rallies, there won't be on-time graduation, and who knows who else won't come back." I rubbed at my face with the back of my hand, hoping that Mack wouldn't see the tears that had formed in my eyes. "Everything changed, Mack. For three years, you and Mom got me into a really awesome place. As much as other kids would complain sometimes, I loved that school. I don't want to go back and see a shell of it. Not when the world is struggling so much."

Mack and I were quiet, and save for the occasional bleeps and call-outs from his radio, the silence held like sound caught in a vise.

It was petulant and self-indulgent, but I said it anyway. "No one I knew died before. Not like this, Mack."

Mack nodded, once. We let Josh's name stay unsaid.

"I don't want to see any more loss. And there's worse coming. I think I'd just rather make camp with Mom for a while. Ride this out. And then get back to school when things settle down."

"There is worse coming," echoed Mack.

My eyes narrowed. "You are not doing as good a job of comforting me as you think you are."

Mack shrugged. "Little Man, I can't lie. I can see it out here already. It's why I was so desperate to get the state police here. And it's why it took them as long as it did to arrive. They don't have the manpower. They lost people too." Mack took a deep breath and rubbed a meaty hand underneath his large chin. In a softer voice than he had used so far, he added, "Don't hate me, Little Man. But that's exactly why you have to go back to school."

"How's that?"

There was no hesitation now. "The world will restart. It will take time. It will be a painful disaster. Everything that existed before—all the depression and stress and drug use, that's going to be magnified."

"Cool. Sounds like fun. Absolutely something I want to see."

"Time marches on, Corey. Humanity took millennia to get to this point. We have survived wars and plagues and tyrants. I've seen more than my share of it overseas. More than I care to count." Mack began looking over at me, intense eyes alternating between the road and my face. "Even in the face of death and destruction, humanity moves forward. Those who wait have an awfully hard time catching up."

I thought of the pictures of Mom holding me, taken by my former dad. Mom was young. If you just glanced at the picture, you saw the smile of someone whose face glowed with the beauty that came from someone in the prime of their life. But if you knew what you were looking for, you saw something else. The little fading bruise around her right eye that could easily be mistaken for discoloration caused by a lack of sleep. The catch in her smile. The slouch in her posture.

When I thought about my mom's youth, I thought about the years she lost as a result of… well, me. Not that I could help it, but it was reality.

"Isn't it my turn to return the favor?" I asked Mack. There was no transition there, no way for him to easily follow my thought patterns. But he knew what I meant.

"Corey. Your mom survived your dad. She survived your three years at school and was able to pay what your scholarship didn't cover. She will have her work, and her friends, and Jill and me. We will take care of your mom to whatever extent she needs it."

I sighed. Mack had said the words I knew he would say.

"I will admit to being a little afraid," I said softly.

"You know what I'm going to say to that, Corey."

"That there is plenty to be afraid of?"

Mack nodded once. As much as I sometimes hated his honesty, it fit the moment. Mack was only telling me what he thought I deserved to hear. "Only thing I can tell you is this. You can't retreat. Not now. Not ever. The world needs people in it. Helping each other. Caring for each other. Isn't that why you and I are together now?"

Mack's radio squawked, leaving the question unanswered. Not that I needed one. Mack was right, of course. When it came to the real world, Mack was almost always right.

I couldn't understand a word that the voice on the other end of the radio said, but I did see the cloud flicker across Mack's face. He reached for his radio and said, "Copy that," in his police voice. The next thing I knew, Mack flicked the sirens on, and the car was doing a 180 on gravel.

"That can't be good."

"Another D.V.," Mack said.

D.V. meant domestic violence. Somewhere, a woman—well, most likely a woman, anyway—was running from her husband… or worse. I nervously rubbed my thumb across my fingers. "All right."

"I'll be able to drop you off at home first. Just get out quick, okay? We're heading right by your place."

"Okay, Mack." My thoughts drifted to the important questions. Where was the woman now? Was she bleeding? Was she okay?

And then my mind went one step further, to the idea of Mack, throwing himself in harm's way. He wasn't that old. He was in pretty good shape and worked out on a regular basis. I teased him sometimes— he looked like a wall with a head and a hat. Normally, he laughed. As I looked at his face, I found no joy. Just a steely, professional resolve.

Mack made a sharp right on Winchester, and we found two cars in front of us. One blast of the sirens and the cars abruptly slammed on their breaks before skittering off to the side of the road. "Mack. Why this way?"

"I'm dropping you off at your house first."

"Yeah, but you said my house was on the way, and it's not like—"

"Not now, Little Man." Mack's voice was firm. So firm it made my heart beat faster.

As we came up over the rise on Winchester, I knew. I knew when I saw the pattern of lights in front of us at the Ford's house.

"Oh." The streaks of sadness that had seemed to cover Jason Ford's face, and the withdrawn glaze of his wife's eyes when they had been over, a pain I had simply chalked up to our impending death.

"Yup," Mack said. His mouth was open to say something else as we prepared to drive past the Ford's on our way to my place, but an explosion of glass through a lit window cut off any idea of that. With a curse, Mack slammed on the brakes and flung the car ninety degrees to the right, sending it skidding for a moment before the tires caught. Mack drove another fifty feet forward before abruptly hitting the brakes. A thick hand undid my seatbelt and pulled me down in the car, while Mack's other hand reached for his radio and called out some code. The only part I understood was the most terrifying. "Shots fired at Thirty Wellington."

Mack undid his seatbelt, kicked open his door, and looked at me very closely. "All right, Little Man. Here's the deal. I need to be a police officer. You are not—under any circumstances—to leave this car. I don't care what you hear or what you see. Do not—"

"Got it. Staying right here." I was certain Mack could feel my heartbeat thundering through the hand that was wrapped around my shirt. If it was anyone else, I may have made a show of bravery. With Mack, I had no such delusions. Mack knew exactly what I was at this moment—a terrified teenager who was way too close to an angry man with a gun.

"All right." Mack pointed beneath the dashboard. "Now."

Slithering like a cowardly snake, I slid under the dashboard. Unwittingly, my mind raced to the last time I had been forced to cower in the dark when I was much smaller, and Mack was the rescuer, not the one ordering me to hide.

There was not another word, no tender expressions of love to the son he had always wanted. Mack dropped to one knee beneath the open door and unholstered his pistol. I sat there, a crumpled-up ball of terror, staring in horror as the closest thing I had ever seen to a dad pointed his gun at a house.

Three more retorts. Sharp. Echoing in the otherwise silent night. They were gunshots—there was no way they were anything else. And they were followed by a sharp, high-pitched, female scream.

Mack ran for the house.

I gasped. At least, I tried to gasp, but it probably sounded more like the noise of a strangled animal in pain. It took everything I had, all of my self-control and restraint, to avoid screaming Mack's name. Trying to block out the sound of my own heart, I attempted to shimmy upward, but my limbs were locked in a paralysis of terror, unlike anything I had experienced since I was seven years old. All I had of those moments were flashes of memories—agonized screams, the wet sound of flesh meeting flesh, and muffled cries which could not be restrained. Those memories haunted me, weighed me down like ghosts of iron.

I inched my way upward, peeking out over the dashboard. I could just make out Mack, his weapon at his side. He was screaming something, but I couldn't tell what. Adrenaline was flushing its way through my veins, narrowing my vision, crowding out my hearing, somehow making me feel small and large at the same time.

Whatever Mack said didn't have the desired effect, and I watched in horror as he jiggled the doorknob, turned it, and pushed his way into the house. There was a shadowy light off to the side and Mack left the door open, giving the appearance that the house was bleeding a dull yellow.

Mack was gone, into a house of horrors. I'd heard him say it to Mom before, talking in a knowing, quiet voice. Domestic violence calls were the ones that cops feared the most. They were the most volatile, the most emotional, and often the deadliest.

"What can I do?" I said to myself, my voice ragged. "What can I do?" Mack told me to stay put, and it's not like I have any combat training, unless you count the Call of Duty game I was in the middle of when Mack decided it would be a good idea to deputize me.

So, I was stuck in a police car, waiting on other officers to arrive... oh. Crap. Taking me along for a joy ride while he was on duty was most definitely not legal. We'd done it before, but Mack had always told me to keep it our little secret. I suspected that other cops knew about it and had looked the other way because everyone liked Mom, liked their Chief. And besides, we'd never gone on an actual call during that time, but this was clearly very different.

Could I get out of here? I probably should because who knew how much trouble Mack would get into if I was found. This was stupid. I should have known better.

But, that meant leaving the car, slipping past a house where there were men with guns. How could I escape when a barrage of bullets was liable to erupt at any moment?

Crack. Another bang in the night.

My breath caught in my throat, and I let loose some sort of gargle before abruptly understanding just *why* people peed their pants when they were afraid.

Bang. Bang bang. I caught another few retorts and jerked downward. I was now completely curled underneath the dashboard of this police car, hands over my head, and I lost track of the number of gunshots, but there's no way they were all coming from the same gun.

He's shooting. Mack's shooting at someone and someone is shooting back at him. My neighbor? Was Jason Ford, a mild-mannered business owner... was he killing my Mack?

The shots concluded as abruptly as they started, and I took a deep, shaky breath, straining against the silence to hear any noises outside. Nothing. No hollering, no cries of pain. And certainly, no approaching sirens.

There was the slightest noise outside, and I tried to peak over the dashboard, slipping awkwardly on the fake-leather seats. For a millisecond, the shadows on the front porch danced in front of my eyes, and black forms appeared, spectral against the moonlight. I squinted harder, but my eyes found nothing. With a fearful grunt, I levered myself up and was able to just see over the window. The direction of the car, I realized, had left the passenger side exposed toward a view of my home in the distance. I wondered, briefly, if Mom could see or hear what was going on. I bet she could hear the gunshots, and the thought filled with terror at the sound froze me.

Then another cry. Barely audible, but no doubt, a cry, something that sounded like a wounded animal. I peeked over the dashboard and was surprised by what I saw—Mack.

"Little Man. Get out here. It's okay."

I was crunched in the ground, and it took my shaky hands a moment to wrap around the passenger door, but the instant it opened, I fell into the snow. Clambering to my feet, I ran, stumbling. "Mack." I cried plaintively.

Mack extended a hand forward, palm down. "It's all right. It's all right. Take a deep breath."

I did, my lungs unsteady and shaking.

Mack spoke again, his voice astoundingly level. "I got him. He's bleeding from the shoulder and handcuffed." Mack placed a gentle hand on my back and walked me closer to the house, and I was embarrassed by how warm his palm felt on my back.

Jason's hands were locked in binding silver. He had been immobilized against a thin column in their ragged living room, surrounded by fast-food containers and Walmart bags. I could see his chest rising and falling deeply. His eyes were closed, his shoulders slumped, and his head curled against his chest.

"Where's Missus Ford?" I asked.

Mack shook his head. "I don't know, and he won't say. Help is coming. I need to find her and see if she needs aid. You stay here and wave the officers to Jason when they get here. I'm going to find this asshole's wife."

My mind reeled to fear… Mack was going deeper into a darkened house where he had just exchanged gunfire? But… no. There were no other assailants. Only ghosts and memories. "Okay, Mack."

Mack nodded once and hesitated as if he wanted to say more. Then he was gone. I positioned myself against the doorframe of the house, staring at that bastard Ford while keeping one eye on the road, eagerly awaiting Mack's compatriots. *I'll have to say that I heard the gunfire and came down. We're only a little ways away. Will they believe that?*

From behind me, a noise. The slightest of squeaks that sounded completely out of place in the dark night.

Chills fired through me as I remembered the shadows I had seen on the porch. The small cry I had heard when I had first seen Mack.

I ran to one end of the porch, pushing aside upturned furniture and garbage cans. My foot caught one can and ripped it open, injecting the cold evening with an odor as pungent as raw sewage. I coughed and reached the end of the porch—nothing. I turned and ran the other way, gagging on the garbage as I moved.

On the other end of the porch, lying in the snow, was a woman. Her collapsed form was shivering in the snow, her eyes barely open slits that looked deadened against the weight of the world. On her leg was a crimson bloom, just above her left kneecap, and I saw it slowly expanding through her shredded pajama bottoms.

A rush of bile charged into my throat.

Then I was moving, charging down the stairs, skidding in the snow, on my knees, next to Mrs. Ford. The wind chose that moment to pick up, gusting across us like ice, and I had to wait to call Mack, lest my words be stolen by the night.

When the wind abated, I cried, "Mack! Mack!"

Mack, thankfully, was on the left side of the house—I could hear him. "What—oh." Mack had thrown open a window and peeked out of it. "I'm coming."

"Call help," I said, and a little voice in my head said, *What, you need to tell him that?*

Mack was outside now, racing to his car. I watched him run—faster than I'd ever seen him run before—then turned my attention back to Mrs. Ford.

With a groan that bordered on the noise that you make just before you throw up, I lowered myself farther, trying to ignore the sharp cuts the frozen snow was leaving on my skin.

Mrs. Ford's eyes had taken on some semblance of life. They were now open wide, with big, shining pupils black in the night. I had the most absurd thought possible. *Do I introduce myself?*

Instead, I settled for a strangled "Hi" and looked at her leg. The blood had sluiced down, following gravity into the frozen ground. A small, rust-stained discoloration had formed just where her pajamas, blood, and the ground all met. "Oh, God." I struggled to stifle my nausea.

Her face. Find her face. I did, and she was absolutely terrified, streaks of dirty blonde hair covering her wide, wide eyes.

I had no idea how much blood she had lost. I had no idea if she was even going to live. She looked so, so pale and so scared. What the hell was I supposed to do here, anyway?

Bleeding. She's bleeding. Right. She's bleeding. Okay. I could focus on that. I could focus on actually doing something, not the potentially dying woman, lying on the ground in front of me, aware that the last person she saw alive may very well be a scared high school kid who didn't even know her name.

I took off the belt from my uniform pants in an awkward yanking motion and dropped back down to the ground, still staying as low as humanly possible. With an awkward jerk, I lifted her left leg to slide my belt under her, and she *screamed* something so fierce that the sound piercing my eardrums felt as physical as a knife.

"Shh. It's okay, it's okay," I said lamely, but of course it wasn't okay, and however much pain this poor woman was in, she must have thought that I had no idea what I was doing. Well, I didn't. But it was still better than nothing, so I swallowed and said, "All right, fine, it's not okay. In fact, this is going to suck a lot, but it's better than bleeding to death on your front lawn, so…." My voice trailed off as I looped my belt into my buckle, and with a pull, tightened it as hard as I could. Mrs. Ford screamed again. The octave of her cries was so high I would have thought only animals could have heard it.

I waited for her voice to trail off, and eventually, it did, the scream dying out with a wet gargle. There was nothing now. Moving her was absolutely out of the question, but Mack was calling for help, and that had to count for something. From the sound of her scream, something was very, very broken inside of her left leg, and I had a bad feeling that moving would make it worse.

Her screaming had ceased, and she was crying softly, whimpering in the darkness. For a moment I couldn't figure out what to do, and my silence felt like an insult. So, still keeping low to the ground, I looked over at her and said, "Missus Ford?"

She didn't say anything, but her crying briefly halted, and she angled her head toward me. "Missus Ford, I'm so sorry, but we only met a few times… what's your name?"

And she laughed. Well, at least she did the closest thing I think she could have done which sort of sounded like a laugh, and it actually sounded like a less painful cry, so I took that as a win. She took a little intake of breath and said, "Kristy."

"Kristy. Okay, Kristy. I'm Corey Walker." I wanted to say something poetic, but I was feeling lightheaded. My armed neighbor had shot at least one person—his wife—and tried to shoot at the guy who was basically my father.

I whipped off my coat and balled it up into a semblance of a pillow that I shimmied under Kristy's head.

Her teeth chattered. With shaking fingers, I unbuttoned my shirt and covered her with it as best I could. Then I pressed myself deeper into the snow, trying to ignore the needles of cold that shot through my soaked skin and bare chest. I took Kristy's hand and was relieved to discover just how strong her grip was.

"Let's ride this one out together, Kristy."

We said nothing else. Heard nothing else. I just stared East, toward town, desperately waiting for the cherry and blue sirens of safety to get here as fast as they could.

Chapter 4

IT WAS A startling *boom* that woke me from the couch, and I swear, I fell right off of the damn thing. It wasn't funny like when that happens in movies. It was terrifying, and for a moment, I didn't know where I was or why my heart was beating so fast. Then I felt the familiar marks in my cheeks which happened whenever I crashed on the couch and remembered why I had woken up so afraid.

The clock said it was a little past four in the morning, and as I looked out the window, I realized what had startled me awake—Mack. His car had pulled into the driveway. The "boom" wasn't a boom at all, but the slam of his car door.

A second slam startled me almost as much as the first, but this one was from behind me. I turned around just in time to see Mom bolt out of her room and make a beeline for the door, faster than I'd seen her move in some time, her hair still tousled and her face splotchy. With a jerk of her arm, she flung open the door and kicked the screen door open.

"Mack. I… I… god damnit, just get in here, so I can figure out if I want to hug you or kill you."

Mack trundled up the steps. He looked sore. "Don't worry. Jill already handled that one."

"Which one?" I asked as Mack reached the door.

"Both, Little Man. Both."

Mom moved aside and let Mack into the living room. She screwed her face and bared her teeth, and for a second it looked like she really was going to slap him.

"It's all right, Cara, I deserve it." Mack's voice had a weight in it that I'd never heard before.

Evidently, Mom heard it too. Her face slackened like someone had hit an off switch.

"Oh, Mack…." She hugged Mack, her arms tightening around his broad back, and Mack put his head on her shoulder.

I walked up behind them, and as soon as I did, Mack disengaged from Mom and wrapped me in his arms. "Little Man, I am so, so sorry."

"It's all right, Bigger Man." Mack squeezed me tight.

"I did not think there'd be any danger. There never had been before." Mack stepped back and stared. "You still in your deputy pants?"

I looked down. "Guess I am."

The night had been hectic. Thankfully, it hadn't been more than a few minutes before the entire Robinette Police Department and half the state troops from this side of the Susquehanna River arrived on Winchester Road. EMTs had strapped Kristy into an ambulance, hooking her up to every piece of equipment I could imagine as they drove. Once free, I'd run to Mack and thrown my arms around him. "I came from the house," I'd whispered to him.

Mack had nodded once, and that was that. A set of interviews later, and a state trooper had dropped me off at my house, where my mom stood, waiting for me to explain everything.

"You look natural in those pants, Little Man."

"And he's never wearing them again," Mom said.

"God, that is so true." Mack took off his hat and hung it on a nearby hook while keeping his eyes locked onto me. "That could have been so much worse. Cara, that's the most dangerous call I've had in my sixteen years as an officer. I've only had to unholster my weapon one other time."

With a heavy sigh, Mack eased himself onto our couch as Mom shuffled around in the kitchen, filling the coffee pot.

"Jill okay?"

Mack inclined his head and paused, thoughtfully, before saying, "She thinks it might be time to see what my pension would be."

"Got that right!" Mom shouted. "Go into private security, Mack."

"You'd be the second woman who runs my life to tell me that today, Cara." Mack sighed again.

"Are you okay?" I asked. I realized we hadn't asked yet.

Mack nodded tightly. "I'll be fine. From a legal perspective, there's no trouble. It's pretty clear what happened. Ford and his wife had an altercation. It turned violent, very quickly. I called the hospital—Missus Ford was covered in bruises and had a couple of broken bones. Some were weeks old."

A wave of shame washed over me. We'd seen them. Lived down the street from them. I'd never noticed, never known. "I had no idea," I whispered.

"You weren't supposed to either. What counts is the action you did take. You're a bit of a hero, Little Man. The EMTs said there was some pretty major blood loss. The shot that Ford hit her with nicked Kristy's femoral artery. A few more minutes before you or the EMTs get there, she doesn't live."

I know Mack was trying to make me feel better, but I couldn't get the image out of my head. The Ford's lived fifty yards away. I could hit their house with a frisbee and a stiff breeze. And he'd been smacking his wife like she was a punching bag. And she only lived—maybe—because I was able to stumble into the snow and wrap a belt around her leg? God damnit.

Then I realized Mack was snapping his fingers across from me.

"Hmm? Sorry."

Another heavy Mack sigh. "It's all right. I don't blame you. Rough night. Just… make sure you take care of yourself after this, okay?"

I wasn't sure what Mack meant, but Mom came in with our coffee a few moments later, a steaming cup in front of her face.

"I guess going back to sleep is out of the question," I quipped.

"You were asleep?" Mom snarked back.

"Touché."

"And I won't be going back to work until the investigation is completed, so I can just sleep in today. Hope Jill doesn't need any help around the house." Mack put his feet up on the coffee table with slow, exaggerated movements, and Mom and I let loose a snicker.

"I suspect Jill will spend the day just wanting to hold onto you," Mom said.

"And I suspect you're right," Mack said, his voice grave.

"Mack, what else are you hearing?" Mom asked. When Mack tilted his head to the side, Mom added, "The rest of the area. The surrounding towns. Anyone else struggling like this?"

"Oh yeah," Mack said.

I stared at him, suddenly feeling as cold as when I had held Kristy Ford's hand in the snow. "What?"

"Arrests and paramedic calls are up all over the place, Little Man."

"What for?"

Mack sat back and looked up at the ceiling. "Well, a lot of domestic violence, like I said before. But it's more than that. The past couple of days brought a whole bunch of overdoses."

"I would have thought that anyone who was going to overdose already did," Mom said. Oof. We thought we had a drug problem before Perses. We had no idea just how bad things could get.

And now? "Why is it getting worse?" I asked.

"Lots of theories on that. I'm sure there will be more in the upcoming days," Mack said, before gesturing to the flat screen that he had mounted in the corner of the Living Room. "Little Man, you see what's going on out there. The riots, the gang killings, the weird cult activities."

I thought of the CNN report from the day after Perses had missed— the men and women in purple, flowers in one hand, gun in another. "Totally normal response."

Mack ignored me. "Perses didn't hit, but some piece of it did. It knocked something loose. People suddenly realized that death was only an accident away, and everyone reacts differently. Some get scared. Some get sad." Mack gestured over his shoulder, in the general direction of the Ford's home. "Some get angry. Really, really angry."

I shifted, trying to ignore the itch burning its way up my chest. "Things have to go back to normal at some point, right?"

"Sure," Mack said, but his voice was devoid of conviction. "For that to happen, people have to start believing in civilization again. In society. In our ability to care for each other. Otherwise…." Mack's voice faded into dust. I took a big gulp of my coffee, and almost spat it out when Mack said, "That's why what we were talking about was so important."

"About school?" My voice cracked as I said "school."

"About school," Mack echoed and shifted in his seat.

"Bigger Man."

"Corey," Mack said, abruptly shifting tone. "Corey, they need you there. The world needs you to be a part of it."

"Did tonight not teach you anything?" I looked to Mom for support, but her face was as stern as stone. "Mom. I'm staying with you until the world calms down. I'll go back eventually but let me stay home for a while."

"No dice, Corey." Mom shook her head. "I was supposed to go back too. I didn't. And I regret it every day."

"You sort of got pregnant with me."

"And I don't regret that. Most of the time." The corner of Mom's mouth turned upward. "But I do wish it had been later. I could have been able to provide better for you."

"You've done okay." My voice cracked and a tear sprang into my eyes. I tried to wipe them away with the back of my hand.

Mack resumed what he had been winding up to say. "There is no perfect time to go to school, Little Man. But your mom and I talked about this quite a bit. We're agreed. You have to go back."

"Why?" I was genuinely shocked. Mack had almost died fifty yards from where we were sitting. Mom had heard the gunshots that almost killed him. How could she want me to leave?

"Because you need to be there," Mom said.

"No." The conviction was rock-solid in my voice. "No, Mom. You need me here. There was a shooting next door. The world is ripping itself apart at the seams. I am not traveling two hours away to go to a school and be surrounded by rich idiots who can't stand the sight of me."

Mack fixed me with a hard stare. "Those idiots have never bothered you. You laughed at them on a regular basis, and you told me that every time we talked." There was a pause. "Tell your mom what you told me."

"There's no way," I burst. "No way."

"No way what?" Mom asked.

"That place…." I stumbled on my words, tripping on them like they were loose stones on shaky ground. "Augustus isn't gonna be what it was, Mom. I felt it change that last day. School won't be the same. It never will be." The words felt useless and melodramatic as they came out of my mouth. They came anyway.

"Everything everywhere is undone," Mack said. "Your job must be to fix it."

"I'm seventeen, Mack. Hell of a burden to place on me."

"I didn't place it on you, Little Man." Mack gestured to the sky.

Abruptly, Mom stood, walked over to me, and knelt. She gathered both of my hands in hers. "I know you think that staying here can shield you from the world. I know you think you can stop the world for me."

"You did for me," I spluttered.

Mom shook her head. "That was different. That was very different. I was young, and I was stupid, and I didn't have anyone else to turn to. I thought I'd go back. I should have realized what would happen." Mom pressed my hands together. I felt her warmth through my fingers and hands. It was all-encompassing, like comfort personified in my bones. "Corey. The world will not wait. And I can't have you wait for it. Don't do what I did. Live your life."

Then I was crying again.

"The gun was too close to you, Mom," I whispered, and Mom took my arm in her hands, leaned me against her as I started to cry softly.

Images of the night swirled in my head, the panic I felt while I cowered underneath the dashboard, the uselessness and the impotence, and then the blood….

"Little Man," Mack said, after a time.

I sniffled. "Yeah?"

"What you did tonight. It's exactly why we need you to go back."

"I hid under a dashboard, Mack."

"And then you found Kristy. You saved her life," Mack said, his voice firm. Firmer than I felt at that moment.

"I should have…." But my voice trailed off. Should have done what? Run into the house with Mack, with no guns, no protection, and no training? Yeah, okay, I wasn't that dumb. But the truth was, I wasn't sure how to feel right now. I only knew how I had felt at that moment. "It was terrifying."

"Of course, it was," Mack leaned over and rubbed my shoulder. "It's supposed to be terrifying. A bloody, beaten woman is supposed to make you feel afraid and useless."

"But that doesn't change where we are right now," Mom said.

"We?" I asked.

"We," Mom repeated with a sad smile. "All of us. This world needs people who are going to run into the snow."

"The world belongs to those who are willing to seize it," Mack said, and his eyes acquired a faraway look, one I had seen before. When he described his time in Iraq. When he told stories that never had an ending, that resembled the parts of a page which had been blacked out.

Mack's eyes locked with mine. "But a man with a gun was yards from your home. Violence will come into all of our safe places. It may come as a domestic abuser, or a criminal gang, or a power-hungry cult. And if we aren't there to meet it, the fear creates a box. And it locks you in."

"If we all withdraw into our own little enclaves, our own little worlds, civilization stops, Corey," Mom said. "This world only works when we believe it does. And yes, it probably is going to get ugly." Mom paused. Gathered herself. Brushed her hair out of her face. "But you cannot let that ugliness win. Otherwise, Mack doesn't save us from Jim. Otherwise, you and Mack don't save Kristy Ford from Jason. And thousands die because we're too afraid to make the world a better place. To make ourselves better."

Mack took a deep breath and ran a hand over his stubbled cheeks, massaging his temples gently. His face was shrouded in darkness and his eyes were wide. Mom reached over. Wrapped a hand around his wrist.

"Little Man. I almost lost my life tonight to a piece of white trash who should have been arrested ages ago, but Kristy Ford had no one she could go to. She didn't have any help until I knocked down her front door and you stopped her leg from bleeding. She was surrounded by alcohol and enough firepower to take down a small army. Your generation has to change the world, and you have to be able to make that change. The asteroid missed. At some point, we're going to have to stop living like it hit. Go back to Augustus."

We were quiet for some time as I pondered Mack's words. All I wanted to do in the world was to go to sleep, wake up in twelve hours, and play Xbox. I did not want to check my email. I did not want to go on Facebook or Snapchat. I didn't want to see what I knew was the truth. Portions of the world were starting again.

But they were. And I knew which part of the world I wanted to belong to.

Chapter 5

MY FIRST THOUGHT as we passed the majestic homes on West Chew Street was that it felt like a twisted homecoming. The first time I had ever seen the gorgeous houses on this magnificent tree-lined street, I was a thirteen-year-old kid. Mom had gotten tired of sending me to a school that was built when the Civil War was just starting and had an internet connection that seemed straight from the 90s. When we'd driven down the street, I had marveled at the wealth of the houses and wondered what their occupants did to be able to live in such stately manors. These homes were immaculate brick mansions, complete with grandiose columns, grand porticos, and perfectly manicured lawns that glowed green. A piece of me had wondered if I'd ever be able to afford such opulence and if Augustus Boarding School would put me down a pathway that would lead me to one of these gorgeous homes and shining futures.

Today, the trees were barren for winter. Slushy snow from yesterday's storm melted in the soupy, fifty-degree heat, a reminder that Perses was gone, but a warming planet remained behind. Most of the homes had withstood the Perses Fall, the name we gave the Autumn before the near impact… when things got bad. Really bad.

Some homes made it through with minimal damage—a set of tire tracks on a lawn here, a broken window there.

One home was a charred mass of burnt wood and melted glass. I wondered about those who had been inside. Where they were right now.

Everything we had seen—everything I had feared—was just getting reaffirmed, over and over again. I shifted uncomfortably in the car, the site of one disaster after another rolling past my window. None of this was a surprise, of course. Everyone had warned me as much. That included Jill, Mack's wife. I had frantically tried to pack my life into a bunch of boxes and bags last weekend, and Mom, quickly determining that I was a train wreck and would break all of my things, had enlisted Jill to help while she made the trip north to Scranton. Jill had been all too happy to oblige and calmly folded my shirts while I frantically tried to jam my shower caddy into a shopping bag.

"Corey? Corey?" Jill had asked.

"Hmm?" I turned the caddy sideways.

"Corey… Corey, give me the damn bag."

I obliged. Jill had the caddy in the bag in seconds and was tying the bag while I smiled meekly. "Thank you."

Jill's smile grew, even as she returned to folding shirts. "I didn't think we'd be doing this again."

"Doing what?"

"Packing you up for a second first day," Jill said. I snorted. "I thought once was enough."

"I still think it is."

Jill shook her head. "The world makes the circumstances, Corey Walker, but it's up to you to meet them or fold to them."

"I don't know if not going back would be folding."

"I don't necessarily think it would be either. But I do think you have to at least try."

That thought got me out of my head. I sat there, wondering about what my life would be like, back at school. What kind of condition would the student body be in? Did anyone really give a damn about school right now?

These thoughts crisscrossed my mind, bouncing around like pinballs with a multi-ball activated, crashing into each other, colliding… and then Jill was snapping her fingers.

"Hmm? What?" I asked.

A patient smile crinkled Jill's face, and I realized why. I was trying to jam a fitted sheet in a duffle bag without even attempting to fold it. "Oh, Corey, are you so worried about this?"

I looked at the sheets. Then back at Jill. "Wouldn't I be nuts not to be worried?"

Jill took two steps and closed the distance between us. "Yes. You would be. I cannot imagine the pressure you're going through." A thoughtful pause. "Well, actually, that's not true, yes, I can. I see it in my ER every day. The patients who… well, I suppose this isn't really helping, is it?"

Jill took a deep breath. "Life can be like driving. The roads and the background and the pathways look familiar. And then, sometimes, you run into a traffic jam and can't go forward. Or you have to leave town to find what you are looking for. And everything looks so unfamiliar that you can't imagine how you will keep driving."

"So, how do you keep driving?" I asked, biting my lower lip.

Jill had shrugged. "One mile at a time."

«◊»

THE WINDOWS WERE down in Mack's car, and that's when I first heard it—the crisp flap of taut fabric whipping in the breeze. It was the sound from the Augustus banners that dotted streetlights, with their cardinal red background and bright white text. I smiled at seeing those banners that had been stolen like they were candy during Senior week. For five months, I hadn't thought I'd live to see those banners again.

The streets around Augustus grew more crowded as we reached the center of campus. Augustus had no grand entrance, no grand gateway. Just a stone sign, engraved with, *Augustus Boarding School—Founded 1848*. In smaller print, the school motto, *Ubi Doctrina Annectit: Where Learning Connects.*

I hope so.

Anyway. I wasn't sure what I was expecting when we pulled in. I knew what I was hoping for. An atmosphere like my first day of freshman year, one rich with promise and potential. Knots of students, alternately looking up from their phones to the surrounding architectural grandeur, not even bothering to hide the fact that they were gawking. Old friends reuniting and embracing. Couples holding hands as they ambled along sidewalks, staring at everything and nothing and each other.

What I got instead was a knot of cars, half of which were occupied by drivers who seemed to have forgotten where they could park. The air was filled with the sounds of horns and muffled cursing.

Mack, unfazed, smirked. "Were people this stupid before Perses?"

"Human stupidity is a constant," my mom sighed. For all her encouragement about returning to school, she had been the most upset when the email came two weeks ago, announcing that the modified semester would pick up where we left off.

We reached the car line for my dorm, Florence Fabrizio Hall, so named after a wealthy alumnus. We just called it Flo.

I bit my lip in frustration. Everyone on the streets in front of us acted like they had forgotten how traffic laws worked. But in front of Flo, emptiness. On my move-in day last August, an orderly line had snaked its way for two solid blocks. We unpacked, and I had eagerly greeted friends who were ecstatic at having returned to Augustus. We'd laughed together at the Freshmen who had brought way, way too much stuff as if they were moving to an ice station in remote Antarctica.

And now? Nothing. No one in front of me. Just a fine mist falling from the sky, and deep puddles that had formed in macadam potholes.

Sid was around here somewhere. He had told me he was getting back before me. That meant we were still roommates. At least I had that to look forward to.

Mack parked in the designated move-in area, and I hopped out of the pickup, stretching. He got out next to me and clapped me on the shoulder. "You ready, Little Man?"

"Sure?" I was unable to hide the question in what should have been a statement.

Mack nodded once, knowingly, and pulled the rear of his truck gate down. Mom hopped out next to me, and we began to unload, dragging my stuff off to the side so Mack could move his truck. I had packed relatively light, and I doubted this would take the three of us more than a few trips.

The parking lot where Mack had parked was only halfway filled, and that struck me as odd. Well, okay, everything struck me as odd right then, and it wasn't like I had much of a baseline for, "Civilization almost ended and now I'm going back to school." But I had figured more cars would be there. Even weirder was that a few cars had been loaded with bright orange tickets and had windows that were caked in dirt and dead leaves. At least one had a bright orange boot.

And there was a news van in the parking lot. Bright blue and yellow lettering—Channel 69. Yes, really. Yes, we had all giggled like nine-year-olds when we discovered that was the major news channel here.

I turned around to walk into my dorm and almost crashed into her.

"Hi," said a perky voice with a hard edge. It took me a moment to realize I had almost careened into a petite blonde woman. My first thought was that she was a student—she certainly looked young and energetic enough, even if she didn't seem to carry herself with the same level of dullness that was permeating campus. My second thought was that she wasn't familiar. That was weird since the school was only 1,000 or so people—small enough that you should recognize everyone.

Then I saw the microphone.

"I'm Stephanie Perkins. Channel Sixty-nine," said the blonde.

"Uhh… hi?" What the hell is a reporter doing on campus?

I think the look on my face must have asked that question because the next thing Stephanie said was, "We're doing a story on Augustus reopening, and how students are adjusting to life after Perses. Would you like to be interviewed for the news?" From the way her voice gained in pitch when she said, "for the news," I could hear that she was trying to somehow flatter me into thinking that I was someone important. Her cameraman wasn't waiting for my answer, and he had already hauled his camera to his shoulder and smooshed his face next to the viewfinder.

My thoughts, however, went elsewhere. "Isn't the campus private property?"

Darkness fell across the reporter's face. "Why?"

"Did the campus give you permission to be here?"

I think I heard Mack chuckle.

"So, do you want to be on tv or no?"

"You didn't answer the question."

The reporter's face froze like ice hardening. For a moment she was still, fixing me with a look that mixed anger and admiration.

The spell broke. "Whatever." She dug a hand into her jacket pocket, and I almost jumped backward, not sure what she was going for. Then she removed her hand, which was pinching a thin business card between her fingers. She jammed the card into my front shirt pocket. "Let me know if you change your mind. I can't get anyone here to talk."

With a huff, Stephanie Perkins of Channel 69 walked away, her cameraman racing to keep up with her angry steps. I watched them go, blinking, not really too sure what had happened.

"That was probably a good move," Mack said. "And well handled."

"No guns were involved, so that was a lot easier."

Mack snorted a laugh. "Lay low. Unless you can't avoid it." Mack didn't elaborate on what he meant. I didn't ask.

The first thing that struck me when I walked into Flo was the smell. My mind whirled right back to the way it had smelled when I first walked into this building in August, like Lysol and unpacked luggage. Before Perses. Before everything.

The hallways were largely empty. This disconnect was startling. I nodded at someone in recognition, and every face brought the slightest spike of joy. I found Michelle Quinn, the girl who had been the first friend I'd made my freshman year. There was Jason Moses, plucking awkwardly at his guitar, his face placid and his hands moving like they were in jello. These were kids who I'd known since Freshman year, and it was like I was seeing them for the very first time.

I tried to stop in at Dr. Drake's office. According to the email I'd gotten from the school, he'd be one of two teachers in the dorm who would be responsible for check-ins, with Dr. Skinner being the other. Last year, before Perses, we'd had eight teachers.

Of course, it didn't matter. Drake didn't answer his door when I knocked, no matter how hard I pounded.

Disgruntled, Mom and I walked into the elevator, and I hit the third-floor button.

"Not exactly a lively group today," Mom said.

"Tell me about it," I grunted, thumbing open my phone and opening the Augustus app. I'd have to check in on the phone. "Remind me why you wanted me here again?"

Mom sighed and ran a hand through her hair. I worried for a moment—was she about to tell me she had changed her mind? Smash the Ground Floor button and demand Mack turn the car around?

She didn't. "Because it has to be."

"Yeah, but everything is broken here."

The world's slowest elevator dinged on the third floor.

"I know. I see it everywhere."

My room was just off of the elevator, and we turned the corner before hitting Room 305. Two cardstock race cars cut against neon paper glowed at me—Corey and Sid.

God, those stupid nametags from the Prefects. The email from the school hadn't mentioned who would be filling that role this semester, or if Brian Bogart would even be coming back. He was my year, and he hadn't made an Instagram post in months.

Then I laughed with a memory. The last nametags on our doors had been of space and shooting stars.

I was still laughing like an idiot—and trying to ignore the confused look on my mom's face—as I waved my student ID in front of the keycard entry. With a pleasant beep, the red light turned green, and I pushed the door open.

There was Sid. He was sitting on his bed, staring at the door, having probably heard the noises outside. Sid was broad-shouldered… at least, he had been. He'd clearly lost a few pounds. That wasn't a good thing. Sid used to have a belly. He was tough and jolly. Now, he looked like a scarecrow, with hollowed-out eyes and a disproportionately large nose that was too big for his shrunken face. His soccer jersey, red and grey, looked like it was hanging off him.

"Corey." The scowl on Sid's face turned into a wide smile that lit up the room. He was off his bed in a flash, and the next thing I knew, I was off the ground. Maybe Sid hadn't lost as much weight as I thought.

It took my arms a few moments to catch up, but eventually, they did, and I hugged Sid back. Christ. His back felt boney. We'd hugged when we said goodbye back in September, having planned on seeing each other before our fiery deaths. The lack of law and order on the highways put a stop to that one pretty quickly.

"You lost too much weight." I smiled through my tears. Reflexively, I thought of Josh, and the tears came again, burning as they filled my eyes.

I heard Mom slide past me to fling a bag on my empty bed, and that snapped Sid and me out of our bromance. "Hi, Missus Walker," said Sid. To my surprise, my mom's eyes were also wet.

"It's good to see you again, Sid." Mom hugged my roommate. "Did you get in today?"

"Yesterday. Coach wanted us here early. He thinks the season will restart soon."

"How'd practice go?" I asked.

The dark look on Sid's face answered for me. Mom picked up a bag and heaved it onto my bed, the clattering sound interrupting me before I could ask any more questions. Instead, Sid shook his head like a wet dog, and I almost laughed. That was an old habit of his, one I'd seen him do since Freshman year. I hadn't realized I'd missed it. "You see the Twins?"

"Not yet, but we basically just got here. The only person we ran into on the way up was a reporter. Which was weird."

"Which part was weird? The reporter or not seeing anyone else who lives here?"

"Yes," Mom and I said at the same time.

I sighed and exchanged a discrete glance with my mom. "Let me get the rest of my stuff from the car."

"Sounds good."

A few minutes and some awkward lifting later, all of my stuff was in my room. "Go," Mack said quietly, gesturing out the door with his head. "Your mom and I will unpack your stuff." Mack's eyes flashed toward Sid, and I could hear the conversations we'd had in the past couple of weeks.

Sid and I left and started walking the dorm, taking the stairs to the fifth floor, and working our way down. The words came easily.

"We barely got to explore this place last year," I said.

"I remember, Corey, I remember," Sid said. I suspect he was thinking what I was thinking—all the memories we had made, and all that we'd never had a chance to experience. The few weeks we had spent at school had been poisoned. Tainted. "He's everywhere."

"Yes. He would have loved more time being connected to the girls' dorm." Flo was the only dorm for seniors and was a monstrous structure, one that divided the boys and girls sections via two thick sets of doors in the middle. In theory, you were only allowed in the section of the opposite gender during certain hours. In reality....

"He only waited three years for it." Sid shook his head. "He couldn't have handled coming back, seeing the school like this."

"He's not the only one."

We were silent for a few steps, our lack of volume matched by the quiet of the surrounding dorms. When Sid spoke again, his voice was wet. "It feels like everything is in a fog."

My heart ached, and I stumbled on my words.

"You know what I mean," Sid said as we pushed open a fire door. Thankfully, this section of the dorm seemed to have a bit more life. Pockets of conversation were audible here and there. A couple of rooms were open, and music blared from them. The stale smell of cheap incense and bad pot emanated from behind a door.

Sid's nose wrinkled. "That's one way to deal with life, I guess."

Sid had never smoked or touched alcohol. Throughout his entire time at Augustus, he'd abstained. I'd asked him about it once, trying to keep my voice as neutral as possible. With a wry smile, Sid had said it was simple. He'd made a promise to himself. That was it. And it wasn't like we were swimming in booze or pills, but they were both on campus, and they weren't hard to find if you wanted either.

I looked at the door where the weed was coming from. "Guy's gonna get back to school and get kicked out right away."

"Hence the bad call nature of that decision," Sid said. "I can't believe anyone would be that obvious on the first day." We both stopped in front of the door, staring at it. "This is wild."

"It is," I said quietly.

We moved on, eyes roving the hallway. Yeah, there were normal pockets of activity here and there—gunfire from video games, terrible music being blasted way too loud, that sort of thing. But the silence and absence of people were louder than any scream. I couldn't help but notice how many rooms I knew were doubles that had only one name on them. How many whiteboards had been removed from doors, leaving behind discolored paint which seemed to glow like a scar. By the time we got a quarter down the hallway, I saw at least five rooms that had names missing.

Sid saw too. "That happened at practice today too."

"Hmm?" I asked, looking up, catching the twist of pain on Sid's face.

"We couldn't practice. Not really. Too many people missing. Coach thinks they'll get here tomorrow."

I bit back a wince. When we weren't hanging out or he wasn't in class, he was doing something soccer related. Sid was a great student too—his grades had consistently been better than mine last year, and I was no slouch. And yet, he played and played hard. I'd watch him pour over his playbook. Review tape from prior games on his computer, studiously making notes. Anyone who didn't think that athletes worked hard, that sports weren't a craft to be taken seriously… I wanted to introduce them to my roommate.

We reached the halfway point of the hallway. I'd never noticed it before but did this time because the fire doors had closed. Apparently, the magnetic holds which kept them open were busted.

"It's like no one knew we were coming back." Sid grabbed one door and opened it with ease. I did the same with the second, and we both tried to reattach them to their openings. We failed. The doors closed behind us with a resounding thump.

"Yeah." I scratched my head. "Yeah, that part sucks."

"Everything sucks," Sid mumbled darkly.

I squinted at my friend, but before I could say more, I heard a high-pitched, "Siiiiiiiiiiiiiiiiiidney."

At the same time, another voice echoed, "Cooooooooooorey."

"Oh, great." Despite his dour tone, the corners of his Sid's lips cracked upward.

I turned to face the thudding footsteps, and there they were—the Twins. Okay, I mean, they had names. Maurice, who went by Mo, and Mika. Members of Augustus's track team, they were blurs of light when they ran. Right now, they were running at us hard, with big, broad grins on their wide-set, goofy faces.

The biggest smile sprouted on my face. "We're about to get tackled."

"We are." Sid's voice was unpleasantly level.

I planted my feet as Mika left the ground—he was the broad jumper—and launched into me, grateful for the fire door's closure behind me, or I would have been flat on my ass. Mo had less success, and Sid stood like a wall, grunting only slightly upon impact.

For a moment, Mika and I embraced. Then, as if synchronized, he and Mo disentangled themselves and switched between the two of us.

"It's good to see you," Sid said.

"You too," said Mika.

When I spoke again, my voice was a gasp. "What he said, but you're strangling me, Mo."

Mo pulled back, clasping my shoulders. "We live here now."

"What?" I asked. They'd lived on the second floor when we left.

"Yep. School called. They said this floor was too empty and asked if we wanted a bigger room," said Mika.

Mo gestured upward with his arms. "We were like, 'Hell yes.' So, we're here now."

"Why the hell would you want to move up here?" I asked.

"Duh," said Mo.

"Better WiFi," finished Mika. I laughed, but it was true—the fifth floor did have better WiFi. The damn lounge in front of us was called The Netflix Lounge.

"Seems like people are slow to move back." I gestured around me.

Mika flapped his arms around. "Tell us about it. Dad made us get here early. He was all convinced that there'd be a mad rush to get back here."

"Dad's been like that since Perses missed. He swears everyone would want to rush back to school," said Mo.

"'Go back to fantasy island' was how he said it."

"I think he just wanted us out of the house," Mo finished.

We laughed, but the conversation trailed off, threatening to veer into everything we didn't want to say. Instead, Mika and Mo walked toward the lounge. I started to follow, clapping Sid once on the back to make sure he did the same.

The four of us sat in the four prime overstuffed chairs and spun them into a loose semi-circle, facing the rest of the hallway. There was no wall near the entrance to the lounge, and we'd have the perfect view to see other people. We chatted about this and that, commenting on the crappy condition of the roads and the burnt-out homes in the area. As we talked, my eyes roamed the large lounge. It was replete with threadbare chairs, beat-up tables, and massive bay windows that seemed to tower over campus.

It was also silent. That almost never happened.

"This is crazy." Mika's voice turned low for the first time since we'd begun to speak. "Feels like we're living in a post-apocalyptic film after the credits rolled."

"Right?" said Mo. "That's exactly it, Mika. Where is everybody? Don't they want to get back to normal?"

"I don't think they can," I said. At that moment, we saw our first person—a girl with a short-blonde haircut and an all-black outfit. Megan Buchanan. She'd transferred in our sophomore year.

Mika waved his hands in the air. "Hey, people! Yay, people." He began to hoot and holler, giving Megan a standing ovation. Not to be outdone, Mo leaped to his feet and began applauding while lightly jumping.

"Oh, sweet Jesus," I put my hands over my eyes and slunk down in the chair. Between my fingers, I watched Megan, her face filled with frost as she carried a duffle bag over her shoulder and walked out of sight.

"She seemed like she's in a good mood," Mo quipped. "Very friendly."

"In all fairness, you did just start cheering for her for no reason," Sid said.

I gestured at our friends. "Yeah, but it's the twins. No human being on earth has ever taken them seriously."

Mo's face assembled itself in mock horror. "Excuse me!"

"Right here," echoed Mika.

I waved a dismissive hand at them, and they laughed as they sat back down.

This was how it was supposed to be. We were back at school, in stupidly large chairs, making fun of each other.

Abruptly, Mika's gaze darkened. He licked his lips. "Do you guys hear from Josh's parents at all?"

Mo didn't react, but I swear, the little color in Sid's face drained quickly.

The awkward silence threatened to stretch, broken finally when I spoke. "I didn't. I reached out afterward… told them I was sorry I couldn't make it to the funeral. They never responded."

"I don't blame them," Mo said, all pretenses of having a good time having evaporated like a puff of smoke in a stiff wind.

Mika looked at his brother, his face unsure. "We heard from them." Mo nodded slightly, and Mika continued. "They told us to say they were sorry. That they understood."

My mind stuttered. "When was this?"

"Last week," responded Mo.

At that, Sid stood up, stuffed his hands in the pockets of his sweatpants, and walked over to the bay windows of the lounge that faced the campus outside. I stared at him. Willed him to come back to the conversation.

"Sid?" My voice was whisper soft.

In a voice which equaled mine in volume, Sid said, "Wish I heard from them."

I looked over at Mika and Mo, found their expressions loaded with sympathy and pain, their usual goofy smiles wiped out with the force of a nuclear detonation.

"Did they tell you what happened?" I asked Mika.

He shook his head. "Not yet." He ran his hand over his close-cropped hair, raking fingers over his scalp like he was trying to dig something out of his skull. His fingers came to rest by his temples. "They said that now that things may be returning to normal...." Mika's voice trembled, ever so slightly. I hadn't heard his voice shake like that since he called me to tell me that Josh had died. "...now that things may be returning to normal, they may ask the coroner to run some tests."

Mo was shaking his head. "We couldn't tell them, man."

What Mo didn't have the heart to tell Josh's parents was that the dead and dying were everywhere. That there was no way anyone would care about whether a teenage drug overdose had been accidental or intentional. That they would join the scores of people in this world who had survived Perses, but who hadn't survived it whole.

I hadn't seen Josh since Thursday. Thursday, September 12, if I want to be exact. That was the day that the Wikileaks story broke. That was the day the world basically ended.

The school had tried holding a big school meeting… it was an absolute disaster. There was crying and screaming. The counselors looked utterly overwhelmed by the situation—after all, when in their training did they read the chapter on, "How to comfort the young adult in the prime of their life who is about to die in a fiery, Earth-ending explosion?"

When they told us the school was closing, they screwed up. And I mean really screwed up. They announced they were closing the school the next day, not that night. Some students left, but Augustus was prime educational real estate for a lot of the nation's youth, and an awful lot of kids couldn't catch the flights they needed to get home.

So, what happens when you have a bunch of depressed teenagers with absolutely no consequences in front of them? Bad stuff. Only bad stuff. No one packed. Everyone partied.

I remember watching my classmates, drinking, fighting. It was so depressing. Without fear of repercussions, the veneer of civilization had been largely torn away, and suddenly, we were playing our parts in *Lord of the Flies*.

I watched my dormmates get absolutely plastered and the prefects and teachers that lived in the dorm give up, lost in their own pain. Everyone was just trying to forget that the entire planet had essentially turned into a massive version of the Titanic and that no amount of praying, screaming, or kicking could get us a seat on the lifeboat.

Sid and I didn't drink. We sat in the dorm. We talked.

Josh came by our room at around eight that night. His long, blond hair was hanging in front of his eyes, and his tears were so heavy it looked like a storm had unleashed on his face.

And suddenly, it was like some circuit clicked into place in Josh's mind. He brushed the hair out of his face, looked at us, and with red-rimmed eyes said, "Hey, I'm gonna go grab a smoke. Not like I need my lungs anymore, right?"

He'd slapped my knee and left the room without another word. And that was it. We didn't see Josh again.

Mika gestured with his head down the hallway. "He's not the only one, you know. I heard of a few other of our classmates who didn't make it."

I didn't want to say it, but I did too. Death turned social media profiles into into digital tombstones, a place for all of us to go and wonder what the world might have looked like if not for the cosmic accident that sent Perses our way.

"Yeah." I stared down the hall at the approaching footsteps, trying to arrange my face into something which didn't look like it was about to explode into a storm of tears. A tall girl walked by, her long red hair trailing behind her. Her expression was hard until she caught my eyes. Then her face softened to something approaching sympathy and a gentle smile appeared on her face. I nodded, once, trying to place who she was. And then she was gone, around the corner.

I looked back at Sid—you could have been forgiven for thinking he was a statue. He hadn't moved, as if the pain had turned him to stone. "Sid?"

Sid's shoulders slumped, and he turned back around, returning to his seat while casting his eyes furtively about. He looked lost, like the events of the past few weeks had untethered him from the ground.

Mika and Mo stared at Sid with concern, alternating their looks between him and me.

"Think this gets better?" Sid asked quietly.

Mika whistled softly. "You might have just asked the most important question, Sidney."

Suddenly, I felt electricity in my legs, like I needed to stand up and walk around.

"I think it has to," Mo said solemnly.

"Yeah?" Sid asked, and I stared at Mo with a fierce urgency, hoping he knew something which I did not.

"Yeah." Mo was standing, having walked around to the back of his seat, flashing an uncertain smile. "There are too many of us who are here. Too many people have returned to their lives and are trying to live them as best they can. We're alive. We're alive, and after spending four months dying, we get to live. This should be a big party."

"I have a different idea," I ventured cautiously. I didn't want to burst Mo's bubble, but that take wasn't rose-colored glasses, that was rose-colored glasses in technicolor and then with 3-D glasses. And then spotlights. Bright, red spotlights. "Look, you're right, we should be thrilled. We're alive. But I guess there are two things that I see."

I held up a finger. "First, we all spent four months contemplating our deaths. Yeah, we're alive now. But we spent all that time trying to figure out why we had been so screwed and screaming at the stars and praying to God. Four months not working. Four months doing nothing but planning for the end, thinking of what our last moments would be, wondering which scientists would be right, if the fire or earth would kill us first...." My voice trailed off, and I shivered.

"That leaves scars," said Mika.

I pointed a finger at him. "Exactly. That leaves a scar. And scars...." I knocked my forehead, touching the wound from my dad. "Scars don't heal so easily. None of us can snap back to normal. As much as we desperately want to."

I think Sid knew where I was going. Either that or his grief had rendered him incoherent. "Josh."

"And Josh," I said. "Do they have any estimates on how many people died in the lead-up to Perses? How many suicides, stunts gone wrong? How many died in the Kashmir war, or when Russia invaded Poland or all those cults that committed mass suicides?"

"No," Mika said.

"But probably in the millions," Mo said.

"This is going to take so much time." I put my hands in my head for a moment. "We're living in a broken world. And I think we'd be stupid to pretend otherwise."

Around us, the relative silence of the dorm stretched on oppressively. Mo was silent, his face a sentinel of thought, chewing over the words I'd just said. Mika's face was twisted, rippling with an unknown emotion, but I was almost relieved to see that. At least he was processing.

Sid was silent, his face inscrutable. Was he lost in a memory? Seeking happier times? Or had the hard first day back simply stunned him into a relative silence?

I looked past Sid, staring at the clouds in front of us which had overtaken the sun. Slush striated the ground, covering most of the school's green, save for the periodic pockets of grass which stubbornly poked their way through the snow. Someone had thrown a bright red scarf over the granite statue of Francis Augustus which stood in the direct center of campus, his stony, regal eyes seeming to touch all of us who looked in his direction.

His gaze stretched across a silent campus.

Chapter 6

A FTER PARTING WAYS with Mo and Mika, Sid and I wandered back to the dorm, each of us quiet. I tried to stifle the pain which I imagined shimmering from behind the closed dorm rooms. Did they feel less sorrow than me? More? What was going through their minds at this moment?

Mom, Mack, and I said a relatively quick goodbye in the parking lot.

After I thanked them for unpacking my stuff, Mack said, "Take care of your friend. He looked ill."

"He did," Mom echoed.

Mack stepped closer. I could smell his aftershave when we hugged. "And take care of yourself. You know how bad this may be. Be the person we know you are."

I stared at Mack, my head tilted like a confused puppy when Mom wrapped me in her arms. She was squeezing me tighter than I think she had since we'd found out just how bad Perses was going to be. "I'll be all right. You do you."

I tried to look confused, but she wasn't having it, and her voice dropped to a whisper. "I'm fine, Corey. I made it for a long time because of you. Made it when my parents said goodbye. Made it when your dad turned ugly. I didn't do it for you to be worrying about me."

"Bit of a reflex, Mom."

"Well, learn some new ones now, okay? All I need out of you is for you to go to school. Learn something. Have fun."

At that, I rolled my eyes. Looking around the hollowed-out campus, I couldn't imagine what "fun" could be had here. The place reminded me of a piece of rotting fruit.

But still. Mom needed to leave here thinking that I was going to be okay, that this would just be another semester of school. And she wouldn't be alone—Mack would check in on her. She still had friends. She'd have her job soon enough. I hoped.

So, with a sigh, I put on the best fake smile I could. "I will, Mom."

Mom pecked me on the cheek and drew me in for another tight hug. I could feel her warm tears on my neck. "You freakin liar."

I laughed through the moment. "Well, I'll try. That much I can promise you, Mom. I'll try."

I laughed as we said goodbye, the darkness encroaching on the school. I stuffed my hands in my pockets as I walked, marveling at the bright white lights which lined Academic Row. For a moment, I paused, overwhelmed. I'd always been drawn to these lights. They were massive, stretching about twenty feet into the air with three distinct bulbs, each slightly taller than the next. They threw off a deep, bright glow that could be seen from almost anywhere on campus. Carved into them were intricate patterns of weaving and intertwining brass.

On more than one night, I'd seen students stop at the lights and swirl their fingers around in the patterns. I distinctly remembered doing the same the night of my freshman orientation, my first night here, when I was scared and lost, overwhelmed by what was in front of me. With a heavy sigh, I found my feet carrying me over to the nearby light, and I reached out, touching it with three fingers, running them up and down its cool metal skin.

Under normal circumstances—it was still early evening—I would have been too embarrassed to stand there, caressing a streetlight. Tonight, however, there was no such fear—no one was around, save for a couple of students in dark clothing at the end academic row. I lost them as they walked, their dark silhouettes disappearing into the glare of the light.

The lights stuttered and blinked as I walked back to my room. I tried not to think too much about that.

I got back to the dorm and still felt utterly useless. Sid was in a funk that I absolutely, positively could not get him out of. I tried talking about normal things, like how weird it would be to resume classes. I tried to get him to look at pictures of last semester. Hell, I tried to get him to look at pictures of Junior year. Nothing. And yeah, the noise outside got a bit louder, but not much. Not what it should have been. People were moving in silently like they were unloading furniture into an active library. The dorm was as quiet as a tomb by nine o'clock, an unearthly silence which I'd never heard before.

Sid went to bed thirty minutes later. What the hell kind of student goes to bed at 9:30? We were supposed to savor every second until lights out.

Around 10:00, I took a selfie of myself in front of my door and uploaded it to the Augustus app. Even as recently as a decade before, a teacher would knock on the door to make sure students were in their rooms. Those days were long gone. If I opened the door—even for the bathroom—the app would detect it, and I had to recheck in. If I didn't upload a photo, Dr. Skinner would be pounding on my door sometime in the next thirty minutes.

When I climbed into bed, my blankets sounded as loud as cannon fire.

《◇》

MY CLASSES STARTED the next morning, and I was grateful for it. Sid was gone at 8:00 a.m. when my alarm started blaring. He liked to work out early, and I was relieved to see that he was trying to stick to that schedule.

Breakfast was at 7:30 a.m., classes at 8:30. I blinked, trying to figure out what scared me more—seeing students, or not seeing the students that were no longer at school.

The thought made me shiver as I pulled up my slacks and smoothed out my cardinal red blazer. No, I was not going to breakfast.

My first class was Critical Thinking—one of my electives. Before Perses, it took copious amounts of coffee to get me through it. The teacher was dry as sand. Dr. Drake had been the longest-serving teacher at Augustus, and it showed. Oh, God, I could hear him, droning on about argument structures, thinking he was talking to everyone when he was talking to no one, wispy white hair bouncing on his mostly bald white head….

I got to class and found I was only the third person there, five minutes before nine. I didn't think much of it and whipped out my phone, thumbing my way through Instagram, allowing myself to sink into the gentle numbness that was the scroll hole. I liked every picture I could find of friends who had moved back to Augustus and were talking about how they couldn't wait to move #PastPerses. Technically, our phones weren't supposed to be out during classes, but I had a hard time seeing Drake yanking my iPhone out of my hands.

It was only when I heard "Where is this guy?" that I realized fifteen minutes had passed since I first sat down. It was now ten minutes after class was supposed to start, and that was weird. Really weird. Dr. Drake was a lot of things, but late was not one of them.

At fifteen minutes, the dozen or so of us who had gathered looked at each other. "Do we leave?" Jessica Falgaraes asked, and I realized she was nervously bothering the collar of her Augustus blazer.

I was genuinely confused. Was I in the right classroom? Had my schedule changed? "Maybe?"

"I feel like leaving for our first class back is a terrible idea," Barry Bamber said. His face was bright red—just like always—and he seemed to be breathing a little harder than usual.

Eleven of us were looking at each other, trying to figure out what was going on. One student was in the corner of the room, a dark hoodie closed over his face, his blazer nowhere in sight.

And, thankfully, that was when an actual adult walked in…. But it wasn't Dr. Drake. It was a youngish guy—probably in his thirties, with unruly, curly hair poking in every direction. He was out of breath and his button-down shirt was halfway removed from his wrinkled khakis.

"I apologize. Doctor Drake will not be in class."

Groans around, except for the hoodie. I looked at him, and he appeared to slink incrementally into his form.

There was a weird lilt to wrinkled khaki guy's voice that gave me pause.

My eyes narrowed. "Will he be here tomorrow?"

Khaki looked flustered. I suspect his face would have flushed if it wasn't already. "We'll have more information for you shortly."

There were no groans now.

Khaki stepped out of the door frame, and with a forced casual tone, gestured to the doorway. "Please, go enjoy the beautiful day until your next class."

It was forty-five degrees, the sky was slate gray, and a thin mist was falling from the air.

"Jesus Christ." I whipped on my blazer and was first out the door. I was in such a rush to leave that I banged into the door frame as I moved.

It wasn't until I had burst into the wet winter morning that I realized I had no idea where I was going. With nothing better to do until my 11:00 a.m. class, I stormed into the Student Union, my foul mood matching the weather.

A cup of coffee and a cold bagel later, and I sat alone, watching people walk by. I had loved doing this before Perses… staring at everyone as they walked. Examining their stony expressions, their joyful smiles or angry eyes, pondering what lay beneath. Most of the time, people's faces were easy enough to read. On nights when Sid had an away game or the Twins were doing whatever they were doing, probably trying to sneak off campus. If I'm being honest, there were times where I'd just get a cup of coffee and watch.

Those nights were the worst. Friday nights in school brought out a swarm of emotions—the bloom of new relationships, the violence of love scorned, the comfort of a good friend. The array of faces that I saw never ceased to amaze me… that so much complicated emotion could exist in the same space.

Now? I'd give anything to see it again.

I stared at the ground, anxiously scanning for wet footprints as I jammed a half-thawed cinnamon-raisin bagel down my throat. Groups of students sat in twos and threes, talking in hushed tones. I'd say at least ten of my classmates were buried in their phones, thumbs absently scrolling. But among them, one constant—a slack, emotion-free face, one covering up whatever they didn't want to feel.

Time stretched like taffy. One second, it seemed as if the clock was stuck on 10:03, and the next it was 10:45 and time to go. I reluctantly moved off of my perch and went back outside. The mist had turned into a damp, cold rain, one which soaked my blazer as I trundled down Academic Row.

By the time I barged into my class I was soaked and chilled to the bone, but I was also relieved. I wasn't the only one in this class, and Dr. Poll was already there. Reed thin and tall, with his small chin covered by a black goatee, Dr. Poll was pretty much exactly what you thought of when you imagined a teacher—erudite and bubbly. Thankfully, his brilliance was matched by his friendliness. Poll's Introduction to Psychology class was the stuff of Augustus legend. Students fought over slots for it. I'll never forget my first class with him—he walked in and proceeded to stare at his pencils, lining them up in size order, before even saying his name. Then he asked what he was doing, what the behavior might be a symptom of, and how we knew. It stuck with me.

Poll's easy smile found me when I walked in. "Mister Walker, welcome back."

I fought back the urge to hug him. "It's really good to see you again, Doctor Poll."

"You too, Corey, you too. I'd ask how your Fall went, but I suspect not well."

The other three students who had walked in laughed, and I couldn't help but do the same. I could feel my spirits lifting like they'd been exposed to sunlight. "I've had better."

"I think we all have. Hopefully, the transition back to this semester will be easier than the past few months have been. After all, they can't get much worse."

More small laughter. I noticed one of the girls who was sitting in the back row put her phone away. Then, noticing the smile on his face, I thought of my last class. "Any idea what happened to Doctor Drake?"

I worried about asking the question as the words tumbled out of my mouth, afraid that it would alter the easy vibe of the classroom, but, thankfully, Poll nodded knowingly. "I don't, unfortunately. Was he not there?"

"No," said Josh Dunphy, one of Sid's soccer teammates. "Dude must have surprised people. Some guy from the Dean's office came running in to tell us."

Dr. Poll placed his hands on his hips. "I think we're going to see a lot of that these days. I understand a good portion of the student body hasn't returned."

Nods everywhere. No one seemed capable of speaking though. More kids were piling into the classroom, looking immediately at Poll, who welcomed them with a nod or a smile as they entered.

"Jen isn't back. I hadn't heard from her during the whole fall," said Jessica Good, her eyes wider than I'd seen on most humans. I think her roommate was Jen O'Neal… oh, damn, was she gone?

"Ditto," said Jason Schroeder, a big guy sitting in the front row. I was pretty sure he played basketball. "One third of my teammates didn't come back yet."

Poll's head bobbed slowly. "That's about the number I heard." He took a quick glance at his wristwatch. "Well, tell you what, I think this is the perfect segue for what I planned on talking about today." Poll took a step backward and centered himself in the classroom. When he spoke again, the conversational voice was gone, and he sounded like a teacher. "Welcome back, everybody. It's good to see you all again."

"It's really good to see you," shouted a voice from the back, much too loud. Nervous titters everywhere.

"Same, Mister Maddox. Same." Poll scanned the room. "I see that we're missing a few faces, but by and large, most of you are here, and under much happier circumstances than the last time we were together, certainly."

Oh, God, that's right. All of our phones had gone off at the same time about five months ago. The government had used some special alert system to instruct us to watch a Presidential address that would start in fifteen minutes. Poll had thrown the stream up on the computer… and the screams followed shortly thereafter.

I wasn't the only one who had forgotten or at least chosen to forget. A slew of students were shifting in their seats, uncomfortably remembering those terror-filled moments.

"I suppose my first question is this. How are you?" asked Poll. My barely suppressed twitch must have been visible enough to grab Dr. Poll's attention because for a moment, his eyes locked onto mine. "Mister Walker. How you doing, kid?"

That earnestness. It was just so irresistible. You wanted to answer Poll's question. Even if you didn't want to answer truthfully. Even if you were still washing your hands to get the blood of an abuse casualty off of your fingers, even if you could still smell the gunpowder as a domestic violence victim lay dying in front of you. "I'm okay."

"Yeah? No lingering fears from the Perses Fall?" There was more laughter now, but it was more sympathetic than anything else.

"Oh, no, everything's just fine." I matched Poll's vocal tone, earning more laughter. Poll, bless him, laughed as well, before turning back to the rest of the class.

"I'm sure things for all of you went about as well as they did for me." Poll's eyes acquired a far-away look. His facade of eagerness broke for a split second. "I understand it has been a difficult few weeks. I know I'm the first teacher many of you have had since returning, and the school has asked me to remind you to take it easy over the next days and weeks ahead. I'm sure we can expect more out of them, but for now, they've asked me to reiterate that the counseling center is open—"

Groans around. Poll put his hands in front of his chest as if to ward off the murmurs of protests. "What? What?"

"You know why we're groaning, Doctor Poll," said Jess Good.

"We couldn't get in there in the best of circumstances," said another guy behind me. "I called first thing this morning because their online system was down. They are already fully booked."

"It's like they don't care about us at all," said Megan Buchanan.

"I think they're trying to get other counselors in," said Poll, meekly. "I do know that this has been a relevant topic of conversation. The school is concerned about all of you as we try to reacclimate to the world. And, for whatever it's worth, I'm also concerned. All of us have experienced some very significant events."

"To put it politely," groaned a voice.

I shifted in my seat, staring at the faces of those here. What was remarkable was the anger fixed on people's faces, and I suddenly felt bad for Poll. Save for one or two people, the vast majority of the people in this classroom looked furious.

"Doctor Poll?" I asked tentatively. Poll looked over at me, and I continued. "I do have a question, and it's been bugging me since we got back. How are we supposed to go back to normal?"

"That's a great question, Corey," said Poll. "But there's also a very easy answer. I don't think we ever will get back to normal. I think—and I hope—that we can use what happened with Perses to better ourselves."

"What do you mean?" asked a male voice from the back.

"Well, let's think about this." Poll extended both of his hands and looked at his left. "The world has just experienced a tremendous tragedy. We all thought, for four months or so, that we were going to die. We spent all that time staring down the barrel of a gun, waiting for our death, spending our savings when we could, looking at our children and mourning the future that they would never have."

"Don't forget the collapse of civilization," chimed in Ryan Wild, a short kid who had been on my floor sophomore year.

"Yes, that little thing," Poll said. "The near-collapse of the global financial and banking system. The law and order breakdowns. The suicides and the drug overdoses. The reckless behavior. Did you all see the bungie-less jumpers?"

Nods everywhere. I'd seen the clips on YouTube. Pure nightmare fuel.

"And now, here we are. Alive. Like we are supposed to go back to normal." Poll clasped his hands in front of his chest. "I don't think we ever go back to normal."

"Then why are we here?" said Megan Buchanan, her voice clear and crisp.

"How do you mean?"

"Why would any of us participate in a society that caused us all so much pain, and so much anxiety? Even before Perses, it's not like any of us were having a great time." Megan's voice toned down an octave, but her words were sharp. Just like yesterday, she was wearing an all-black outfit, only this time, her red blazer covered her shirt.

Megan continued. "I mean, come on. How many of us were depressed or anxious or scared and couldn't find help anywhere? How many of us couldn't stop checking Instagram because of what we were scared of missing?" Students were nodding. I felt a pit opening in my stomach. "The world was out of control before Perses. What incentive do any of us have to give back to a place that never cared about us in the first place?"

"These are excellent questions." A wide smile appeared on Poll's face. *He thinks this is an academic exercise. It's not.* "What do you propose we do?"

Megan shrugged. "I have some thoughts. But right now, I just want to make sure I'm not the only one who feels this way." She looked around the room and found students nodding in her direction. "This world sucks, Doctor Poll. I'm not sure any of us have any real incentive to return to normal."

A heavy silence fell, thick as molasses, and I wasn't sure what to say. This world did suck. The planet was melting. We had just missed dying in a fiery apocalypse, and we were supposed to go back to class and act like nothing was wrong? Come. On. I wasn't sure where Megan was going, but I appreciated that she was at least speaking a fundamental truth.

"That is, without a doubt, the biggest load of crap I have ever heard in my life," said a deep female voice from the corner of the room.

A bunch of giggles and a couple of hoots of awkward laughter followed. I turned in the direction of the voice and found a redhead, her hair like fire, and a facial expression that seemed to match. The intensity on her face was downright frightening, and right now, she had fixed Megan in her laser sights. "What planet are you living on?"

"Earth. The one which was almost destroyed," said Megan evenly. More giggles. I glanced over at Dr. Poll, but he had folded his hands behind his back and seemed content to watch this play out.

"'Almost' being the important word." Red extended her arms. Her face looked familiar, but not enough for me to identify her. She looked like a memory I'd forgotten. "Yeah, the world kinda sucks right now, but it will keep sucking if all of us just stop 'participating' like you just said. There's got to be an upside here. We're the only ones who can actually fix things."

"And how has that worked out so far? Anyone in here happy right now?"

"We just almost died. No one is going to be happy," Red huffed.

"Kristy," I said to myself, softly, so no one else could hear. She was in my mind again—blood pouring on snow.

"And no one was happy before Perses either," snapped Megan. "That's who we have always been. Since birth. That's where 'staying connected' has gotten us. We're all in this together, but we're all going downhill."

"So what do you want to do, Megan? Throw all of civilization into a tub of acid?" Red's skin tone had flushed, nearly matching the color of her hair. "Do you want to go back to caves? Did you miss the part where the advances of human civilization actually allowed us to avert the extinction of the human race? Would that have happened if people stopped 'participating' in society?" Red's mouth was open, her eyes wide, her facial expression flashing to utter disbelief.

Megan issued an icy smile, one which practically radiated the coldest snow, and said no more. The flash in her eyes said that she was holding something back.

Red sat back in her seat and looked at Poll. "Whatever." Then she bounced back up, like the back of her seat had springs. "Wait. No. I do have one more question. What do you mean?"

Now Megan looked taken aback. "Sorry?"

"You say civilization sucks. The world is out of control, and no good comes from participating with each other. I mean, social media is pretty evil, I'll give you that." Red tapped her phone. "I'm pretty sure that human civilization means more than liking a TikTok video, but whatever. If things suck so much, why didn't you just stay at home with everyone else? What do you mean when you say you have some 'thoughts' about what to do going forward? Do you just want to spread your misery to the rest of us?"

I jerked my head back at the question—what was this girl's deal? The redhead was right… why was she here if everything sucked so badly? Before Megan could answer, Poll interjected, a hand extended. "All right, I think that's enough for now."

My head swiveled between Megan and the redhead. I kind of wanted to hear Megan's answer to that question.

«◇»

CLASS WENT ON, as Poll made a valiant effort to discuss disorders like depression, but honestly, no one needed to learn about it from a textbook. When class ended, the redhead practically bolted out of the door, fueled by jets of fiery anger. I walked quickly after her, nearly barreling through Megan, who was holding court with three other students.

I was within a few feet of the redhead, trying to figure out what I wanted to say. Her words in the classroom had been heated, fueled by some sort of anger inside of her. I wanted to figure out why. But then she whirled in my direction, now walking backward and staring at me with these striking blue eyes. Her eyes were slightly widened and her expression open.

I opened my mouth to respond and then realized something. I had absolutely no idea what to say.

So, instead, I grunted, put my head down, and thundered forward like I was being chased by a ghost. I closed my eyes as I bolted to the cafeteria, trying to ignore the waves of shame and awkwardness that were crashing into me like I was a low beach at high tide.

Fifteen minutes later, I was in the cafeteria, with a plate of pasta and a salad that had been soaked in blue cheese dressing balanced awkwardly on a tray. Sid wasn't around—which was weird—and I couldn't find the twins—which wasn't weird. I had no idea where they went during lunch. Probably with a girl.

I sighed and poked at my salad, one hand listlessly moving my lettuce with a fork, the other hand precariously balancing my face on my fist. I was too miserable to even bring out my phone.

The clatter of dishes startled me so much that I jumped, knees hitting the table, jostling the drink in my tray. It was the redhead. Smoothly, she placed a linen napkin on her lap, grabbed her fork, and jammed a mouthful of steamed carrots into her face. Then she made eye contact. "Do you believe that?"

"Believe what? Megan?"

"Yes, Megan. The ice queen who wants the rest of the world to fall down around her. I couldn't concentrate on the rest of that class, and I actually wanted to. Poll was an amazing teacher the first few weeks we had him, and I wanted to learn something." Red paused to take a drink. For a second, I thought that maybe she was trying to rein herself in, but that wasn't it because she swallowed way too quickly and started talking way too loudly. "And did you see how she didn't answer the question?"

I was starting to regret not scampering to my room. There was no warmth in this girl's expression. No joy in her eyes. And there was no name to her face. "Umm… who are you?"

Then she smiled. "Paige. Paige Lynn."

That startled me. "Your… your hair."

She fluffed out her mass of red curly locks. "Yep. This is my natural color. I died it black before."

Now it hit me. Paige—her face covered in freckles—had always looked slightly off, like a golden retriever with silver fur. "Why would you do something like that?" *Oh. Oh, no. I didn't open my mouth and say the stupid thing again, did I?*

Paige just gave me this little smile, and the subject was behind us.

"You've got friends who aren't here this semester, right?" she asked.

The abrupt change of conversation snapped my brain like a rubber band, and my mind went to Josh. To his empty room that I hadn't yet gathered the strength to walk past. "Yes."

Paige heard the husk of my voice, and for a moment, her eyes softened. "Not just that, but I'm sorry. Me too. But that's not exactly what I meant. I mean people who haven't come back."

I thought of my Instagram feed, replete with #IJustCant status updates. "A few, yeah."

Paige jerked a hand over her shoulder, where I found Megan Buchanan holding court with four other students at a round table. "If Buchanan is so content on blowing up the world—if she thinks that everything is terrible and that humanity should just fall back into itself— why is she here? Wouldn't she want to just go hide out in her bedroom and watch Netflix?"

That was a good point. "You're right, but I don't get why that is such a big deal."

Paige's spoon froze on the way to her mouth. A bit of soup dribbled back into her bowl. "That question you asked in class."

"How we get back to normal?"

"Yeah." Paige's eyes narrowed. "Don't you know the answer?"

"If I did, why would I ask the question?"

Paige's voice was devoid of the anger which had characterized our brief conversation. "Because you want confirmation. You're here. I'm here. So many aren't. And we're here because we want to try again. You do want to try to resume life, don't you?"

And there we were, sitting in the middle of the crowded cafeteria but feeling like we were the only ones in the room, hitting on the haunting heart of the matter. And it occurred to me, for the first time since I'd gotten back, that it felt like I was actually at school again.

"Of course, I do." I swallowed and pushed my plate away from me, my stomach feeling light and heavy at the same time. "I'm here because I have to be here."

Paige waggled a finger. "Exactly. We want to try again, even knowing just how screwed up the world is going to be for a little while."

"You don't think that's what Megan was talking about?'

"Oh, hell no." Paige waved a dismissive hand. "She was talking about not caring about society. About not investing in its future. I can't get over that she said that. What good would not caring anymore do?"

I thought of the Perses Fall. All of the aspects of our world had seemingly been ground to dust, falling apart due to entropy or our own inability to maintain order at a time when we needed it the most. "I get where she's coming from, though. There are a lot of people who didn't come back because they aren't ready."

"A lot of those people are here. They're looking for a voice to carry them through this moment."

I shivered, and I don't think it was caused by the weather. "Yeah. When people are scared, they'll listen to anyone."

Paige made a noise that sounded like something between a grunt and a snort. "Didn't we find that out over the past five months or so?"

"Oh, for sure." The conversation seemed to have trailed off and could feel the sweat starting to pool in my lower back. Crap. I hated this part of the conversation. When you went quiet because you didn't know what else to say. I clawed through my mind for something to say as Red stared at me expectantly. "What made you so angry about this?" *Oh, sweet Jesus, did I really just ask the girl I just met why she's so angry? Why am I so bad at this?*

But God bless the world, Paige put on that little smile again. "We almost died."

"True."

Her smile broadened a touch. "We almost died, and I spent seventeen years in near silence. Almost dying gives you clarity." She broke eye contact and stared off into the distance, her vision falling to the students who somehow seemed to be everywhere and nowhere around us. Then her gaze wandered. I wondered if she was staring at the blank spaces where students used to sit. "Look, I'm not an idiot. This isn't supposed to be easy. Rebuilding five months of destruction will not come without a price. But I don't think I'm angry. I think I'm just saying what's on my mind. I wish everyone else was doing the same right now. I think we all need to be more honest about what we are afraid of. And what we want."

A wave of warmth washed over me. I hoped it hadn't hit my face. "There's going to be a lot of pain over the next little while. I've seen it." There was Kristy Ford again, bleeding on my shirt, and from the way the smile fell from Red's face, I could see that she saw the pain on me. "It's beyond overwhelming."

"It is. But there's not much we can do but say what we want."

"And be honest about the days ahead." Slowly, I extended my hand forward. "Corey."

Paige's blue eyes sparkled ever so slightly. She extended her hand. Folded it into mine. Her nails were each a different neon color. "I know who you are." Her lips turned upward again.

Chapter 7

Meeting Paige and trading numbers with her was the high point of the day. It was all downhill from there.

Okay, take the campus. It was beautiful. We always heard about "Augustus Pride" and how the school spent so much more than the average school on keeping its immaculate campus green and gorgeous. As jaded high school students, we had always rolled our eyes and whispered snide comments to each other at appropriate moments, but deep down, I think most of us loved just how beautiful Augustus was. The massive dining hall that looked like something out of Harry Potter. The arboretum on the west side of campus boasted dozens of tree types. At its center was a stone fountain by which every new Augustus couple was supposed to have their first kiss.

Now? The campus looked like a shell of its former self. Yes, it was February, but snow-capped trees were supposed to be inviting and warm, not foreboding and haunting. And yet, here we were, surrounded by dead trees and overgrown branches and roots that seemed to claw through the pavement to send you sprawling to your hands and knees.

They found a substitute teacher for Critical Thinking, but it became clear from our first class with him, a week after classes started, that he was in grad school and only a few years older than us. The library—my favorite spot to go and study—almost never had a clerk at the front desk. Books lay scattered on tables for days at a time. The one librarian who

I'd gotten to know, Mrs. Jones—a sweet, older woman who asked me about Mom and gave me homemade brownies in Ziplock bags—was nowhere to be seen. No one knew where she was.

I saw way too many kids stoned in the middle of the day. Before Perses, that happened now and then. But not every day. And not this brazenly, this consistently. It was a cry for help that was being left unanswered.

It was with this background in mind that I trudged toward the Student Union about a week after classes had started. The sun was out and there was an almost unnatural warmth outside, causing damp sweat to soak my neck. I was with Sid, Mika, and Mo, and only half paying attention to the conversation.

I hated it. Watching classmates walking next to each other but wearing headphones, not even attempting to talk with each other. Pairs of students dressed in all black outfits that clashed awkwardly with their deep red blazers. They weren't even speaking, just holding hands, with glassy, still expressions locked on their faces.

It wasn't until I saw the third cluster of students in all black that it registered.

I scratched my head. "Did we enter a new emo phase?"

"Is emo a thing?" asked Mo.

Mika shrugged. "After Perses, anything is a thing."

"Also, nothing," grunted Sid.

I laughed. "No, but seriously, what's with the all black?" We entered the Union. "Is there a protest going on that I don't know about? Do these kids realize how dumb they look?"

Sid kept looking ahead as if I hadn't said anything.

"Oh, Sidney," I ran a few steps ahead and walked backward. "I know that look, Sidney."

Sid glanced off to the side, trying not to crack a smile. "There's no look."

"Oh yes there is." When Sid trailed his eyes upward, I raised my voice an octave and said, "I think I'm gonna have to do it."

"Oh, dear God," said Mo. "Just tell him what he wants, Sid."

"Not in public. Please not in public," Mika begged.

I grinned and dramatically shook my hands. "Tell me what's with the people in all black."

Sid groaned. "You'd never do it here."

I looked around. The crowd was lighter than it had been at dinnertime pre-Perses, but there were still dozens of students milling around and a line was just starting to form in front of the Dining Hall.

Then again, I kind of thought everything around us would be a smoking ruin at this moment. And here we are.

I cleared my throat, fixed a big smile on my face, and mustered up my highest-pitched voice. "Oh, Sidney." I extended the "eeeee" sound at the end of Sid's name. Everyone in an immediate vicinity turned and looked at the noise coming from my throat, one which, I admit, sounded like a dying cat had been stepped on.

Mo, Mika, and Sid all brought their hands to their ears.

"Stop, stop." Sid was practically begging through his laughter.

"Tell me…." I said, adding the high-pitched noise to the "eeeee" at the end of "me."

"Fine, fine, just shut up." Sid waved his hands frantically. I stopped shrieking, trying to ignore the ringing sensation in my ears. "Why am I friends with you again?"

"It ain't his looks," said Mo.

I stared expectantly at Sid. "True."

After a moment's hesitation, he rolled his eyes. "Fine. Can we just get our food first?" He cast a surreptitious look around. "Also, can we move, please? I don't want it to look like I know you."

I eyed the makeshift pasta bar which was in the corner of the Dining Hall. "I respect that."

A few minutes later, the four of us sat down with our trays. Sid had already started jamming some sort of beef down his throat… at least that hadn't changed.

He was probably hoping we'd forgotten the earlier conversation, but we hadn't. Mo, Mika, and I stared expectantly at Sid, and for a moment, his eyes bounced between the three of us. Then he sighed and put his fork and knife down. "Fine. But you're keeping me from food."

"Don't care." I absent-mindedly twirled my spaghetti. "What's up with the black?"

Sid sighed. "I'm really not supposed to say anything."

I couldn't help but notice Mo and Mika lean forward. They traded looks, and Mo said, "Yeah, not gonna lie, we were wondering about that too. We couldn't find anyone to talk about it."

That was weird. Particularly for the Twins.

"I first started noticing last week," said Mo. "First I thought it was some theatre kids prepping for a play."

"It's not." There was such a certainty in Sid's voice that I almost didn't recognize it.

"Okay, Sid. Seriously. What is going on?" I asked.

Sid looked around the room again and lowered his voice. "They're called 'The Refuge.'"

"The Refuge?" Mika, Mo, and I repeated at the same time.

"What, like from another country?" asked Mika.

"No, you idiot, those are refugees," Sid said. "This is The Refuge. There's a difference."

"And what's that?" Mika snapped.

"It's a group," Sid responded.

"Like a club?" I was practically laughing. The school's closed-circuit TV system used to periodically flash announcements for clubs. The only thing it announced these days were advertisements for support groups and texting hotlines for counseling. "I don't get it. What do they do?"

Sid paused, thoughtfully, and tilted his head to the side. He was staring upward as if he was making some great calculations. "I think it'd be easier if I showed you."

"Showed us?" Mo and Mika said.

"Yes." Sid nodded. "Yes, absolutely. There's a meeting later tonight."

"Oh. Cool. So… is it…." My voice trailed off, and I looked over at Mo and Mika.

"What our tongue-tied friend is trying to ask is what happens at these meetings," Mo said.

"Yes, that."

Sid looked past us, out the cafeteria door. "It's… honestly? I think it's just a group of people getting together."

"Kind of a weird name, no?" Mika asked.

"I think it's perfect," Sid said.

That gave me pause. "Perfect?"

"Yes," Sid said. We stared, expectantly, waiting for him to elaborate. He did not.

"All right," Mika said, crumbling up his napkin and throwing it on his plate. "Well, now I'm too damn curious not to go. Mister Stoic over here isn't gonna fill us in on the grand secret unless we go to this meeting with him."

"Honestly, this whole thing is perfect." Sid was smiling more than I had seen him smile since we arrived on campus. "I wasn't sure about inviting you guys, but if you're noticing them, you'd be a great fit."

Leaning forward, Mo opened his mouth to speak, but I cut him off. "Wait, you weren't sure about inviting us to this meeting? Then why didn't you just tell me when I asked?"

Sid popped a hunk of a bread roll into his mouth. "I wanted to see you make a complete fool of yourself." The hint of a smile formed on his face.

I threw a piece of lettuce at him. "Asshole."

Sid laughed.

«◊»

THE MEETING WAS in Hillside, a dorm located on the southern end of campus. Hillside was one of the nicer and newer dorms, usually occupied by juniors. It had a huge lounge on the Third Floor, one that held a gorgeous view of campus, albeit a view that terminated abruptly thanks to our large and newly renovated student union.

A student wearing all black was holding the door to the dorm, some underclassman that I didn't recognize. "Hi! Come on in. Third Floor Lounge."

"Thanks." Mo's voice sat on the edge of friendly and mocking. When we walked past, Mo looked over at me, his face a warning. I shrugged as we trudged over to the elevator. None of us were saying anything. I suddenly felt awkward, like I didn't know what to do with my hands.

"Third Floor," the robotic voice in the elevator announced, its doors sliding open.

It hit me right away—people. Friendly conversations. Laughter. A good thirty students were crammed into the smallish space, milling around, holding drinks and small paper plates with food. The room wasn't overly crowded, but people were packed in tight enough that we had to thread through clumps of conversations in order to get out of the elevator.

I glanced around the room and caught a few things. First, not everyone was in all black. That was good—I had been nervous that I would stick out like a sore thumb. People in all black were intermingling with people who were dressed normally. Here and there, a few students still had their red Augustus blazers on, a sign that they had run over straight from our mandatory study hall.

Sid ambled up to us, handing out name tags with our names written on them in his barely legible handwriting.

"Dude. Really?" Mo asked.

"Nametags? There aren't even seven hundred people on campus right now, homie. Just about everyone knows everyone," said Mika.

"Also, you can't write. At all. I think you hit the ball one too many times with your head. Is that an M in my name or a Q?" asked Mo.

Sid's face froze, and he looked at the ground.

"Thanks," I said softly, taking my name tag from his fingers and slapping it to my chest.

From behind, a hand with black nail polish grasped Sid's shoulder. Sid turned, and just before his face disappeared from view, his whole expression brightened, widening into an open-mouthed smile. He wrapped his arms around the girl, and she wrapped her arms around his back, hugging him in greeting. A second later, they disentangled, revealing Megan Buchanan.

If she remembered the last time she had seen Mo and Mika—when they had attempted to serenade her with applause in the Netflix Lounge—she didn't show it. "Hey, guys. It's wonderful to see you." Her face creaked into a smile, and her eyes didn't move. Then she looked at me. "I'm really glad you could be here, Corey."

"Same." I tried to force a brightness into my voice. "It is awesome to see this many people together again."

"I forgot how much I missed seeing people together," Mo said, his voice sincere.

"Well, that's what we are trying to do," Megan said. She looked at Sid. "Did you bring these guys?"

"Oh, yeah." Sid laughed. "We've basically been inseparable since we got here three years ago." Then he pointed at me. "Especially this one. We've been together since we first got here."

"He snores." I shrugged.

Megan laughed. "So, that whole thing in class, didn't throw you off?"

I shifted my weight on my feet. "Nah, I get it. We're all gonna have a hard time getting back to normal."

"Very true," Megan said. Everyone nodded solemnly, even Mo and Mika. Then, Megan said, "Still though. Is that what any of us want? Normal?" Megan gestured around the room. "I mean, if this is normal, great. I'm just not sure if normal is possible out there anymore."

Sid nodded thoughtfully. I tilted my head and stared at Megan, willing her to say more. I'd heard Paige's thoughts on this one. I kind of wanted to hear the other side from Megan.

Next to me, Mo opened his mouth to speak but was slapped in the stomach by his brother. Megan pretended not to see it. "Anyway, enough of that for now. Make yourself at home. Corey, I think you'll find that everyone here is struggling with the same questions."

"Everyone outside too," Mo snapped.

Megan made a non-committal grunt and turned to Sid. "Glad you guys all came," she said, flashing him a warm smile. Then she was gone, melting into the increasingly crowded room.

"Everyone here is struggling?" Mo said. "What, here, and only here, are people having a tough time getting used to things again?"

"Yes. All of the universe's pain. Centered right here, in this very room." Mika laughed.

"Ehh, I get where they are coming from." I couldn't miss the sharp tightness that seemed to have clasped Sid's shoulders.

"I guess," muttered Mo.

We drifted sideways, heading in various directions. I made my way to the snack stand and grabbed a fist full of pigs in a blanket, jamming them into my mouth like I hadn't eaten dinner three hours ago.

"Corey, hi," exclaimed a girl behind me. I turned around and recognized her. Marleen Vaver and Danielle Brown. Both a year younger than me. I'd had AP History with them last year. They were utterly inseparable. Both were in black outfits.

"Hi, Marleen and Danielle," I said, pronouncing their name like a unit, and in the right order. Of course, my mouth was crammed with hot dog meat, and I probably had mustard on my face, but I was hoping they didn't notice that.

If they did, they were polite enough not to comment. We chatted for a few, engaging in what I had found was the new ritual—avoiding the past five months. No one wanted to talk about where we had been, what we had experienced, whether or not we had run into the supply shortages that seemed to permeate so much of the country and still hadn't fully abated.

The conversation drifted to safer ground—classes so far. How strange everything on campus seemed. Then, a change in the usual pattern. Somehow, Danielle started to discuss the first few weeks of getting back to normal, and she said, "I still can't believe it missed." Her voice dropped as she said it.

"I know," Marleen said, squeezing Danielle's hand once. "Me too. It's crazy."

"Yeah," I echoed.

"I was watching Gold on CNN when he started crying. I didn't believe it."

"None of us did," Danielle said. "We barely had internet, and I kept getting it in drips. We didn't know we were safe until an hour after the rest of the world did."

I winced at that. I couldn't imagine not knowing whether or not you were going to live.

"We exploded." Marleen gestured outward with her hands. "I mean, totally exploded. My dad started running around the house, just cursing every other word."

I laughed. We all did. The conversation felt easy for a moment.

"I just thought... that the happiness of that... that it would keep going like that, you know?" Marleen said. "That we wouldn't have to face everyone being so depressed again."

"The whole world feels like it might slip out from you at any second," Danielle said. She bit her lip and her eyes swam.

"I know what you mean," I said.

Danielle's eyes seemed to brighten. "You do?"

"Oh, yeah." I gestured around. "Everything feels so off. So unsure. It would be nice to find something more stable, more real. As scary as things are right now."

Danielle and Marleen's eyes seemed to flash at the same moment. "What if it didn't have to be this scary?" Marleen asked.

I cocked my head sideways. "Huh?"

Danielle and Marleen shimmied closer to me. The movement was oddly synchronous, like it was planned. "Corey, we found something here," Danielle said.

Marleen leaned in closer, her voice low and reverent. "The Refuge."

"Oh… sure." I tried to keep any tenor of agreement out of my voice. "So, this is like… a club?"

Marleen grunted with mock offense. "Please! More than that."

"Much more than that," Danielle said.

Marleen gestured around again, her hands almost flailing. "People, Corey. Actual people are getting together. Doing something. Not just sitting around talking, but actually interacting. I never thought there were new people to get to know on this campus, but here we are. Having our horizons expanded. Even at this place."

"Is that what this is about?" I asked.

"Among other things." Danielle laughed and gestured at herself. "Corey. They have these tests to make sure that you are right for them." When I tilted my head, Danielle quickly added, "Don't worry, it's just to keep out the psychos and stuff. Anyway, once you pass, they introduce you to people who you are going to be friends with."

"So… they make it easy for you to make new friends?"

"They don't make it easy for you, Corey. They do it for you!" Marleen cried.

"What if you want to make new friends with others out of the group?" I asked cautiously.

"But why would you *want* to?" Danielle asked.

Marleen nodded eagerly. "It's like Tinder. For High Schoolers. Also. Better. You know what? Here." Marleen reached back into her pocket and came back with a white pamphlet with black lettering. "The Refuge" was written across the top. "We're both pretty new. Read this. I think it can explain what's going on better than we can."

I took the pamphlet and glanced around the room. Others were also looking at similar brochures while chatting with others. Directly in front of me stood a red-headed kid, small, wearing his Augustus blazer. His arms were folded firmly across his chest, and he wasn't talking to anyone.

I brought my attention back to Danielle and Marleen. "Okay, I'll check it out."

We said goodbye, then I opened the pamphlet and scanned the document. The first sentence that I read made me raise my eyebrows.

In our darkest moments, we became each other's light.

"That's a lot," I muttered to myself.

Around me, the din of conversations seemed to dissipate as I disappeared into the document in front of me.

At what we thought would be The End of the World, The Refuge was formed. Our founders came together to give each other solace and comfort in our planet's final hours. Using social support, sheltering techniques, and a variety of other methods, our members were able to endure the worst days in the history of our civilization, believing that they would at least find peace and joy in our final days.

And then, we were saved.

But the fight to save civilization was just beginning.

Too many of us know the pain of loved ones lost, of unfulfilled dreams, of a civilization designed to enrich the few at the expense of the many. What if there was a better way? What if there was a Refuge?

I looked up. Mo and Mika, I realized, were nowhere in sight. They had disappeared.

I found Sid again, talking with two underclassmen I didn't recognize, along with Dave Thomas, a junior. Seeing me, Sid broke away.

"What do you think?" he asked.

"Kind of interesting," I kept my tone as noncommittal as possible.

Sid heard through it. "I get it, Corey. Just enjoy yourself. We're here to meet new friends. That's all."

I looked around the room again. Conversations were popping off everywhere. More people were talking and more smiles were blooming than I had seen since I had come back onto campus. And yet, every conversation had a weird pattern to it. After a moment, I realized what it was. In almost every conversation, two people wearing the black outfits were talking to one person wearing normal clothing.

I looked back at Sid. "Did you read the pamphlet?"

Sid shrugged. "Glanced at it. Why?"

"This isn't just an Augustus thing. It sounds like this was something that started during Perses and then got stronger afterward."

"Oh, yeah, I think someone said something about that. That's the brochure with their history and everything, right?"

"Yes…." I let my voice trail off. When Sid didn't add anything, I said, "I don't know… doesn't this seem kinda weird to you?"

"How?" Sid's voice was sharp.

I knew what I wanted to say. "A movement started during the end of the world that talks about wanting to help people and makes you wear all black doesn't seem weird to you? Or a social club that picks your friends for you and…." Sid's eyes were almost cross with anger. My voice fell away, but every alarm bell in my head was firing off at record speed. As I tried to form the words, my mind turned over like a broken engine. Sid's arms were folded across his chest, his muscles bulging against his t-shirt. His head was tilted. One of his feet was bobbing up and down, waiting.

So, instead, I said, "Just a club? You're sure?"

Sid was nodding. "Just a club, Corey."

I scanned the room again. "Why are so many people in all black, Sid?"

For the first time since we'd gotten back to campus, Sid's face changed, like a coolness that spread across it. His features hardened, and I could feel my lip twinge uncomfortably. Eventually, like ice crackling, Sid smiled slowly and said nothing.

I opened my mouth to speak, but the words caught. So, instead, I said nothing too.

Chapter 8

THE MEETING MADE me uneasy. Okay, yeah, a lot of things made me uneasy lately, but this weirdness had a new layer. The world made me feel like I was standing on quicksand, and every day, we sank a little bit deeper, and it became a little bit harder to move.

Before Perses, I had spoken with Mom every few days and Mack about the same. Since I'd come back to Augustus, our conversations had become more frequent, and we texted a lot more too. That night, after Study Hall, I got back to my room and walked into the Netflix Lounge. It was blissfully empty and the best place on campus to get good reception.

"Hey Corey," answered a deep voice that was most decidedly not my mother.

"Jill?"

"Oh, yes, it's me." Jill had a smile in her voice.

"Oh, Lord."

"Yes, your mom is enjoying herself. Don't worry, all is well here. How are you, young man?"

"Well, nothing's on fire on campus."

"Give it time," Jill said. Something rustled in the background. *"Hang on, your mom is coming."*

"Love you, Jill."

"*Love you too, Cor.*"

With a clunk, the phone was transferred. "*Hey, Corey.*"

"Mom." I tried to keep the snicker out of my voice. I failed.

"*Corey Shannon Elizabeth Walker!*"

"None of those are my middle names."

"*Fine. But they would have been if you were a girl. Anyway, Corey, I've had two glasses of wine—*"

"Lightweight."

Mom ignored me. "*I will have you know that I am with Mack and Jill, and Mack is driving me home, and he has not even had one beer.*" I was smiling until Mom added, "*And if anyone deserves to drink right now, it is someone whose son is away at school.*"

I groaned. "Stop. It's not that bad."

"*No?*" Mom sounded angrier than necessary. Then a pause, and a deep breath. "*I know. And I'm sorry. I wanted you to go back. And I'm glad you went.*"

"So am I. Most of the time."

"*Same.*" Mom paused. "*But that isn't why you called.*"

"No, it basically is." We'd spoken about how strange things were on campus—"I'm paying a small fortune of our very limited income to send you there, and they hired some kid barely out of college to teach you?"—but when I filled her in on The Refuge, a frost spread over the conversation. I told her about the kids in all black and the mystery which surrounded them.

"*That… that makes me very uncomfortable,*" Mom said.

"Me too."

Then another pause. "*Sid doing okay?*"

"Sure?"

"*So, no.*"

"No, I don't think so," I said. "He's not who he was."

"*Are any of us?*" Mom asked.

"The pain at this place, Mom. It's overwhelming. And the school can't get their arms around it."

"And they will continue to struggle to for a long, long time." There was a pause that lasted a second too long. *"Here, let me give you to Mack. Tell him about this campus group, okay, Corey?"*

The pleading quality in her voice left me distinctly uncomfortable. "Sure, Mom. Love you."

"Love you." Then a clunk and a rustling.

"Corey?" Mack's voice was questioning. I imagine he was staring at the look on my mom's face. *"What's up?"*

"Campus is weird, that's all, Mack."

"Weird, how?"

So, again, I launched into the new mystery group. Or at least, got to the part where I described students running around in black.

"Is this a group called 'The Refuge?'"

My blood ran cold, and for a moment, the world blinked out of focus. "How did you know that?"

There was movement on the other end of the line, and when Mack spoke again, his voice was much lower. *"All right. The D.A. still has me on leave after the shooting, but they're letting me update my MOPETC in the meantime."*

"Your what?"

"Training. They're letting me do my training, Little Man. Anyway, last week, the State Police held a training on some of the terrorist groups which are proliferating in the post-Perses chaos."

"Terrorists?" I screamed, my voice uncontrollably loud. "Terrorists are running around Augustus?"

"The definition of terrorists has changed, Little Man. When you think of terrorists, you think of religious nutjobs, running around and blowing themselves and everything within a hundred feet of them up, right? Or some lunatic who wants to start shooting at anyone whose skin is darker than white?"

"Something like that."

"Right. That doesn't hold true anymore. The new version is more inclusive." There was a sharp edge to Mack's voice now. An anger which was previously saved for criminals Mack arrested. For people we discussed

around the dining room table on Friday nights when Mack would decompress over a homemade meal. *"Now, terrorism means people who are intent on slowing the recovery of civilization."*

My eyes narrowed. "I don't get it."

"Little Man, there's an awful lot of chaos out there right now—"

"Painfully aware."

"Then this isn't a surprise for you. Where some see chaos, others see opportunity. The end result is groups like this Refuge popping up in various parts of the country. There are a lot more of them, but their goal seems to be to provide people a safe place. Somewhere they can go and shut their minds off."

Now I paused, dumbfounded. "Is… is that bad?"

Apparently, that wasn't the response Mack expected. *"What?"*

"The Refuge. If they are giving people comfort, a chance to escape the world… I don't know, Mack. Yeah, it seems intense, but no one had guns at their meeting."

That got Mack's attention. *"You went to their meeting?"*

"Yeah. Sid invited me." With that, I stood, letting the silence settle in as I stared out the big bay windows of the lounge, staring at the darkness and the periodic burst of light from the streetlights below.

Finally, Mack said, *"You remember why your mom and I wanted you to go back so badly?"*

"Because life goes on."

"Yes, Corey, exactly. Because life goes on. And because the world needs you to be a part of it. All of the problems we had before Perses are back. They are just bigger and louder and now the world is filled with millions of people who are destroyed by everything they saw during the Perses Fall. Because of this, we also have to contend with those who are savvy enough to take advantage of the chaos."

"How does this come back to The Refuge?"

"Groups like The Refuge don't care about giving their followers peace. I'm sure some in the organization do, but I guarantee that their leadership is as corrupt as a tree that's rotting from within. They see people who are vulnerable and need solace. And they take advantage of them, and their money, and their sadness." The words were tumbling faster and faster out of Mack's mouth now. *"Corey, I joined*

the military and then became a policeman because I really, truly believe that we have a social obligation to each other. A contract to take care of the weakest and the neediest. And these bastards—these Refuge monsters, and their ilk—they want to unwind that contract and put us back into clans, warring with each other with torches and pitchforks until there's nothing left but ashes. They want to control others. Control their decisions. It's insidious, Corey. It starts off slow—the clothing you wear. The friends you make. And then you can't call your loved one or go outside. I've seen it in foreign countries. I've seen it in America. And I am seeing it more and more now."

Whoa.

"So… so how are they doing this?"

"*We don't know yet.*" Mack's voice sounded weighted to the point of exhaustion. "*These groups popped up so fast and the government is still in such shambles that no one has had time to conduct a proper investigation. Combine that with the secrecy of groups like The Refuge, and we have a problem.*"

"Fine. But who's funding them? How do these groups get their money?"

"*Little Man, you've got an awful lot of broken people in the world with an awful lot of cash. People who cashed out their retirement savings. People whose sense of time and long-term planning were destroyed as if Perses had hit. Millionaires and billionaires searching for meaning and investments. And the world is never short of people who want to separate the wealthy and the naive from the naivete which their wealth has bought them.*" Mack paused, and I could hear the rustling of him rubbing his big hands over his face. "*Plus, you've got whatever these bastards can wrangle out of their new members. That's more than enough money to push up the food chain.*"

I thought of the students in all black and briefly wondered whether or not their black jeans had room for their wallets. And where those students were going. Had they been heading to the same place? Oh, and another thing, why the hell does a secret cult wear all black? Are they trying to signal their presence? To whom? And why?

"*Little Man?*" Mack's voice was loud and insistent.

"Hmm?" I realized I'd ignored him.

"Be careful out there, and tell Sid to do the same. Don't lose him to this Refuge. Don't let someone else steal his sense of agency."

"Right." The words weren't fully computing. This was a boarding school, not Communist China.

Talk trailed into the mundane. The state of home. The rest of Mack's police force. Patrolman James, who still hadn't been seen.

The whole conversation had an undercurrent of sadness and tension to it. Mack was distracted. I'd called home to try and find comfort. Now I was more lost, and by the time I got off the phone, I think Mack felt bad for upsetting me.

For a few moments after hanging up, I stared blankly out the window before shifting my gaze to a worn-out fireplace that occupied one corner of the room. Finally, I curled my head into my chest and took a deep breath.

"You all right?"

I think I partially jumped out of my skin. "Jesus."

Paige was sitting at one of the tables, the only other occupant of the Netflix Lounge, a broad smile on her face. Her books were spread across the table and a highlighter perched between her fingers with rainbow-tinted nails. "In my defense, having a deep, emotional conversation in a public area may not be the smartest idea."

"Point taken." We stared at each other for a moment before I decided that her smile was an invitation. I moved to sit across from her.

"Fun meeting?" she asked. I stared at her for a moment. Her voice was thick and deep. She sounded like a professional singer, not a high school senior.

"Just great." I smiled wanly. "None of them were doing any chanting or anything."

Paige arched an eyebrow. "Any animal sacrifices?"

I waved a dismissive hand. "Only a goat. I think he was dead before I got there though."

Paige chuckled. "Did you see my new friend?"

"Megan? Oh yeah. She was one of the first people we spoke with."

"Did you know her before class?"

I shrugged. "I had a few classes with her, I think. We never really spoke."

In response, Paige tapped her phone with a magenta fingernail, bringing up screenshots of Megan's Instagram page.

"That's not creepy at all," I quipped.

The harshness from that first day of class reemerged. "If you think this is creepy, you ain't seen nothing." Paige gathered herself up, sitting up straighter and pushing her books aside. "You should have seen some of the stuff Megan wrote after they announced Perses."

A couple of button taps later, and Paige handed me her iPhone. It was opened to a series of screenshots. They were statuses from Megan's Instagram page, and Paige wasn't kidding. They started normal enough—the usual stuff, I'd call it. Sadness about our impending doom. Pictures of a moonless sky. Selfies that accompanied a list of things that she never got to do. God, I had forgotten how self-indulgent the #WhatIWish movement was. Then, sometime in November, things took a dark turn.

November 2, a selfie in black and white, with Megan's face barely visible: Has it all been a lie? The vile truth behind our existence is that none of it was for any point. All the poverty, all the wars, all the pain, and all the peace… nothing. We're all dying together.

The status rung in my heart like a bad note at a concert.

"Yikes."

"Was that the continuing one?"

"Oh, no." I flipped over to the next shot.

November 3, just a picture of a bed, again, in black and white: All this pain. There's no point in continuing. The replies were from friends, urging her not to commit suicide.

"Poor girl." I rubbed my forehead and tried to ignore the disconnect in front of me. The girl I had spoken with seemed so far removed from the depressed kid who was posting suicide notes on Instagram.

Paige leaned forward on the edge of her seat. "Keep going."

November 4, another selfie, her face clearly visible this time: I'm fine. I don't know why, but I'm still here. But I wish I didn't know. I wish that I could just live my life, stay at Augustus. That place was like a bubble. A blanket, warm and safe. I don't know how to find it, but I want peace and calm and tranquility. If there was a pill I could take to make me not know everything that was happening, I'd find it. There's too much now… too much pain, too much death, and too much uncertainty.

And at once, my mind went back to the recently ended conversation with Mack. "The Refuge."

Paige knew what I was talking about right away. "Is *that* what their name is?"

I nodded, each movement of my head feeling like I was stuck underwater.

Paige's face scrunched. A lock of straight red hair had fallen across her forehead, directly over her left eye. If she noticed, she didn't make a move. For a few moments, she sat, frozen, and when she spoke again, her voice was small. "These people scare me."

"You're not the only one." I was referring to Mack more than myself. "I get their motivation, though."

"I do too. I think that's why they scare me." Paige drummed her milky-white fingers against the laminate table. I hadn't realized how pale her fingers were until just now, and I found myself transfixed by them, watching them rhythmically bob against the table. Abruptly, Paige stopped and stretched her hands. I looked back up at her face. "I think what scares me the most is that we're in uncharted territory."

"Completely." I looked around the Lounge. A few months ago, it would have been off the wall crowded, replete with study groups and video games and conversations taking place under the watchful eye of one of the teachers and prefects. We'd probably be doing some activity. Sitting in a circle, drinking hot chocolate, discussing college applications and what came next.

Instead, it was just Paige and me, sitting under pale, dim lights, trying to move forward in a world that didn't seem to have any idea of which way to turn. "It's like the world is embracing nihilism as one."

"Holding hands and jumping off the cliffs." There was a strand of hair in front of Paige's face, and she brushed it away with a smooth twist of her arm. "The entire planet needs therapy."

"That may be a start." I thought of my evening routine during the Perses Fall. Watch CNN. Try not to cry. Look at TikTok. Usually cry. Climb into bed. Cry into my pillow. That routine had been replaced by an increasing gnawing in the pit of my stomach, a fear from watching the world devolve around me.

"Or we need to just be more honest with our pain."

That snapped me out of my reverie. "Come again?"

Suddenly, Paige was sitting up, leaning close. I matched her gesture as much as social norms would allow... and then maybe a little more. I could feel the tail end of her warm breath. "Did you know me before Perses?"

I searched my memory, trying to remember a pale-skinned girl with long black hair, not the vivid shade of red in front of me. I smiled meekly and said, "I remember that you... you know... existed... and were a person... and such...."

"We were in five classes together."

I tightened my mouth. "Oof. Well, I...."

Paige waved her hand aside. "It's okay, between the darker hair and the fact that I never spoke in class, I don't blame you."

Now I stared at her, blinking slowly. She had been generic. A girl who never said a word, who just blended into the furniture. Someone who moved through the hallways like a ghost who was afraid of their reflection. "I can't imagine you not talking."

"I'm glad. This is who I'm supposed to be."

"What?" I blinked in confusion. Paige found the space to lean even closer. Our noses were practically touching, and my heart was starting to pump like I was exercising.

"Can I tell you a secret?" she whispered. I nodded, slowly, scared of bonking noses. "Perses was the best thing that happened to me.

All right, I couldn't help it, I pulled backward. "It was the what now?"

Paige issued a delightful, throaty laugh. "The best thing."

"How is almost dying a good thing?" I asked, but I could see where this was going.

"Clarity." There was a lilt of brightness in Paige's voice. "Almost dying comes with clarity." Then her voice turned serious again. "Look. When I thought we only had a few months to live, I decided to live it on my terms. I wanted to be noticed but was always too afraid of my own shadow. You lift the consequences, the ridiculous fears of getting mocked, and you're left with nothing but yourself. For me, the pain of death was clarifying. I'd spent too much time trapped in a shell of my own making. So, I let Perses make me an honest woman." Paige gestured to her hair. "I let my hair be what it wanted. I let my voice go. I'm free. Free." Paige shouted the last *free*, and I giggled like a kid. "Don't you laugh. I heard you, yelling at your friend today in the Dining Hall."

At the mention of Sid, my face must have dropped because Paige tilted her head.

"Sorry. Sid's having trouble."

The other day, Paige's eyes were hard and fiery. Today, her face was soft and kind. Wherever that hard-edged girl had been, she had withdrawn, pulled back into a coated shell, and left me staring at the face of someone who wanted to hear more.

So, I kept talking, finding the words as I went. "Sid was solid. Before. He was at ease with his life. He was the one who people went to when they were in crisis. Not me. Not Mo or Mika or anyone else that I'm friends with. When they didn't know where else to turn, they turned to Sid."

I let my voice trail off, trying to leave the rest of that statement unsaid. I didn't want to keep going here. Sid was my best friend, had been since the first day we found out we were roommates and followed each other on Instagram. I still barely knew Paige.

And there were her pale blue eyes. Blinking slowly and flashing me a little quarter smile, encouraging me to complete that circuit of thought. "Perses knocked something loose from Sid. Like a brick from his foundation. And the rest of it is just collapsing around him. He's quieter now. More withdrawn. Like he's trapped in his own head."

"Why?"

I waited for a beat, then said, "I remember having this conversation with the therapist that Mom took me to after my dad put us in the hospital." *Wait, what? Why did I do that?* If Paige was taken aback, she didn't show it. Her arms were folded across her chest, but her face was still warm and calm. "I remember a lot, actually."

"I don't see how you couldn't. That sounds truly awful."

I nodded, my voice sounding apart from my body. "I was a kid. And a lot of what the doctor said to me stuck. But there's one thing that I keep coming back to when it comes to Sid… trauma isn't our fault, but healing is our responsibility."

Now Paige was leaning forward again, her stare burrowing a hole into my eyes.

"I don't think a lot of us are acknowledging just how scared we are," I said.

"Are you?" Paige asked.

Here I paused, trying to collect my thoughts, torn between the urge to be impressive and honest. The latter won. "Sort of. I'm not any different than anyone else here. I'm not any less afraid. I think I'm just more experienced. What happened with my mom and dad. How I spent my first seven years, and how Mom and I spent the next few recovering. I think I've just been there. I think I'm just unlucky enough to know what trauma looks like, and lucky enough to know you can get back from it."

The answer seemed to satisfy Paige. She was smiling.

I tapped my phone. "Thank God for this. Talking to Mom and Mack really helps."

"Mack?" Paige asked.

I smiled as I launched into the explanation of my slightly confusing family. No, Mack wasn't Mom's boyfriend, he was happily married to a wonderful woman who took me on a shopping spree when I was seven so I had pants that didn't stop at my ankles. Mack was just the cop who had arrested my father, who had seen a terrified kid hiding in a closet, and who saw in me the child he never got to hold....

The time melted away. Paige was from California. She wanted to go into the business world until Perses. Now she was thinking about becoming a therapist because the world couldn't find enough people who could help. We talked about what we wanted to be before Perses. How the disaster which had taken a bite out of humanity had still provided clarity for so many who were willing to try and find it. How scared we were about the condition of the school. How even the quality of the food had dropped off.

Hours later, when the clock was pushing 11:00 and we heard Dr. Skinner begin his check-ins, we decided to say goodnight. We hugged, our cheeks grazing, and for a moment, my heart lurched. But then Paige spun away with a little giggle, and I realized something. Maybe Paige was as scared of me as I was of her.

Chapter 9

"WHAT THE HELL are we supposed to wear?" I asked Mika.

"Something that doesn't make me not want to be seen with you."

"Got it. Muppet Babies t-shirt."

Mo gently smacked me upside the head.

"Ow."

"Don't say stupid things." Mo's teeth were visible as he smiled.

I'm not quite sure how, or why, but Mo and Mika had convinced Sid and me to go to a party. A group of students who had graduated last year was having their "break year" at a nearby mansion. They'd picked it up at a steal during the Perses Fall—courtesy of their dad's money—and now were apparently opening their doors to the lowly students they had left behind.

I'd asked Mo earlier in the night how we were going to sneak off-campus. He'd just given me a wry look. "Dude. Like anyone cares anymore?"

I turned to Sid, who was fitting a tight t-shirt over his barrel-shaped chest. "No soccer team party tonight?" When we didn't hang out, that's usually where Sid spent his time, even dragging me on occasion.

"No," he barked.

Wait, what? "Sorry," I said quietly. I stared at Sid, giving him a chance to explain what he was so angry about. For half a moment, I held his stare, but Sid turned and looked back in the mirror, busying himself with fixing his hair. He barely had any hair… just the stub of a crew cut.

I looked over at Mo and Mika, surprised to find them looking in different directions but with the same facial expression. Mo was staring at Sid, pain, and confusion stamped on his face. Mika was doing the same but looking at me.

The house was on the other end of the school, just a couple blocks off campus. I stared at Sid as we walked, watching the red skin on the back of his thick neck. This wasn't my friend. I knew he was in pain, but he didn't have to be alone.

I took a deep breath. Opened my mouth to speak. No words came out. I shook my head and tried again. "Sid?" Mo, Mika and Sid all stopped and turned.

Without waiting for a reply, Mika grabbed Mo by the arm and continued walking. "We'll catch you there."

Sid stared at me. There was no malice in his eyes. Just a glassy stare. "What's up?"

I could feel my heart start to run away from me and tried to ignore the sick feeling in my arms and legs. *Maybe you can help him*, a voice in my head said. So, I swallowed and ran a hand through my hair. "You tell me." I hoped my voice projected confidence that I didn't feel.

For a moment, Sid's bushy eyebrows practically touched. He didn't look like my friend. He looked like a stereotypical angry jock who was staring at a math book.

And then the moment broke. Sid's face fell, smoothed over like a still pond. We made eye contact for an aborted second before Sid looked away and up at the cold night sky. "I'm sorry." His voice was barely above a chalky whisper. His hands started shaking so intensely that his arms shook as well. "I'm sorry for all of this."

Was that a tremor in his voice?

I reached out. Wrapped my hand around a thick bicep. "Hey. It's all right. Talk to me."

When Sid looked back, his eyes were slightly pink and watery. I could feel the pain burning off of him. "Soccer's canceled."

"What… what do you mean? You can't cancel a sport."

"No." Sid wiped his nose with the back of his hand. "But you can cancel a season. And that's what happened. We were only looking at exhibition games in the second half of the year, anyway, but coach could see it, and he was right. A fourth of the team didn't come back to campus. Another half didn't show up at our first three training sessions. No one cares about soccer, Corey. I'm still trying to figure out what anyone does care about."

There was a pause as I searched for the right words to say. For ten seconds, we stood silent while I racked my brain, my sense of uselessness doubling by the moment.

"What am I supposed to do now? I mean that literally. What do I do with my time?"

I followed the hypothetical Sid had laid out, and I didn't like where I found him at the end. All Sid had in front of him were empty hours, vast stretches of time previously filled by comradery and training and practice, and a feigned hatred of the coach that they all really liked deep down. Soccer for Sid wasn't just a game. It was a way of life. And now…?

"I can help." My voice was soft.

Sid snorted. "I appreciate that, man, but that's not enough." He paused to lick his lips. "You get this, Corey. You know that this isn't some stupid club that people went to once a week."

I was starting to form a response. "Of course, Sid. But it's not like everyone is gone."

Another sharp snort that sounded like it was coming from an angry dog. "Most of them are."

"Yeah, but a lot aren't. Look, I appreciate you telling me." I paused. "Is this what's been bugging you?"

Sid looked off into the distance again. He stared intently at the statue of Francis Augustus, who stared back at us through a dim spotlight, stone eyes looking just to our right. "Sure," Sid said, with a voice that hid the truth.

"Sid… I got nothing, man. That was the one part of your life I never understood. I mean, I never played. Hell, you never allowed me to play."

"There was that one day you tried out to score on Marley."

"I remember that day. I still have the bruises." I was laughing, and it was a laughter that got more robust with every second. "You had to let him full-on slide tackle me?" Even if it was funny now, the sight had been terrifying at the time—a six-foot four-inch guy charging at me like a truck. The video of the slide tackle had made many rounds in my dorm that night. Mostly by Sid, who had knocked on the doors of half the people on our floor to have them watch me spin through the air, landing like a broken ballerina. I'd gone quasi-viral on TikTok for the one and a half flips and the way I'd jumped back up, screaming, "I'm okay!" only to immediately fall back down again.

"See, but that's it, Corey. That's it. That was soccer. Every day had some sort of memory. Some new challenge. Someone else got to be the hero."

I thought of the kids in black, searching for a refuge. "The school isn't what it used to be. I don't know what will be next. I do know that there are an awful lot of people who can't deal."

"How are you not one of them?"

I stared at him as if he had suddenly grown a third head. "You think I'm doing well?"

"Compared to others? Hell, yes." Sid snorted, ignoring my disbelief.

"Why do you think that? Dude. I thought I was going to die holding onto my mom for dear life. Then I watched a woman almost bleed to death in my arms after her husband shot her."

That got Sid's attention. "You what?"

I waved it away. "Sid. I am many things. But okay is not one of them. Classes. This school. My home. You. A lot has changed."

"You're making new friends, though." And there it was. The whisper of jealousy. If I hadn't had any luck with women, Sid had done even worse. Which was weird. I watched girls stare at him. They looked at him a hell of a lot more than they looked at me. I think he knew that too. I think he was just too scared of his own shadow.

"I am." I thought of Paige. Wondering where she was right now. Wondering what her hair looked like if it was wrapped around one of those cream-colored fingers… stop, stop, stop. "But I just started talking to someone who sees the same things that I do."

"And what's that, Corey? What do you see, now?"

Easy answer there. I gestured around us. "Sid. Everyone was so ready to die that they forgot how to live."

"Or if they even wanted to."

I nodded. "Exactly. Look. I'm no expert. I'm not a doctor or therapist. I'm just a guy who has seen my share of pain."

"I know." Sid knew about my "Dad."

"And I know there are only a few ways through. Yeah, everything seems awful… but it doesn't have to be forever."

"That's some real therapy nonsense, right there." There was a note of playfulness to Sid's voice.

I laughed and shrugged. "Well, I've seen my share of therapists. The only way to get back there is to try. Can we try? Can we please just… go to this party, be awkward for a few hours, try to hit on women, fail miserably, and go back to our room and play video games?"

That earned me a full-throated laugh from Sid, and for a moment, there it was. My big roommate and me against a school we didn't understand, in a world that never really felt like ours. Maybe this was it. Maybe Sid needed this… just to talk, to connect for the first time, really, since we'd gotten back. Maybe the old Sid would be back. Would be better. Maybe this laughter would stay.

"Fine. Let's go."

The cloud was still in his voice as he spoke, but when I slapped him between the shoulder blades a couple of times, he smiled, and it looked real, not forced.

《◇》

We caught up with Mo and Mika in the line to get into the house. Mo and Mika hadn't been kidding—it was a large, sprawling property. The main section looked like it had been built at the turn of the century, with its chipped brick facade and cracked stone columns. But it also had an awkward addition jutting off the sizable main building, which had obviously been built decades later, clad in aluminum siding and devoid of any decorative charm. It looked like we were entering a building that had been created by slapping together different Lego sets.

Mo and Mika were deep in conversation when we caught up to them, and they barely acknowledged our presence. I think they were trying to give us space.

I rubbed my hands across my arms and jumped up and down a couple of times for warmth. It was freezing, and the line of kids stretching down the main walkway gave me pause. Was this place asking to be busted? How would the school react if we had to explain that one to them?

By the time enough kids in front of us finally moved forward to allow us entry, my mood had sunk considerably, and my stomach was starting to churn.

If Mo had similar feelings, he was doing a great job of hiding them. "All right," he said, adjusting his jacket as I stuffed my hands inside my pockets. His mouth was brimming with a smile that didn't quite reach his eyes. "Let's do this."

We threw our coats in a pile and began our trip around the house, saying hi to people as best we could. There was no quiet space. Someone had paid to install speakers in every hallway, and the narrow halls ensured that loud music assaulted us from every angle. That, combined with the dimmed lights and crush of bodies, made me feel like I was in a cave, only instead of stalagmites, it was filled with drunks.

Mo and Mika seemed at ease, laughing, accepting shots as we passed a room. Sid and I exchanged looks and nodded to each other. He leaned in, whispered something to Mo, and we took off in the opposite direction.

"Good call," I said.

"What?"

"Good call!"

Sid nodded, and we kept moving, our feet sticking to the tacky floor as we moved. Not for the first time—and probably not for the last—I found myself questioning my decisions.

"Where we going?" Sid shouted over the din.

"Main dance floor?" I shouted back. "Is that a thing? Is there a main dance floor here?"

Sid shrugged and continued awkwardly moving his head in tune with the music. I'm not sure what he looked like to someone who didn't know better, but to me, he looked like he was trying too hard. Then again, at least he was trying. I felt like a lump.

Somewhere along the way, we made a wrong turn—Sid had been following me, and that was clearly a mistake. The music had actually died off, which is probably why Sid and I went this way... even if we were trying to get to the dance floor.

"Thank God," I muttered.

"I've been to soccer parties that were quieter," Sid said.

"How the hell are we supposed to actually talk to anybody in there? I never understood that."

"I think that's the point." A wry smile popped up on Sid's face, and he pointed toward a dark set of stairs. "Come on, let's go up. I think I know a few people who live up there."

"I got nothing better." We trudged up the stairs, sharing in the mutual relief of not feeling like we were surrounded by people.

We hadn't been on the third floor for more than a few seconds before we heard it—a loud acceleration of voices, followed by five seconds of silence... then more screaming.

Sid and I exchanged looks. "Do we want to know?" I asked.

"Come on. Where's your sense of adventure?" Sid slapped me on the shoulder and walked toward the noise. I grimly followed.

There was no one else in this hallway and the noises from the floor below were muffled. If I hadn't known any better, I would have thought

I was in an old dorm on an ordinary night. But the noise at the end of the hall was starting to pick up again, and now I was curious.

We walked into the open room to find a gaggle of thick guys and a few scantily clad girls in tank tops that left little to the imagination.

A couple of the girls looked familiar, but I think they had graduated the previous year, and I had already expelled them from my memory. They looked bored. Uncomfortable. Turning toward the back of the room, I realized from the muscles on the guys in front of me that we were dealing exclusively with soccer players.

From the back of the room, a voice screamed, "Sid! And smaller guy!"

"Corey," I muttered, recognizing the goon in front of me.

"Tony," Sid bellowed in return, and they hugged. "What's happening?"

"You're just in time. Watch this." Tony moved out of the way and revealed… uh-oh.

Perched on the window, about ten feet away, was a guy in a baby blue T-shirt and dark black jeans. "Do it, do it, do it," chanted the room.

Do what? I thought, before registering what was happening. Without even realizing it, I bolted forward, but Tony grabbed a fistful of the back of my shirt, and I snapped in the air like I had been grabbed by a seatbelt. With an almost casual lean, the guy in the window disappeared into the darkness.

"What the hell!" Sid pushed Tony aside, off of me, and ran to the window, sticking his head out. I watched in horror… the room had gone deathly quiet.

Sid pulled back in the window. He was breathing heavily, but his face was relaxed. "It's all right. There are mattresses down there."

"Mattresses?" My voice hit an uncomfortably higher pitch than I would have liked. Now I joined Sid at the window and stuck my head into the cold winter night. Sure enough, there was the kid in the blue t-shirt, lying on one of three mattresses, doing snow angels.

"He's fine, man," said Tony. "The pills relaxed him. He just flops when he hits the ground."

From the darkness, a tinny voice spoke. "Weeeeee."

"Shut up, David." Sid shouted. "Tony, I love ya, but this is a bad, bad idea. Dave the Drunk could easily miss the mattress."

"It's nothing, Sidney."

"It's three stories, Tony."

"Aww, he's fine!"

Sid held Tony's stare, his eyes as unyielding as granite, and the tension in the room held and expanded, like a balloon filling with air. "All right, all right." There was a hard, slurry edge to Tony's voice, and I scanned the room. The three girls. Five meatheads. Sid and me. Not good.

"Tell you what, you stop. I'll go get you a few beers, all right?" I spluttered. These guys lived here. Did they need a beer? Would they let me get them a beer?

"We're good, homie." Tony gestured to his dresser, where an array of hard liquor and plastic shot glasses stood. Next to the alcohol were a couple of opened and unlabeled bottles—the kind you got when you filled a prescription.

Now Tony was starting to look from Sid to me, and I wonder if he was making the same calculation I'd be making if I was him. Just how pissed are these two? Pissed enough to get the police?

The answer was hell yes, I was absolutely pissed enough to get the police. And the scowl must have been visible on my face because Tony looked at his friends and said, "Tell you what. Let's go grab a bite."

Nods and murmurs. Tony picked up a set of keys and flicked it to one of the girls, a pretty one with long dark hair. "You good?"

"Sure, baby." The girl stuffed her phone in her pocket.

The eight silently filed out of the room. They didn't even look at us until Tony placed a meaty hand on each of our backs, pushing us out of the room, locking it behind him.

"Jesus Christ." My heart rate only started to slow when the crew and their girls had disappeared down the stairs. "Were your buddies always that dumb?"

Sid's eyes hadn't left the stairway. "No." There was a sharpness to his voice—an angry edge—that I hadn't heard before.

"Huh."

An awkward silence fell.

Sid kept staring. "This is our world, now," he muttered under his breath.

My heart filled with revulsion. I didn't want this to be our world—stopping twice as many guys who were twice as big as me from jumping out of windows for the thrill of it. I just wanted to try to enjoy a school party. Wasn't that what I was supposed to be doing?

«◊»

WE FINALLY MADE it back downstairs and were staring over the second-floor railing, overlooking what should have been a colossal dining room but was now serving as the party's main dance floor. It was, predictably, a mess. In the center of the room, sloppy drunks grinded to bad remixes, holding flesh in one hand and cheap beer in the other. The edges of the room were lined with beer pong tables. We spotted Mika and Mo, easily crushing Jameson Sonco and Jeffrey Scalion at a game on the floor below. They saw us and waved. We waved back.

"Should have stuck with them," I muttered.

"Apparently," Sid said.

We stayed for a few minutes, watching the fun but feeling apart from it before I heaved a sigh. "Come on. Let's get downstairs, see what we can find."

Sid nodded sourly, and we walked toward the stairs, past the main entrance, where kids in various states of inebriation were still waddling into the party. That was when I saw the sign. It was on a cheap poster board and half-hidden behind a freshman who looked as out of place as a flower growing in nuclear waste.

The paper was neon green, and the handwriting was sloppy, but it was still legible. *NO ONE IN ALL BLACK ALLOWED—WE MEAN IT.*

"Sid, check that out." I pointed out the sign.

Sid paused, thrust his hands into his pockets, and allowed something resembling a smile to approach his face. "That's… interesting."

"Yeah. Wonder what caused that."

Sid waved a dismissive hand. "I doubt anyone in all black would want to be here anyway." He pointed forward. "Whatever. Let's get in there."

The din of the party was overwhelming in the hallways, but as soon as we hit the balcony of the main floor, I felt like my ears and eyes were being actively assaulted. Some Hip-Hop song blared from three-foot-tall speakers on elevated stands while colorful lights splashed around the dance floor in a way that probably would have given anyone even slightly epileptic a seizure. The forced-rainbow effect was made worse by the way the lights bounced off of the glass windows, and I resisted the urge to squint.

It took my eyes a few seconds to adjust, but once I did, I was able to find a few people I recognized, including Mika and Mo. We weaved our way over to them and were greeted with excited half-hugs.

"Play," Mo screamed over the music, miming himself throwing the ping-pong ball that was lightly grasped between his thumb, pointer, and middle finger.

"We'll drink for you," Mika shouted, but his timing was perfect and the song that was playing ended just as he spoke, resulting in a comedically loud statement that sounded like a desperate plea to drink. Everyone within a five-foot radius cracked up. "What. I will!" Mika waved his hands. "Give me all the beer!"

More laughter, even from Sid and me. We locked eyes, and I shrugged easily, trying to will myself to let go. "Sure, why not?" I said, just as the music started to blare. Sid and I assumed our positions, him with Mika, me with Mo.

I hate to admit it, but this really wasn't that bad. I had a knack for beer pong and sank three shots in a row at one point, earning cheers from the surrounding players and jeers from Mika and Sid. Mo, I think, was happy to have an excuse to just keep drinking.

We won our first two games and were losing our third—Mo's shots were starting to get comedically wide—when I first saw a splash of red hair, highlighted momentarily by a winking white strobe light. I blinked and looked in that direction, but it was gone in a heartbeat.

"Hey. It's your throw, man," exhorted Mika.

I shook my head. "My bad." I threw a shot while catching a glimpse of something on my right. The end result of the throw was a miss that hit a girl three feet to the left of the table.

"Dude," Mo said.

"Sorry." I looked at the window. "I was…."

Thud. Thud. Objects fell in the darkness, loud enough that it was heard over the din of the music and everyone in the immediate area turned in that direction. Ridiculously, my first thought was, *Well, at least people know I wasn't imagining that crash.*

"Uhhh… what?" A confused smile formed on Mika's face.

Sid and I locked eyes as a third, rectangular shape fell from above. "Was that a…?" I started to ask.

Sid nodded, horror crossing his face. "It was."

"Was that a what?" asked Mo, confused.

"Mattress," Sid and I said at the same time.

Two seconds later, the music cut out and was replaced by an "AIIIIEEEEEE," as a flesh-colored shape appeared from above, the form blurring as it crashed into the mattress, bounced on an angle, and then slammed into the ground, limbs akimbo as they became reacquainted with gravity. The guy skidded, face first, before disappearing into the darkness.

Gasps and laughter followed. I wasn't sure if anyone else realized what had just happened, but Sid and I did. Some idiot had just jumped into a pile of mattresses from thirty feet above.

With a curse, I spun around, crashing into Jill Torsella and spilling beer all over her shirt. I muttered an apology and pushed my way forward, searching for a door. Finding one, I barreled my way through, ignoring the cries of protests along the way. I stumbled into the snow, the sudden shift from a crowded party into the freezing February night making me feel like I had just stepped into a block of ice.

Lurching forward, I raced toward where the drunken asshole had landed, cursing him and praying for him at the same time. I found the prone boy in the snow, groaning slightly. *Well, that's something.* I knelt down, not even sure what I would do, so I just started with, "Hey man, you all right?"

His face was scraped as if a Brillo pad had run down the right side of his hairline to his jaw, dozens of small cuts oozing blood. He was shirtless, and his right shoulder was higher than his left. He was giggling woozily. I couldn't believe he was even conscious.

Do I touch him? Move him? No, those both seemed like bad ideas. *Get help.* I stood and started to turn back to the house when my ears were assaulted by an array of screams and joyous shouts—a group of guys from the party were barreling their way outside.

"Hey. Over here." I waved frantically.

"Wooooo!" screamed one of them, thrusting a solo cup into the air.

"Yes, woo, over here," I waved. I recognized one of the guys instantly.

Tony reached me and grabbed a fistful of my shirt, pulling me close enough to smell his liquor-scented breath. "Hey, you. I remember you. Get outta here. Go get me some beers." The push seemed casual to Tony, but the next thing I knew, I was skidding six feet backward and flat on my ass.

I bounced up, adrenaline surging, but Tony had already turned away from me and lifted the drunk on the ground like he was a toy. The kid screamed—his shoulder had to be totally dislocated—but Tony adjusted his grip and the kid stopped crying. "You. You're the man," slurred Tony, half walking and half carrying him toward the back of the house. "Statues for you, buddy. They're gonna make statues for you." Tony and the rest of his crew laughed as they waddled around the house.

"Get him to a hospital." Pinpricks of light danced in my fingers.

"Piss off!" screamed Tony, and the rest of his friends laughed.

I cursed, spat, and stomped my feet a couple of times before I began to trudge back to the house.

I'm done. This place sucks, and I don't want a drunk landing on me. Maybe I can pry Sid out of here. I bet he's had enough….

Standing in the doorway, framed against a rainbow of lights, was a tall girl, pale-skinned, with long, flowing red hair. She looked delightfully out of place, wearing a red and white baseball shirt, with sleeves that reached three-quarters of the way down her arms. She was holding onto the doorframe, almost as if she was barring my way back into the house.

I could feel my sour mood melting away like butter on warm toast. "So, you saw… all of that?" I raised my voice slightly to make sure that Paige heard it over the din of the party.

"I did." Paige leaned forward slightly, and I was struck by the sultry quality of her deep, deep voice. "That was nice."

Failing to hear the expected bite of sarcasm in her voice, I cocked my head sideways. "You did just see me get pushed into the snow by a guy who could literally eat me, right?"

"Sure. But before that, I saw you be the only one in a room full of people who ran to the guy who might have been hurt. I mean, if you're gonna get knocked on your ass, it may as well be for a good reason."

"Let's go with that." I smiled slightly, suddenly feeling the warmth of pride.

We stared at each other for about five seconds. She had gorgeous, sparkling teeth, framed by a pair of lips my eyes were drawn to like gravity. I watched them move as Paige spoke. "Wanna go for a walk?"

It was freezing. I barely noticed. "Absolutely."

We crossed back into the house, threading our way between the gyrating couples and knots of conversations. *The guys.* I turned over my shoulder while still walking, catching Mo and Mika's penetrating glances. At that moment, it was evident that they were twins, and even in the dim light of the house, I could catch the identical hint of a smile that was just starting to sprout on their faces. I raised an eyebrow at them, and I swear Mika doubled over laughing.

Sid was nowhere in sight. I swiveled around, looking for him, but found nothing.

Paige and I made our way to the front of the house, and after five minutes of wandering, and an awkward silence because conversation was just impossible, we grabbed our coats and made our way back outside. I stared at her for a moment, trying to gauge just how much she had had to drink. Her cheeks were flushed, but was that the alcohol, or the cold?

"You, my friend, are a sight for sore eyes," Paige said. Her voice was even and smooth.

"How's that?" We marched up the hill, back toward campus, my eyes scanning for any campus police officers while we walked.

"That has never been my scene."

"I thought you only did what you wanted now?" I was aware that I was pushing my luck. Paige snapped a look over at me, and I silently prayed that my raised eyebrows and slight smile were enough to show that I was kidding.

She laughed. It was a deep, throaty laugh, and I felt it rush along my spine. "Fair point. But no. I promised myself that I would try to broaden my horizons a little bit."

"Even if it made you miserable?"

"I wouldn't say miserable." Paige's arms crisscrossed over her chest, and I couldn't help but notice a sterling silver heart locket with a P on it, the charm jangling softly in the cold breeze. "More like somewhere between 'God, I hate this' and 'Hey, the world almost ended, so let's try something different.'"

"Speaking of something different... I know you saw the hurt guy, but did you catch the reason I ran outside?"

"Yes." Paige turned toward me for an instant and placed a hand on the arm of my jacket. "Nice jacket. Can't go wrong with leather."

"Glad someone thinks so." Sid always told me I looked like I owned a bike, and I always responded that I wasn't nearly coordinated enough for that.

"Oh, yeah. Leather jackets. Mmm." *Mmm?* I liked the sound of 'Mmm.' "But anyway, yeah. Did some guy really jump out of the window?"

"He did. He wasn't the first either." I filled Paige in on my earlier run-in with Tony and his drunk buddies.

"So, you thought you got them to stop, and they really just waited you out."

"Something like that." I was annoyed again and felt the wetness in the seat of my pants from where I had landed in the snow.

There was a lull in the conversation before Paige said, "What a bunch of tools. Is that normal?"

"Jumping out of windows? I'm going with no."

Paige laughed. "Okay, clearly not, but that's not what I meant. Is it normal as far as parties go?"

"Better question, and I'm not sure. I can't say I've spent too much time at parties like that."

"Ahhh, so you let yourself get dragged to this too." Paige said, smacking me on the arm. "See, I knew we had something in common."

More than that, I hope. "But, yeah. I don't know if this is normal for them. I mean, those guys jumped out of a third-floor window just to see how far they'd bounce. Are people usually that stupid?"

"Yes?" Paige asked uncertainly. "Maybe?"

We weren't saying what we were thinking. *Don't do it. You've got a beautiful redhead who left a party with you. Shut up. Shut up.* "Perses?" God damnit.

But, thank everything that's good and holy in this world, Paige didn't recoil. "Yeah. Perses. People are trying new and exciting ways to make sure that if the asteroid didn't do its job, Darwin's laws of evolution will."

I laughed. "Ouch."

"Well, it's true. There are people who are so desperate to run from thinking about what happened that they'll try anything to get a rush, to get a jolt. To feel."

My mind went toward the ugly YouTube videos I had seen during the Perses Fall. Convinced the world was about to end, countless daredevils had decided they'd go out with style. Elaborate car stunts, skydiving, and challenging each other to see how long they could wait before opening their parachutes, that sort of thing. It had chilled me at the time. Now? It seemed like people were still doing it. Just for entirely different reasons.

"That's a frightening thought." My voice was almost lost in the wind.

"There's a lot of frightening things in this world right now. Perses was just the start." She stared into the distance.

Well, I'd ruined it. "Let me ask you something."

Paige looked up at me, and I realized I had absolutely no idea what I was going to ask her.

I spluttered for a moment, mind turning over, before settling on, "Does this stuff overwhelm you?"

"Perses?"

"Yes."

Paige went silent for a second, before she nodded wordlessly, her lips pressed into a thin line.

"Me too. All the time," I said. "I'm worried about my mom and Mack and Sid and that Refuge group and this school. I'm terrified about a future when everyone seems completely incapable of imagining the next day."

"So, how do you deal with it?" Paige looked at me, her eyes wide and unblinking.

"I think that one is above my experience level," I answered with a smile.

"No, it's not." Paige's voice was suddenly serious. We stopped walking, and she was grasping my arm again, but this time, her grip had a strength that came from urgency. "That story you told me about the woman whose life you saved. That guy today that you—that only you— ran toward. The way your heart is breaking for your friend. You have something. Say it."

My mind went to my mom, to the fleshy sound of a hard fist meeting soft skin. To a terrified, injured seven-year-old, cowering in the closet, horrified at the sound of a metal baseball bat and a lion-like male roar.

To the rough, thick hand of a police officer, gently lifting me as if I weighed no more than a bucket of straw.

"You have to care. You just have to. Perses, the Perses Fall, everything that's come after… it means that we all need each other to deal. Now, more than ever."

Unexpectedly, Paige reached up and kissed me softly on the cheek. When she pulled back, her eyes were smoldering.

It was at that moment that I realized that, maybe, just maybe, I wasn't as much of an idiot as I thought I was.

She took my hand and started dragging me across the grass. I didn't ask where we were going. I think I already knew.

About a minute later, we were back on campus, wandering through a grove of trees—the Augustus Arboretum. People from across the state would stop here and lose themselves in the wooded maze. At the center stood a stone fountain, five feet tall, with gorgeous white lights that gave it a heavenly glow. Decades before, men had brought their sweethearts to this place, where they'd give them their pins or letter jackets.

The fountain was heated to keep the water going, even in the middle of winter, even in the dead of the night. Paige pulled me forward, stumbling only briefly over roots and branches, but as we made our way to the center of the grove, the lights from the stone fountain became more and more visible.

We arrived in a clearing, ringed by benches and trees and places where flowers grew in warmer weather. Paige let go of my hand the instant we reached open space and spun around, her eyes locking with mine.

There was no sound, save for the gentle tinkling of the fountain. It was almost as silent at that moment as it had been the night that Perses was supposed to arrive. There was nothing but the fierce urgency of the moment, nothing but cold hands and warm eyes.

Very gently, I slipped my hands inside Paige's open jacket, running my fingers along her waist. My leather jacket was zipped up, and slowly, so slowly, Paige extended a shaky hand and unzipped it, moving almost one notch at a time. When my jacket fell open, her hands curled inside.

There we stood.

"Is this… too fast?" I asked softly, removing my hands from the inside of her jacket to brush aside a strand of red hair the wind had blown in front of Paige's face. Her skin felt chilled and new.

"Yes. Of course." The silent, sparkling smile on her face told me the rest of her answer. *It doesn't matter.*

The pain of the world had led to chaos. It had altered my life in ways that I couldn't even begin to imagine at that moment.

But, in the heat of the moment, a force crashed into me with the same emotional impact as an asteroid hitting the planet. Perses hadn't just altered mass psychology. It had altered interpersonal physics. The push and pull of objects. Fundamental laws of attraction.

Those new laws were operating on overdrive, pulling my lips closer to this gorgeous redhead named Paige Lynn, one of the few people I'd met since the start of the Perses Fall who seemed committed to finding a real way forward.

The air was sharp and pure. The trees were woody, mixed with the scent of pine needles and steam from the fountain.

Paige's lips felt like fresh water on parched skin. All I wanted to do was drink.

Chapter 10

THERE WERE A few iron-clad rules of boarding school, rules that you only messed with if you really wanted to push your luck. One of those rules—don't get caught having a sleepover in a room of the opposite sex.

Perses had changed a lot of those rules. And when we got into Paige's room and the lights went off, I began to calculate my indiscretions of the night. I hadn't checked in at 12:00 a.m. I'd sneaked off campus. Been around alcohol. What was one more rule broken?

As Paige whipped my shirt off and flung it into the dark, I realized I was absolutely, positively making the right decision.

Afterward, I set an alarm for 8:00 a.m. This would let me sneak downstairs and back to my room before everyone woke up. Maybe I could check in on the app then and hope Skinner didn't notice the time.

Eight a.m. arrived. The trill of my alarm woke me with a sharp start, and for a moment, I blinked, disoriented. Then the night came back to me in a wave of joy, memories of pale skin and red hair beneath me, and I smiled so wide I think I giggled.

Paige turned over with a groggy smile. When she opened her eyes, the first thing she saw was me, grinning like an idiot. "What're you doing?" Her voice was thick with sleep.

I swear, even her morning breath was sweet. "I wanted to get out of here so Skinner wouldn't catch me."

"That's nice." Then Paige pulled me in and kissed me deeply. My arms clenched around her back, almost of their own volition, and I found myself buried in a warm wave of soft hair.

Two hours later, I actually did leave.

《O》

I DIDN'T SO much walk back to my dorm as I did skip. It was 10:00 a.m.—might as well have been 4:00 a.m. as far as the dorm was concerned—and I didn't encounter anyone when I walked downstairs. I was humming to myself, trying to imprint every memory of the evening into my head, staring straight forward, seeing everything and nothing at the same time.

I was still smiling when I opened the door to my room. It was unlocked, and that meant… yep, there was Sid, in a T-shirt and shorts, his head snapping toward the sound of the door opening. He was staring at a black piece of paper, and when he saw me come in, he crumpled it up and threw it at me.

I snickered as the paper bounced off my chest. "You!" Sid screamed, but there was laughter in his voice.

"Me." I grinned so hard it felt like the ends of my lips were touching my eyes.

"I don't think you could be less cool if you tried." Sid rolled his eyes. I giggled some more. "You know, if you're gonna do the walk of shame—"

"—there's no shame, here," I said, and I continued giggling.

"Well, you should at least have the decency to button your shirt right."

I looked down, and Sid was right. My buttons were mismatched so that the collar of my shirt was hooked awkwardly into the button below it. I looked like a nine-year-old who had tried—and failed—to button his shirt for the very first time.

"That's my bad." I unbuttoned my shirt, stripping and throwing it in the laundry.

We were quiet for a minute, but I knew that Sid was dying to know more. Not specific details, I mean. Sid wouldn't ask, and I wouldn't tell, and in our brief romantic successes last year, we'd always just sort of smiled knowingly at each other, laughed hours later when we sent each other texts which read, *FOR THE LOVE OF ALL THAT IS GOOD AND HOLY FIND SOMETHING TO DO THAT DOESN'T INVOLVE OUR ROOM.*

"Who is it?" he asked.

"Paige Lynn."

Sid thought for a moment, his face pensive as he rubbed a meaty hand over his large chin. "I feel like she was in one of my classes last year. Economics?"

I nodded. "Sounds right. She's more interested in Psych now. I met her in my intro class. She got into a screaming argument with Megan Buchanan."

"Yeah. Speaking of." Sid pointed, and I followed his finger, looking at the crumpled up black piece of paper Sid had just thrown at my chest. Puzzled, I bent down, unfurled the paper, and smoothed it out over my desk.

I read the first three words and felt my heartbeat gallop. The accelerated blood flow which followed chased my afterglow away.

Seeking A Refuge?

Let's Find a New Way Forward, Together.

Monday, 7:00 p.m., Taylor Lounge

I looked at Sid, and my eyes must have been flaring because he raised his hands defensively and said, "Calm down. It was slipped under the door in the middle of the night. I don't know if they even realized I was here."

"Someone flier-dropped a dorm on a Saturday morning? Really?"

Sid nodded slowly. "Must have. They're all over the hallway too."

I spun around and moved toward the door.

"Please don't make people see you shirtless," Sid called, but I ignored him and threw the door open. Sure enough, Sid was right. The fliers were all over the hallway. Creepily, they were evenly spaced, about twenty feet apart, hung at an almost identical height. Five doors down, two of my floormates were glancing at one of them, talking softly to themselves.

With shaky fingers and a sickening feeling, I took my phone out of my pocket and opened up Instagram. Sure enough, there it was. A promoted ad from The Refuge, featuring a racially diverse array of students in all-black outfits.

I looked at Sid. "Who are these people?"

Sid shrugged, his movements slow. "No idea, Corey."

I kept staring, waiting for him to say more.

Instead, after a moment, Sid turned back to his computer. I let the flier drop out of my hands. "You're not gonna go, are you?"

Puzzled, Sid turned back around. "Why not?"

"Cause these people are creepy as hell, Sid."

"Come on, Corey. I told you. It's a new club."

"Where all the members wear the same thing. Where they are advertising a 'new way forward.' Where they make your friends for you. That doesn't weird you out?"

"Not really." Sid typed away on his laptop. I said nothing, did nothing, just stood there, staring at the back of my friend's head, glaring bullets into his buzz cut.

Finally, Sid turned back around and said, "Hey, man. We're not all doing as well as you are."

I didn't know what to say to that. What *could* I say to that? My night had been great. Sid's evening clearly hadn't been nearly as good, and I could feel my good mood evaporating like air escaping a pinhole in the skin of a balloon.

Be honest with your pain. The conversation with Paige was echoing in my head.

"I just got lucky," I said quietly, and now Sid turned, a stupid grin on his face. "No, no, not like that."

"Oh, no?" Sid wiggled his eyebrows.

I laughed and sat down in my desk chair, staring at Sid, leaning on my knees. "Sid, man… this is gonna take some time."

"Of course, it is," Sid's voice was easy. "I'm just looking to see what else is out there." He turned back to his computer and began typing again. "After all, I have the time."

"If classes keep getting canceled like this, I may need to find something to do too." Three of my classes that week had gotten axed as teachers disappeared, only to be replaced the next day by a revolving array of poorly prepared substitutes.

"At least you found something new." Now a sharp edge cut through Sid's voice. He still wasn't looking at me.

"That's not fair." After a moment and a handful of typing from Sid, I added, "This sucks for me too."

"It doesn't seem like it." Sid's voice was sulky, almost petulant. Abruptly, his hands stopped flying over the keyboard, and he turned, slowly, before matching his position with mine. "Yeah. That wasn't right. I'm sorry, man."

Relief flooded my veins. "It's okay. But this isn't as easy as it seems."

"How?"

I gestured out the window. "Dude. Have you seen what's going on out there?" When Sid just stared at me, I pointed at his computer. "Fine. You know what, go to CNN right now."

Sid did, reluctantly. His body was blocking the computer, so I asked, "What are the headlines?"

"Uhh… mass shooting in New Jersey…."

"Another one?"

"Yep, four dead, ten wounded. Was in a club last night or something."

I shook my head and looked down. "What else?"

"Terrorist groups on the rise… ISIS in America, oh, that's happy… ahh, see, you were wrong, Corey. It's not all bad news. Here's a story on how pollution is at an all-time low, thanks to Perses."

I rolled my eyes. "Genius. You're going to be an economics major. You know why."

After a moment, Sid sighed. "Yeah. Because the economy tanked, and no one was buying anything. Oh, hey, here's another nice story. Congress says that they probably won't be able to reimburse people who spent all of their retirement savings when they thought they were going to die."

I stood up and leaned on my chair, suddenly regretting my decision to have Sid visit CNN. I'd tried to avoid it since I'd gotten back to Augustus. Most of the time, I failed miserably. "Yeah. Like I said, Sid. The world still sucks. We're all living in it together."

Sid pointed at the flier on the ground. "And that is exactly why I'm going to this meeting."

I flung my arms in the air. "Sid, man…."

"No. No buts about this one. You're right, and you're proving me right. The world is terrifying. I know what I saw at that last meeting, Corey. There were people who actually want to try and be normal again. If there's a group that wants to band together and try to make everything less terrible, I'm more than happy to hear them out." Sid spun his chair around and looked at me. "And you're coming with me too."

I eyed Sid carefully. We were rapidly getting to the crux of the issue here, and I didn't really know the right way to talk about it. "Sid… Sid, I don't want a refuge."

Sid's eyes narrowed.

"Well, I don't." I stuffed my hands into my pockets to keep them from flailing all over the place. "I just want my world back." My mind flashed to my conversation with Mack the other day. "I don't know what this group is hiding. But I do know that anyone who wants to spend that much time and energy in setting up someone's social group, maybe limiting contact with others…."

"This group isn't limiting contact with others!" Sid tapped the paper. "It's about figuring out how to not make the same mistakes we made before Perses!"

I raised my eyebrows. "It's literally called 'The Refuge,' Sid. I don't think that means they're going to be doing community service projects."

Sid gestured around the dorm. "So, what do you want to do, Corey? Sit here, do nothing? Wait for the world to reboot itself?" His voice was elevated, and his face was a tinge of pink. "I am not sitting still, watching this school fall down around us. I will not catch drunks when they land on top of me. I will *not* be their mattress, Corey. I'm going to this meeting, and I'm going with or without you."

Not going to lie… the intensity in Sid's voice was disturbing. And I had the briefest flash of insight at that moment. We couldn't possibly be the only ones having this conversation right now, and there were already kids running around this campus in all black. How many people didn't have a Mack to warn them about what was happening in the real world? How many people had lost their Mack and were aching for a replacement?

Sid hesitated before speaking again. "I'd still rather go with you. You can help me figure out if this group is legit. What they're looking to do."

I know what I wanted to say. I even opened my mouth to say it. No, Sid. There's something deeply, deeply wrong here. You don't need a Refuge—we have each other and Mo and Mika, and some weird group in all-black outfits can't take away what we have in front of us.

But I saw the mixture of emotions all over Sid's face. The wide-open, sad eyes. The slack features begging for help. Sid found something that could maybe pull him out of this. Was that really that bad? If it was what he needed?

So, I closed my mouth, and when I opened it again, I said, "Guess I don't really have a choice."

Sid stood, patting me on the shoulder as he got up. "You never did."

《◊》

THE NEXT DAY, we met up at Taylor, and I realized right away The Refuge was onto something. I got there fifteen minutes early and a steady flow of students was already pouring into the room, marching down the stairs into the basement lounge which doubled as event space. Sid and I wandered in the front, joining a few other students who were standing around.

And I noticed something right away. I turned to Sid. "You seeing this?"

"Hmm?"

I gestured to the front door and lowered my voice. "Most of the people who are walking in are by themselves."

"So? That's probably just the ones who don't have anyone to meet with. Those people are standing here with us."

"I guess....." I let the subject drop and watched the people walk into the room. Over the next three minutes, I watched ten people shuffle in. All of them had a bit of bounce to their steps, the slightest smiles on their faces, a sparkle in their eyes that existed despite the bitter cold. And every one of them was walking in by themselves.

A gaggle of familiar-sounding voices was approaching from the opposite direction. I turned and found Mo, Mika, and Paige, laughing like they were old friends.

Paige and I made eye contact. She smiled. I smiled. The world smiled.

Of course, that was when Mo hit me square in the face with a snowball. Paige's smile turned into a stream of laughter as I wiped the slush from my eyes.

"I'm sorry, I'm sorry man," Mo said. He paused, dramatically, before adding, "All right, maybe I'm not sorry, that was pretty perfect."

Mika sighed. "Never take your eyes off my brother."

Meanwhile, Paige stepped forward, still laughing as she embraced me. "Your face is wet."

"On account of the snowball," I said.

Paige laughed again. "Here." She unraveled her scarf and dabbed my face. "All better."

Sid snorted.

"Meet Paige." My voice was muffled by the scarf.

"Hi," Paige said.

"Hi." Sid awkwardly waved his hand before stuffing it back in his pocket. His smile trembled.

I quickly tried to talk over the moment. "I wonder what they'll have down there." We started to walk in together.

"Ohh, maybe they'll have balloons." Paige exaggeratedly clapped her hands together. "And I bet we'll know what color those balloons will be."

"Black? Will they be black?" Mo asked, leaning forward in fake enthusiasm.

"I bet they will," Paige said.

"Oh, God, how do you three know each other?" I asked.

"We just met in Flo," Mika said, referring to our dorm. "She looked familiar from the other night."

I tried to stifle a grin at the mention of the other night. Paige's eyes met mine. She raised a single eyebrow, and I felt a lurching in the pit of my stomach.

We started to go down the stairs to enter the lounge.

"Hey, where are your friends?" Mo asked.

Mika's voice dropped to a mock sulk. "We were promised friends."

"Women don't talk to you two," Sid laughed.

"Yeah, we had a class together last year, didn't we?" Mika asked Paige.

"We did."

"Right, and I remember you always walking around with that girl with the short black hair. The tan chick with the nose ring."

After a moment of hesitation, Paige said, "That would be Sara. My old roommate."

Ahh. Guess that explained the bare mattress in her room that I never asked about. Mo and Mika took the hint and shut up.

I pulled closer to Paige. "Your friend?"

Paige looked at me, her eyes slightly glassy. "Yep. Still haven't heard from her."

I winced. "She okay?"

Paige's shrug was a painful response. "She was alive in the final few weeks leading up to the miss. After that, I wish I knew. She hasn't answered any of my texts or calls, and the number I found for her parents isn't in service."

Oh, God. That had to be hell. Not knowing. "I'm sorry."

Paige nodded, slowly. "Me too." She said nothing else, and I clammed up. I mean, what I wanted to do was put my arm around the waist of this obviously wounded girl… except we'd just hooked up for the first time yesterday and that was clearly too much, too fast….

Of course, it's too fast. Paige had said when we were in the arboretum.

I put my arm around Paige's waist. Pulled her in slightly. And she looked at me and gave me a hooded, secretive smile that I think only I could see.

"Damn," Mika said suddenly, his voice dipping.

I wasn't sure what had caused the sudden surprise until the big guy in front of me moved off to the side. Then I stifled in a gasp, just as Paige let one loose.

Normally, the Taylor Lounge was exactly what you would imagine a dorm to look like—tables, some standard office-type chairs, outlets, chargers, the works. In the middle were some pretty comfortable chairs and couches that had seen more than their fair share of overstressed students crashing in them. I'd spent a few evenings in here with some clubs, but never a ton of time—it was in the basement of a Sophomore dorm, so I hadn't made it in there too often.

What I knew, though, was that the lounge was nothing special. It was a place for large groups to meet and watch TV. It was where a roommate who had been sexiled could escape. That wasn't what I was looking at now. The lounge, apparently, had been remade.

There was brand new furniture strewn around the place, comfy leather couches which looked virtually untouched, complete with built-in leg rests that students were lounging in. Tables of food dotted the sides of the room—trays of cheese, vegetables, fruit, sandwiches, and desserts stood gleaming, and I spotted a few students I knew loading up large plates.

All of the chairs, leather couches, and cushions were arrayed around the center of the room, where a series of lights had been hooked up around a stool. On the stool was a hammer, its clawed edges glinting under a spotlight.

Directly in front of us stood four students. Two were underclassmen, and I didn't recognize them. But I absolutely recognized Kate Arney, a blonde girl who was a senior. Kate was wearing all black and holding an iPad, smiling as she greeted people.

"Hi, there," she chirped when my slot in the line reached her. Kate's smile was stretched so tightly against her cheeks that I could only imagine how sore her lips were going to be in the morning. "Can I have your name, please?"

I blinked. "Kate, it's Corey Walker."

Kate smiled back dimly. "Sorry, Corey. Bright lights. What's your email?" When she asked for my cell, I balked. After a moment's hesitation, I gave her my number, one digit off.

She smiled broader, somehow, and pointed forward, toward the food. "Help yourself. We'll be getting started in a few minutes."

"Thanks," I stepped backward, allowing Kate to talk to the next person.

The line which had started behind us was only growing deeper. If they wanted to get everyone into the room before the event started, they wouldn't be beginning anytime soon.

Paige stepped next to me and tapped my shoulder. We exchanged severe looks and got out of the way.

"Did you give Kate your cell?" Paige asked.

I shook my head. "No. Faked a digit. You?"

"Hell no." Paige raised her eyebrows. "She almost didn't let me in because of it. That guy next to her said to let it go, so here we are, ready to listen to a lecture."

Mika appeared behind me then, and in a rare moment, Mo was nowhere to be found. Of course, Mika had a plate of what looked to be cured pepperoni and Swiss cheese. "This is good."

"Can't go wrong with food," I muttered.

"I think they know that, Corey," grumbled Paige.

"Look. This whole thing is creepy as hell," Mika said. That was when Mo slid next to us, holding two glasses of juice.

"How did you get across the room so fast?" Mika asked.

Mo flashed an easy smile. "Uhh, I ducked around the registration table. Obviously. I'm not giving these people my name."

"So, you agree that this is weird?" said Paige.

Mo looked at her like she had six heads. "It was weird the other day, and it's weirder now. Some random group parachutes onto campus that no one has ever heard of, refurnishing a lounge and coming with a small restaurant worth of food. That's gonna set off a few alarm bells in my mind, hell yes."

This room was approaching capacity, fast. Fifteen percent of the school was going to be in here at this rate. "Jesus," I muttered.

"They hit a nerve," said Sid. His hands were still empty, but I caught him eyeing the sandwich tray pretty hard.

We went silent for a few moments, and I took the chance to glance around the room. I knew a few students in here and waved a couple of awkward hellos, but by and large, it was people who I hadn't seen since returning from Perses. Some were sitting in groups of twos and threes, but most of the people who were there were staring awkwardly at the center of the room, waiting for something to happen, or scrolling through their phones, their thumb and eyes the only parts of them that were moving.

"Let's grab a seat," Sid said.

"Sure," Mo said.

We wandered toward the first large couch we found, one close to the back of the room and the exit. I slung an arm clumsily around Paige and caught my thumb in her hair for a moment. "My bad."

"I don't mind," she replied. To my extreme relief and joy, she nestled into my chest, and for just a second, I was able to forget where I was and why I was there.

Mumbled talking filled the small space, which grew hotter as more and more students piled in. As the clock grew closer to seven, the room became quieter, as if the assembled masses were waiting in anticipation to see what would happen next.

Finally, at 7:00, the lights to the lounge dimmed, and a slim figure in all black walked toward the center of the room, moving between the students who were assembled. Her movements were smoother than silk. She looked graceful and poised, and the only thing which gave her any substance against the dim light was her short, blonde hair.

"Great. Her…." Paige started to say, but her voice trailed off as the figure entered the light.

"Hello, friends," said Megan Buchanan. Utter silence invaded the lounge, save for the small hiss of the microphone and the echo of Megan's voice.

Even if I hadn't recognized Megan's physical attributes—the short blonde hair, all black clothing—I absolutely would have been reminded by the way her face was set. There was a blank sort of serenity on it. I felt like I could have thrown a water balloon at her nose, and she wouldn't have blinked. Even in the dim light, I could see her alert, green eyes, scanning the room, taking everything in, the smallest shade of a smile decorating her small, almost elfish face.

Megan placed her hands in front of her stomach, folded them, and spoke. "It is so wonderful to see so many of you here, to know that you're willing to give us some of your precious time to learn more about our movement. How we can be together. How we can forge a new path in a new world." Her voice echoed over the small space. I hadn't even realized she was wearing a microphone.

Megan scanned the room, turning in a slow circle as she spoke. "I'm sure many of you have questions. Who we are. What we want. Why we're in these strange outfits." Megan gestured downward across her black-clad body, and the room laughed softly.

I flexed my hand behind Paige. Paige wasn't moving, and when I glanced at her, I spotted the fire in her eyes.

"I don't want to start by talking. I want to start by listening." A dramatic pause and Megan's hands were extended outward as she stalked across the small, elevated platform. "How many of you have been scared in the aftermath of Perses?"

For a moment, the room stood stock still. Megan Buchanan may have been the first one who asked this question.

No one's hands were moving, and Megan's smile extended ever-so-slightly. "Go ahead. It's all right."

Somehow, that coaxed the first hands loose, and a smattering went up across the room. Slowly, like a puddle extending over concrete, more hands extended to the ceiling, and soon the entire room had their hands upward. Reluctantly, I put my hand in the air, joining Mo, Mika, and Sid. Paige's hands remained locked in her lap, the twist of anger on her face impossible to miss.

"Okay. Thank you." Megan extended her hands to the side and pushed downward. "You can put your hands down." The crowd obliged. "Let me ask you a related question. How many of you have felt uncertainty lately?"

Now there was hesitation, and I could see some people around the room look at their neighbors.

"I should elaborate." Megan took a deep breath. "I know that none of us were living in the greatest of times before we got that alert on our phones. Politics, world events, climate change, shootings… was anyone really happy? Was anyone really certain of what they were going to do? Who they were going to become?"

"We're in high school, we're not supposed to know anything," Paige mumbled, only to be shushed from behind. She spun around and cast a dark look in the direction of the noise.

"And then, Perses." Megan stopped her pacing and looked down. Her back was to us, but her head was slumped and her hands had gone limp. "Our generation's defining event. We spent months—months—convinced that we were about to die. That all our dreams, every one of our passions, and all the people we loved were about to be evaporated in a cloud of smoke and dust and fire."

"That's a weird way of putting it," Mika said, only to be shushed by Sid.

"And then, January third. We were saved. Shouldn't we be happy? Shouldn't we be ecstatic that we were given our lives back?"

I shifted uncomfortably because I knew where this was going.

"Why didn't we feel better, having been given the second chance that we all wanted for months? Why weren't we rejoicing, dancing in the streets, living our lives to the fullest? Why did it feel like the world was covered in this much uncertainty?" Megan paused here. The crowd was leaning forward, almost as one. "Our world has been clouded by it. It seems as if there is so much darkness, so much evil, that we're being attacked from every direction." Now Megan was staring in our general direction. "That's how I came to The Refuge."

"What… what does she mean?" I whispered to Paige, making sure to keep my voice low.

Paige glanced up at me, her mouth tight. In a different context, the look would have sent me running… to her or away from her, I honestly wasn't sure. Definitely running, though.

Megan was speaking again. "The Refuge isn't a club. It isn't a social circle." The sweetness and earnestness of her voice were starting to grate on me, rubbing my nerves like saltwater on skinned knees.

"Here we go," Paige said. "Everything we got before was the windup. Now the pitch…."

"It's a national movement. One run by leaders who have experience well beyond their years. Our Leader—Cameron Bellevue—is one of the wisest people I have ever met. I had the chance to shake his hand once. To listen to him philosophize about how the world can change if we're willing to take charge of our lives. To create our own future by creating our own social circles. To learn from our ancestors and reject the evils of the modern world."

"Oh, did you hear that, Corey? They have a leader," quipped Paige, looking at me with a smile that practically screamed, *I told you so.* "He's wise, Corey. Very wise. He has so much wisdom to give us."

I shifted uncomfortably. "Dude kinda sounds like God."

"Our first goal—to heal. We want to give back the certainty that world events and the Perses Fall stole from us."

"She has a magic wand?" I was getting angry. "What kind of fresh nonsense is this? The world has no certainty. That's the point of living."

"Here's what that means." Megan began to tick off items on her fingers as she spoke. "We may not have the ability to change the world, but we can create a structured society which reduces the pain we all face. Our movement is built on kindness. A culled social group. Charitable activities. Shared respect. Our behavioral code—one that all of our members adhere to—creates a culture of mutual admiration."

"Huh?" said Mo.

"Yeah, I'm with you," said Mika. "These guys giving out magic kisses too?"

Whew. I glanced to my right at Sid to find him leaning forward, a large fist supporting his chin.

"We know you're all in pain. We know that virtually everyone in here lost someone." The room's breath seemed to catch collectively. Our grief was communal. But it was left untouched, like mold in the kitchen you tried to ignore. "Be honest. How many of you lost someone in the Perses Fall?"

Virtually all the hands in the room shot up, without hesitation. I saw Josh and his curly blonde hair in my head as I raised my hand. Only Paige kept her hand down, her arms firmly crossed.

Sid looked back at me, a pained smile on his face.

Megan raised her hand. "Me too," she said, the smoothness in her voice breaking like a lake of ice crackling. "But for us to move on, we have to move together. Our organization has access to grief counselors and newly developed ways of coping with our pain."

That caught Paige's attention. Mine too. We looked at each other, her eyebrows raised, my mouth slightly ajar.

Leaning into Paige, I whispered, "What the hell is a 'new way of coping?'"

"This pain that we share—we can heal it, together."

There were murmurs throughout the crowd, toneless noises as people whispered to each other. Megan waited for them to die down before she spoke again, holding up two fingers.

"Second. We're here to help. The Refuge was built on the promise that once we heal, we move on by helping each other survive." At that, Megan reached into her back pocket, withdrew a slim iPhone, and held it up for the crowd. "It's a brave new world, everyone. And a huge part of that is thanks to these things. Another question for you. How many of you spent most of the Perses Fall separated from these things by no more than a few inches?"

"A few inches?" screamed a voice from the other side of the room. "It was glued to my face."

Murmurs of agreement, and the slightest smile from Megan. "Exactly. They never left our sides. And let me ask—how did this make you feel?"

Now there was a pause. No one answered. Megan spun around the room, slowly. "Anyone? No? Okay, let me ask you this. When you put down your phone, did you feel better?"

"I didn't put it down," said the same voice.

This time, Megan whirled on it and said, "Why not?"

No answer. Absolutely none.

"I think I can tell you why." Megan tapped her phone with a free hand. "It's because these things give a false sense of connection. They make you feel that, somehow, if you know what's happening in the world, you can control it. But do any of you feel better when you're reading the news? Looking at TikToks of the latest bombing or shooting or riot? Do you feel more or less hopeful about your chances of living a better life when you learn that another European government has fallen? The terrorists have taken over another Middle Eastern country? That climate change is accelerating?"

No one said a word. It was as if Megan had opened up their heads and poured bleach into their minds.

She gestured to her phone again, tapping it now, but more aggressively. "Here's my theory. These aren't connective lines. They're chains. They are chains that weigh us down with useless knowledge, painful memories, and experiences that can never be ours. They are designed to make us want, to make us need, and to make us suffer." A pause. The room was as still as a stone. "Wouldn't you like to be free?"

Megan put her phone on the stool. For one heartbeat—then two—she stood, stock still. As if she were moving in slow motion, she picked up the hammer. Expertly twirled it in her hand. Then, quick as lightning, she flung her hand back and arced it forward. With a tinkle of glass and circuitry shattering, the ball of the hammer met the screen of the iPhone. The phone's screen sparked and shattered, and the crowd gasped before applauding.

When Megan looked back up at the crowd, there was a beaming smile on her face. "Do you have any idea how freeing this is? To not feel as if a phone is pulling you into a black hole, demanding constant attention, stroking, poking, and prodding? To know that life is only what I see in front of me?" Megan gestured broadly. "When was the last time any of you saw what the world really looked like? What do you actually want to see?"

Megan went silent, patrolling her square on the stage. The room was stock still, staring at her, hanging on her every word.

I could feel acid spreading throughout my stomach as I watched the room react. It was a poison born from the power this one woman seemed to have over a room she had just walked into. Who was she? Why did she sound so possessed?

Here and there, I found people looking around the crowd as if disbelieving what they were thinking. But those faces were few and far between.

"We know, we know, that there is a better way—that modern society and the aftermath of the Perses Fall have meant that all of us have to forge a new path. That's what The Refuge is about—helping us move forward together. That's why we are so dedicated to personality screening. We want to make sure that we help people find new friends and build new relationships with the right people, and we want to make sure that the people who stand with us will truly benefit."

The crowd murmured.

"How many of you have struggled to replace what you lost in the Fall?"

Hands shot up around the room. To my dismay, one of those hands belonged to Sid.

Megan was nodding, her hands on her hips. "Exactly. It's like Perses has changed the basic rules of civilization. Our goal at The Refuge isn't just to help build a new way forward, it's to replace the holes in your life. We'll help match you with friends—and maybe more—who can help make you whole again."

"Oh. Cool." I shook my head. "It's like Tinder for dummies."

Paige laughed, too loudly, and heads turned. We were out of sync with the rest of the room. "What do you think their third principle is?" Her voice was brash, unbothered by the stares.

Paige's voice echoed with a dark humor, but I was filled with a righteous anger, and when I spoke, my voice was intentionally loud. "Well, we're at 'help' and 'heal,' so the third one has to begin with an *H*."

"How about 'Hell, I can't believe these people are falling for this?'" Paige asked.

A "SHH" followed.

"Too long." In my mind, I could see Kristy Ford, bleeding and pale and scared. I remember what it felt like—the cold snow on my bare skin. The sensation of Mack's loose arms around me, the gentle tremor in his biceps as he squeezed me tight. Images flashed through my head. Sid in all black. Sid, not talking to me anymore because some charismatic "leader" in another state had told him he had to make new friends.

This world was filled with so much pain. But people like Sid were in it. He deserved better than the garbage that was being served to him on a silver platter.

Then, I snapped my fingers. I was standing when I screamed it. "Hide!"

That, to my horror, got Megan Buchanan's attention. Slowly, she turned and looked at me. "Sorry?" Her voice boomed over the microphone.

I swallowed and hoped that when I spoke again, I wouldn't stutter. "Your third principal. Is it 'Hide?'" The words practically tumbled out of my mouth at lightning speed, making it sound more like I had said, "Your-third-principle-is-it-hide?"

Megan was nonplussed. If anything, she almost looked pleased. "It's not, but I can see why you'd say that." She turned away from me, back to the rest of the room. "Does this feel like hiding to any of you? Working together to find a better path?"

Voices rang throughout the small lounge. More voices than I expected. "No."

But there were some that were silent. I could see them peppered throughout the room, and their silence recharged me. When I spoke again, I was speaking to them. "Joining a club is going to take all of their pain away?"

"This isn't a club." Megan looked back at us. "This is a new way forward. A movement."

"Who funds it?" The deep voice of Paige rang through the lounge, and I swear, I heard it echoing off the walls. For a fraction of a second, Megan's perfectly arranged face stumbled. Her hand went up, brushed her hair, and she spoke again.

"Benefactors who understand the pain of today's students. Of us." And again, her hands were spread, wide open. "You'd have to be blind and without a heart not to see and feel what's happening today."

"And you want us to be blind, don't you?" asked Paige. Then she stood and was beside me, and that was when I felt it—the eyes of every person in the room, locked onto the two of us, two matchsticks against the madness. "That's why you want people to smash their phones with a hammer."

"No one has to do that. No one has to do anything that they don't want to."

"No one has to join them," shouted one voice.

Then another. "No one's keeping you here." That got a few cheers and hoots.

I flexed my fingers and thought of Mack, alone, firing a weapon into the dark. "No, we can leave. I get that. But I want to know why you want the people who stay to run away. Why you want them to join some exclusive club—"

"Movement," snapped Megan.

"Fine. Movement. Why is your solution to the pain of the world to run away?"

"How is making new friends running away? How is using new techniques to cope with grief and pain hiding? How is learning to restore our communication habits to something more rational a problem?"

Paige gestured around the room. "Why are you only targeting people who are overwhelmed? Why don't you want people who are doing okay? And what happens if someone wants to join your group but keep their old friends?"

When Megan stared blankly at her, Paige continued. "The name of this 'movement' is The Refuge like you can somehow shield people from pain. Your fliers talked about finding a new way forward, whatever the hell that means. This isn't exactly geared toward people who feel like things are great."

Megan's hand went to her hair before she spoke. "Take a look around, Paige." There was a bite in the way she said Paige's name, one that made my heart clench. "Does it look like there is a shortage of people who need help? Don't you think that maybe we're talking to people who aren't okay precisely because they are the ones who need help the most?"

"You think they're so scared that they'll fall for anything."

"And you think they're so far gone that they aren't worth your time," said Megan. Now it was Paige's turn to stumble, and she lifted an eyebrow. "Just because you're lucky enough to not be in pain doesn't mean the rest of the world feels the same." Then a pause. "Empathy can be developed, Paige. We can help."

"Not worth my time?" Paige said. "My solution to everything isn't to find a 'movement' and shut the door behind me."

"Do you think we should keep going? Like nothing is wrong?" asked Megan. "Maybe you could scroll through Instagram without wanting. Maybe you didn't worry about being shot in the middle of a class or about what would come when we left this school? Maybe your dad could buy you a ticket anywhere." I think I felt Paige flush, and I'm pretty sure I heard her growl. "But for most of us, that wasn't an option. For most of us, the world left us incapable of functioning without panic. So, let me ask you again, Paige and Corey, what was your way forward?"

"Forward." I kept my voice even, not betraying any of the fear I felt in my chest. "And with no one left behind."

Megan blinked and cocked her head sideways. I took it as an open invitation to speak, and I tried to find the voice for the anger in my heart. "You get some things right and some things wrong, I'll give you that. Things are falling apart. Too much social media is pure evil. And everyone in this room is in pain. We all lost someone. All of us feel like Perses hit anyway."

"Josh," said Sid, in a voice so soft it cut through my ribs like a knife.

"But this isn't when we run away and hide, even if it is with a few people who pass your screening or whatever." I waved my hands in disgust, before turning them into a jabbing, pointing, shaking finger. "If society is falling apart, then the way to save it isn't to pull backward and make your relationships more exclusive. It's to connect with more people, not less."

"Do you really think the chance exists for all of that?" Megan's voice was gentle to the point of patronizing.

"You're the one who seems to think that withdrawing into little cliques can save the world."

"Yeah, dude, things were going really well before," someone said, and I tried to stifle a curse.

"Listen to what you just said!" I screamed at the voice in the crowd. Yeah, screamed. I even saw a couple of people pull backward, away from my voice. "What happens when you pull away? What happens to everyone left behind?"

I took a deep breath, disturbed to find my chest heaving a bit. There was Kristy Ford again, her pale face glowing in the moonlight while blood oozed from a nicked artery in her thigh, wondering if she would die in the snow with a stranger....

"Seriously, answer that for me, Megan." My hands were on my hips, gripping the sides of my shirt. "What happens to everyone who doesn't join the movement?"

"Well, won't that be for you to answer?" A slight smile was on Megan's face. Snickers crisscrossed the room.

"Corey...." whispered Paige. I looked down, saw Mika and Mo staring up at me. Sid was still looking at Megan.

"Nothing in this world has ever come easy," I said. "No one has ever survived by pulling away. Not really." I straightened my back. "When I was seven, my dad almost beat my mom to death. He wasn't a drunk, he wasn't addicted to anything. He was just a bad man. He shattered my mom's orbital socket, right here." I touched my face above my eye, then moved my finger to my left temple. "He gave me a concussion so bad that I had to spend two days in the hospital and attended months of therapy later. All kinds of therapy."

And, suddenly, deathly silence.

"My mom called the police and Officer Mack Miller was the first one at the house. He kicked the door in and screamed a lot of words I didn't understand. Then there were a lot of wet noises. Then there was crashing and breaking. It was my dad attacking Mack. That ended when Mom hit him in the face with a baseball bat." As I spoke, I could smell the sour scent of blood, wafting its way under the closet door. Seven-year-old me had wrapped my hands around my knees and tried to pull away from the smell as if it were poison.

I shook myself free of the night. "My point is that someone came when I called. Someone was there to help my mom. And it wasn't just someone who had passed some weird screening test. It was someone paid for by our community. Those men saved my mom's life. Mine too. And if they were in your Refuge, I'd have been in a body bag." The last sentence exploded from my voice like it was fired from a rocket launcher. "This is a lie. Everything you are preaching is a lie. No one ever made the world a better place by pulling away from it. And I know that because I lived it."

The silence extended, morphed, and for ten solid seconds, held. For a moment, I wondered if I hadn't broken the spell.

"That's terrible," whispered Megan. "And I'm sorry. But your pain then and your reaction to the world now doesn't nullify the experience of everyone else."

"Absolutely wrong," I spat. I leveled a finger at Megan. "Mack answered the phone of a stranger because he had an obligation to. What happens when one of you joins this Refuge and someone tries to call? What happens to the seven-year-old that was me when no one answers the phone?"

"But what would have happened if the world that was created never pressured your father—evil though he was—into hitting your mom? What if the circumstances that led him there didn't exist?"

"There will always be evil in the world, you naive idiot," Paige said. "There will always be assholes and bullies. The question isn't if you can run away from them or control them. It's how you punch back when they punch you."

I looked over at Paige, noting the way her skin was flushed and her features were contorted in fury, and I swear, I don't think I have *ever* been so attracted to someone.

I put a hand in the air and looked around the room. The fear that I had been suffocated by when I started speaking was long gone, shed to the ground like a snakeskin that I had outgrown. "If you believe you can create some false facade where bad news doesn't exist because you can turn off your phone, you should sit here. But if you think this is a hell of a lot of nonsense and that we need each other, leave. That's what I'm doing."

I looked at Paige, and she nodded, and with hundreds of eyes on us, we started to thread our way through the tight space, stepping gingerly over legs that didn't seem too eager to move and allow us passage.

For a moment, I wondered if Paige and I really had lost our minds because we were the only ones moving. But then, as one, movement from where we were sitting. I turned, hoping to see Sid, Mika, and Mo, but only found the Twins rising.

Sid was sitting and looking at Megan as if I didn't exist.

"Thanks for the food," Mika said, a smile plastered on his face. "Tell your movement's donors that they buy the good stuff."

"You're welcome back any time," Megan said kindly.

"Yeah, no," said Mo. "Hard pass. I'll stick with TikTok and therapy."

Nervous laughter across the room, but it shook something loose. In ones and twos, groups stood and left, moving toward the exit, following Paige and me. As we climbed the stairs, passing the dirty looks thrown our way by the other Refuge volunteers in all black, I heard Megan say, "It's good that they left. Please don't be angry. These are people who wouldn't have been happy with what we have to offer."

Paige and I were halfway up the stairs, and out of microphone range. I could feel the cold from the door ahead by the time we looked at each other. Wordlessly, we took hands, and I was relieved to discover her fingers were wet with sweat too.

Snippets of the confrontation began to play in my mind. I could see all the things I'd said. All the ways I'd looked stupid.

My skipping mind was interrupted by Paige. "Intro to Psychology is gonna be real awkward on Monday."

And just like that, the thoughts were pushed aside—if only for a moment—and I began to laugh.

Mo slapped me on the back as we reached the door. Mika did the same, albeit gentler, for Paige. "Damn," Mo said. "Damn, damn, damn, Paige. What did you do to our boy here?"

"I don't think I did a thing," Paige said. "I think that was Perses."

I realized I was shaking as we made it outside, the cold breeze feeling as refreshing as a hot shower. "That wasn't Paige."

Paige smiled, and there was a twinkle in her eye.

I took a deep breath and tried to pull together my thoughts into something vaguely coherent. "These… people." I practically spat as I spoke. "They're snake oil salesmen. They're acting as if running away and secluding themselves is the solution to all the world's problems."

"They never actually said that," said a quiet voice, and I whirled on the guy so fast that he actually took a step backward. He looked tiny. He had a lanyard with his student ID in it, for God's sake. It was like a big, awkward nametag that blared "I am Kevin." Still, when he spoke again, his voice was solid. "They never said anything about wanting to run away."

The squinted eyes and red hair gave him away. I pointed at him. "I remember you. You were at that meeting the other day in Hillside."

"I was." The kid's voice crackled as he spoke. "I thought these people were out of their freaking minds then, and I think it even more now."

I smiled. "The Refuge did say that they would be screening people and using personality tests. And if that doesn't just scream 'Hey, we don't want all of you,' I don't know what does," I responded.

"They're targeting people," Mo said.

I pointed a finger at him. "There you go. Exactly. They're targeting people who they think are too afraid to push back. But no one on Earth can ever convince me that the way out of this is by smashing our phones and making fewer friends. The only way we heal together is… is to heal together. The way forward is Mack Miller. Not that group in all black."

I was dimly aware of the crowd forming around me, watching me. The twenty or thirty or so who had piled out. I swear I glimpsed a phone pointed at me, a bright light recording me as I spoke, and it threw me for a loop. *Why the hell is anyone recording this? And how long have they been filming?*

"Guess we won't be getting an invite," quipped a girl and murmurs of laughter rippled through the small group.

"That's probably a good thing." I tried to smile. My mind was running away from me now. I felt like I'd left a piece of me in the basement of Taylor. "Still. There's an awful lot of people down there who are lost and in pain."

The laughter abruptly stopped.

"So, what are we supposed to do about it?" someone asked.

"I'm not sure," I said honestly.

"Wait for the world to heal?" Paige said, but there was a snark in her voice that broadcasted that she was kidding, and the crowd laughed mirthlessly.

"We can't wait that long," I said.

"No. We have to heal it ourselves," Paige said, and there was that sparkle in her eyes again. Now she had turned to me, her body shifting in my direction.

"That one might be a little above what a few pissed off boarding school kids can do," said the redhead from earlier.

"Agreed," I said. "I have no idea what the answer to this is. Particularly given how much things really do suck right now." I became dimly aware of a couple of people moving toward us, their slow gait ambling in our direction. Security? Yup. The on-campus security force stopped under a streetlight, about twenty yards away, their uniforms announcing their presence louder than a crappy garage band at a talent show.

Others had noticed them too. "Wonder what got them here."

"Probably my screaming," I muttered. "All right, let's get out of here." I started to walk away before inspiration struck me. "Hey, wait, one more thing." The crowd turned and looked at me. "Don't... if you've got friends in there. Don't be a dick to them. Be nice. Don't laugh at people who make a bad choice."

No one said anything, but a few nodded thoughtfully. I hoped it was enough.

We turned and left, walking in separate directions. Security was definitely staring at me.

"Nice ending." Paige was on my right and slipped her left hand into mine, intertwining our fingers.

"Thanks," I muttered, stroking my chin. "Felt like I had to say that part."

"Why?" Paige asked. Mo and Mika walked beside her, wordless, their gaze alternating between her and me.

"Because otherwise, if there's a fight tomorrow, it would be my fault. That I didn't try to tone it down."

"That's not the only reason," Mo said.

"No, it's not," I said.

"You said it for Sid."

"I had to," I said. "He's my friend. And he wouldn't leave with us."

"And it wasn't for a lack of trying," said Mika. He mimed lifting his arms underneath a person. "I tried to drag that dude with me when we left."

"Did he say anything?" I asked.

Mika broadened his shoulders. "I want to stay. Be big sulky soccer player. Smash all the things."

"He's in pain," I snapped, my voice white-hot.

"A lot of us are in pain, Corey."

"And here we are. Walking away anyway," Paige said. "The motivation that made us stand up and leave that room. That's what we have to remember."

Mo looked to Paige, confused. "What do you mean, remember?"

Paige picked up the pace a little. We hustled to keep up, already fifteen minutes late to study hall. "That isn't going away, Mo. Nothing that we just saw is stopping. Not anytime soon."

Chapter 11

I SLEPT IN my room that night, despite Paige's very sweet and not-so-subtle offerings to have me sleep in her room. She had taken her bed and her roommates' old bed, lofted them and pushed them together. Later that night, she even sent me pictures of what the beds looked like.

Sigh.

No, I had heard that Skinner had actually busted a few kids for being late to check-in, and I didn't want to push my luck. Besides, I had to wait for Sid.

So, instead of sneaking off with my brand new, smoking hot, red-headed girlfriend, I waited for my dejected, depressed roommate. I laid down in my bed, my pillow rearranged so I could see the door easily, and stared at my phone, waiting for the telltale sound of the door turning. While I waited, I wondered which version of Sid I would see. Would it be the dejected one, the one who felt lost in a world unmade? Would it be the awkward one, quiet because he was angry with me but too afraid to say it?

Then, a thought of terror. What if he came back in an all-black outfit? What if he was already gone?

As 11:00 leaked toward midnight, my mind became hazy and drifty, and I hit the point where consciousness and dreams sloped into each other. Skinner never came, but I heard no shortage of fantom knocks at the door, and by 11:30, I fumbled with my iPhone and used the virtual check-in. Flashes of the night replayed over in my mind—yelling at Megan. Paige standing next to me. Sid sitting, immobile as a tree stump, ignoring his friend's pleas to leave the room. The hundreds of people we left behind.

I don't know when, but at some point, sleep took me. When I opened my eyes again, the room was gray with light from the early morning sun. I rolled to my right. Sid's bed was untouched.

«◊»

I DIDN'T SEE Sid until that night, and when I did, he acted as if nothing was wrong. He might have been a little more guarded than usual… I don't know, maybe he was leaning over his phone a little more. Shielding his laptop tighter with his body.

Maybe it was just me.

We didn't talk much. I searched for an opening to bring up the rest of his night, but Sid never gave it to me. When I finally worked up the courage to ask how the rest of the event was, Sid just said, "Fine." He didn't elaborate. And I was too scared to push, too worried about pushing him further away.

So instead, I said nothing, an acquiescence to the chasm that was forming between us.

The black shirts seemed to be multiplying, and I swear, every one of them was giving me dirty looks. I found out a few days later my entire performance from the night of The Refuge meeting was circulating on social media. Just what I'd always wanted—to go viral on campus. Ahh, well. At least it wasn't because I was naked and drunk on academic row.

I wasn't the only one. Paige was also on the reverse end of some awkward encounters. She could hold her own, but still. To watch someone you care about be vilified for no good reason isn't a fun experience, and it multiplied the sadness I felt.

Thankfully, someone in Augustus's Dean's office had made the relatively smart decision to hold a Parent's Weekend.

Friday arrived, and it was as if the campus had been transformed. Gone were the half-filled bulletin boards and the busted garbage cans that had been broken by bored kids the prior weekend. The unkempt lawn and slushy walkways were replaced by sparkling pathways and cozy Adirondack chairs. Driveways were plowed, stairs salted and shoveled. Even the administration building was washed from the top to bottom, giving the building a sparkle I hadn't seen since the prior August. It was like I was looking at the school I had selected when Mom, Mack, and I had walked onto campus four years ago.

When I saw Mom and Mack walking onto campus, I had to remind myself not to run. Then I saw the dampness on my mom's face and my resolve broke. Into her arms I went. We touched cheeks and her tears mixed with mine.

"I know I'm supposed to be a grown-up," I said in my mom's arms. "But it feels really, really good to see you."

Mom pushed me aside but held me tight in her arms. "Corey Elizabeth Shannon Walker. You are seventeen. That is as far from grown up as you can get."

Mack was next, and his arms still felt as safe as they had that day when I was seven. He pulled me into a tight hug, and I instinctively shifted to my right to avoid bumping against his gun. It had been returned the day before—the Ford shooting had been ruled justified.

We started walking easily toward campus, my mom and Mack scanning as they went. "Looks like they cleaned it up at least," Mom said.

"Didn't you say it looked like hell?" asked Mack.

"Oh, it did. They made it nice for you. You cut the check."

"Technical school, Little Man. All the money and none of the college debt."

"Can you imagine me using my hands?" I said, extending my arms and staring at my fingers. "I feel like that ends with me losing a few of these."

"I take that back. You have many skills, Corey. Handywork isn't one of them."

"I'll stick to scrolling," I said, with a hint of a smile. "I still remember when Jill asked me if I wanted to be a surgeon. I think you both laughed for about five minutes."

"Jill sends her regards, by the way." Mack tilted his head toward me while stuffing his hands in his pockets against the bracing wind. "She couldn't find anyone to cover her shift. An increasing problem these days."

We talked as we moved toward the Student Union, chatting about everything and nothing. I was ecstatic that all the students around me were wearing beat-up hoodies or designer jeans. Not a fleck of black around, and no more than a couple of kids in pajama pants.

We were going to meet with Sid, whose parents worked weekends. We'd done this since our first year as roommates when we were terrified freshmen. I'll never forget the look on Sid's face when Mack took us to some Italian restaurant in town and let him order whatever he wanted.

There came the tears again. I blinked them away rapidly and hoped Mom and Mack didn't notice.

"I don't see any of your friends around," Mack said, his voice dripping with sarcasm. I had told them of The Refuge meeting, the video, and corresponding reactions. My big mouth had earned decidedly ambivalent reactions from Mom and Mack.

"No. Thank God. I'm not sure those people have parents to hug. I feel like they were hatched."

Mom smacked my arm. "Didn't you say you told people to be nice to the people who were thinking about joining?"

I sighed. "I did. But that's easier said than done. And besides, it's not the regular members I hate. It's whoever is in charge of it that I really want to strangle."

Mack's police voice came out. "Is there a leadership on campus besides Megan Buchanan?"

I shrugged. "I don't know. I haven't seen any of them besides her, but they must be around. Hell, Megan looked right through me the other day in Psych. It was like I didn't exist."

"How about your new friend? How'd she look at her?" Mom asked. Now her eyebrows were raised.

"Like she was a fly that she wanted to inspect. Or dissect. Probably both."

"Well, I want to see how your new girl is going to look at me."

"Oh, hell no," I shook my head vigorously. "We started dating a week ago. I'm not exposing her to you two yet."

"What, I just want to say hello to this wonderful young lady." Mom's hands were clasped exaggeratedly, and she was practically twirling. Then she actually did a twirl. "My son, my little boy…."

"I hate you."

"I can just see the wedding."

"Oh, dear God, please stop, she might be around and running away as we speak."

"It's too late for us, Corey," Mack said solemnly. "But this young lady still has a chance."

"Sid. Help me. Wherever you are, help me." My voice was loud enough to carry.

As it happened, Sid was in front of the Student Union, staring at us disbelievingly. "You know, you make a lot more sense when I see your mom."

Mack extended his hand, and Sid warily shook it. "Hello again, Sidney. How are things?"

"Fine, fine," Sid said quickly. He moved to my mom, who embraced him before he could slink out of the way.

"Wonderful to see you again, Sid." She held him at arm's length. "You've definitely lost weight."

Sid's eyes darted from side to side. "Yeah. That's what happens when you don't have a coach riding you."

Moments later, we were in the cafeteria. "Is the food always this good?" Mack asked as he loaded up his plate with chicken parmesan that had been flecked with parsley. God, the smell was so appetizing it was making my mouth water.

"I think we both know the answer to that," I said with a laugh.

"Hey, gotta make the food look good to the folks who are paying for it," Mom quipped.

"And the Board of Trustees. They are on campus too," I said. "Then again, maybe we can compare notes on their food later."

A weird thing had happened. Yesterday, I'd gotten a text from the Dean of Student's office. They'd invited me to attend a campus update with the Board of Trustees, Teachers, Alumni, and "selected students." Why? I had no idea. I'd said yes, and that was where Mom, Mack, and I were headed in a bit. After some asking around, I hadn't found anyone else who was going.

Whatever. That didn't change the fact that I was hungry now, and I loaded my plate with as many pieces of chocolate cake as I could cram onto my tray. Sid looked at me in horror. "What? I'm hungry. Besides, this cake is good."

"I have no idea how you can eat like that," Sid said. "I eat more like that for a few days and someone would have to carry my ass from place to place."

I laughed. "Hey, man. You don't have soccer to worry about anymore. Get twelve pieces of cake. Go nuts!"

I thought Sid would laugh. Instead, his face morphed like a dark cloud appearing over a clear sky. My smile twitched and faltered. "Hey. Dude. Kidding."

Sid blinked and seemed surprised. He turned and moved on, shaking his head slightly, and left me with Mack, who was staring intently in our direction.

The rest of lunch proceeded almost exactly like that. Mom and Mack prodded Sid to talk. Sid gave one or two sentence answers, and the conversation lapsed into silence. There was this weird, tenuous balance in the conversation. On one hand, I knew Mom and Mack wanted to talk to me and hear about our struggles on campus. On the other, they clearly didn't want to exclude Sid from the conversation, so they kept trying to bring up topics that would get both of us talking. Classes. Campus life in general.

They steered clear of The Refuge.

Eventually, by the time I started digging into my second piece of cake, Sid more or less gave up talking. Instead, he jammed his pizza into his mouth, wolfing it down at a speed normally resolved for a five-minute lunch when you were ten minutes late for class. I stared at him, wondering where the food was going and how his esophagus was pushing it into his stomach fast enough to prevent him from choking. Mom sighed and began talking about work and how relieved she was to be back. Clients were starting to call again.

Finally, the painful lunch ended. Sid made up some obvious excuse about needing to study for his first round of tests and stood. He gave Mom a quick hug and Mack an awkward wave before turning in the other direction.

I knew where the conversation would go the second Sid was out of earshot.

"Wow." There was no malice in Mom's voice, no mocking edge. Just sadness. "You keep hearing about kids on the news, trying to cope with the aftermath of Perses. That's the first time I've really seen it."

"I swear, if I hear the phrase 'a world in chaos,' one more time, I'm going to go on a rampage myself," Mack grumbled. "No wonder everyone is such a mess. All you can hear about on the news is what a mess everyone is."

"Don't joke," Mom said quietly. "The news is all terrorists and cult groups and religious nutjobs shooting places up and closing down malls and standing in the middle of the highways, talking about how God's plan hasn't been fulfilled so it's their job to bring His wishes upon us." Mom had grown paler.

"Stop," I said quietly. There was enough on my mind. I didn't need to add to it by fearing something I could do absolutely nothing to stop.

"How much do you think this Refuge has to do with his mood?" Mack asked.

I shrugged. "Tough to say. We haven't spoken about it since I went nuts."

Mack's eyes narrowed. "Has he not brought it up?"

"He has not."

Mack put his fork down gently and folded his hands over each other. "That's worrisome."

My mind went back to me losing my mind at The Refuge meeting. "I don't know, Mack. I did sort of crap all over what they're doing. He knows how I feel about that group."

"True. But don't you think he'd try to convince you about how wrong you were?"

I shrugged. "I have no idea, Mack. Honestly, I'm not even sure if he's gone to another meeting."

"He has," Mack and Mom said at the same time. They made eye contact.

"Golden rule," Mom said.

"Ugh." It was a running joke at home. When Mom and Mack came to the same conclusion independently of each other, it had to be true. They had very different backgrounds. Mom was an abused teenage mother turned social media marketing maven. Mack was an army veteran turned grizzled rural police chief. If they agreed, something had to be up.

"How has security been on campus?" Mack asked.

"Fine? I guess? I haven't really thought about it."

"Have you noticed an uptick in their presence?" asked Mack, gesturing with his fork.

"No."

"Any additional security measures? People sitting around, looking like they are trying to blend in but actually sticking out like a sore thumb?"

"Not really."

"Okay, how about local police? Are you seeing them more?"

"No?"

Now Mack threw his fork down. "What are they doing here?"

I glanced at my phone. "Well, tell you what, let's go find out. The Q&A with the Dean of Students is in ten minutes."

"Oh, I'm looking forward to that." Mack stood up so quickly that he almost forgot to take his tray with him. Mom and I smiled at each other as Mack stormed ahead.

"It's only because he cares," she said.

"I know. I'd rather have it this way than with someone who wasn't worried."

Mom paused for a second and looked like she was starting to say something. She stopped… then started again.

"You can't make anyone do anything." Mom touched my arm gently. "The world isn't your responsibility, Corey Walker. You just do all the good you can. Don't make other people's problems yours."

It really didn't feel like enough.

《O》

THE EVENT WITH Dean Sumner was in the main administrative building. Normally, it was a wide, cavernous space and deathly silent, with footsteps echoing off of the chapel-like ceiling above. Today, it was filled with chairs and ringed with fancy cocktails and drinks. The space was also crowded, with attendees ranging from students to parents to well-dressed individuals with "A" pins and nametags.

To my pleasant surprise, this seemed to be one of the few places on campus where there seemed to be an energy in the room. Well-dressed butlers—I'm pretty sure it was the same people who worked in the dining hall, but whatever, they had food—circulated the room, carrying trays of heavy hors d'oeuvres. Even Mack looked pleased with the spread as he and Mom grabbed a drink from the open bar. In one corner of the room, a four-piece student band played classical music, just loud enough that you could hear their obvious skill but not so loud as to crowd out conversation.

I'm sure people were wondering what we were doing there. Mom must have sensed my discomfort because she leaned into me and whispered, "Don't worry, Corey. There's a reason they invited you."

"My skill at friend selection?" I quipped angrily.

"Stop," Mom said. "Seriously, relax."

"Yeah, but why am I here? I've seen a couple of other students but it's the student government types. No other... I don't know. Normal people."

And at that moment, the soft clinking of silverware meeting a champagne flute. We turned in that direction as a crowd cleared in front of Dean Sumner, who was at the front of the room. Sumner, I could see, was trying to look relaxed, wearing a charcoal grey suit and white button-down shirt that was open at the collar. His lapel was decorated with the ubiquitous script "A" that it seemed all high-level Augustus staff were required to wear. His sandy-blonde hair was perfect, parted slightly to the side. My Mom said he looked like Brad Pitt.

"Good afternoon, my friends. And welcome. We're so glad to have you here. Welcome back to Augustus. Welcome back to our wonderful school." Sumner clasped his hands in front of his chest and smiled glowingly. He was the second to the President of this school. A likely successor whenever she decided to retire. I could see why.

"We celebrate this Parent's Weekend at a difficult time." Sumner paused and looked appraisingly at the room. I'm sure he saw a group of nodding heads. I was among them. "Now, normally, this is the part where I tell you how wonderful the campus is doing. How admissions are at an all-time high, how our student enrollment is bursting, that our alumni engagement is strong and that our students are setting new records in academic achievement and extra-curricular activities."

The smile on Sumner's face evaporated like steam. "You all know, of course, that I can't do that this time. The campus is a wreck."

Behind me, Mack whistled softly.

"Our soccer season was canceled because not enough players returned, and barely any clubs have started meeting again. Demand for our counseling services—which was already at an all-time high before Perses—is through the roof. We can't keep up and have begun petitioning the state for emergency assistance. Admissions for next year are non-existent—we didn't have any students enrolled during the Perses Fall, and we're scrambling to make up for it. Alumni engagement is largely absent, and we're only now looking to reinvigorate our base with financial donations. In short, we're a disaster. We're also no different than virtually any other boarding school in the country, or the world, right now. We are supposed to be preparing a future generation for entering the next levels of their academic careers. Instead, we've become a holding tank as the rest of the world tries to right itself."

Mack wasn't whistling anymore. No one was making a sound.

Sumner eyed the room slowly. Despite the words he had just said, there was confidence in his voice. An evenness in his stare. "I'm not telling you this to frighten you. Rather, to engage you. And I firmly believe—as does President Helm, as does the rest of our senior staff—that the only way to rebuild our school and our society is by transparency and trust. So, I don't tell you these things to scare you into opening your wallets—though, if you do so, that would be awfully nice of you."

Soft giggles floated around the room as Sumner thrust his hands into his pockets.

"I'm telling you all of this to prepare you. Difficult days are ahead for Augustus, as they are for many other boarding schools and colleges. While I believe we will survive, as you all know, the decision to reopen the school this semester was a difficult one. Not every school has made the same choices, and already, certain campus events—including a rise in vandalism, alcohol poisoning, and even assaults—have made some question the wisdom of that decision. We're under a microscope, here. And there are certain people on campus—and outside of it—who want to take advantage of that chaos."

That got my attention. I looked from Mack to Mom and found they were staring at me.

Sumner again. "Our motto on this campus, as I am sure you all know, is, 'Ubi Doctrina Coniungit—Where Learning Connects.' That is the creed that this campus has lived by since it was founded in 1848. This means that learning must bring our students to the outside world. Our role, as educators, is to train our students to seek the knowledge that will prepare them to function in society, no matter how ugly that knowledge may be." Sumner paused, somewhat awkwardly, and scanned the room. He stopped moving his head when his eyes found mine. "No matter how much pain the truth brings to others."

Huh?

"Already, there are students on campus—as well as staff, as well as members of this administration—who are working to give students the help and support they need. But we will only get where we need to go as a school if we are honest about our challenges. If brave voices—voices with authority, credibility, and compassion—speak their truth, engage on this campus, and remember that everyone here needs redemption. They just may need a little bit of help finding it."

Son of a bitch.

He might have been talking to some of the richest and most connected alumni on campus. But he was definitely looking right at me.

Chapter 12

MOM WAS PATTING my shoulder excitedly as we left. Sumner had tried to move toward us but had been intercepted by a couple of guys in suits. I had lit out of there more or less as soon as the Dean had finished. I had a feeling a conversation with him would come sooner rather than later. But I didn't want to have it there. Not with that much money in the room. And not before I had any idea what I wanted to say, or what he wanted.

"I guess he saw the video," I mumbled.

"Of course, he did." Mom gestured back to the Administration building. "You think these guys don't see all those viral videos that you all think you're so clever shooting and sharing? Corey, these people are smarter than you give them credit for. Do you think they don't know that check-ins are falling apart, that all of you are breaking curfew?"

"Holding sleepovers," Mack muttered, a little smile on his face. I felt myself turning bright red. "You got on his radar, Corey."

"Me and my big mouth."

"Yes. You and your big mouth."

"You should be proud of that mouth," Mom said. "How many people do you think you convinced to leave that room with you and Paige?"

"A few," I mumbled. That was true. I'd gotten a few messages from people, including from freshman and sophomores I didn't know. They were texting me to say thanks. I had no idea how they had gotten my number.

Jesus. What the hell was I doing? I scratched the back of my head. "This seems a little bigger than I intended."

"It is," Mack said. "And it's going to keep getting bigger."

It was that sentence which caught Mom's attention. "Just be careful, okay, Corey?" she said, all previous enthusiasm gone.

"Hmm?"

"These people." Mom shivered slightly. "The Refuge. All these other nutty groups that are running around in campuses and cities and the country. It is not something I've seen, Corey."

"And it is not something law enforcement is prepared for," Mack said. "We have no idea how to tackle people who want to withdraw from society and take others with them."

My head was starting to spin. "Yeah, but if they want to withdraw, why does that involve law enforcement? I think these guys are absolutely out of their minds, but I haven't seen them do anything illegal."

Mack kept staring at me. It was a cold, hard stare.

"Not yet, anyway," I added.

Mack leveled his finger at me. "Exactly. Not yet. Corey, The Refuge isn't as bad as some of the other, more violent groups which have popped up. They aren't anything like the Unfulfilled or Borderlanders or anything like that." The names Mack spoke had some meaning, like a song I'd heard before. The truth was all of these groups and all of these names were starting to run together, blending like they had been put in a spin cycle of the world's pain, playing in my ears like a symphony of the damned.

Mom stared at Mack like she was annoyed. "But they may be."

"It's true. They may get there." Mack stared from Mom to me. "I don't think your mom and I would ever urge you to back down."

"No. Not at all," Mom said. "Just use your head, okay?"

I nodded meekly. "Okay."

We tried going to the basketball game that night. They were able to field a team, but just barely—nine guys instead of the usual twelve. It felt like we were sitting on a balloon that was slowly leaking air. Barely more than a few dozen people attended, and by ones and twos, the room emptied as the night went on. Soon, it was just us and a few others, probably parents of the kids playing. Augustus won—I guess—but the score was as lethargic as the crowd. Mom, Mack, and I stayed for the whole game, mainly out of pity.

So, we said goodnight, with Mom and Mack going to their hotel rooms.

"Maybe tomorrow we get to meet this girl of yours?" Mom asked.

"God, no," I said, and Mom punched me with surprising force. "Ow. I hate when you do that."

"Well, don't be embarrassed by me, then."

"Then don't do anything embarrassing."

"I never do that."

"You screamed about our marriage in a very public place earlier today."

"All right, all right, stop it you two." Mack was laughing. "Be safe, Little Man." Mack hugged me.

"Always, Bigger Man." I returned the hug.

Mom gave me a gentle kiss on the cheek. "We'll see you at breakfast."

"Fine, fine." I relented with a smile.

It had only been a few weeks since we were back on campus, but seeing Mom and Mack felt like putting on my most comfortable pair of sweatpants. I was lucky… I had them. And in this chaos, I'd found Paige. That had given a lot of insanity meaning.

But… what about those who didn't have meaning? Who didn't have a Mom or a Mack? Who had lost their Paige? What about all of those who had lost a Josh and were still struggling to replace what they would never find again?

"I'm lucky," I muttered to myself. I was in pain, but I could see it. I had the people available to help me deal. I'd seen trauma all my life and knew how to cope. I knew what pain was in front of me. But Sid? And others? They didn't deserve my scorn. I don't even know if they deserved my sympathy. I just knew they deserved my kindness. That was the only thing I could give.

I texted Sid. *Hey. You around?* We really hadn't gotten a chance to discuss Josh. My phone said it was only 9:30 or so, and I doubt Sid had any plans. He'd probably be playing video games in the room. Maybe I could find the Twins and the four of us could just hang out. Figure out how to get through this a little better.

I started to text the Twins when I keyed my way into the room but was greeted by its emptiness. The lights were on… but no Sid. I almost called his name to search for him, as if my voice would somehow magically make him appear.

Okay, Sid not being here wasn't that strange. But he didn't come back after ten minutes, and I stood, confused.

The Twins were around but hadn't seen Sid.

lmk when he's in, Mo texted.

And yet, nothing. I looked around the room, trying to suppress a gnawing feeling of dread. I was about to text him when I noticed it, out of the corner of my eye. Sid's shower caddy. He'd always been pretty religious about putting his shampoo and soap in the exact same spot… in fact, I teased him about it all the time. To mess with him, I used to put his shampoo in random spots around the room.

Now, the space was empty. And when I looked in his closet, I realized it was also missing his deodorant and comb.

"God damnit." I put my hands on my hips. He was obviously sleeping over somewhere. But where?

I was too afraid to ask. Even though I probably knew the answer anyway.

Sid wasn't going to come back that night. I went up to Mo and Mika's room, and they confirmed what I figured after firing off a few texts. The Refuge was having a big event at some off-campus house some of their members were renting. It was not a party. Mo's friend had insisted. It was a mixer, and no one was getting in without an invitation.

"You should totally try to get in though, Corey," Mika said with a mischievous smile on his face. "I'm sure Megan would love to see you."

I rolled my eyes. "Absolutely. I'll go with Paige. We can be Mister and Miss Refuge." I chucked an empty can at Mika's gut with more force than I intended. He didn't seem to notice. I cursed again and put my head on Mika's pillow, staring at the ceiling.

We puttered around for a little while longer and debated trying to find something to do, but it was no good. All I saw when I closed my eyes was Josh, that stupid smile and his stupid curly hair and the stupid way he had died, scared and assaulted by an apocalypse that would never actually arrive.

Paige texted an hour later. And then I was in her room, crying. There was nothing she could say, nothing she could do, but it felt as if something between my best friend and me had snapped horribly and fractured forever. She just sort of held me as I made an ass of myself and wept into her shoulder.

At some point—I don't remember when—I fell asleep in her arms.

«O»

WHEN PAIGE AND I woke up the next morning, we decided we'd try to get together at breakfast with my parents. So, I'd stumbled back to my room, hoping against hope that Sid would be there, even though I knew better. I had no idea where I thought he'd be, but I just knew it wasn't in our room.

Sighing, I threw on a nice Henley shirt and the most wrinkle-free pair of jeans I could come up with. Truth be told, I wasn't so much worried about Paige meeting Mom & Mack. Mom was young enough that she knew how important this moment could be, and how awkward. It was one of the benefits of her having me so young. Mack, of course, would be fine… steady, solid, quiet. He knew how to read people. He knew how to talk, and he knew when to listen.

It was meeting Paige's parents that was making my heart skip a bit. This was a significant moment. I was smart enough to know that. And

Paige had said that her parents were pretty cool people… but how cool could they be? Was her dad going to take one look at the guy who was dating his daughter and want to punch me in the mouth?

When I confessed this fear, Paige said, "Stop. Come on. He's not an idiot. He's my dad."

"Yes, but is he a violent dad?"

"What the hell is it with some of you guys?"

"Hmm?"

Paige's voice took on an exaggerated, caveman cadence. "Ohhh, look at me, I am man. Man think little girl his property. Not strong woman on own. Man punch other man that touch his." Paige smacked her chest to emphasize the caveman point. When she spoke again, her voice was normal. "Dude. Relax. My dad is cool."

"Seriously, though." I didn't bother to try and hide the insecurity which was sliding into my voice. "Is he that cool?"

"He's cool enough that, when I was twelve, he sat me down and talked to me about the decisions I get to make. He told me to wait until I was older. He told me that if I was going to ignore this advice—or even if I wasn't—that I should be smart and use protection. He told me he'd help me if I ever got into trouble or if anything bad ever happened to me. He said I could always talk to him. And he told me that the decision should be mine, and mine alone."

I linked my fingers with Paige's, thinking of a similar talk I'd had with Mack when I was old enough to wonder why girls no longer seemed that gross, and all the talks we'd had since. "I like your dad."

"Me too," Paige said, with just a hint of a smile. "I can't wait for you to meet him."

"But not at breakfast?"

"No. Later. The plane was delayed, so they'll be here in a couple hours. They said they'd try to take us out to lunch."

I couldn't say the idea of eating real food off-campus was something I'd object to.

And then we were at the Student Union, marching toward the Dining Hall. Finding Mom and Mack was difficult. The space was teeming with people, everyone from anxious freshmen who were pointing out the sights to their parents—"This is where we scan in… yes, Dad, it's automatic…."—to jaded seniors who just looked miserable and hungover. The Student Union was more crowded than I'd seen it since before Perses, and the realization made me smile. It seemed like this decision to schedule a Family Weekend on this day had been a wise one, like it had invigorated some sort of life into the campus's stagnant bloodstream.

Paige squeezed my hand and said, "That them?"

I followed her gaze and nodded, waving with my free hand. "Yep. Nicely done."

"Duh. I looked at your Insta profile. Wanted to have some stuff to talk about."

"You actually did research?"

"This is important," Paige said solemnly. "I'm not winging this."

I swallowed wordlessly. I had absolutely not done the same. But, before I could say anything else, we were there.

"Hi," Paige said evenly, her voice calm and steady. She extended her hand and shook Mom's. "I'm Paige."

"It's so wonderful to meet you," Mom said, her voice even and her smile bright. "It really is."

"Nice to meet you, Paige." Mack extended a meaty hand, almost encasing Paige's in his.

"Likewise, Officer Miller."

"Mack is fine, but thank you." Mack popped a friendly smile. He scanned the hallway. Wide as it was, we were being jostled by people moving in and out of the Dining Hall. I was starting to feel like a rock in a fast-moving stream. "I think we should get out of the way."

"Yes, please," I said. "It's a family weekend and dinner yesterday was ridiculous. I can't wait to see what they do for breakfast."

"Do you remember those crepes last year?" Paige asked.

"Crepes?" Mom and Mack said at the same time.

Paige and I nodded enthusiastically.

"Crepes," I said. "Delicious, tasty, fruit-filled breakfast crepes. I vaguely remember jamming half a dozen down my throat."

Paige laughed. It was a breathy, sweet sound. "Did you get filling all over your face?"

"Oh no," I said. "No, no, the first real conversation the two of you have will not be about me getting cherry filling all over my face."

"So, it was cherry filling you got all over?" Mom teased.

"Everywhere. I got it everywhere."

"Paige, honey, let's go get your breakfast." Mom threw her stuff over a small circular table in the corner of the room. "When you get back, I'll tell you about the first time Corey ever had spaghetti."

Mom and Paige walked toward the omelet station. Mom's hands were moving like it was raining from her head, clearly indicating that she had launched into the story early.

Mack was still standing there. When Paige and Mom were out of earshot, he leaned near my ear and said, "Good start."

"Bonding over making fun of me. You can't go wrong."

"I've seen that picture too. You looked like you had tomato sauce hair."

"Was this from last week?" I quipped.

Mack chuckled. "How's everything going?"

And just like that, my good mood was gone. "Been better." I filled him in on what had happened last night.

By the time I finished, Mack's face was stern. "Aren't you supposed to have people in the dorm, doing check-ins?"

I shrugged. "Hit or miss, Mack. We've only got one teacher and it's a big dorm. We've been leaning on the virtual check-ins, but so many kids aren't doing it. The story is that Doctor Skinner has a kid in college that is in some sort of trouble."

Mack raised an eyebrow. "What sort of trouble?"

"I don't know, Mack. Lots of options."

Mack exhaled through pursed lips. "I couldn't help but notice the presence of a few of those folks in all black. They look like piss-poor entries into a Johnny Cash look-alike contest."

I looked Mack in the eyes. "I'm scared, Bigger Man. He's drifting."

"Well, ease your expectations," Mack said, and I cocked my head. "You can't save everyone."

"I saved a few." I thought again of the messages I'd gotten from people, thanking Paige and me for snapping them out of their daze and pulling them out of The Refuge meeting. "Why can't I save him?"

"Some people can't be saved. I've seen it a million times before. You have to want to be helped."

Mack's words bounced around my head as I loaded my plate, but the implication behind what he said… that some people couldn't be saved because they didn't want to be… that was enough to keep most food off of my tray. I came back with only three crepes. Thankfully, Mom and Paige were too engrossed in their own conversation to notice my—relative—lack of appetite. Also, thankfully, they had moved on from making fun of me.

"Paige was just telling me that she lost a friend too," Mom said. I looked at Paige and slightly raised my eyebrows. She responded by raising just one.

"Yeah. Something I think we all have in common," I said.

"Our office too," Mom said. She looked at Paige. "I work in marketing. Things have actually picked up. Our biggest problem is trying to get qualified staff back. Or in, I should say. At least two of my coworkers are gone, and we were never a firm of more than ten to begin with."

"The dollars always flow." Mack's smile was thin.

"I'm just grateful they're flowing our way. The work we do is something I can be proud of. Getting people to spend money again is important, or this recession will just get worse." Mom popped a forkful of scrambled eggs into her mouth. "People are too afraid to spend."

"If they have anything left. You're right, Cara. I joke, but getting people working again—back to doing something productive—that's more important than ever."

I took a good, hard look at Mack then. Saw the slump in his shoulders, the bags under his eyes. Had those always been there? What else had I missed since I'd been away? The faucet of guilt that was on a constant drip in my mind opened slightly, its flow expanding to a slow trickle.

I gestured to one of the televisions which were studded around the dining hall. Since we'd come back, I hadn't seen them on. "Kind of hard to care about the world when all you hear about is it that it's failing all of us."

"Thank God they haven't turned those back on yet. They used to be locked in on CNN. Now they're just silent. They should stay that way forever," Paige said.

Mack made a noise, something that sounded like a toneless *harrumph*, and Paige looked at him. "You don't agree?" Her voice was an octave sharper than usual. Fortunately, one look at Paige, and you could she see wasn't trying to be rude—her chin was propped up on her fist, and her face was calm, eyes blinking slowly.

"If I'm being honest, I don't know. On one hand, you can't run from the world. On the other, I'm not convinced that having it constantly in your face is a good thing." Mack patted the front of his flannel shirt, where his iPhone was lodged in his pocket. "Besides. It's not as if you can get very far."

"True." Paige poked her breakfast. Then she looked at me. "Corey and I have been running around screaming at people to be honest with their pain, after all. Maybe that means facing the world for what it is."

"There's such a thing as too much truth," Mom said.

"And too much information." I pushed my tray away from me, marginally aware that my voice sounded louder than usual. "I wish we could go back to the way things were. I wish for it all the time. But it's never happening."

"No. It never is," Paige said. "That's why those bastards in black are having so much success...."

I kept staring at Paige, but her voice had trailed off, and I realized that she was no longer looking at me, but past me, staring intently at the table behind me. I turned and realized why. They were looking at their phones with an intensity that couldn't have possibly been maintained for any TikTok or Reels. I stared at the group, trying to get their attention, but their eyes were locked on their phones. Three boys, two girls. One girl and one boy looked near tears.

I turned back at Mom, Mack, and Paige, dimly aware that the noise in the cafeteria had now dropped to a series of urgent whispers. "Uh-oh."

As one, Mom, Mack, Paige, and I went for our phones. I thumbed open X with shaking fingers.

Mom and Paige cursed simultaneously. "Shooting," Paige said. "Mass shooting at… MTBS?" A wave of ice shot down the left side of my body. MTBS was Mountain Top Boarding School, one of the top boarding schools in the country.

It was also just two hours from Augustus. They were our rivals. Kids with cars pulled pranks on each other's campuses.

"No, not MTBS," Mom said, her face crinkled. "Western University of Pennsylvania. Shooting inside a dorm. Multiple gunmen… they went room to room, my God, my God…." Mom's voice had trailed to nothing. "I think you have the wrong school."

In response, Paige held up a shaky hand, showing a picture of the campus I remembered from my sporting events—students running in terror, down a hill, phones clutched in their hands, moving from Mountain Top's Student Union as fast as possible.

Now Mom looked down at her phone and scrolled further. "At least three campuses had mass shootings today. All in Pennsylvania." Her voice had gone toneless, deadened, as if she was reciting a grocery list.

I looked to Mack.

My father figure knew enough not to cause a panic but also had become acutely aware of the potential danger. By the time Paige said, "Make that four," her eyes still locked on her phone, Mack had swiveled his head around the room and was standing, looking toward the main entrance of the Dining Hall with a fire in his eyes. Through the glass doors, I could see students, maybe walking a little quicker than usual.

One or two looked blissfully unaware of the danger facing us. More than a few people were heading toward the exits.

The loudspeaker crackled to life at that moment. I heard multiple cries.

"Attention students and family. Due to recent events, we are in a lockdown status. I repeat. We are in a lockdown status. Assume active shooter."

The message droned again, but no one heard it. A mix of reactions circulated through the cafeteria. Like different blood cells traveling through an artery, different students reacted differently. Some students shrieked and wept. Others rolled their eyes and tried to feign indignation that I knew wasn't there. The fear in the air was palpable. It had an unmistakable weight to it.

Other students grabbed empty tables and began to push them to the massive doors of the cafeteria, but not before security jogged into the room, their heads swiveling, looking for danger. The room was growing darker, and glancing up, I discovered why. Black-out shades were dropping from the ceiling, inching their way after down after having been activated by an unseen switch.

Mack turned to me, his voice an urgent whisper. "Little Man. Stay with them."

"Okay," I said, aware of a thudding in my fingertips as my pulse drummed louder. Mack took off to the front of the room, making his way to security. Paige and I spun around, looking, making sure that all entrances were blocked off with a mass of chairs and tables.

Students looked around, waiting. Watching. The same message droned on about an active shooter.

"Under the tables!" one of the security screamed loudly, eliciting more shrieks. "This isn't a drill, people!"

Mack got closer to the man, and my mom's eyes widened. I wasn't sure what terrified me more—the look of terror on her face, or the way her gaze slowly met mine, like she was looking to me for reassurance.

"I…." I shook my head. *Stop. Lead.* "Let's get under the table."

We did. Others were doing the same.

I crawled under a table, wrapping my legs to my knees. Mom jostled me from the left, Paige from the right.

"What's he doing?" Paige whispered, staring at Mack, who was now standing with the police officer, one hand safely nestled under his jacket.

"He's watching," Mom said. "Watch his eyes. Look how he's looking around the room. He's watching for a gunman."

There was nothing I could say to that. There was just cold, brutal reality—some group was running around the state, shooting schools like mine. Maybe someone was on their way here now.

Bizarrely, I wanted to look down. Check my phone, read more about the terror. I wanted to run and scream. More than anything, I wanted to go home.

But where could I go that was safe? What would happen at home, when even Mack couldn't protect the rest of my small town? Safety was gone, and the illusion of it had been shattered when Perses bounced off the sky.

Chapter 13

AN HOUR LATER, we were still hiding under the table, looking at pictures of the dead and dying across the state. CNN's Breaking News Twitter feed blared *CAMPUSES ATTACKED* and news of more shootings rolled in.

Our campus remained quiet, filling me with a sensation that was equal parts gratitude and guilt.

Northampton police stormed into the cafeteria an hour later, announcing that the campus was secure, and ending the lockdown. Their hands were on their weapons. Shakily, students began to emerge from tables, folding into the arms of their friends or loved ones.

The shades began to slowly lift, re-revealing campus to the inhabitants of the cafeteria. On a normal day, you could see the outline of the bleachers for our soccer field, a near-perfect view of Academic Row and the campus lawn. Today, it gave us the ideal view of SWAT teams, no longer running, but certainly not looking relaxed.

We stumbled out of the cafeteria, tears streaking down the faces of far too many present. Students were with their parents, who limply hung their arms around their children. I saw more than a few students stagger off toward the visitor's parking lot, pile into cars with their families. I wondered if they'd come back.

Someone had turned the TV on in the lounge. The text blared the headline. 29 DEAD, 107 WOUNDED AT COORDINATED

SHOOTING ON PENNSYLVANIA COLLEGES AND BOARDING SCHOOLS.

Some talking head was saying something. I didn't hear a word. I just felt a burn inside my nerves, a fire so hot that it deadened all my other senses. A waterfall of emotion fell over me. I knew I should try and wrap an arm around Paige, who was every bit as shocked as I was. I knew I had responsibilities. Obligations.

But I could barely lift my arms.

I don't know how long we stood in front of the television, barely breathing, immobile. Eventually, Mack touched my shoulder. "Little Man."

"Yeah, Bigger Man?"

One of Mack's solid hands wrapped around my left shoulder. Mom did the same with my right, and after a moment's pause, she put an arm around Paige. Paige soundlessly leaned into the affection.

Mom and Mack left a little while later. It was clear that the campus was under heavy guard and there was nothing they could do but get in the way. Mack, I knew, also had promises to keep. There was a community college the next town over. I'd seen him look at his phone and discretely respond to texts. He had people who relied on him.

Mom and Mack exchanged hugs with us, and Paige had tried to cover up the fact that she was crying. We exchanged words, but I couldn't tell you what they were. I saw dead bodies everywhere I looked.

Paige and I watched CNN and doomscrolled for the rest of that day, locked in Mo and Mika's room, with Paige and me alternatively curling up in each other's arms. Even Mo and Mika sat closer than usual. We barely spoke—there was nothing to say. We just watched the carnage on a campus which could have very easily been ours, wondering why we were so lucky. Wondering why it had been our friends to the north, and not us.

Sid still wasn't responding to my texts. Bastard.

The pictures were unending. Students, the dead and dying, bloody splotches covered by matching white sheets. If you believed enough, you could almost pretend that they were dolls, just dolls. Not people who had survived the end of the world, only to be killed by the aftermath.

It was a coordinated attack, of course. A group of religious extremists called the Left Behind had taken responsibility, according to CNN. Their manifesto held that God had found us unworthy for heaven, and it was their job to send as many people as possible to the Devil as quickly as they could manage.

They had gone into dorms and killed sleeping students while Paige and I drowsed in each other's arms. Shot up two student centers while we walked into ours. Obliterated another two dining halls with small arms and automatic rifle fire while Paige, Mom, Mack, and I ate our breakfast, blissfully unaware of the degree to which this planet was broken.

We finally went to the dining hall to get dinner late that night. It was a Saturday. The place should have been packed with students getting ready to attend some social event, or seniors preparing to get off campus and see a movie or go to the mall. Instead, there was only a handful of us, eating under the watchful eye of a police officer. I saw a couple of members of the school administration there, eating off of trays. I even saw Dean Sumner, his blonde hair mussed, and his skin an off-shade of grey. He didn't see me, and I didn't go to try to talk to him. He looked ill. I could only imagine his burdens.

When I handed my tray in, I heard overheard two custodians talking. "It's like nine-eleven again, man," one said to the other. "It feels like nine-eleven all over again."

I hadn't understood what that day felt like until today.

Somehow, exams were supposed to go on next week. The school had said as much in a campus-wide email that came around 10:00 p.m. that night. The world may be sputtering, but life had to go on, and the teachers on campus had been instructed to not cancel classes and continue teaching. I couldn't tell if I was angry at their indifference or grateful for the distraction.

The same email promised increased coordination with local police and enhanced patrols from campus safety. It was most decidedly short on details.

The day began to pass in phases of grief and anguish and images of blood and terror. When we got sick of the television, we waddled out into the Netflix lounge. We weren't the only ones. The school had tried to put together a campus-wide rally, and prefects had dutifully fliered the dorm. From the look of things, most of our dorm had decided, like us, that leaving the safety of the building was too frightening a prospect. Instead, we stared out of the massive glass window that overlooked the school green. It didn't look like there were more than a few people out there, holding candles against the nighttime sky. It was a nice effort. But I don't think anyone in the school administration fully understood our devastation. We knew the world had drifted into chaos. But this was the closest the chaos had ever felt.

《0》

I HAD EXAMS starting on Tuesday, as did a huge chunk of the campus. It was supposed to be something approximating midterms, although the school wasn't calling them that. I think that was mostly out of the fear of looking callous.

We woke up early after a fitful night's sleep. My eyes were swollen. So were Paige's.

"How ya doing?" Paige's voice was slushy with sleep, any thoughts of prefects or teachers catching us long gone. They would have had to tear me out of there.

"Fantastic." I groaned at the morning light that was streaming into the room, knifing its way through my eyes. The heaviness which had settled into my chest as we'd slept last night had not dissipated, as I'd hoped. Instead, it had metastasized. My arms and legs felt stiff with grief.

"Come on. Let's go get the twins up."

"Uh-huh." I threw off the blanket.

Thirty minutes later, we were in vaguely presentable clothing and stumbling toward the Dining Hall. I shivered at the thought. Not that I wasn't hungry—I was—but….

We were all walking slowly. With a bitter laugh, I turned to my friends. "You guys see how slow we're moving?"

"Yeah," we all muttered at the same time.

Tears welled up in Paige's eyes. "I don't want to go in there."

I debated ignoring it for the sake of not embarrassing her, but Paige had preached honesty above all else, even in your most pain-filled moments, so I wrapped an arm around her waist. We all kept staggering forward.

To their infinite credit, Mo and Mika looked at the ground and said nothing.

At the cafeteria, the attendant greeted us with the saddest smile I'd ever seen.

"It's okay, honey," she said to Paige, evidently spotting her splotchy face. "We're all scared. My son didn't want me to leave today."

Paige didn't say anything. She just started crying again, ran around the desk, and gave the woman the tightest hug I'd ever seen two strangers exchange.

"I don't even know her name," Mo said.

I just sort of blinked.

The woman finally disengaged the hug and whispered something into Paige's ear. Whatever it was, it made Paige laugh. It was a laugh wet with tears, but it was a laugh.

As we moved forward, I said, "What did she say to you?"

Paige rubbed a fist to her face. "Take care of your boys."

Now I laughed too.

We were the first ones in the Dining Hall that morning. When we reached a table, I was pleasantly surprised by what I saw. Every table had a gorgeous, blood-red rose on it, encased in a thin, simple glass vase.

"That's nice," Mo said.

Mika nodded approvingly, but Paige saw it first. She pointed at the rose. "What's that?"

Underneath the rose was a black piece of cardstock. The letters on the note were printed in light grey.

It's Not Too Late

Don't Let It Be

2446 W. Liberty. Tonight. 5:00 p.m.

"Those bastards." Paige looked over my shoulder. "Those absolute, complete, total bastards."

My mouth hung open in an "O" of horror. "They're using the shootings as a recruitment tool." Mo and Mika simultaneously ripped the note out of my hand and began to emit a stream of cursing which was usually reserved for anonymous internet comments.

"What the hell do we do with this?" Mo asked.

The question was answered for us by a campus security officer who I hadn't seen earlier. With shaking fingers, we handed him the note. The man blanched.

"These shouldn't be here," he said quietly. He looked toward the door. More students were starting to arrive in packs of twos and threes. I guess we weren't the only ones who couldn't sleep. "Help me remove these. Please."

With a lurch, the man spun around and began to move from table to table, scooping up black fliers with indelicate hands and knocking over more than a few vases in the process.

Paige, Mo, Mika, and I looked toward each other, smiled, and nodded. Screw these guys. Not now, not at this moment.

Heart in my throat, I began to grab at those evil black fliers.

《◇》

WE HADN'T BEEN quick enough, of course, and it obviously hadn't been the only spot that The Refuge had fliered. By the time we got back to Flo, giggling at our little punch against The Refuge, the black fliers were covering the hall. Paige and Mika ran down one side of each hallway, ripping down fliers as they moved, laughing all the way.

"This a good idea?" Mo said.

I shrugged. "No idea. But security did it, so it can't be all that bad. Race you to the next floor?"

"Hell yes."

Minutes later, every floor in the dorm had been cleansed from The Refuge's propaganda. Paige, Mo, Mika, and I were now on the fifth floor, gasping for breath, and smiling at each other. I don't know if the smile was from joy, the sheer absurdity of the situation, or having finally felt like we were doing something. For whatever reason, I was smiling wider than I had in some time.

"Now what?" Mo asked. Halfway through our run, Mika had run into his room and come out, hollering, holding a small garbage bag. It had filled up with remarkable speed, and all of us still had fistfuls of fliers in our hands.

"Hang on." Mika shuffled his papers around and freed up a hand, dug into his pocket for a few seconds, and withdrew a lighter. "Heh."

"Okay, wait, let's not actually start a fire," I said.

"What if we used a fireplace?" Mo gestured behind us.

Son of a bitch. I'd completely forgotten. "Best idea you've had in years."

"Thank you," Mo said brightly.

Minutes later, the fliers had been unspooled from our fists and unloaded from the garbage bag. Each of us took a turn, feeding the growing flames one by one, a twisted smile on all of our faces.

"There is something deeply, deeply cathartic about this," Paige said. We all murmured our agreement and kept feeding fuel to the flames.

When we had finished all of the fliers a few moments later, we took a step back. Mo adjusted the chimney damper, pushing it to the maximum open position.

"It's beautiful," I said, a wistfulness to my voice. The world may have been burning around us, but at least we were fighting fire with fire.

"It is," Paige said, and for a moment, we were silent, staring at the fliers as they burned. Around us, students were starting to move, leaving their rooms and probably wondering why the hell a group of us had crowded around a fireplace and looked so happy watching things burn.

Paige spoke again. "You know, this isn't enough."

"Not even close," Mika's voice wavered. "These people scare me. They are so quick."

"And there's a lot of 'em," Mo said.

"We're going to have to fight back." Paige poked me gently in the stomach, snapping me out of the hypnotic hold of the flames.

"Yeah." I didn't know what to say to that. Paige was right—these people were frightening, and a push back was necessary. I ran a hand over my face, dimly aware that Mika and Paige were staring out the window. "What's going on?"

Paige pointed. "This looks weird, right?"

"Yeah," Mika said. "Yeah, it really does."

I pushed myself out of an overstuffed chair. "What does?"

Mika waved me over. "There's a lot of them."

I looked out the glass window and followed Mika and Paige's pointing fingers. Like swarming locusts, students in black were converging. They were moving in clumps, not rushing, chatting mildly with each other as they moved. Like maggots drawn to rotten food, they were all moving in the same direction—the Student Union.

"Do they have a big breakfast date or something?" asked a deep voice. I turned as Auron Connor approached, his disgust evident. Connor had joined us in our abrupt exit of the first Refuge meeting.

"I… I don't know," I said, genuinely puzzled. I looked back at my friends and down Academic Row. We'd counted a few dozen of them moving into the Union, and there were more coming.

"Maybe they're all going to breakfast?" The words rang hollow, even as I spoke them.

Paige's hands were balled up into fists. "Not this many. Not at the same time." We all looked at each other, gazes bouncing between our own faces and out the window. My legs tingled with electricity.

I nodded. "Let's go."

As one, we tore off toward the elevators.

"Show of force," Paige said. "Has to be."

"Force for what?" I spluttered.

"Yeah, that part scares me," said Mo.

"Ditto," snapped Mika, mashing the elevator button. I fished my phone out of my back pocket and fired off some texts to a few people who I thought would be in the cafeteria.

The first one to respond was Kevin Thompson, the freshman who had joined us when we left The Refuge meeting. *Uhhh what the hell is this?* He sent me a picture, and we instantly crowded around it. We were stopped just in front of the elevator, oblivious to the two students who almost had to shove past me to get in. The picture was of a crowded cafeteria scene that looked relatively normal—students chatting, buried in their phones, or cramming scrambled eggs down their throats.

I looked around the photo for a mass of black shirts, expecting... what was I expecting? A protest? An animal sacrifice? A group of students firing semi-automatic weaponry?

It wasn't any of those. But there was one black shirt—and only one black shirt—at every table in sight.

"They're recruiting," I said. "They're recruiting for their meeting tonight."

Mo whistled softly. "Yeah. They are definitely taking advantage of everything happening."

We exchanged horrified glances before Paige slapped us both in the back and began to briskly walk out of the dorm. "Come on, you three. Move it. Back to the Dining Hall."

"Right," I was hot on Paige's heels.

I texted Kevin to call for reinforcements.

Way ahead of you, he responded instantly.

«◊»

THE DINING HALL was buzzing with activity and energy. It almost seemed alive.

Kevin practically tackled us when we walked in. "They're persistent assholes, I'll give them that!" His hands began to gesticulate wildly, his lanyard bopping with his every movement. "They all just came in like a wave and just started sitting, one by one, at all of the tables. At first, I didn't think it made any sense because there are still a bunch of open tables, and—"

Paige held up a hand. "Whoa. Whoa, whoa. Slow down."

Kevin took a deep, practiced breath, his eyes closed. "Sorry. Little excited. Very excited." One more deep breath, and he continued. I eyed the room, my gaze roaming from table to table. There were a couple of hundred tables in the room—way too many for The Refuge members to cover, thank God. But there were dozens of them, and from what I could tell, they were actively engaged in a good amount of conversations. At some tables, they were actively talking, hands moving, mouths smiling. At others, they were listening patiently, hands propped under their chins, nodding now and then.

A few of them were circulating from table to table, hands easily leaning on chairs while they talked to the table's occupants. Most people seemed to be listening intently.

I cursed.

"Yeah, exactly," Kevin said, any calm the deep breaths he'd taken having apparently been flushed by my expletive.

"What are they doing, exactly?" Mika asked.

"Trying to get people to their meeting tonight." Kevin pulled a flier out of his pocket. "Leaving these."

It was the same flier we'd taken earlier in the day. Was that today? It already seemed like a week ago. Time was moving at a rate I couldn't understand.

I looked around the room and felt the rage boiling my blood. "Their meeting… that's one thing. But now they're just…." I ran out of words. This felt so wrong. Like a violation.

"Intruding. This is our cafeteria." Paige was staring at me. There was an angry glint in her eyes. "We're stopping this. Now."

I whipped my head back to Kevin. "You text people?"

Kevin ripped his phone out of his pocket and tapped it with anger. "Everyone that was there with us. There's a few already here." He gestured back to the mass of tables.

"Great. Let's go." I looked back at Paige, Mo, and Mika.

Mo had a massive smile on his face as he extended his arms and cracked his knuckles. "I love making friends." He took five easy steps and sat down in an empty chair at a nearby table. Even over the din, I heard him talk to the person in black. "Hi there! What's your name, new friend?"

I lost it laughing.

"Atta boy. Guess I gotta outdo him." Mika weaved his way down the tables, thankfully turning around to avoid seeing me shift uncomfortably. Getting emotionally fired up and screaming at a group of ugly people was one thing. Forced, intimate conversations against a movement that was spreading like a virus… that was something else.

Paige saw it. The smile on her face was golden. She extended a fist in my direction. "Don't screw up."

I bumped her first with a chortle, and we turned in opposite directions. I found a table with a short kid in black.

"Hello, everyone." I started to sit down, but another kid extended her hand.

"Thanks, Corey, but I got this," she said.

I blinked, scanning my brain before remembering who the girl was—Ayla Robin. She'd also left the first Refuge meeting with us. She was tall, with curly hair, pale skin, and a hard stare that kept shooting back to The Refuge member at this table. "I was just asking my friend in black here why they are called The Refuge. They are having a really hard time answering."

Oh, man. Her smile was just ear to ear.

"I think I'll find somewhere else." I winked. I stood up, feeling warmth and confidence firing through me. The kid in black looked distinctly uncomfortable.

I didn't have to look for long before finding another table with someone in black. I inhaled sharply and sat down in an empty seat.

"Hello." I forced cheeriness through my veins. "I'm Corey." I looked at the guy in black. He was thick. Broad-shouldered, with long hair. Almost looked like Sid if he had skipped a barber for a few months. The thought filled me with sadness, and I made an effort to put that sadness somewhere useful. "David, right?" I extended my hand, and the long-haired Sid shook it with a finger-crushing grip.

"Yeah." The words escaped out of a tightly closed mouth.

"Great to meet you, David." I looked around the rest of the table. Three guys, two girls. I couldn't get a read on their year, but they all looked young. "Who are you folks?"

Mumbled introductions followed, so soft and hurried I barely understood who I was talking to. The one girl whose name I'd managed to catch—Alexia, I think—said, "Are you in The Refuge too?"

"No," muttered one of her guy friends. "He's obviously not. There's color in his outfit."

I laughed at that. David's face was unmoved. "No, I'm not in The Refuge, Alexia. Actually, I'm a little curious about what they are doing." I sat back, folded my arms across my chest, trying to fake a sense of comfort I knew I didn't have. "Go on, David. Tell them what you want them to hear." The bite in my voice was impossible to miss.

"Well, before I continue, let's make sure we're all straight on what Corey here wants," David said. "I think that Corey and his buddies are part of that 'harming' group I was telling you about earlier." And David looked at me with this menacing chomp, his lower lip slightly curled in.

I tried to ignore it. Tried to forget the fact that David could absolutely kick the hell out of me if he wanted to. "I've been called a lot of things, Dave, but that's a new one."

"The Refuge is built on three principles—heal, help, and harm."

"That last one doesn't seem to fit," I quipped.

"Sure, it does." David's voice was slow. Methodical. He sat up, pinning me to the back of my chair with a glare. "We can only help the world heal if we take care of those that would harm us."

Pinpricks shot through my legs. "That's your third principle? You're being that open about how hostile you are to others?"

David leaned upward. "Corey… did you see the news yesterday? The shootings? Those weren't randomly targeted. They are coming for us if the college doesn't shut down first." David poked a finger into his own chest. "Me. I lost a friend at Mountain Top."

That took the air out of me. "And I am sorry for your loss."

"That's so scary," said Alexia.

"But what does 'harming' have to do with anything?" I asked, speaking quickly.

"Easy," David said, and I had to suppress a shiver at the smoothness with which he slid from bereaved student to salesman. "We are here to help. And we will harm anyone who tries to get in our way."

"That doesn't sound threatening at all," I said.

David spread his arms wide. "These aren't normal times. And we aren't a normal group. We want to start a fresh society within a failed one."

"A cult," I said. "You mean you want to start a cult." Something clicked inside me as I said those words. I scanned the eyes of everyone else present. Alexia looked disgusted and confused and angry and scared, as if the emotion of every student in the world had somehow made it onto her face.

"Cults are built around isolating yourself from the outside world. It's a little difficult to do that at a boarding school," said David.

"Right now, sure. But what happens next week?" My head was swirling, and I was having trouble getting thoughts to form coherently. I kept drifting back to Sid, to the moments that I had let pass. *Forget about David. Look at Alexia.* I did that. "Does this make sense to you? You have to wear all black to join a club and make new friends?"

"No one has to wear all black," said David, picking at his shirt. "Some of us choose to as a mark of faith."

"Yes, clothing marks your faith. This is all very normal and healthy."

"You can be as sarcastic as you want, but I think that speaks volumes about your disconnection from these people. I wear black for reasons no different than why Christians wear the cross or Jews wear kippahs."

My eyes narrowed, and I looked back at Alexia. Her friends were staring coldly at us. Alexia was the only one who seemed to hear what I had to say. I stared at her. "A brand-new group shows up on campus, and they're telling you that wearing black is like wearing the cross?"

Alexia swallowed. "Sounds a little excessive."

If David was offended, he didn't show it. "It's a new world. And new worlds call for new emotions. New feelings. We can use Perses." David, I realized, was now looking at the other four rapt students sitting here. He'd chopped Alexia from his view completely. "We can make it better than it was before Perses."

"Or we can make it worse," I said. "Look. I thought I was going to die with the rest of you on January third. Hell, I thought I was going to die when I was younger—"

"We know. We were there," said one of the guys, his eyes rolling.

Right. I lost that one. I looked at Alexia. Her face was relaxed, her eyes wide, and she was looking right at me. "I'm not the only one who endured pain and hell for those few months. But the way forward is together. Experiencing the world and sharing our pain, not cloistering it away with people who demand loyalty."

An eye roll from David. "Again, Corey, you're being obtuse. No one is demanding anything—"

"—yet," I snapped. "No one is demanding anything yet."

David was tellingly silent.

I let that silence spread. Alexia had a small smile on her face, and now it looked like her other friends—save for that asshole who'd taken a shot at me—were looking at me pretty hard.

I looked around the room. There were other tables. And if I left now, I could end the conversation on my terms, and on a high point.

I stood and extended a finger at David. "What this guy is promising you is a mirage. It's not a Refuge against anything but reality."

David extended his arms. "Reality is what we need to reshape. And we offer a refuge until then."

"A false one," I snapped. "And one that comes with a cost."

Enough, said a voice in my head. I turned around and walked away, whipping out my phone and swiping through my contacts as I walked to the next table.

《O》

"That was a frightening exercise in gaslighting," Paige said as we left the cafeteria. Her voice took on a high-pitched falsetto. "Oh, no Paige, you're just being excessive. New times demand new solutions."

"Did they tell you how their third principle is actually 'harm?'" I asked.

"Oh, yeah, we got there."

Behind us, a group of twenty or so was also walking, having basically left at the same time. Yeah. Twenty. Between the texts that Paige and I had sent out, plus Kevin and his group, we'd pulled in a lot of others to start pushing back. I was kind of floored. And more than a little frightened.

"Man, I almost lost it when I heard that one," Mika said. His eyes were wide and unblinking. His stare resembled that of a combat soldier's. "It was too late by the time I got to that table. These people were looking for a ten-foot sand dune to bury their heads in."

"And The Refuge offers it," Mo said, shaking his head. "I had a little bit of luck. Maybe. I think I talked a couple of them out of going to their event tonight. But for a lot of them, it was way too late. They were at the meeting. And that smiling little bastard got them there, I know it, I just know it."

"These people are all gonna screw up their midterms," Mika gestured behind him.

"Damnit to hell. Midterms," I said. "I barely studied. You guys?" Muttered agreements. We were almost back to our dorm. I looked at Paige. "Want to—"

"No, I don't," Paige said with an eye roll. "Okay, I mean yeah, I definitely do want to study in the same room. But that won't work. We both know why."

Paige smirked. I smirked back. And she leaned in for a quick peck on the lips, wrapping her fingers against the zipper of my jacket. Our cheeks brushed, and I could feel their flush. "Besides, we gotta talk more about this."

"This?"

Paige gestured behind us. "Yes, genius. This."

I turned. Some of our original group had peeled off, but there was still a good dozen or so trailing behind us.

"We got a little bit of an army now."

"I don't want an army." I stared at the sky. "I want people who can think for themselves."

"They can," Paige said. I had stuck my hands into my pockets to guard against the breeze, and Paige stuffed one of her hands into my pockets. The contrast of the warmth of her hands against the cold of the February afternoon was delightful. "That's why they followed us."

There was no need for other words. The footsteps echoing off the stately academic buildings surrounding us felt like tiny imprints of hope on my heart. I drew comfort from them, almost enough comfort to avoid seeing the dozens of students in all black clothing.

《◇》

Studying for my Psych midterm was akin to trying to break through a wall of hard, thick ice. I'd take a pick to the cold surface and jab. Barely a pebble chipped out of the surface, and my attention wandered.

Eventually, I brought it back to my textbook and highlighted notes, reading like it was an exercise. The harder I pushed, the more ice I broke through. Eventually, the surface broke away, and I fell deep into a subject I loved, swimming in neurotransmitters, dancing in nerve endings, absorbing the side effects of anti-depressants, leaving The Refuge, Sid, and all my troubles behind me.

Time flowed, and hours melted. Self-quizzes went well. Chapters dissolved into the grey matter of my mind as I forgot myself. By the time I glanced at the clock—4:45—the day's light had started to leak away from the window, having been replaced by a pre-sunset haze. I emerged from the rabbit hole of the difference between internal and external validity, blinking as if I had awoken from a deep sleep. I stood, stretched, and cracked my neck. It popped with a delicious snap that sounded like a celery stalk breaking in two. I warmed up some Mac & Cheese in the microwave, and with a sigh, I pulled out my Statistics textbook. The ice pick would have to be a lot sharper here.

That's when the door opened with a bang that sounded like a cannon.

I spun, knocking my snack off the desk in the process. It exploded with a gooey splat over our green throw rug, and I cursed and knelt to pick up the mac and cheese. "No, Mo, I do not want to play Call of Duty, and yes, I was ignoring your texts—"

"Hey," said a slushy voice. I looked up and found Sid towering over me, his figure occupying the full doorframe. He was in a black shirt and blue jeans. His face was cherry red, and the cold was radiating off of him.

"Hey." I tried to sound casual and failed miserably. "I was wondering when I'd see you."

"Yup," Sid said, nodding. He still hadn't moved from the doorway and his head was still bobbing like it was on a string.

"You okay?" I pursed my lips and stared at Sid.

"Sure." Sid finally detached himself from the door and waddled into the room, his steps slow.

"Uhh… Sid?"

He looked at me, his eyes glassy, red, and swollen. "Hmm?"

"You asshole!" I screamed.

Sid's face was motionless. "What?"

The door was still open. I slammed it with a jarring crunch. "You're so, so high."

That seemed to get through, and Sid cracked the slightest of smiles, like a little boy who had been caught smuggling cookies upstairs to his bedroom. "Maybe." He drew out the "ay" sound for a good three seconds.

I ran a hand through my hair and took a deep breath, remembering what I had said before. All these lost people. All of this pain. This wasn't the moment for judgment. This was a moment for kindness.

"Sid…." I started. He just stood there, looking dumbfounded, his eyes slowly skating across the room. "Sid, sit down." I grasped both of his shoulders with my hands and gave him a gentle shove into his desk chair. It creaked with the sudden weight, and I pulled up my chair next to him. "What made you do this, man?"

Sid shrugged. Everything took twice as long as it should have. Sid looked like he would have been very happy if he was watching his hand wave back and forth in front of his face.

I was heartbroken. It felt like Sid had lost something special. He had been so proud of the fact that he hadn't touched alcohol or weed since coming here. It was one of his trademarks, one of the things I respected the most about him—not that he didn't drink, but that he said he was going to and never did.

"Was this because of soccer?" I knew the answer. I wanted to see if Sid said it.

He stared blankly back at me. So, that was a no.

"The Refuge?"

Now a small smile appeared on Sid's lips. "Yeah. Yeah, it was." There was a twinge of sadness in his voice. A piece of me wondered if Sid realized he'd just given this group a piece of what made him… him. I also wondered if I should try to wait on having this conversation with him. He was stoned out of his mind.

I was screaming at myself to slow down. It didn't work. "Why? Why are you doing this to yourself?"

Sid blinked slowly, achingly slowly. Every movement was through molasses. "What do you mean?"

I gestured at him. "Being stoned. Avoiding Mo and Mika and me. I know the school sucks at staying in touch with people, but are you even going to class now?"

"Sure."

I stared. I couldn't tell if he was being honest. Then another dark thought crossed my mind. "Sid… Sid, man, you're on a scholarship."

"Yeah, it's fine."

"Sid, it's not."

"Sure, it is," Sid said, but the mellowness was now gone, replaced by a vague annoyance.

I leaned in closer to Sid. "Sid, it's not. I've been to your house. I know what your money situation is like, and I know it's worse than mine." Sid's head lolled off to the side, and I followed. "Sid, if you lose your scholarship, then that's it, man. There's no coming back from that. You will not be on campus next semester."

Sid said nothing. Maybe my words were cutting through. A pursed frown had overtaken his lips, and tiny beads of sweat had started to form across his brow.

I got off my chair. Kneeled in front of him. "What's happening, Sid? Talk to me. Please."

Sid's pupils looked enormous, black holes in a red-tinged sea.

I thought about the past few weeks, what it was like to watch my friend slip away. "You know I get this, right? How terrible everything is? You're not the only one who is scared of what is going on, but the same people trying to stir up a separated campus aren't the ones to try and find hope from."

Sudden wetness appeared in my eyes, unbidden, and I quickly wiped it away with the back of my hand.

I continued. "You… you act like your pain is somehow unique. That you can only endure it by finding a new group that offers magic. That's not how this works, Sid. When my dad almost killed my mom, I didn't start hanging out with the school bullies. I moved to the people who offered to help me get through."

I stared at his face. It was as blank as a fresh whiteboard.

Trying a new tack, I said, "Sid, this world's gonna suck. It's gonna suck for a while. But the only way we make it is if we stick together. Find the people that care about us, old and new. And hold onto them for dear life."

I looked anxiously at Sid, hoping against hope that my words had made a difference.

Instead, his head went backward, almost parallel to the ground, and he stared at the ceiling. "Hmmm?"

Something inside me broke, and all the empathy, all the sympathy disappeared as if bombed away in a small nuclear explosion. My friend had let himself deteriorate—I had let him decompensate—and here he was. A proud, tough, calm soccer player reduced and seduced into *this*. It wasn't who he was supposed to be, Perses or otherwise.

The anger flowed through me. "Look at me, you asshole," I screamed, clasping his shoulders like he was a small child who I could just yell at into submission.

Sid flung out his hands, striking my biceps and slamming my left hand against the corner of my bed. It caught me right between two bones in my hand, and I leaped up, cradling my right hand in my left.

Sid showed no remorse. He showed no feeling. He just stared at me, blankly, as if he couldn't understand what had just happened.

I felt a surge of adrenaline pulse through my veins as if I'd been injected. My fingers began to shake, and the pain in my hand numbed like it had been dunked in ice.

Slow down, a voice said. Slow down, or he's gone forever.

Abruptly, Sid stood. He looked surprisingly steady on his feet. He looked at me, one last time, a near sneer on his face, and when he spoke, he sounded like a bitter, broken version of his old self. "We can't all be like you."

The words cut. I almost winced.

"Sid…." I started, but whatever euphoria Sid felt from his high was gone, and he was marching out the door. I could feel him leaving forever.

Before he got more than three steps out, I followed. "Sid—"

Slam. I didn't know what had happened, but I was pinned against the hallway wall, unaware of the transition between standing in the doorway to my dorm and being smushed into the space next to my door. I was vaguely aware of stinging pain in my back, legs, and elbows. Could feel Sid growling at me, hot breath in my face, the sour scent of his sweat radiating off of him. His teeth were bared, and at that moment, I lost all empathy or kindness. I just felt fear, like a fly trapped in a spiderweb.

Then I was released, but I refused to let my legs sink. I stood and watched Sid march down the hallway, not even bothering to turn around, shouldering past Kyle Tahan, one of my dormmates who had seen the exchange. "You all right, Corey?" Kyle asked, staring at me through thick glasses.

"Yeah," I muttered. At least, I think I did, but my hands were shaking so much I don't know if I actually said anything. The next thing I knew, I was in my room, the hard slam of the door echoing in my ears, vaguely aware of the smell of microwaved mac and cheese and the faintly woody scent which Sid had left behind.

My textbooks were on the ground, spun open to random pages. My phone had landed face up, the overhead light reflecting on the blank screen. The corner of my pen was stuck in the remainder of the mac and cheese.

I wasn't picking them up tonight.

Chapter 14

And still, in all the chaos and all the noise, midterms went on.

Paige and I walked together on the way to take our first midterms. "I don't get it," I said, quietly.

"I don't think you are supposed to."

"How am I not supposed to get what happened to my best friend?" I was louder than I intended. In a different, normal world, I bet someone would have looked our way, given the sharp tone of my voice. In this universe, no one blinked, and that somehow made my shame worse. I shook my hands. "My bad."

"It's okay. I know who you are yelling at."

"Who? Sid? Myself? The universe?"

"Yes?"

I chuckled.

"Look, I think there are a few things we all have to understand. The Refuge. What's happening to Sid. What happened to my Sara." Right. Paige's old roommate. The reason she had a double bed. "It's a whole lost generation. I keep seeing more kids throwing on all-black outfits. Did you see that Rosanna Stein joined them the other day?"

My eyes narrowed. "She was our homecoming queen last year."

We stopped in front of Harring Hall, where our Psych midterm was. "It's like watching people turn into holograms."

"They turn to smoke," Paige said, softly. "They turn to smoke, and the more you try and pull at them, the more they disappear into the wind." Her voice caught. I extended my hand. Paige shook it off. "Not now. Game face, Corey. Midterm time."

I looked at the glass facade of the building in front of me. "How could I forget?"

We started to climb the stairs. "Remember what Mack said. Someone has to want to be saved to actually get there."

"Sure." My voice had no conviction. There was nothing else to say.

Paige filled the gap. "Good chunk of the bastards in black in this building." Again, she made no attempt to lower her voice, but this time, I just laughed.

"You noticed that too, huh?" She was right. Their numbers were growing. There were five of them sitting in our class of fifteen when we folded ourselves into the uncomfortable desks of our Psych class.

That's where we sat until Dr. Poll strode in, gave us a beaming greeting, and promptly handed out the midterm from hell.

By the time it finished, I was red-faced and sweating. No matter how hard I tried, I could not get my head to stop swimming long enough to focus on the various pieces of human memory. Time swam by in misleading waves. In one blink, five seconds passed. In another, twenty-five minutes.

By the time it was all said and done, I knew I was dead, and I handed my midterm back to Dr. Poll with slick hands. He gave me a sympathetic smile. "Hang in there, kid," he said. I nodded grimly and moved on, excited to get out of this class and shake the memory of failure which had imprinted itself on my brain stem.

Students congregated in the hallways. Some were obviously waiting to take their midterm, their faces tight with tension. Others looked relieved and were smiling. Guess they'd done better than me.

Paige and I stood still for a second, flipping our phones back off of Do Not Disturb.

"That went well." I swallowed, moving past a text from Kevin, asking if I could join him at a local coffee house meeting to talk strategy. *Jeez. Even the Freshman are breaking the rules.*

Paige was shaking her head. "I don't think I did much better." Then she paused. "This sucks. Who gives a midterm, with all of this going on?"

"Kind of hard to study," I embraced the bitter taste flooding into my mouth. I opened up my texts and found a bunch in the group that included Mika, Mo, and Paige. When I opened it, I found a link to a video on Instagram, sent by Mika. Mo's responses were a string of profanities.

"Oh, this can't be good," I moaned.

"I got it." Paige thrusted her phone in front of me.

Black screen. Growing white text, fading in one word at a time. *We Are Your Refuge.*

"Oh, Lord," I said.

Cut to a tall blonde girl with shaggy, curly hair and clothing that seemed to fall off of her emaciated frame. Danielle Deasy. I hadn't seen her since we were back. "This wasn't the way it was supposed to be. It was supposed to be high school…." Danielle was being interviewed right on the campus green, the statue of Francis Augustus in the background. I still remembered her crying the first day we came here, our Freshman year.

Her stutter caught my heart, just like it had four years ago.

"I'm supposed to be graduating soon. Graduating into what?" She gestured around. "This world isn't meant for us. Not like this. No college, no future."

"She's right about that," Paige said angrily. I put my hand on her back.

"What kind of world is this? What am I doing here?" said the girl. She paused. Swiped at her eyes with the back of her hand.

Cut to… David Parks. My friend from the cafeteria yesterday. "When baseball fell apart, I knew things wouldn't be the same. I'm so glad The Refuge was there."

Back to the Danielle. "The Refuge gave me hope."

Back to David. "It gave me something to believe in."

And then fast cuts. Different faces, different races. All in black.

"It gave me a social life again."

Now a couple on the screen. "It gave us each other."

"Oh, for the love of all that's good and holy," Paige groaned.

More cuts, rapidly accelerating, and new faces every time. "I found hope in The Refuge."

"I found the friends I lost."

"I found my bearings."

"I found a reason to believe again."

"I found the ability to help."

"I found hope." The shot had changed, and there was my old buddy, Megan Buchanan. I sighed. Her face looked so peaceful. So serene. Like she actually had faith in what she was selling. "I found a reason to believe again. And I found something to fight for. The Refuge is more than just a club. It's a way of living. It's a group of people dedicated to a common cause of rebuilding ourselves, together. We're united in the idea of helping ourselves, then helping each other."

"What does that even mean?" screamed Paige, so loud that others looked our way. I ignored them.

"The Refuge—Our Refuge—is here to help you. If you are lost in the aftermath of Perses, come our way." Text flashed across the screen. *#FindYourRefuge, FindYourRefuge@TheRefuge.com, @TheRefugeAugustus.*

"The Refuge dot com?" I said. That one caught my eye more than the other two.

Paige must have noticed it, but she held up one finger to shut me up.

"We're here to help. And we know that there are others who aren't on board with our mission," said Megan.

"Uh oh," I said.

"What we offer is hope and a new path forward," Megan said. "We understand that not everyone is comfortable with that idea. That's okay. But ask yourself this. Why is your choice any of their business? What do they have invested in maintaining the status quo? What do they offer you besides fear and a need for your participation in a failed world?"

"It's called empathy," I spat.

"You bitch," added Paige.

"Our way forward is together. Theirs is apart. Come see what we have to offer." Megan extended her hands. "Together."

"Together," said a series of voices. "Together." And the voices echoed, interspersed with the smiling face of everyone in the video before circling back to Danielle. "Together, I found my Refuge. And I hope you will too."

The video faded to black.

I looked up and scanned the hallway. Here and there were others looking at their phones, and I saw the video on at least one. The viewer was smiling. God damnit.

I ran a hand through my hair, hoping against hope that it would cover the cold sweat that was now prickling its way across my skin. The world was spinning. This morning's coffee was threatening to make a reappearance.

Paige took my arm. Grabbed it tightly. "Hey."

She started walking, and I let myself be led by her for the first twenty steps before the feeling began to return to my legs.

《◇》

I STARED AT my Stats textbook and tried to make the numbers make sense. I went through the motions, did the practice formulas, but it was no good. Trying to study with everything going on in my mind was like trying to start a car with no gas.

Eventually, I gave up and stared out the window, watching the sunset and listening to the relatively sedate noises of the campus in front of me.

Sometime later, Paige shut her books and rubbed her eyes. "I died. I think History killed me."

I snickered and gestured to the wreckage of my stat worksheets. "At least you tried to fight back against your impending death."

That got a chuckle out of Paige. "You know what time it is?"

"Little past seven," I said.

"That explains why my stomach feels so empty," Paige stood.

I shifted, realizing suddenly that I had a dull headache. Probably from trying to smash numbers together in my brain until they made sense. "Yeah. I feel like God-awful pizza would be fantastic right about now."

"Ohhh, yes," Paige purred. "Pure grease and cardboard, please."

I pulled my phone out of my pocket. "Yep. I'll call Antonio's."

Two hours later, fat, dumb—really dumb, in my case—and happy, Paige and I went to sleep. My rest that night was tortured, replete with snippets of images that wafted away like smoke. Apparitions in black. Crowds chanting my name and screams of terror. The unending vibrating of a cell phone in my right ear.

By agreement, Paige and I were blowing off breakfast the next morning, knowing that there was no way we'd want to eat before our test. When my alarm sounded at 9:00 a.m., it was almost a relief. I groggily turned over and smacked at my cell phone, desperately reaching for the snooze button but only succeeding in knocking my phone to the ground.

"Damnit," I muttered.

In a state that I can only describe as barely conscious, Paige growled, "Turn it off."

"Trying, trying." I stumbled out of bed and picked up my phone, which had skittered across the room. Mercifully, I was able to gain enough control of my fingers to hit the snooze button, and I was about to stumble back into bed for a glorious eight more minutes of sleep when I realized that I had a slew of text messages. Thirty-seven, to be exact. "Huh?" I squatted on the ground in my boxers, trying to keep my skin from touching the cold linoleum floor. I unlocked my phone and scrolled to the start of the long chain, catching words like *Hospital* and *Fractured* as I did. It was a group text message, and my heart was now in my throat.

Finally, I reached the top of the text. It was a big group—thirty people—and the top text was from Kevin. He'd sent it at a little past midnight. *Hey, guys. Sorry for the group message. I was jumped last night walking back from Jay's.*

I screamed a strangled curse, suddenly wide awake.

That got Paige's attention. "What? What?"

Hands shaking, I read the rest of the text out loud. "I have a broken eye socket, a broken collar bone. They took my wallet and only missed my cell because I screamed."

"What the hell!" Paige screamed.

"I'm at Sacred Heart Hospital. They're keeping me here until my parents get here. Yeah, I'm really scared." Followed by a bunch of sad faces and a skull and bones emoji.

I handed my phone to Paige. It was still vibrating.

"Looks like people are still commenting," Paige said. With shaking fingers, she scrolled through the text chain. "A group of them went to Jay's Coffee to talk about having some event against The Refuge." Jay's was about four blocks off campus. It shouldn't have been that dangerous. "It's like half the campus is commenting and just getting up now… why do you have that look on your face?"

"When's your midterm?"

Paige's face scrunched up, and she rubbed a hand against her face. "Uhh… eleven. Why?"

"Same." We had almost two hours. I looked in the corner of the room, finding my pants. Then I looked back at Paige. She was already leaping out of bed. "I can be ready in ten minutes."

Eight minutes later, our hair not even combed, we were running to the Student Union. Paige ran in and got coffee. I got a Lyft and tried to ignore the fact that we were both absolutely going to get expelled if we got caught going to the Hospital. Then again, I hadn't even bothered checking in the last three nights, and no teacher had come knocking at my door, discipline slip clutched firmly in their hands.

By the time the Honda pulled up to the curb, we were both practically bouncing. Paige thrust a coffee into my hands. "As soon as you can get there, please," I said to the driver.

"About twenty minutes."

"Faster would be good." Paige said. "We're seeing a friend."

Our driver didn't respond, and Paige and I buckled in. For the first time since stumbling out of bed, the adrenaline was beginning to fade, and Paige and I had a chance to actually look at each other.

"Was it them?" Paige's eyes were wide. The eye shadow which she hadn't bothered to remove yesterday was smeared.

I shrugged. "Maybe? I mean, it was a big meeting of freshmen. They're loud and probably didn't realize they should keep their voices down. Or it could have just been a random mugging. Crime's up everywhere."

"Yeah, but coming back from a meeting about how to fight back against The Refuge? At a time when more and more people are becoming loyal to the group?"

"Yeah." I tried to ignore the stares our driver was shooting us.

"I'll try and text him back." Paige whipped out her phone. "See where in the hospital he is. And what happened."

I had finished catching up with the group text. "He didn't say anything else about the circumstances of it. Just that he was walking home, and three guys jumped him."

"Did he say what they were wearing?"

I scrolled down. "Black. But I mean…." My voice wilted against Paige's stare. "That poor kid. He must have been terrified. Never even got through a semester of school. Finally gets back and this happens."

"Freshman year is bad enough without getting mugged," Paige's voice acquired a heavy quality. She looked like she was repressing a shiver.

We didn't say much else for the rest of the agonizing ride. It was only five miles to the hospital—they'd even showed us where it was during a bus tour of the city during our freshman year. But Northampton was a traffic disaster, and our estimated time of arrival kept slipping. I could feel the minutes passing between my fingers, sliding through them like buttered silk while I anxiously bounced my leg in the back seat.

Traffic light by traffic light, we moved through the city. Thankfully, our driver was smart enough to sense our mood and made no effort at conversation. Paige finally put a hand on my thigh to stop my leg from bouncing. I smiled wanly and stared out the window, resigned to my fate, and trying to slay the dual demons of worry for Kevin and my impending Statistics disaster.

Finally, we pulled up to the hospital, the two of us hopping out with a mumbled thank you. We charged through the main entrance, dodging patients, and wheelchairs. One of the nice things about being in the hospital was no one ever blinked at two people running through a crowded lobby, worry stretched across their faces. Everyone was locked in their own pain.

We hit the information desk, the two of us slightly gasping for breath. I gave them Kevin's name, and we waited. After a few calm taps on her computer, the pleasant woman behind the desk said, "I'm sorry, but I don't have a Kevin Thompson in the ER."

"What?" Paige exclaimed. I had a moment of panic—had I somehow gotten the wrong hospital? But no—I looked at my phone again and confirmed it. This was the right place.

"Can you tell us if he's been discharged?" I asked.

"I'm sorry, no." The woman looked genuinely crestfallen.

Paige and I fell back. I was trying to call Kevin, but it went automatically to voice mail.

We looked at each other. "What do you think?" I asked.

"He was in the ER. Maybe he was discharged already? Especially if it happened last night."

I closed my eyes and tried to ignore the storm cloud building in my chest. I hadn't so much as laid eyes on Kevin until that day with The Refuge. He'd been inspired by my words. So inspired that he had tried to organize his friends to push back against The Refuge in the fight for those who were lost but didn't know where else to turn. "He was the only one who actually tried to do something when The Refuge invaded the cafeteria," I said, my eyes wide. "And look where that got him."

Bruised, broken, bloody, and scared. And I had no idea where he was, or how to make it up to him.

I thought of home. Of my couch and my Xbox and nothing but empty land around us. I could put aside the ghost of the Ford's house. I'd attend Robinette High School, poor internet connection and moldy classrooms and all.

I wanted to go home. I wanted to go home so badly that I could smell my tiny, cramped room.

Amazing. I'd spent months wanting nothing more than to be back here. And now that I was back, all I wanted to do was escape.

Paige looked at me, her face marred with a fear I hadn't yet seen. "Hey. Hey." She wrapped a hand around mine. I tried to shake it free, but she held me tighter. "Please."

I relented and folded into her arms.

«◊»

Fifteen minutes later, our original—and probably very confused—Lyft driver returned to take us back to campus. Somehow, the traffic was even worse. It was now past ten, and I had no idea how we were going to get back to campus on time.

Paige and I were using our phones, calling random numbers on the group text to try to figure out what the hell had happened to Kevin. Finally, on her third call, Paige lucked into calling Kevin's roommate. She put a hand over her mouth to talk and avoid driving our surly driver nuts. I couldn't read her face until she hung up.

"What's going on?" I asked.

"Physically, he'll be okay… eventually." Paige barely made eye contact with me. "His parents drove up from New Jersey so that's how he got out of the hospital. His injuries are just as bad as he made them sound."

"But he's okay?"

Paige shrugged. "I mean, he's not gonna die. But he's scared out of his mind." Paige brushed a stray hair out of her face. "Dean Sumner met him at his room. They tried to talk but Kevin's parents apparently wouldn't let him."

"That can't be good."

"It's not. Whole big screaming thing about how the school isn't doing enough to protect the students."

My eyes narrowed. "This was off campus."

"Exactly. His parents couldn't stop screaming about how lax security at the school was, how appalling it was that he was allowed off campus in the first place."

"They should be more understanding," I said softly.

"Corey, what do you want? Angry parents lose control."

"Well aware," I said coldly.

Paige didn't miss the anger that flashed past my eyes. "I'm sorry. I'm really sorry. That was insanely stupid of me." Her lips quivered.

I sighed. "It's fine. Not like either of us is thinking clearly." I ran my hands over my face, blinking away the sudden wave of exhaustion that was building up again.

Paige's hand was on my knee. When my eyes met hers, there was an urgency on her face that spoke to the moment. "Corey. We can't let this happen."

I knew what she meant. "We can't let these guys hurt us."

We were silent for a second. Whatever flash of anger I'd felt melted onto Main Street. Then Paige said, "So, Kevin went back with his parents. They grabbed some stuff and stormed off campus. Something about lawyers."

I could see Kevin—curly hair. An aura of self-possession and confidence that most Freshmen didn't have. A leader in this fight. And now he was gone. "We're not going to see him again."

"I don't think so."

The rest of the ride passed in the silence of road construction, honking horns and a silent Lyft driver.

We made it back to campus in time, but barely. And I mean barely. "I'll see you later." I yelled at Paige as she ran one way, me the other, her red hair bouncing as she jogged.

My phone said 10:58, so I'd be able to bust into the room in time, but this wasn't exactly the ideal state to take my midterms. I was exhausted, stressed, hadn't eaten anything, and hadn't had a chance to check my notes. When I finally crammed myself into a desk and stared at the page in front of me, the numbers simply swam back and forth, shifting like a mirage in the desert. I blinked once. Twice. Tried to make the numbers hold still.

Ninety minutes later, and I was experiencing a sense of failure so deep it made my midterm the day earlier in Psych feel like I had won the World Series. My mind was utterly blasted, and all I wanted to do was get naked, shut off the lights, and climb into bed for the next eight hours. Students were chatting amiably with each other as they left, but I did hear at least one group of friends telling another about Kevin's attack. So that was getting around. Awesome.

I flipped my phone out of my pocket, almost dropping it on the tiled floor. That would have been the cherry on top of this sundae. Whatever. Paige should be done with her midterm. Maybe we could get pizza again… uhh, how would Mom react if I spent more money? Could my stomach handle any more cheese? As it was, my gut felt like a sack that contained a series of heavy, awkwardly shaped bricks.

A text from Paige greeted me. *Campus green. Now.*

"That can't be good," I said to myself.

I stopped in the middle of the hallway and students flowed around me, moving like water veering around rocks in a babbling stream. Like a moth to a flame, they were being drawn out the door, talking to each other as they moved. Those who weren't looking at a friend were looking straight ahead. Some were pointing.

"Oh, no." I started to move.

Paige was standing just off of the entrance of the Administration building, and I realized right away what she was looking at. About fifty yards in front of us was a group of students, just in front of the main administration building. I couldn't make out what they were saying, but I could absolutely hear a dull, angry roar coming from their direction, sounding like a drone of angry bees who were sharpening their stingers.

They weren't wearing their red blazers, a heretical action in the middle of the day. But they were most unquestionably wearing all black.

I looked at Paige, the terror from my poor Statistics performance morphing into a dread that touched the marrow of my bones. "What is this?" I looked back at the crowd.

"I ran past them when I was trying to meet you. I was gonna ask if you wanted to do pizza and drown our sorrows in grease."

"Yeah, we may still want to do that after all." I gestured back to the crowd.

"I didn't get too close. Bad vibe."

We started walking toward the protestors. Other students were joining us. "What are they doing?"

Suddenly, Paige gasped, as if she had been shocked. She moved ahead of me and wrapped her arm around my wrist. "Don't lose it," she said.

I didn't need to say anything else. Somehow, I knew.

We made it to the group. They were a mishmash of Refuge men and women, some students who looked familiar, others who I didn't recognize. They held makeshift signs, saying things like "Where's the help?" and "Are we next?" with a bloody gun. The one that got me the most was, "For Kevin."

"Oh, you're kidding me. You are absolutely...." The rage coursed through me, sharp as lightning, angry as blood. "They're using him?" I spat.

"The only question is if they know they are gaslighting us or if they have been tricked into it."

"He was trying to organize against them."

The Refuge was chanting now. "For Kevin. For Kevin," they plaintively cried.

My mouth hung slightly open, as if my jaw was a broken hinge. The outrage of the moment—the flagrancy of The Refuge's actions—had rendered me utterly mute.

"I can't believe this." Paige's voice was like chalky dust. "He'd be murderous if he were here."

Other students—kids not yet Refuge members—cautiously approached the clutch of protesting monsters. Every time one appeared, an older member of the group would approach them, a serious smile on their face. They would talk. I watched it happen over and over again, my feet and mouth unwilling to move.

I spotted a face I recognized. Tom Decker, my hallmate. He was walking away from me, a thin palm card clutched in his right hand but turned just as he passed. "Hey man," he said, spotting Paige and me. "Crazy, right?"

"Yes." I gestured to the card.

"Oh, you know…." Tom had a slim smile on his face as he adjusted the straps of his backpack. "They just gave me one of their pamphlets when I asked what they are protesting."

"What did they say?" Paige asked, her voice spiked like venom.

"Pretty much everything," Tom said, shifting from side to side as he spoke. "The security issues. All the teachers seem to have given up. The lack of counseling. That freshman who got jumped."

"Kevin," Paige interjected.

"You know they're lying, right?" My anger was bubbling, threatening to erupt.

Tom blinked, his eyes assuming the stare of someone unaccustomed to confrontations. "Yeah… sure," Then his voice perked up as if he had remembered the entire conversation. "About what?"

I gestured wildly. "Everything, Tom. They're lying about everything."

Tom stared, incredulous, his eyes bulging. "Everything?"

"Kevin Thompson hated them. He was probably jumped by one of them." The words felt like poison as I said them, the accusations sharp, scratching at my throat. "People are stressed because of them. They don't want peace. They want more of this." I whipped my hands above my head, aware that Tom was staring at me as if I'd lost my mind. His stare was half sympathy, half concrete. His eyes kept twitching left like he was trying to see what The Refuge was doing behind them.

And it hit me. "Tom… Tom, man, better question. What are they offering?"

That seemed to set Tom back. "I don't know. A group, I guess?" Paige had folded her arms across her chest. She unclasped them and brought her hands together, staring at Tom dead in the eyes. "You know we're creeped out by them, right?"

"Who isn't?" A smile snaked across Tom's face.

"And we're not the only ones," I said.

Now, Tom was nodding. "Okay, yeah, that's true. Other people are kinda creeped out by them."

"Do you know what they want?" I asked.

Now, finally, I think we got through. "No… not really."

"These guys are telling people to change their outfit and their social circle. They're getting people drunk and living off-campus."

Tom's eyes widened, like a bug who had been caught. "Wait, what?"

"I haven't seen my roommate in days," I said solemnly. "I guess the school knows where he is. Last I saw, he was wearing a black shirt."

"Their points aren't wrong," Paige added. "The reason The Refuge is here is that people are terrified. But there's got to be a better way to get back to the real world than… I don't know, dressing like nighttime and cutting off all your friends."

Tom didn't say anything. His hands were firmly lodged in the pocket of his jeans. His eyes looked like they were buffering. Processing. Trying to find the truth.

Finally, Tom nodded. "Yeah. I getcha. Okay."

He didn't make another move.

《◊》

THE PROTEST PULLED students like a magnet, gathering strength, mass, and energy. Paige and I were set to the opposite pole and compelled to push away.

We didn't leave. We spent the rest of the afternoon on the periphery of the protest, talking to students we knew and ones we didn't. We knew The Refuge saw us. We could feel their stares burning into our backs. It didn't matter. We already had a few hundred students who hated us. What was a few dozen more?

After a few hours, the protests dissipated. I was disheartened. We'd stopped some. We hadn't stopped all of them.

The angry, twisted look on the face of more than a few reinforced the ugly undercurrent coursing through campus. People wanted protection and were finding none. And that only made more of a space for The Refuge.

The sun was just starting to dip below the clouds by the time Paige and I trudged back to the Netflix Lounge. It was Friday, and we were exhausted. For a few minutes, all we did was stare at each other, blinking on occasion. My life felt like trying to jam a key into a lock that didn't fit, as if the individual tumblers of the locking mechanism had rusted away into nothing. There were no answers, no reasoning. Just rage and anger and threats and a cloudy sky.

Mo and Mika joined us. I think Mo grabbed me, and Mika gently hoisted Paige, and then we were walking past the campus green again, marching to the Student Union under strict orders. The hollow echoing in my stomach was kind enough to remind me that I had missed breakfast and lunch. Too many of those moments lately. A few moments later, we were seated at a table. There was a lot of pasta in front of me. I pretty much went in face first.

Paige was laughing by the time I came up for air. "Well, I'm glad you're not so miserable you can't eat anything."

"Is that a thing?" I asked.

"For normal people, yes," Mika said. "For you, I doubt it. And how the hell are you so skinny?"

A garlic knot was in my mouth. "I have no idea." The words were intercepted by a starchy obstruction.

"Huh?"

I swallowed and repeated myself.

"Oh."

"You two okay?" Mo asked abruptly.

"Just freakin' great," I said.

Paige sighed and pushed her plate away. "I think we will be. Today was frustrating."

"No one ever said fighting an evil cult was easy," quipped Mika.

"I didn't want to do that," I said and abruptly my tray was away from me too. "I just wanted people to think for themselves."

"We've made an awful lot of enemies," Paige said.

"I hope some friends," I muttered. I thought of Kevin. He hadn't texted me back yet, and I sure didn't feel comfortable calling him. "And we saw too many go toward those protestors."

"You can't blame them though," Mika said. "They're looking for a reason to fight, Corey. They want to believe in something."

"And isn't school when you're supposed to protest? Get angry? Set stuff on fire?" Mo asked.

"Most of that," I cracked. "Not one hundred percent sure about that last one."

"If you want people to remember that there's more to life than anger and looking like a miserable cloud, you have to remind them why they are here," Mo said, his voice uncharacteristically serious. "You have to give them something to believe in beyond, 'Hey, don't go over there.'"

"Okay…." I said. "I don't know what that is, though."

"I do," Mo said. His face was so serene, so calm, so certain, that I believed him.

"What?" I begged.

"A party."

"Oh, come on." I threw down my fork. I stared at Mo, waiting for his expression to crack and his face to return to that goofy smile he wore so naturally.

"I think he's being serious," Paige said.

"I absolutely am."

"I may be the smarter twin, but my brother is not wrong," Mika agreed.

"How does a party solve anything?" I blurted.

"Because it reminds people why we are here." Paige's voice was trance-like.

"A bunch of alcohol?" I said to Paige, suddenly feeling lost. "Come on, people drink to forget, not to remember."

"No, people drink because they are awkward and want new experiences, and if they are sad, yeah, they drink to forget," Mo said. "But you're missing the point. I don't want the booze. I want the people."

And suddenly, things made a little more sense. Gears started clicking into place.

Mo read my face. He was already smiling. "You know, Doctor Skinner isn't on campus today. I heard it from Dave Cassidy, who got out of his class early. Something about his kid in school." Mo's face was brightening, his eyebrows rising. "They don't want to tell anybody, but we're alone for the night."

Mika had a look on his face that implied he was trying to tell me the Earth was round, not flat. "People aren't going to follow you if the only thing you do is give them a negative to push against. You have to remind them what real life is."

"Gotta give people something to smile about, Corey," Mo said, continuing his brother's speech. "Gotta give them a reason to feel joy if you expect them to avoid wearing all black."

I got it. "The Refuge exists because all of us are just… existing. We forgot what the real world is." I paused and put my hands on the table. "Still. A party doesn't do anything to stop The Refuge or these protestors."

"Will you get off of that, man?" Mo said. "A party doesn't need a profound statement. We just need to remind people why they are in school. What the real world can be. It gives them normalcy. Adventure. A chance to hang out and make new friends. There is no 'goal' for a party. It's just… to be."

I tried to remember what life was like before Perses, my mind stumbling on memories. There had been hope then. Yeah, Megan Buchanan wasn't wrong, things were tough, but there wasn't a feeling that we could get blown out of the sky at any moment. There had been a chance to be what we wanted. It was *school*. It was fresh and new and exciting.

Wouldn't it be nice to remind people that was still an option?

It must have shown all over my face. Mo was already walking away. "See you in an hour?"

"We won't be that long," Mika shouted back. While Mo walked out the door, Mika pulled out his phone and began texting furiously.

"Eight p.m.?" Mo said. "Start easy and early."

Paige and I looked at each other. Her face was absolutely, positively shining.

"What the hell," I said, not sure if I was making a statement or posing a question.

Paige took it as a statement. "What the hell," she repeated, a smile bright on her face.

Chapter 15

MO HAD A lot of food. I eyed it cautiously. There were fields of pizza. Skyscrapers of chips. "Uhh… you need some money for that?" I asked.

Mo waved a hand. "Nah, I got it, buddy. You talk to people. Take their pulse."

In another room, a stereo was going strong, playing a song that I didn't recognize. "And Brian… Brian's cool?" Brian was our prefect. In the absence of Skinner, he was the closest thing to "in charge" that the dorm has.

"Man, Brian doesn't care at all," Mo said, stopping to bro-hug a kid who had just walked into the room and ripped a six-pack out of a box in the closet. I pretended I hadn't seen it. "That's one of the benefits of the spread of nihilism."

"Good?" I offered.

Mo shrugged. "Sure."

Paige and I had spent a good hour on our phones and weren't surprised when people began waddling onto the fourth floor. Yes, the rules of the universe had changed substantially, but food and beer still drew students.

The night began with fifty or so students who I honestly think were just looking for a distraction and some joy. We all had a few things in common. We hated The Refuge, and we were scared out of our minds about the state of the campus and the state of the world.

The rest flowed easily from there.

Too many other students wanted to talk to Paige and me, and they were serious conversations. It sort of surprised me, at least at first. This was a party. Isn't that what everyone wanted? A distraction? A chance to blow off some steam?

I realized pretty quickly what a dumb thought that was.

People didn't want alcohol. Well, okay, they did, but not that much. More than anything, I think people were looking at the booze as a chance to loosen up. What really surprised me was just how much alcohol never left Mo's room. People were just looking to talk. They were looking to reconnect.

I watched more than a few games of beer pong. I got a big kick out of watching this one gangly, tall kid, buried in the corner. He looked like a sophomore, and I never got a chance to get his name. He seemed to need to psych himself up with every drink of alcohol. Then, finally, he put the beer down, took a deep breath, picked the beer back up, took a long drag, and marched over to the blonde I'd seen him eyeing. With an awkward poke of the shoulder, he got the girl's attention. I almost lost it laughing.

"Were you that smooth?" Paige had a beer in hand, her head moving along with the beat of the music.

"I think I was worse." Then I smiled, watching the kid. At least he was trying. "Much worse."

Paige and I just leaned against the wall for a moment or two, our pinkies linked.

We actually didn't get much of a chance to talk that night. Our attention kept getting snapped in different directions. More than a few students waved me down to say hi, and I could see that Paige was in the same boat. Mika and Mo were basically cruise ship directors, setting up games and making sure no one was drinking too much, so it was on Paige and me to watch everyone's emotions.

And that took effort. A freshman came up to me—Danny Lorber was his name. I think. I recognized him from when he had been introduced at the Freshman Indoctrination ceremony, before Perses, a lifetime ago. Danny had a mop of unruly, curly hair, and he was wearing a wrinkled polo that made me think he had actually bothered to dress nicely for a party with an upperclassman.

"Thank you," he exclaimed, coming up to me, his eagerness both earnest and grating. I raised an eyebrow. "For The Refuge. I wasn't going to join… I mean, yeah, not for me. But for my roommate."

Now I was confused. "What do you mean?"

Danny shrugged. "The guy lost his dad. Suicide. They think. His mom sent him here to get him out, he said." Danny paused. I don't think he knew what to say. I didn't blame him.

"He must be so…." I left the statement unfinished. What could describe it? A kid whose dad had been driven by madness caused by the end of a world that never actually finished….

"Yeah." The sadness streaked down his face. Abruptly, Danny's eyes welled. For a moment, I was set to ignore the tears, as dictated by the guy code. *No. Don't do that,* a voice said.

"You're a good guy, Danny," I said. Danny wiped his eyes and stared at me. "Empathy like that. I think we need more."

"I have no idea what to say to him." The tears spilled down Danny's face. "He's been moping around all year. I barely knew him. I didn't think we were going to be close. And then he lost his dad, and he has no other friends, and he barely talks to his mom…." Danny's arms flapped once, knocking his own hips. "What do you say to a kid, besides 'everything is going to be okay,' when we know that's not gonna happen?"

From ten feet away, Paige looked on. We caught eyes, and she threaded her way through the crowd.

"Hey," she said, her voice soft and sweet. Danny seemed to shrink for a moment, as if the attention of a pretty senior was too much to bear at the moment. "I'm Paige. You okay?"

We filled Paige in.

"Danny was just wondering what to say to his roommate. You got any ideas?" I asked. "I sure as hell don't."

Paige had the bottom of her lip firmly lodged underneath her teeth, and she stared at the ceiling. "You know there is nothing that you can say, right?"

"That's not an option," Danny retorted, with more confidence than I would have thought possible.

"But it has to be." Paige gestured at the two of us. "Danny, there's no answer to these questions. No one has ever been here before. No time in world history has ever seen a spike in suicide and death and all that other stuff like this. You're not supposed to have the words. None of us are."

"So what am I supposed to do, eh?"

Paige and I made eye contact.

"I think you try to bring him to the party," I said. "And just be his friend."

"That won't make him feel better," Danny said. "A party isn't going to make him forget that his dad drove their car off a cliff."

"Of course not," Paige and I said at the same time, and I found the groove in the conversation. "It's not supposed to. We're not gonna have the answers, Danny. We're not supposed to either. You're just supposed to… live. To be this guy's friend."

"And show him that people care," Paige said. She waved her hands above her head, grabbing Mo's attention, and began to whisper into his ear. Mo's goofy smile abruptly disappeared.

"Oh, man," Mo said. Sunglasses were covering his face, and his breath was sour-scented.

Paige put her arms on Mo's shoulders. "This is our friend Mo."

Mo's smile reappeared. "What's going on, buddy?" Mo slapped Danny's hand. It hadn't been outstretched.

"Mo, you're on a mission. Find Danny's roommate. Bring him here," Paige ordered.

Mo fired off a mock salute. "Aye aye, boss." He wrapped an arm around Danny. "Where's your friend at?" Mo said as they left the room. "I need a new pong partner."

We watched them go, not even bothering to look at each other as if the stare behind our eyes would reveal more than we could bear at that moment. Instead, we just hooked pinkies again.

The night wound on, and coherence collectively seemed to leave the group around 11:00 p.m. I prowled the hallway, looking for signs of trouble, but thankfully, finding none. Most were drinking cautiously, like it was brand new, nursing beers like bunnies taking steps on an icy pond. It was weird for us to be drinking so openly. If you had told me five months ago what would be happening in my dorm, I would have thought a violent revolution had taken place. Of course, something like a revolution had happened. Just one that I never would have thought possible.

Throughout the night, I found only two kids that had clearly had too much to drink. Both were stumbly, overemotional, and largely incoherent. Both were in tears over their alcohol. For the girl, her tears were openly flowing. The guy kept wandering from one room to another, looking dazed.

In each case, I moved toward the kid, ready to open my arms and talk.

In each case, someone beat me to it.

For the girl, it was Spring Finneran and Jessica Good who swept in, appearing to be a couple who had found someone in pain. They moved the girl into a corner of the Netflix lounge and began to talk. For the guy, Josh Dunphy—I think he was one of Sid's teammates on the soccer team—slapped a meaty paw on his shoulder and steered him to a video game. It was clumsy, maybe, but I don't think the kid who was crying gave a damn what he was doing. You could see it written all over his face when Josh took him by the shoulder. He had been seen. In all the insanity that was the world, maybe two guys playing a game of Smash Brothers was all anyone would get—but maybe it was all anyone really needed.

The music boomed, the alcohol flowed, hips swayed. In twos and threes, people started drifting out around midnight. By 2:00 a.m., even the most hardcore of my classmates were starting to blink heavily, and by 3:00 a.m., everyone was gone. We only saw Mo again when he came back to the dorm at 2:30 a.m. I thought about asking him what had happened, but the pain was written all over his face as he sat down in a chair. The four of us stayed in the Netflix lounge, arrayed around the oversized fireplace, languidly drinking warm beer and trying to keep ourselves awake long enough to see the sunrise.

Paige and I mushed ourselves into an oversized lounge chair that was only big enough for one and a half people. Of course, given the way that we were pressed together, I wasn't complaining. Mika caught Mo up about the evening's events, trading gossip, comparing notes. Somewhere around 3:30 a.m., I started realizing my eyes were getting droopy, and even Mo and Mika started letting their sentences trail off into an absence of sound. I found myself staring at the hypnotic flames, losing myself in their sparks and embers. It was as if the warmth had grabbed me, had wrapped its arms around me, and pulled me into its comforting embrace.

Eventually, the heat took us.

《○》

The slam of a door jerked me awake with a sharp start. This, in turn, bounced Paige, who was pushed uncomfortably into the side of the chair we were sleeping on.

"Owwwww," she moaned. Grunts across from me. Must have been Mo and Mika. "Asshole."

"Sorry," I mumbled.

A beat. "Okay. Maybe you're not an asshole." Paige wiped the side of her mouth and the shoulder of her shirt, where a thin river of drool had pooled. "Ugh. My neck hurts. What time is it?"

I blinked and used my right hand to rub the sleep out of my eyes. "I don't know… can you stand? My phone is in my left pocket."

"Sure," Paige said, but instead, she rolled onto the floor and closed her eyes again, stretching like a cat, knocking into discarded beer bottles. "Holy hell, that's better. How did I sleep like that?"

"No idea. But my face hurts."

"Ughhhh," Mika groaned. His eyes were right in the middle of a sunbeam. "Ahhh. Damnit. Consciousness."

"Consciousness is stupid. Also, you're loud. And stupid. And shut up," said Mo. His eyes hadn't opened yet, and from the grimace on his face, he didn't look like he wanted to open them anytime soon.

I fished my phone out of my pocket and scrolled past a slew of Snapchat notifications and texts. I had barely even noticed my phone yesterday—the drone of the music must have drowned out its vibrations. *8:32*

Groans from the three of them, so loud I laughed. I licked my lips and shifted as my stomach rumbled. "I need coffee."

That got Paige's eyes open. "Coffee. Coffee sounds delightful."

"Pancakes?" I raised my eyebrows.

"It's eight thirty. On a weekend. Go the hell back to sleep," screamed Mo, his voice actually sounding like it was in pain.

"Pancakes at a diner."

Mo opened his eyes a sliver and said, "Real food?"

Paige stood, dusted off her jeans, and extended a hand. Mo took it and allowed himself to be pulled up by Paige. "Yeah, real food. Come on. I'll buy."

"I'll split with you," I said. "Least we can do after yesterday."

"Appreciate it," Mo said.

Now Mika was slowly standing. "If you're gonna buy, I'm in." We laughed softly and began stumbling to our dorms. "Back here in thirty? I'll drive."

Grunts of acknowledgment around.

Thirty minutes later, we stumbled back toward the Netflix Lounge and went to the ground floor. I had freshly showered and changed my clothing. Every one of my muscles felt like it was in a knot that couldn't be loosened. Paige, too, was walking a little slow, but she didn't look much worse for wear. I couldn't say the same about Mo and Mika, who both actually hissed when they went outside, making me momentarily believe that they were actually vampires. Mika stumbled and flung on a pair of sunglasses before we took three steps.

"You okay to drive?" I asked.

"I didn't drink that much," Mika said. "I'm fine. Just hungover."

"I'm driving," Paige ordered.

Without a moment's hesitation, Mika flipped Paige his keys, and she caught them easily. "Bless you," Mika said.

We hit the parking lot and saw it immediately. Two cars in front of us had flat tires. When we saw the third car, every one of us froze.

"What the hell?" I said. We exchanged worried glances and grouped closer together.

"Random?" Paige asked.

Mo pointed. "That's Josh Dunphy'scar. The big soccer player who was at the party last night," he said, pointing at an old Audi that was on its rims. He pointed at a Ford Focus which was in the same state. "And I know that is Jessica Good's car, and she was there too."

We exchanged glances again, fear wrapping itself around me like fog. We quickly walked through three rows of cars, finding more flat tires, all with identical puncture wounds.

We reached Mika's Jeep. Four flat tires.

Mo ran a hand over his hair, and we gasped, staring in shock. All we were staring at was a car with a flat, but it meant so much more than that. Whatever knife someone had used to puncture the car's tires... they'd punctured something deeper.

Mika let out a curse that could be heard across campus. It was one of those screams that echoed at a point deeper than the sound could convey.

Whatever joy I'd felt before from the party was gone now, curled into sour chunks like milk that had been left on the counter for too long. I spun around, my eyes searching. That was ridiculous, of course. Whoever had done this was long, long gone. All I could see were rows of slouching cars, a pothole-filled parking lot that was lined with faded paint.

That, and the darkened figures who I could spot about a hundred yards away.

No one else noticed—Mo, Mika, and Paige were staring at the cars. Mo was muttering darkly about needing to call a tow company and Mika was trying to remember what number to call. Paige was taking charge and had whipped out her phone. And I started to walk, my feet basically moving of their own volition, walking toward the figures in black.

There were two of them, I now realized. One tall, one short, and as I drew closer, I knew. There was something painfully familiar about the larger one's posture. He was a big guy... though not as big as before. I could see it from this far away. I knew that face. I knew that pose. It was the pose of a big, sweet guy who had once danced in our dorm room the night he made a game-saving stop on a breakaway. A guy who had cried in my arms and slammed me into a wall and told me how scared he was. A guy I had mourned with. And now, mourned for.

Paige caught up with me. She knew what I was walking toward.

"Oh, Sid...." I said.

"Hey." Paige put her hand on the small of my back. Her touch barely scratched the surface of what I felt. My skin was ice across a frozen pond. My emotions were everything swimming beneath. "Hey. Corey. Stop."

I still didn't respond. I couldn't. It felt like something had snapped in me. How could someone so close go so far? The Sid I knew was a gentle giant. He would never, ever....

Twenty yards away or so now. I could see his face. There was an expression on it I had never seen before. An odd cross between a smile and a snarl, one corner of his lip upturned, illuminating the shine in his eyes. I stopped, curled my hands into fists at my side.

"Hey. Corey." Paige snapped her fingers in front of my face.

That finally got me. I froze. We weren't far apart now, and I could read Sid's face perfectly. We stared at each other as if separated by a frozen line, each unwilling to cross.

A pinprick of thought bloomed in my mind, and I realized what bothered me so much about Sid's face at the moment. It wasn't the hate-filled expression he wore. It was the absence of anything familiar. It was like I was staring at a character in a movie I loved, but a new actor was playing him in the sequel.

I consciously tried to soften my face. To put aside the rage that I felt and concentrate on what I had said before to Paige… compassion. There had to be compassion. Now, more than ever.

Sid's short friend—Ryan Corbin, I could now see—had a large knife in his hand. He was holding it loosely at his side, not menacingly, but obviously enough to let us know it was there. Paige caught it too, and the hand she had on me tightened its grip on my shoulder.

I looked at the knife, then back at the short kid, then at Sid. I held each of their glares for a second, then broke the silence. "You know… there's still a way back."

No response. No recognition. It was like I had barely said anything.

I put a hand on Paige's back and guided her, so she turned around. When she took her first step in the opposite direction, I followed.

Chapter 16

Campus security was waiting in front of my dorm room when we got back from the mechanics. I wasn't surprised.

"Fun night?" the cop asked. I didn't recognize him, but I'm sure he couldn't miss the smell of alcohol which seemed to permeate… hell, everything.

"It started okay." I wanted to snap at this guy, ask him why he and his colleagues weren't doing a better job of protecting us, but that wasn't fair. I suspected that most of them actually did want to do their jobs. There just weren't enough of them to do it. I stuffed down my useless rage. "What's up?"

"Dean Sumner wants to see you and your girlfriend."

At that, my heart started going. "It's a Saturday afternoon."

"It is. And I'm getting paid overtime." With that, he turned. I stood there, dumbfounded.

I thought of Sid and his friend. The snarl. The knife. Then thought of the fact that crumpled beer cans were visible all over the floor. "Lemme just put on a better pair of pants."

Ten minutes later and in a fresh pair of pants, I walked silently to the Dean's office. I was wondering if, in the course of testing the line, I had finally found the limit. What would that mean for my career here? Was this it?

I felt tired. Tired of fighting, tired of trying to save kids like Kyle. I just wanted a normal life again.

The thoughts swirled through my head like ping pong balls, crashing into each other and emptying over the echoing halls of my mind. My steps felt heavy like my limbs were filled with sand, but I hadn't drunk nearly enough to give myself a hangover. I gazed around campus as the police officer and I walked. Everything was still silent and still, despite the shining sun in the east. Birds chirped. Wisps of snow tickled my feet, blown by a gentle winter breeze. In the distance, I could spot the specks of two students, draped in all black.

"Here's our stop," the cop said, gesturing broadly toward the Administration building. "Dean's waiting for you. Third floor."

"I know." I turned sharply on my heel. That was a lie. I had no idea where the office was.

I took my phone out of my pocket and texted Paige. *Headed in.*

She quickly responded. *Had to take a quick shower. Smelled of beer and potato chips. Bad for meeting with Dean. See you as soon as I can stumble into a pair of pants that don't look like ass.*

I laughed and stuffed my phone back in my pocket. I kind of liked the idea of the Dean gagging on the fun we'd had the night before.

I followed the signs and made a quick left, surprised to find the building mostly full. I guess protests and cults had a tendency of requiring weekend work.

I arrived at a cavernous office space just off of the center of the building. Sitting at an oaken desk was a conservatively dressed woman who looked as if she had been born with a disapproving frown stitched onto her face. Clara Thompson. Everyone said she actually ran the school. If that was the case, it might explain why she looked so miserable at the moment.

"I'm here to see the Dean," I said, brimming with as much false confidence as I could muster.

"Go right ahead," the woman said.

That was it. No ceremony, no waiting. I just walked right in. Dean Sumner was sitting at his desk, tapping away at the computer. His face was lined and strained, and his tie was undone. The wide desk between us was littered with papers that were contained in neat stacks. The office was massive, studded with crystal awards and small sculptures.

Sumner smiled when he saw me. "Corey. It's good to see you." He waved toward his seats. "Thanks for coming on such short notice."

You sent a cop to get me, I almost said. Instead, I wearily sat down. "Of course."

"Can I get you a drink?" Clara asked, using a voice which clearly suggested she'd rather not.

"No, thanks," I said, and Clara disappeared like smoke, closing the door gently behind her.

I stared at Sumner for an awkward moment. It was the first time I had seen him since Parent's Weekend, and I reflected on that for a second, wondering if there had been some missed opportunity, a chance not taken.

"I understand you've been trying to help," Sumner said, and I exhaled so deeply I thought my lungs were going to explode. "I saw that speech you gave, the night that The Refuge held their first meeting on campus. That took courage."

"I wouldn't call it that."

"What would you call it, then?"

"Doing what had to be done." There was more hardness in my voice than I intended. What I meant as a little dig turned into a jackhammer. Where was anybody on this campus when we needed them? Where was the counseling? The teachers? The cops? Where was anyone when Kevin's face was broken on a street corner off of campus? Also, what the hell was I doing here?

Sumner's face stuttered like a buffering YouTube clip. "Whatever the reason, we appreciated it. I appreciated it. I know how hard it can be to stand up, alone, to a massive crowd."

I shrugged again. "It wasn't that massive. And we had friends. Life is always easier with backup."

"Well, that's what I wanted to talk to you about today. Backup." Sumner sighed and folded his hands. "We need your help, Corey. You, Paige, Mo, Mika… anyone else you can get together."

"Sorry?"

The Dean ticked his fingers. "The security issues. The Refuge. The rise in mental health concerns and alcohol violations." The Dean paused and renewed his eye contact with me. I internally withered, praying that the conversation wouldn't abruptly turn. "And that goes beyond the fact that we've lost dozens of staff members and barely replaced a fraction of them. We're not stupid, Corey. We know people haven't been checking in, obeying curfew, staying on campus. We're fortunate that there haven't been more incidents like that of Kevin Thompson."

My phone dinged. I reached into my pocket and turned it to vibrate.

"We'll talk more when Paige gets here—"

"She's on her way."

Sumner smiled weakly. There were dark clouds under his eyes, and the words he was speaking seemed like they were spilling out of his mouth faster than he could control them. "There are things we'd like you to do on campus. The two of you."

My eyes narrowed. "Such as?"

"Put both of your considerable leadership talents toward good ends. We know you've been involved in keeping people away from The Refuge, a cancer on this campus if there ever was one."

I raised my eyebrows. That was interesting.

"We saw you steer students away from the group of Refuge protestors. Trying to take advantage of all the supposed anger on campus."

I shifted uncomfortably. "Dean, there was nothing 'supposed' about that anger."

"No doubt. The anger, I understand. But the militarization of it. The manipulation of it. That's very different." The Dean said extended his hands. "Who would benefit from more chaos on this campus? What group would appreciate more madness? What group could inflate their numbers if things got worse?"

The obvious answer hung in the air. Its implication was punctured by the vibration of my phone. Again, I ignored it.

"What I'm saying, Corey, is that there is a moment for people like you and Paige. A chance for both of you to rise to the occasion."

I thought of all the people who had listened to us so far. What would happen if we spoke more often, and with a larger megaphone?

I had a million questions. What did they want me to do? What did they want me to say?

Sumner mistook my silence as the need to speak more. "Some schools in the state have already looked at shutting down, particularly after the Left Behind shootings. They feel they cannot safely continue to operate in the face of ongoing security and mental health concerns. And, candidly, there are members of our board who feel the same way."

I gasped. "So, those rumors are true."

Now a phone call. I fumbled my fingers into my pockets and smashed the volume button to send it to voice mail.

Sumner was nodding. "Obviously that's the last resort, but it's something that's on the table. We're exploring all of our options, Corey. Some of those involve you and Paige."

"How?"

"We've been approached by a variety of organizations," Sumner said. "As I'm sure you know, this chapter of The Refuge is just a branch of a larger organization. Their actions, and their funding, have caught the eye of some serious players in the government. People who want to use grassroots efforts to push back against The Refuge's efforts to recruit more members and do… whatever else they are trying to do."

My phone rang again. I almost growled in frustration before realizing getting two texts and two phone calls within five minutes was really out of the ordinary.

I whipped my phone out of my pocket. "Paige?"

"*Corey, something's wrong.*" Paige was out of breath.

I exchanged looks with Sumner. "Huh?"

Sumner's face shifted from vague annoyance to confusion.

"I left. I left the dorm, Corey, and I was heading to you, and I saw this one sketchy dude in all black around a tree, about fifty yards from the administration building."

"Okay, so?" Now I was looking at Sumner. "It was probably a Refuge guy playing hide and go seek behind the trees. It isn't that weird."

"Yeah, but when I looked at him, he took off, Corey. Totally took off, and I mean full-tilt running."

"So?" I was utterly bewildered.

"He was carrying a case, Corey."

"A case…" My voice trailed off.

"Yes, Corey. A guy I didn't recognize was running with a small rectangular case."

"Where are you?" I said. "Where are you running?"

"To the Admin building."

"If you think someone has a gun, why—"

There was a shatter. A shatter like someone had dropped a tray of glasses. And then, there was screaming. Sumner and I ran toward the door. I reached it first and ripped it open. Clara was standing, befuddled, but I saw it. Sumner's office was just in front of a railing that peered down into the main chamber of the Administration building. Sun streamed in from the building's domed, glass roof.

I could feel a shift in the air pressure. A coldness that didn't belong. I looked in the direction of the massive, front-facing windows and saw jagged spikes cutting from what had once been a heavy pane of glass.

"Holy—"

This time, I heard the crack. Another glass window exploded, roughly thirty feet to my left. Sumner, Clara, and I dove backward, falling over each other like a house of cards toppling.

Stumbling to our feet, the three of us ran backward, moving back into Sumner's office. I could hear muffled screaming from my hand. *Paige.*

Safely back in Sumner's office, I brought the phone to my ear.

"—I swear, if you don't answer me right now, Corey Walker, I'm—"

"I'm here, I'm here. We're fine. We're—"

"Shh!" Sumner seemed to whisper and scream at the same time. He brought a hand across his neck as he locked his office door, urging me to quiet.

"*I'm coming to you.*" Paige said.

"You're doing *what?*" I screeched.

"Be quiet," Sumner hissed.

"*I'm in the building,*" Paige said. I could hear it through the phone—the chaos and screaming.

"Paige—ahhh, damnit, go hide somewhere!"

"*Gotta go,*" Paige said. Then the cut of the line going dead.

I cursed and jammed the phone back in my pocket.

Sumner, meanwhile, had walked back to his computer. He was working intently, Clara peering over his shoulder. Moments later, Sumner stepped back from his keyboard. Crosstalk blared out of his speakers, and I strained against the din to try and make sense. Every now and then I could catch snippets of words, but by and large, there were too many competing voices to make sense of what was happening.

The look of confusion on my face must have been crystal clear because Sumner said, "Campus security radio." Then, with an element of disgust, he added, "Trying to make sense of this."

"Should you call the Chief? Let him know we're up here?" Clara's voice rang with the first tones of emotion I had heard out of her.

Sumner curtly nodded, picking up the phone and talking quietly into it. "Yes. Thank you."

The third crash of glass was followed almost instantaneously by a fourth. I winced with each shatter, imagining hearing the crack of a bullet that I couldn't hear. The building we were in was being shot at. I was about thirty feet away from a fired bullet. My girlfriend had come barreling in, and I had no idea if she was okay....

The thoughts made no sense in my mind, dissipating like an explosion in space.

I texted Paige, angrily flicking aside a Campus Police push alert that interrupted my text.

You okay?

The response came almost an instant later.

Yeah. Small cut from glass. Few others hurt worse. In stairwell with others. Chilling. We ok.

Relief flooded through my veins, and I was unnerved at how easily the tears leaped to my eyes as if they were searching for an escape from my body.

I can't believe you did that.

This time, the response was slower in coming, but eventually, it came.

I had to. I had to make sure you were okay. I had to... okay. This might not have been the greatest of ideas. A moment later, more typing. *Did we do this? Is this our fault?*

I laughed at that. Sumner looked at me strangely for a moment, then back to his computer, where he was typing furiously. Clara made herself busy by propping a chair against the door.

No one's fault, I typed back. *No one's but theirs.*

I thought about Paige. The way her hair splayed on the pillow like a red-orange halo. The way the corner of one lip turned upward when I told a stupid joke. The way her eyes half-closed when I did something she liked. The way she had looked at me that first night, after we left the party, with a fire in her eyes that rang so, so true.

After a hesitation, I typed, *I'm so glad you are okay.*

Paige responded with an emoji heart.

《◇》

Time yawned forward, crushing downward like a weight. Every thirty seconds, my brain told me to yell at Sumner about the lack of security. About how many people were cut and bleeding in the building now.

Every time I was tempted, I saw the haunted look in his eyes and decided he'd had enough for one day. At one point, Clara, sitting next to him, wrapped her hand around his. It was just a few seconds, and

Sumner's hands twitched when she did. Five seconds later, she released. I don't think they saw that I saw. I don't know if they would have cared.

It was two hellacious hours before we heard a pounding knock at the door. "Northampton Police. Step away from the door," boomed a voice, and Sumner, Clara, and I jumped and stood.

"We're clear," Sumner said.

"Wait," Clara called out in a tiny voice. She cautiously stepped forward and removed the chair that she had propped against the handle.

The door flew open, and I gasped. Two police officers appeared, their eyes barely visible through the slits of their masks, their bodies round and bulky with armor. They both had assault rifles, and they moved like greased lightning, scanning the room with their eyes and their weapons. One whipped open Sumner's bathroom and drew his barrel across the length of the room. The other did the same for Sumner's closet.

They ignored us. I'd never felt so small.

Evidentially satisfied, one gestured toward the door. "This way."

The three of us followed the two cops, moving quickly toward the door. I scanned the damage as I walked. Most of the hallway looked untouched, but here and there I saw signs of something wrong—shards of glass, jagged edges glistening in the light. An upturned chair by the accounting department. A spilled pot of coffee inside a break room, brown liquid poured out like blood.

We made our way down the stairs in shock, one police officer in front of us, the other behind. Their guns were still out. Their eyes were still roaming.

I wondered, briefly, what was going through their heads. Were they scared? Annoyed at this stupid school that was causing so much trouble? Did they care about us?

We got to the ground floor, and I saw Paige right away. Her back was turned to me, arm raised in the air as an EMT pressed something into it. I caught sight of the wound. It wasn't a little cut. It was a nice slice out of the front of her arm.

And then I was running. Because, you know, that's the smart thing to do when there are men with guns around. Strangely enough, they barely even looked at me. I think they knew I wasn't going far.

I was barely able to breathe by the time I reached Paige. Whether it was from the brief run, the sheer weight of the day catching up with me, or the sight of someone I cared deeply about bleeding, I couldn't tell.

"Hey." Paige's voice trembled and her skin was a ghostly white. A second later, her knees buckled, and the paramedic and I both caught her.

"All right, all right," said the gruff voice of the EMT. "We got you. Down you go." We each eased Paige onto the floor. She went to the ground, and the paramedic continued pressing her arm.

I stroked Paige's face. "You liar," I said, no accusation in my voice.

"Yeah. Sorry I couldn't text. Was hard. With the blood." Paige's voice had a dream-like quality. And with her good hand, she reached up and touched my face. Then hers trembled. "All I saw was a bullet, headed your way. I bet that's what they were shooting at."

"They weren't shooting with real bullets," the paramedic said.

That got my attention. "What?"

The paramedic shook her head. "I was on the third floor. I'd know those holes anywhere. I made quite a few myself as a kid." The paramedic said something into the radio pinned to her chest, and like magic, a gurney appeared. Keeping Paige's injured arm stretched toward the sky, the paramedic added, "That was a BB gun."

A series of thoughts fired their way out of my brain at the same time. "You hear that? They weren't trying to kill us."

Paige's face showed no relief. If anything, it simply clouded with more tension and remained pained as they loaded her onto the gurney. "Yeah, but is that really better?"

It clicked then. They weren't trying to hurt anyone. Not physically. But they were desperate to cause us the pain that we felt at that moment.

I looked down at Paige's face. Her lips quivered and her eyes watered. Her hair flowed like mist around her, and I couldn't help but wonder what would have happened if The Refuge—and I knew it was them—had acted with more murderous intent.

I clutched Paige's good hand. She reflexively wrapped her fingers around mine and looked at me with something like gratitude.

Was less than half a semester enough time to tell someone you loved them?

I didn't say the words. Instead, they seemed to float between us. From the way Paige was looking at me at that moment, I wasn't sure words were necessary at all.

Chapter 17

Paige wasn't the only one injured by falling glass, of course. As we sat in an Emergency Room bed, we saw a few other gurneys and wheelchairs rush past us. Some were actively bleeding. Some looked more annoyed than anything else.

At least one person was on a gurney that moved faster than the others. They were surrounded by more people too.

Paige was fine. Physically, anyway. But she was paler than usual, and her normally radiant hair clung to her skull in sweaty globs. They had stitched her arm almost as soon as they had wheeled us into her ER bay, an older nurse humming gently as she expertly threaded Paige's arm back together. The nurse worked with precision and expertise, drawing Paige's skin together like it was a torn blanket… not skin and muscle that had been ripped apart by some cultist with a death wish for civilized society.

Paige's face was as smooth as a flat stone. She didn't wince, didn't cry as the nurse closed the wound in her arm with a needle and thread. It was only when the nurse left the room, smiling gently, that Paige's face broke like a shattered mirror. She had that pathetic look of someone in pain from all sides, of someone who had been found by a trauma they hadn't thought possible.

And when she cried, I couldn't curl into the bed next to her. It was too small. After some pulling and near desperate yanking, I figured out how to lower the railing that kept me from the side of her bed. I pulled up the chair, wrapped my arms around her in an awkward embrace, and let Paige open up the floodgates while weeping on my shoulder.

She cried and cried and cried. I lost track of time.

Sometime later, a gentle rustle as the curtains moved. We both turned, Paige abruptly rising from my shoulder. I expected to see a nurse or doctor, clipboard in hand, with a guide on how to clean her stitched arm.

Nope. Instead, I saw two thick men. One had a crew cut, the other had a thatch of brown hair that was neatly parted to the side. "Miss Lynn?" said crew cut.

"Yeah?" Paige's face was beet red, and her eyes were almost as swollen as her wounded arm, but she still found the strength to sound annoyed at being bothered. It made my heart swell with pride.

"I'm Officer Roca with the Northampton Police Department. This is Officer Dorney. I understand that you may have seen the suspects who fired on the Administration Building. Is that correct?"

"Oh. Oh, yes. I absolutely did." The annoyance was completely gone from Paige's voice, and a hard resolve was in its place.

Dorney smiled. "I'm glad to hear that. We'd like to ask you a few questions, then."

"Absolutely." Paige's normally deep voice cracked, and I laughed. That seemed to remind the cops that I was there.

"He can stay if you'd like," said Officer Dorney, his voice flat.

"I'm kinda hungry," I said softly.

Paige nodded. "Grab me something too?" she asked. "I never got lunch."

"Yeah. Of course. Be right back." I ducked around the other cop's massive frame and edged my way out the door.

Naturally, I got lost following the signs to the cafeteria. Cursing, I found myself back at the main entrance, and I was instantly horrified by what I saw—cameras. Cameras everywhere. They were all outside of the front entrance, arrayed in a semi-circle around a makeshift podium.

"Lovely," I muttered to myself. We were going to be a huge story. Fantastic. Just great.

I ran a hand through my hair and followed the arrows to the cafeteria. This time, I found it. I walked through the entrance and saw her. Short. Blonde. Holding a spiral-bound notebook. Eyes on fire. "You! I remember you."

"You don't remember my name," I said to the reporter. *Stephanie Perkins.*

She waved a dismissive hand. "I ran into you the day the school came back into session."

"I remember."

Perkins and an unkempt guy in jeans were starting to walk toward me. The guy had a little camera in his hand.

I raised my palms. "No. Absolutely not. I don't want an interview."

Perkins gestured to her cameraman, and the guy put the camera down on the table. "Were you there?" The sharpness in her voice had disappeared, replaced by a velvety smoothness that I imagined she reserved for sympathetic reporting subjects.

Before I knew why I was answering, I responded, "Yeah. I was in the building. With Dean Sumner. My girlfriend got hurt. Falling glass."

Perkins raised a hand to her mouth. "I'm sorry. I really am. That must be awful."

I said nothing. Let the silence hang.

"Who do you think did this?" Perkins asked.

I snorted. What a dumb question. "The Refuge. Obviously."

"We keep hearing that. Why do you think no one will go on the record and say it?"

"Fear?" I offered. "They beat up a kid. They slashed tires. Now they shot at the administration building. They're trying to scare people off campus and they're targeting people who speak out against them."

"Why?"

"I don't know," I said before my mouth abruptly reversed course without first checking with my brain. "They view anyone who disagrees with them as a threat."

I could feel my face flushing, my fingers twitching as I spoke. I jammed my hands into the pockets of my jeans and squeezed them into fists. I wanted to talk to this reporter. The world needed to know just how bad these monsters were.

Perkins looked at her cameraman. Looked back at me. It must have been written on my face. "Would you like to talk about it?"

I was nodding, thinking about Kevin and all the suffering kids who were in pain at a school that wasn't prepared to cope with them. "Yes. Absolutely."

《◇》

I took a deep breath before the camera began rolling and Perkins started asking her questions. I was honest with my answers. I couldn't be anything else.

I told them about The Refuge. I told them about the way they targeted kids who were in pain and set up social groups and got people drunk and high. I told Perkins about how they had stolen my friend from me. I told Perkins about Kevin and the flat tires. How the school was trying to help but had no grasp on how much pain people were in. "Kids at this school keep trying to return to a world that just doesn't exist anymore."

"What do you think they need?" Perkins asked.

I looked her right in the eyes. "Hope. Hope and help. Not the false kind that The Refuge is offering. It's only by getting that help that groups like The Refuge can be fought off."

When the interview ended, Perkins asked me for numbers. I gave her Mo's and Mika's and Kevin's and half a dozen others I thought would talk to her. I texted all of them ahead of time and let them know that they may get a call from a reporter. *Talk. Please. Tell her everything. It's time. It's past time.*

By the time I left the cafeteria, I was shaking like a leaf.

Paige was staring at my empty hands when I walked back into the room. "You didn't get me lunch?" Her eyebrows were raised.

I smiled sheepishly and told her about the interview. She was nodding when I finished.

"Good. I'm glad. Had to happen. The only way people understand what we are going through is if someone else says something. May as well be you." Then Paige chuckled. "I mean, they already shot at us, so why the hell not?"

Yikes. I ignored the chill that passed through me and laughed without humor.

A campus police officer was there to greet us when Paige was discharged, his car ready, the heater going. To say it was a relief was an understatement.

We were still in the campus police car when the story aired. I knew because the texts started rolling in. Mo and Mika had caught the tail end of it and sent a long rant of colorful language.

You do know this is DEFINITELY going to get you expelled, right? Mo said.

I don't think that's a thing, I typed back. *Well, I hope not anyway.*

I was kind of floored by how little emotion that thought sent through me. Was expulsion really the worst thing that could happen right now?

I looked over at Paige. Squeezed her good hand.

Before the trip back to school, I had told Mom and Mack to watch the news. In between demands about the condition Paige and I were in, they said they would.

Mack added, *If there isn't proper security in front of your dorm, text me. I will come and get you NOW.*

Two texts hit me harder than all the others. The first was from Mom. *Corey. Oh, my sweet Corey. I am crying as I type this. I am proud of you. I am very proud of you. You are a very stupid young man. And I am so, so proud of you.*

I laughed. My phone trilled a second later. Mack. *From that day in the closet when I arrested Jim. From the first time I laid eyes on you. You may not be my biological son… but I am so proud to know I helped raise you.*

That one caught me, and the tears came without warning and without mercy. Paige looked over, her face filled with concern, and my phone chose that moment to die before I could show her the text. That was all right. Maybe that one was just for Mack and me.

The campus safety car pulled right up to the front of our dorm, and the officer driving it soundlessly hit the brakes and slipped it into park. He hadn't said anything during the entire car ride—I assumed he was mad at us for stirring up all this trouble. Honestly, I couldn't even blame him. Our actions had sort of contributed to a building getting shot at.

However, when he turned to look at us in the back seat, there was a kind smile on his face. He handed each of us a business card. "Here. You call me if you need me."

"Thank you," I stammered.

Then he reached into his front seat and grabbed a sandwich bag. "You two hungry?"

"Yes," Paige and I said at the same time. Breakfast had been interrupted by an act of vandalism. Lunch by a shooting. If dinner was in that bag in front of me, I was a very happy man.

God bless him, the officer handed me the sandwich bag, and it took all of my willpower not to rip it open with my teeth. "Italian," said the cop. "Three foot-longs. I imagine you're starving."

Who IS this guy?

"You're a saint," Paige said. "Thank you."

The cop shrugged. He had grey hair, a ruddy face, and kind eyes. "I imagine you've had a day."

"That's one way of putting it," I said.

He nodded, and I caught his name tag. Officer Harold Baines. "You two get some rest."

"Thank you." I grasped the door handle.

Paige didn't move. After a beat, she leaned forward and hugged Officer Baines awkwardly from the back. It would have looked like she was choking him if there wasn't such a look of gratitude on her face.

We trudged up to my dorm, taking the stairs. It felt good to stretch our legs.

The dorm was as silent as an empty graveyard. There was no music, no muffled conversation. Our footsteps echoed like we were screaming in church, the strangeness of which was matched only by the police officer who gruffly nodded at us as we walked past her.

Finally, Paige spoke. "How do we live in a world with both Megan Buchanan and Officer Baines?"

"Honest to God, Paige, I have no idea."

We reached my dorm and opened the door, encountering no one else as we walked. I did the only sensible thing and jammed my phone into a nearby charger.

That out of the way, Paige and I sat down, leaning against my desk. We sat cross-legged on the floor and didn't say one single, solitary word until three feet of Italian goodness were devoured, every morsel chewed to a pulp, and every sliver of shredded lettuce happily ingested. I burped loudly when I finished, not even bothering to cover it up. Paige just blinked, staring ahead of her. She looked bone-weary.

My phone vibrated a few times, and I sighed. "Should probably look at that. With the shooting and all."

"Uh-huh." Paige stared blankly ahead.

I awkwardly shuffled up, feeling a crick in my neck from having slept awkwardly. I turned to Paige and laughed. "Can you believe that the party was less than twenty-four hours ago?"

"Corey, I barely even know where I am right now."

I snorted and grabbed my phone. More texts from more of our group, but there was one notification that caught my attention—the push alert from Campus Safety. *Attention students: Please check your emails for a very important campus announcement.*

Oh. Oh, no. The air was pressed out of my lungs. That could only mean one thing. I showed Paige the alert. "We out of here?"

"Oh, yeah." Paige's face quivered like the ripples of a pond. She fisted away a tear from her face and sniffled loudly. "Probably for the best. Somebody is going to get killed. Only question is whether or not the closing is temporary or if they are giving up for the rest of the semester." We stayed still for a moment before Paige used her head to gesture to my phone. "Open the email."

I thumbed over to my email. The subject—*An Update to this Semester.*

I cursed and smashed the open button.

I scrolled to the bottom, where I knew the verdict would be. When I got there, I exhaled and said, "Two weeks. Oh, thank God, they're not shutting down. They're sending us home for two weeks. We'll do virtual school, and then they'll bring us back."

Paige laughed and looked aside. "I guess."

I kept scrolling. "Actually, this may be okay. It says they raised some money from alumni and are gonna use it to hire more counselors and security."

I scrolled to the last paragraph. A sentence there caught my eye. *To steal a quote from those of you who have fought for Augustus since the beginning: We will not give this school up to snake oil salesmen. Augustus students do not run away and seclude themselves as if hiding is the solution to the world's problems. We will not surrender this school to those who try to take it from us, or to a world that is drowning in its own sorrow. Instead, we will take these two weeks to resolve ourselves for the battles ahead. Be well. Rest up. And we will see you soon.*

It was signed by Dean Sumner. Paige looked over at me. "Who said that line about snake oil salesmen?"

I thought of that night outside of Taylor, all those weeks ago, surrounded by students who were just looking for something to believe in. "I'm pretty sure it was me."

《◇》

THERE WAS A melancholy in the rest of the night. Paige and I just sort of stared at each other. We responded to a bunch of texts at first, and Paige's tearful conversation with her parents was something I never wanted to see again. I'd slipped my arm around her as she convinced her parents she was okay. The airline industry was still sputtering, and it would take them a few days to get a flight from

California. A call home later, and it was settled. Paige would stay at my house for a few days.

I thought of memories lost, of chances I'd never have. Of nights with Paige and Mo and Mika, and an asteroid that never hit and still killed two of my best friends, just in different ways.

But, strangely enough, the email from the school had been oddly inspiring. They weren't giving up. The semester wasn't lost. They seemed to know what they had to do to get this school running better. And they'd made it clear that The Refuge was a shared enemy. Maybe, going forward, we could do better.

Paige and I stared out my window for a few minutes, blinking, waiting for someone to do something strange. When no sound interrupted the dead of night, save for the footfalls of patrolling police officers, we pulled back into my room and looked at each other.

"I'm ready for bed." Paige was seated on the ground, and her voice sounded lower and softer than usual. It sounded like defeat, and I think she recognized it. "I wish I knew what we could do here, Corey. I am so tired, and I am so wired, and there is no place to go."

I pulled my phone out of my pocket, the smallest of smiles on my face. "Anything good to say?"

"Yeah." Paige scuttled on her butt over to me. I lowered myself to the floor, and there we sat, shoulder to shoulder, her hair touching my face. "Screw those people who try to shoot at you with BB guns."

I blurted out a laugh. "Okay, maybe something a little more articulate?"

Paige thought for a moment, her face crinkled in mock concentration. "Set fire to The Refuge?"

"A little less murderous."

And then, Paige's face lit as if it was filled with electricity. She flung her hand to her phone. "Actually, yes. Yes, yes, hell yes."

Paige thumbed her way over to Instagram, ignoring the red notification buttons and jumping to her status. She took her phone from me and typed, her face alight. "Here," she said, handing me her phone.

Black background. White text. *The World is Our Refuge.*

I hit publish. "Damn, Paige."

"Simplicity is best."

I grabbed my phone and hit the like button.

Twenty seconds later, two more likes. Mo and Mika, of course. They had already gone home with their dad a few hours before. They were not the only ones who left before the email had come.

It wasn't much. Of course, it wasn't much. But the world was our refuge. And for now, that's all I could ask of it.

Chapter 18

Mom was at the door when Mack pulled into the driveway. Her apron was smeared with red tomato sauce, and a smile was on her face. She moved down our small front lawn, coming right to Paige's door, giving her one of the warmest hugs I'd seen. Paige happily returned the favor.

Mom's hug for me burned. Her arms were wrapped tighter around me than I could remember feeling for months. Around two months. When we'd finally said goodnight, drunkenly stumbling to our beds, after the Deflector mission had worked. After Perses missed.

Christ. The school closing again felt like the near-miss of an asteroid.

It was early in the evening, maybe around 4:00 p.m., and the sun was still high in the sky. That didn't stop any of us from being starved. Mom had set the dining room table—that never happened—hell, even the wedding china from my biological dad was out.

Dinner was homemade lasagna. Paige practically sprinted into the kitchen when called, running in to help my mom, leaving Mack and me staring at each other.

"Little Man."

"Bigger Man."

Mack smiled wanly. Then he turned abruptly and moved toward his jacket. "Jill wanted me to give you this." Mack handed me an envelope, and I started to laugh.

"GameStop?" I asked.

"Fifty bucks. Get yourself something nice."

I laughed. "I will, Bigger Man. I can't imagine playing video games anytime soon, but I will try."

Mack nodded thoughtfully. "I figured you'd say something like that." He paused. "Do I want to ask how you're feeling?"

We hadn't had much of a chance to talk on the drive back. Paige and I had each loaded up a good-sized bag, flung it into the back of the pickup, and promptly fell asleep. I think I drooled in her hair.

I stuffed my hands in the pockets of my jeans. "If I had a decent answer, I'd tell you."

"That's about the most honest answer I could ask out of you. It's been quite the half of a semester."

"It has. I honestly have no idea how they are going to bring us back."

"Well, I'm glad they are going to try," Mack said. "The world has to move on. And hopefully, the school can figure out the right way to operate going forward."

"They screwed a few things up. Still. We all made mistakes. I don't think the school realized just how hard we were all going to be affected."

"I don't think anybody did."

"Boys. Sit," commanded Mom.

The smell filled our small dining room with scents of cheese and spices and garlic. Mom wasn't Italian—she often referred to herself as an ethnic mutt—but on nights like this, you'd swear she was from Venice.

I happily sat and reached for the lasagna. Paige smacked me with a serving spoon. "Uhh. No. Guests first."

"Yes, ma'am," I said.

Paige laughed and plopped a serving on my plate. Then she did the same for herself before passing the food to Mom.

"Paige? Is the food good?" Mack asked.

Paige chewed. "Oh, God. I mean, yeah, but I'm not gonna give a complete answer until I'm done eating."

"Oh, good," Mom chirped. Yes, she actually chirped. Abruptly, she stood, then came back into the dining room, a bottle of red wine in her hand.

The image of the alcohol took me back to campus. "Bastards," I muttered to myself. When everyone looked at me, I continued. "The Refuge. They stole our semester. Maybe more."

"I think the world did that," Mack said. "Remember, Corey, yours isn't the only school forced to close. In a sense, you got lucky. You should still be able to finish out the semester."

Paige tore at a piece of garlic bread with a ferocity that made my heart skip a beat. "He's right. You heard all those other schools and colleges that are closing."

"Yeah." My voice trailed off. Something about what Paige said brought me back to Dean Sumner's office. Before the gunshots and the shattered glass. "Oh, hell. I forgot."

Paige twisted her head toward me, eyes squinted. "Hmm?"

"What Sumner said. Before you came. Well, before you were supposed to come." Now Mom and Mack were staring intently at me. I looked at all of them as I spoke. "Sumner. The Dean whose office I was in when The Refuge started firing."

"We remember," Mom and Mack intoned.

"He wanted to talk about leadership and other schools. He was saying that other places were having trouble with groups like The Refuge. That they were part of a larger operation, but that the school had been contacted by other groups too. That they were looking to push back against The Refuge…." I hadn't even thought about the reason that Sumner would have called us into his office on a Sunday afternoon. The implications of this conversation were starting to hit me. "Wait. Sumner wanted to work with us?"

"And use us as part of a larger organization?" Uncertainty crisscrossed Paige's face, her eyes wide and her mouth hanging partly open, a bite of lasagna hanging from a fork that was now suspended in the air.

"Does that honestly surprise you?" Mack asked.

"Maybe a little," I said.

"More than a little," added Paige. "I mean, we kinda held a big party the night before. That's what kicked off our final events at school."

"And why did you hold a big party?" Mack asked, the slightest of smiles on his face.

"To give people a reminder about what a good world could look like," I said softly.

Suddenly, there were no voices. Just the sound of clanking silverware, the thoughts in my head, and the beating of my heart.

I shook my head. "Yeah, but what does that mean? Did the Dean want us to narc on students or something?"

"Corey, I love you, but don't use words like narc, you sound like an idiot," Mom said.

Next to me, Paige laughed in the middle of a drink, sending droplets onto the table. "Sorry, sorry." She cleaned while she coughed.

"This is a conversation with the Dean we have to continue," I said.

"I'm sure you will," said Mack, causing Paige and me to turn in his direction. "Corey, when someone wants something from you, they will keep trying until they get it. He'll call."

"I suspect after a few days," Mom said. "You were in a lockdown scenario together."

"I'd rather not repeat that," I quipped.

I wish I'd meant that comment as a joke. I hadn't. Multiple acts of violence had gotten increasingly closer in the past three months. It felt like so many members of my generation were now wearing a target on our backs.

Paige felt it too. I could sense the fear, the uncertainty, radiating off of her in waves. We made eye contact briefly, and just for a moment, her eyes widened.

And yet, when I looked up, Mom and Mack were staring at each other. Uncertainty was on Mom's face, but relative calm was spread over Mack's.

"What am I missing?" I asked them. They looked over, and Mom shifted uncomfortably.

"Let me answer that by talking about Jill," Mack said. "What have I told you, over and over again, is the thing I love the most about my wife?"

That, I could remember. It was easy. "Grace. Grace under pressure."

"Grace," Mack responded, softly, nodding once. "Paige, my wife is a nurse at our regional hospital. Grace is a requirement of her job."

"And yours," Mom said.

"And mine." When Mack spoke again, his voice intensified, and he stared directly at me. "Corey, you have grace. Grace under pressure. Grace under fire. You have the ability to stand when others duck, and to run into a fire when others run away. That's why you helped save Kristy Ford. That's why you went viral for standing up to that Refuge leader during their first real appearance on campus. And that's why Dean Sumner has called you—and why others will do so. Leadership requires grace."

Underneath the table, Paige squeezed my hand.

Mack's gaze shifted. "Paige, I suspect I'm telling you something you already know."

A Mona Lisa smile crossed Paige's face. "Maybe." Her multi-colored nails gently scratched my wrists, and I felt a lift in my chest.

"And I also suspect that you two are together for a reason."

My turn now. "Maybe."

"Ass," Paige said.

And we all laughed.

《◇》

MACK LEFT THAT night, citing the need to go on patrol. Mom set up a spare mattress in my room, and Paige and I spent the rest of the night curled up on the living room couch, watching 80s movies. Mom spent twenty minutes telling us about what it was like when she saw those movies when she was a kid. Then, mercifully, she took the hint and left. Paige snuggled closer.

At some point, *The Goonies* ended. Paige had drifted off and was unmoved by the closing music as it came to a crescendo. I knew she was asleep from the peaceful sound of her breathing. For a moment, I closed my eyes. Imagined that this was a normal world. One before Perses, before The Refuge.

The music ended. The credits rolled on. It wasn't a normal world.

I sighed and disentangled myself from Paige, taking two empty wine glasses and placing them gently in the sink. It was a little past midnight. Paige and I had decided that we would walk through town tomorrow. I'd show her where I'd lived all my life. The elementary school that had given me so many horrifying memories. The high school where I'd realized I could escape.

Well, for now, I had to get Paige to bed. Could I carry her? No. No, I could not. I would fall. And she would wake up.

"Hey," Paige said groggily, her eyes opening a sliver.

"Oh, thank God. That's one less thing I have to worry about."

"Huh?"

"Nothing."

Paige yawned. "What time is it?"

"Little past midnight," I offered Paige my hand. She took it, and I pulled her up. Then my hands curled around her waist, underneath her shirt.

Paige giggled and reached down, grabbing the bottle of wine on the table and swirling it around. She looked at me, and even in the near dark of my living room, I could see the smile.

Paige took my hand and pulled me into the kitchen at the back of the house. She slid open a screen door and walked us outside. We were both instantly assaulted by a chilling wind. "Oh, that was a mistake," Paige said.

"It was not." I ran back into the house, practically dashing into my bedroom. Five seconds and one stubbed toe later, I was outside with a thick woolen blanket in my hands. "I'm a genius."

"Not bad," Paige said, and together, we sat on the swinging bench that had been a feature of my backyard since a few months after my dad's arrest. The rusted chains creaked under our shared weight.

Wordlessly, Paige took a brief swig of the red wine, sighing happily as she passed it to me. I echoed the movement, savoring the feeling of alcohol that wasn't god-awful beer. Warmth bubbled up in my chest. I wasn't one hundred percent sure of the cause.

Our house was at the top of a big hill. Below us crossed a couple of winding, country roads, with Wellington the most prominent of all, circling past the back of our house and winding toward the front. In the distance was the faintest outline of Route 309, trucks shimmering as they sped toward their destination. To the right stood Robinette, the sign from its Shell gas station standing out like a neon weed.

Nearby, the Ford house stood—dark, abandoned, barely visible against the deep evening sky. It reached for the stars like the husk of a ghost.

I stared at the home and pointed. "That's where Mack almost got killed." My finger slowly dropped toward the floor. I drank again.

Paige grabbed the bottle and took a pull. "You two saved that woman's life."

I nodded sadly. "We did." I pulled Paige closer against me. "You ever read those articles about all the other women who died thanks to their abusive husbands during Perses?"

"Yeah. Hundreds in this country alone."

"And probably more."

"Probably more." Paige must have read my face. "A lot of people endured pain, Corey. We can't save them all."

I shot out a bitter laugh. "Well, we found that one out the hard way."

"Right?" Paige took another drink of the wine, and we sat silently for a few moments, staring at the trucks below. "Still. Doesn't that make you want to know what Sumner was going to talk about with you?"

"It really does," I said. "Like, how did he want our help? What could we have done?"

"Apparently something," Paige said.

I was shaking my head now. "I'm not really too sure what two students could have done to stop a national movement."

"Oh, I have no idea," Paige said. "I mean that. Absolutely none."

"Well, apparently, I'm good at media relations now."

"Right. My parents even saw that clip. You were on the damn national news, Corey."

I winced. "Please don't remind me."

"Too late, rock star." Paige had a twinkle in her eye.

"Let's just remember that I'm not the only one. How many Instagram followers did you gain in the past day?"

"Thousands and growing," Paige said. Her Instagram post—*The World is Our Refuge*—had been on CBS Evening News. That had led to some weird direct messages.

Paige risked bringing her arm out from the blanket and began smacking my arm.

"Ow. Why?"

"Because you are a Goober."

"Goober?"

"Goober. You are a goober."

"What's a goober?"

"Someone who became famous and doesn't want to do anything with it." Paige laughed.

Now I was laughing. "Meh, should have been you."

"I was bleeding." Paige waved her free arm so that her loose sleeves fell, revealing the winding band of stitches that covered the back of her left arm. How many were in there? Twenty? Twenty-one? I'd forgotten.

"Next time."

"Oh, absolutely, next time," Paige confirmed. "You've got a voice, Walker, but I want mine too."

"I can't imagine anyone trying to shut you up."

Paige's gaze was in the distance, and when she spoke again, there was a gravitas to her words. "There's a chance to do something really good here, Corey. The Refuge might have gone too far."

"Or it's just the start."

"It might be," Paige agreed. "It also might give us the momentum to push back against them on campus. Stop anyone else from joining them."

"It was a statement of intent." I remembered the weak denials of The Refuge's national organization, swearing that they weren't involved in acts of violence but reminding schools that they would vigorously defend against any effort to clamp down on them, including using any appropriate legal action. "That might have scared off a lot of schools from doing more to stop them."

"I think any effort to push back against the bastards in black has to come from students anyway," Paige said. "We're gonna be in charge of this world at some point. We're the ones who have to fix it."

Paige's words melted away, fading into the night, and I kept my arm slung around her, lost in my own thoughts. We did have a responsibility to fix the world that we were inheriting. I got that. I just didn't feel particularly up to the challenge.

After a few more minutes, the darkness glided over us like a blanket.

«O»

TWO DULL RETORTS woke me, and my neck creaked uncomfortably. I jerked upward and caught the time—3:03. The night was as dark as death.

Two more bangs followed. Car doors.

I abruptly brought both of my hands to my eyes, rubbing them and jostling Paige.

"Wha?" she said, stirring.

"Hang on," I rasped. My heart was pumping.

Whispers in the dark.

I looked at Paige, whose face was morphing from sleepy confusion to intangible fear.

I whipped a hand into my pocket, and with shaky fingers, punched in my passcode. "Text Mack." I moved off of the bench.

I felt the cold, but the sensation was disconnected from my body like I was feeling what someone else was feeling. Paige was saying something, and it took me a minute to realize she was asking what was going on.

"Something. Something," I said.

She stood to follow me, and as we crossed the threshold into the house, there was a jiggling from the front door. The loose copper handle was bouncing in its socket.

I inhaled a sharp intake of breath and froze for a moment, adrenaline shooting through me, past me. Memories of moments come and gone fought for dominance inside my brain. The sickening sound of my dad's flesh on my mom's jaw. The muffled retort of Mack's gun.

I grabbed Paige and pulled her down, behind our living room couch, just as the door cracked open slowly. We were now hidden from view, Paige's head pressed against mine, her eyes wide with fear and her mouth trembling. We scrunched close together, hoping that we could make each other small. I felt her heartbeat through my chest. It felt like a wild animal that was trying to escape her ribcage.

Footsteps. Unfamiliar, overlapping sensations of weight, pressing into my living room carpet, depressing the floorboards below. It was pitch black behind my closed eyes, and I fought to control my heartbeat and think clearly, recycling all the images of regret and pain I'd gone through from all of these terrible moments gone wrong.

This moment will not repeat.

I broke the invisible bonds of terror that had clawed their way around my spine, wrapped one arm around Paige, and pulled down a blanket that hung on the back of the couch over the two of us. We were covered now, if lumpy. In the light, it would never work. In the dark, it might.

I squeezed Paige close to me, trying to hide our bodies as much as possible, practically pressing ourselves together. She took my meaning and curled her legs and arms into a ball. I could feel her quivering.

How many people were inside the house? Three? Four? I couldn't exactly tell from the footsteps. They weren't speaking at all, just moving slightly, but the metallic *click* that came from one of their hands left no doubt about whether or not they were armed.

I tried to pull myself into as tight a ball as possible, and Paige slowly mimicked my actions. We'd never be able to press flat into the couch, and with a nip of bad luck, one of the men would walk into us… and we'd be found.

The footsteps stopped.

Paige's quivering turned into violent tremors. I was scared they'd hear her teeth chattering.

In the suffocating darkness, the faintest of noises. Words were spoken at a volume designed to conceal their existence. Two sets of footsteps began to move to our left. Two to our right. If they moved past the couch, they'd wash around us like a tide breaking over jutting rocks.

That left us safe. For now. But it unveiled a whole new set of problems.

The men who were going to our left would come to two doors. The first led to Mom's office. The other to her bedroom.

The two men who were going to our right would follow a small hallway to the end of the house. There was only one door there—my room.

Jesus.

Armed men were here. They were in my house. Their intent was unquestionably evil. And they were certainly wearing all black.

I lost track of the men on my right—they'd find nothing in my room and likely wouldn't risk calling out to their friends. The men on the left— the ones with guns who were approaching my sleeping mother—were a more immediate concern.

This was tactical now. It required skill and guile. And I couldn't even play video games right.

My hand reached Paige's and felt something hard and plastic. *My phone.*

And it was lit. Some alert had just flashed across the screen.

With shaking fingers, I pried the phone from Paige's hands and slid it, display screen down, over to me. Using Paige's body as a shield, I tilted it up.

Sure enough, a text from Mack. I covered the phone with my hand to minimize any chance of light escaping the safety of our cocoon. Paige had texted him, *Help*.

Mack's response had already come.

What is wrong?

Corey? Are you safe?

With my free hand, I typed frantically. I couldn't see anything I was saying, but I tried to type *no armed men four. We are hidden behind the living room couch.*

I sent the text. At least, I thought I did.

I kept my left hand on the phone, fearing that any movement would alert the armed men to our presence.

Using my right hand, I tried to touch Paige's arm, but in the dark, I wound up awkwardly pulling her hair. She let loose the slightest of whimpers, one that she bit back a millisecond after the noise escaped her lips.

Now that help had been called, a decision.

I risked moving my head to the left, tilting it as slowly as I could. The men who had gone that way had, as expected, opened the door to Mom's office. I could hear soft rustling and the sounds of paper crashing. Mom's office was a train wreck, a nearly organic mass of papers and books and printers that had died unceremoniously. The men were stumbling around in the dark and depending on how deep into the room they wanted to go, it could take a minute or two to search the room— particularly if they tripped on a dead Lexmark.

But it wouldn't take long. And then they'd be in my mother's room.

I pulled the blanket over our feet, moving slowly, inching it upward. At the same time, I started to bring my knees below me.

Shadows shifted before I heard their movement. The men who had gone to the right were returning. We were like sitting ducks.

If we didn't move, they would see us. I tugged Paige's sleeve, and we scuttled around the front side of the couch and crammed ourselves between it and the coffee table.

Had the lights been on, they wouldn't have missed us.

The men in black came into the living room, crossing behind the couch, walking cautiously and just missing us. I felt the slightest breeze from their footsteps as their feet passed just next to mine.

"He's not in there," urgently whispered one of the voices. Abruptly, a crash and the two men in Mom's office came out. They were all to our left now. One held a flashlight, its beam lazily pointed down toward the ground.

The light reflected back upward, and even in the nearly blinding dark I could make out the unmistakable form of a gun.

"Where is he?" whispered the man holding the gun.

"No idea. Isn't he with his girlfriend?"

Paige stiffened.

"Did they go for a drive?" asked a third voice.

"Car's there," said a fourth.

"Fine. He got lucky. Let's do the mom and go. That's enough."

That was when a bright light filled the living room, coming from the direction of the main window. I grimaced and looked at our would-be attackers, able to see what they looked like for the first time. Their skin was neon white. They were, indeed, covered head to toe in black, everything from black long-sleeved shirts to the black gloves that covered the fingers they had awkwardly raised to their eyes.

Bam. Noises like a cannon. For the second time in forty-eight hours, the sound of gunfire filled my eardrums, followed almost simultaneously by shattered glass.

Bam. Bam bam. Four shots. Dust and plaster fell from the wall behind me.

The two men on my right fell. There was no explosion of blood, no chunks of skin or gore that I could see. It was like a switch had been flipped, and they were down.

There was a pause. The two men still moving clambered forward, one crouching and moving toward the window. His friend was not as lucky. He caught his legs in the crook of one of the bodies, and fell to the ground, gun clattering out of his hand.

That was when Paige let loose a high-pitched shriek that took the air from my lungs, and with a dive, drove her elbow into the nose of the fallen man. The attack had been awkward, but the impact was sharp. Blood exploded out of the man's nose.

Gunfire from the window. The remaining shooter had heard nothing behind him.

The man who had just gotten the business end of Paige's elbow was blinking, his eyes unfocused and wide.

More gunshots now. Occurring in rapid fire. I didn't know who was shooting.

Desperately, I crawled forward and wrapped one of my arms around Paige. In all the absurdity of the moment, I could feel her shaking again.

OUT. GET HER OUT. GET YOU OUT. GO.

The thoughts flashed in the deep recesses of my brain, and I listened, grabbing hold of Paige's shirt and pulling her backward.

I chanced a look out the window. Through the cheap lace curtain, illuminated by the cherry-red and neon-blue colors of the police lights, I could see it. A form, kneeling on the ground, firing into my living room from our front lawn.

Now Mom was racing out of her room, clad in her usual flannel pajamas and oversized sweatshirt. I couldn't see her face, but she moved in flashes. One second, she was at the doorway of her bedroom. The next, she was by our side, wrapping strong arms around Paige and me, pulling us into a mother's protective embrace.

When she wrapped her arm around me, I felt it—cold, long steel. A baseball bat. The one she told me when I was a kid she kept by her side, just in case.

The same one....

There was no conscious thought, no higher-level thinking. Just a boy in a closet, saved by a man with a gun, with a chance to return the favor.

The bat was in my left hand. I whipped around, transferring it to my right as I twirled. The light in front of me was blinding, but the shooter was there, on one knee, firing through the shattered glass.

The siren-infused light flashed like lightning. The police sirens were pure thunder.

I raised the bat as I ran, screaming as I moved, and the goddamn shooter had just enough time to stop firing and look over his shoulder before the metal bat connected with his skull.

The gun fell. Silence reigned. The night was still again, save for the echoing of the gunshots that rang around my home.

I leaned on the window, slicing my hand open on broken glass in the process. In a moment, my hands were slick.

Mom ran out the front door, already open from our attackers' initial entrance to the house.

"The bat, Corey!" Paige's words howled like an animal's yell. Startled, the bat slipped from my left hand, landing on the ground with a hollow thud.

And then Paige was on me, gathering me up in her arms, vaguely aware of the four men—two unconscious and two dead—in our living room.

The hug lasted a millisecond. She turned behind me, grabbing the gun of the man she had knocked unconscious. I did the same for the man whose skull I had pulverized.

The gun was warm. Slick with sweat.

Then we were outside. In the distance from on top of our hill, I could see it, and I knew I'd hear it soon. Sirens were racing their way to our home. The second time in barely a month that they had visited Wellington Road for a call of shots fired. The second time involving Mack.

Mack was on the ground. Mom was on him, and I saw her face, the mixed look of concentration and steel and tightness.

Her hands were pressed on Mack's chest, just below where his arm connected to the rest of his body. In the bloody light of the night, I could see the blood oozing out from my mom's hands.

Loss fired through me. "No." I bellowed. "No, no, no, no, no, no—" I was racing to Mack, the weapons from the attacker dropped on the lawn, disappearing into the grass. Paige stepped behind.

"It's all right, it's all right," Mack gurgled weakly. His eyes were swimming, but he focused on me. "You're all right," he exclaimed. Then he coughed wetly.

"Shut up, Mack, please shut up," Mom said, her face clenching as she spoke through tears. "Shut up or Jill will kill me."

Mack smiled weakly and let his head rest. He looked grateful for the excuse not to talk.

Paige was now weeping. Loudly. I joined her.

There was no joy in this moment. There was no sensation of a victory won. There was only blood and death and fire, and a world that threatened to consume us all.

The police cars pulled up moments later. An ambulance followed shortly after that. More men with guns entered my house. Eventually, the ambulance packed Mack up, hooking him to all sorts of monitors. A cop put my mom in one car and Paige and me in a second. They drove us all to the hospital, a wailing caravan of survivors, the darkness broken by the sirens and headlights.

Chapter 19

E FOUND OUT later, after questioning by the police, that Mack had never gone far from our house. He had patrolled that night but was never more than five minutes away. Jill, through silent tears, told us that Mack had a gut feeling that The Refuge wasn't just after our school or our way of life, but they were after Paige and me. When Paige had sent the text, it hadn't taken him more than a few moments to get there. The only reason he had even hesitated in opening fire was because he wanted to make sure he wouldn't accidentally hit us.

Mack hadn't been hit one time. He'd been hit three. He still kept firing, and that had given me the time I needed to brain the one attacker. Who had lived, incidentally. He was being treated in the Emergency Room, two floors below the room that Mack was staying in.

I was relieved at that. There were already too many things on my conscience. I didn't want a murder—however justified it may have been.

The entrance and exit wounds had been clean, the police said. Mack would need time to recover. But he would recover.

He'd saved me. In my home. Again.

Paige had waited until the sun came up to call her parents. I was in the room when she explained to them what had happened. "Yes, Mom— yes, guns. Yes. We're okay. Yes. Second time."

Her parents were going to love me.

Eventually, the adrenaline faded. The tears passed. The cops packed up their clipboards and notes. Mom, Paige, and I collapsed in a nearly empty waiting room, leaning on each other like a pile of abandoned puppies. When Jill woke us, she was wearing her nurse's scrubs, carrying a tray of coffee and the slightest of smiles was on her face.

When I realized who was in front of us, I straightened so abruptly that I managed to bop Paige's jaw into her upper teeth. She woke with a start and a groan, blinking.

Mom, thankfully, woke clearer-headed than I was. "How is he?"

"He's okay," Jill handed us each coffee. "The bullet passed above his chest and didn't hit anything important on its way out. You may as well have thought he was shot in the head."

I exhaled. Paige, meanwhile, was slowly blinking. "Your husband was just shot."

"He was."

"But you are serving us coffee," Paige said, emphasizing the word "coffee" as if she had never said it before.

"You saved him." The gentlest smile was on Jill's face, and there was a light in her eyes that seemed unobstructed by pain. She looked at my mom. "Thanks for making sure he didn't lose too much blood."

"After he saved us," I gasped. *Again*, I didn't say. *He saved us again.*

"Mack has loved you since he first laid eyes on you." Jill looked at me, and for just a moment, her facade broke. I had been at this woman's house countless times. Been babysat by her since I was a kid. I still remembered playing Mario Kart with her, laughing at her befuddlement on the Rainbow Road, stuffing as many chocolate cookies into my mouth as I could fit. She was the grandmother I had never had. Mack was the father I'd always needed. And he'd almost died for me. Again.

I think Jill saw all those moments and memories too. And I think that explained why her normally stoic and kind face faltered, even if it was only just for a moment. "He did nothing more than any father would do for their son."

That did it. I was done. The tears fell like rain and there was just no way of stopping them.

«O»

An hour later, Jill had convinced the supervising doctor that Mack was in fine shape for visitors. Paige wrapped herself around my arm and Mom walked in front of us.

"You okay?" I asked as we walked.

She nodded. "As much as I can be. With all of the bullets."

A horrifying thought flashed through me. "Is this… my fault?" I asked. Left unasked were the second and third questions. *If it is, what did I do wrong? And what does that mean for us?*

"No," Paige said. "I don't think it would have been your fault before Perses. It sure isn't now. The evil in this world isn't the fault of the good who try to fight it." Her grip on my arm tightened, mercifully.

My head was spinning. I think the lack of sleep and adrenaline storms my body had weathered were starting to catch up with me. We walked through a hallway now, one loaded with medical machinery, the scent of disinfectant, and the sounds of slow beeps and whispered conversations. "So… we're okay?"

"It was never a question," Paige said. There was no hesitation in her voice. No room for doubt or confusion. Just conviction.

For a moment, I put my head on her shoulder. She leaned her head on mine. We walked on.

Mack was in a green hospital gown and his skin was a shade or two paler than I was used to. His salt-and-pepper hair looked greyer, and the area just below his right shoulder was wrapped in a thick, exposed bandage. An IV was pressed into his arm, pricking his skin uncomfortably. A slew of beeping machines and wires told me that the doctors were worried about him, but the half-smile on his face told me I didn't have to be.

"Mack," I croaked. I almost made a move toward him, but Jill had been clear. No touching. Instead, I stood next to his bed, stock still, with Paige's grip on my arm tightening in lieu of her speaking.

"I'll leave you be. Hit the button if you need me, Mack," Jill said, shutting the door behind us.

"Old broad. She's got patients, if you can believe that." Mack's lips were so dry.

Mom pulled forward. "Are you… are you in pain?"

"I was shot," Mack said dryly, and yeah, we laughed, almost in spite of ourselves.

"You were. You were shot," I said, wiping my eyes.

"Little Man. You did good."

I laughed awkwardly. "Thanks, Bigger Man."

"I prefer Holy Man," Mack said. When I cocked my head in confusion, Mack used his good hand to point at his new bullet wounds.

We groaned. "Oh, oh dear God, you're making Dad jokes," I said.

"That might be all the pain killers they are pumping into me," Mack said. "But yes. I'm okay. At least, I will be. May not be operational for some time now." Mack looked at Paige and me. "I hear you got the last two."

"We did," I said. I used my head to gesture at Paige. "She has a sharp elbow."

Paige used her free hand and mimicked driving her elbow into the ground. "I do. It's true." She cracked her knuckles. "I'd be very happy if I never had to use it again."

"Good plan," Mack murmured. His eyes were only half-open.

"You gonna be okay?" I blurted. The words were out of my mouth before I had a chance to filter them.

Mack's eyes opened ever so slightly. "Sure, Little Man," he said. Then, using his good hand, he waved toward himself, IV wire flopping. "Come here."

I did, approaching Mack on his right side. Mack shook his head. "No. The side that wasn't shot."

"Oh. Yeah." I abruptly stopped and moved to the other side of the bed, kneeling down to be close to Mack. He smelled sour, like he had spent the night sleeping in clothing that he had sweated through. There was an added tang to his skin, and it took me a moment to place it—gunpowder.

Mack wrapped a sulfur-scented arm around me, pulling me closer with surprising strength. "Little Man."

"Still here, Bigger Man." The tears were starting to well up again. "I'm glad you are too."

"I am," Mack said. "Three of the most violent experiences in my career as a law enforcement officer, and they all involved you."

I laughed bitterly. "I swear, Mack, I don't go looking for it."

"I know you don't," Mack said. "I know, Little Man. That first time was the fault of that guy who didn't deserve to be your dad. The second time was because of another monster, and you helped save one of his victims. The third time…." Mack's voice trailed off.

"I invited that one," I said, realizing how ridiculous the words sounded as soon as they left my mouth.

"No, Little Man. No." Mack's grip tightened around my shoulders. His eyes were wide open now, and they were blazing. "Would you like to hear a lesson from a wounded man?"

"It'd be kind of a dick move if I said no," I quipped, and Mack laughed.

"Little Man. Listen close to this one. Leadership requires sacrifice. It doesn't usually mean you get shot. But it does mean you may give up things you love."

I looked over at Paige and my mom. Mack followed my eyes. "It also means you find new loves. Didn't you meet Paige when she was yelling at the one Refuge girl?"

"Yeah," I said. "In a sick sort of way, The Refuge brought us together."

"It did," Mack agreed. "Trauma clears the decks of debris, Little Man. You'd be wise to remember that."

"Like Sid?" I asked, softly.

"Sid is lost," Mack said. "Most of them are just lost. Maybe you can help find them again. There are opportunities and pain in your future, Little Man. You're not that boy in the closet anymore. You're not the scared kid nursing a head wound. You're the one with the baseball bat. Take your swing."

I considered what Mack said and allowed the words to sink into my brain like a sponge. At some point, I thought they'd make sense.

For now, I put my head on Mack's chest. Breathed in a scent I had come to associate with safety and home, now tinged with gun powder and rubbing alcohol.

Mack stroked the back of my head. I waited for the tears, but they never came. There was nothing left.

«O»

Jill discreetly sneaked into the room sometime later, kissing Mack on the head and telling us we should get home. It was only after we said goodbye to Mack and left his room that Jill said, "There's actually someone here to see you," looking at Paige and me.

We glanced at each other, then, almost in unison, looked down. I was in a smelly Augustus hoodie and a thin pair of sweatpants, my comfy clothing from the night before. The hoodie had a fresh wine stain on it, and I kept having to pull my sweatpants up, the elastic band on the waist had snapped during the gunfight. Paige was dressed in gym pants and an oversized long-sleeved shirt. She looked slightly better than I did, but her matted hair and blood-shot eyes created the impression that she had just finished a yoga class while hungover.

"Do we have to?" I asked.

Jill's gentle smile was back. "I think you'll want to."

She led us down a maze of corridors, then up a flight of stairs. When we emerged, the smell of disinfectant was gone, replaced by that of wood polish. We were in the hospital's administration wing.

Mom, Paige, and I exchanged glances, but Mom shrugged. "I've listened to this woman's advice for years. I'm not gonna question her now."

"Fair enough," I said.

We arrived at a conference room door, once covered by frosted glass. "Here you go," Jill said, opening the door.

The first face I saw was Dean Sumner.

"Dean?" I almost choked on my words. It was simultaneously incredibly jarring and heartening to see him here. I walked up to him, unsure of whether or not to shake his hand or hug him, and awkwardly stopped a few feet from him.

Thankfully, he shook my hand, then Paige's an instant later. "It is wonderful to see you both, and I am so glad you are all right."

"I don't know about all right," Mom said.

"But we aren't shot," I added quickly.

"Yes. No bullet wounds," Paige mimed running her hands over her body.

"Always a plus," the Dean said mildly.

Then I realized that there were two men behind him.

The first was wearing the most meticulous outfit I'd ever seen. He was wearing a suit that was so sharp I think it would have cut my skin if I touched it. It was bright black, with grey pinstripes, a crisp white shirt, and a black and white tie. His grey-white hair was slicked to perfection, and I wondered absently what he used to keep each strand in place. The man's face was weathered, and when he spoke, his voice was hoarse.

"Corey Walker," the man said, extending a hand. I wearily shook it. "Florence Fabrizio. Call me Flo."

The name triggered a mousetrap in my mind. "I know you."

"You should," said the man next to Flo. He also extended his hand, and Paige and I shook it in turn. He was the polar opposite of Flo— short, close-cropped hair, and a red shirt, covered by a gray suit. "Brian Kavulich. I'm with the Federal Government."

My heart caught in my throat, and it must have shown on my face because Kavulich said, "Relax, Mister Walker. You are not in any trouble."

"Unless you have something you want to tell us," chimed Flo, a sparkle in his eye.

"Which branch of the federal government are you with?" asked Paige.

Kavulich smiled. "We'll get there. Trust me. We're here to help."

An awkward pause, until Dean Sumner said, "Florence runs F.F. Construction. He's also an Augustus alumnus, class of 1970."

"Dean, please don't tell anyone how old I am," said Flo with a chuckle.

Then it clicked. The logo was everywhere in my region. It was also on every construction project at Augustus.

"You're... you're that super-rich guy... wait, holy hell. Our dorm. You're the guy our dorm is named after," said Paige.

"That's me," said Flo, beaming. "Do they even bother trying to say my name when they go into the dorm?"

"God, no," I said. Sumner blanched, but Flo laughed.

"Well, good. I'm glad I could spend my money in places where it counts," ribbed Flo, looking at Sumner and laughing harder at his discomfort. "Relax, Gordon. The checks are still coming."

"I get why you're here," I said, looking at Sumner. Then I looked at Flo. "I... I don't get why you're here." Then the government guy with the bright red shirt. "And I have absolutely no idea why you're here."

"Remember that conversation we were starting to have in my office, a few days ago?"

"Before the first shooting?"

"That's the one." Sumner looked at Flo and Kavulich. "The federal government has an interesting concept for a way to push back against The Refuge and some of the other groups that have popped up since Perses."

"It will take extensive assistance from the very highest levels of the government," said Kavulich.

And there was a smile on his face. A smile that could only be born of confidence. So, I asked, again, "Where in the federal government are you from?"

Smile growing, Kavulich said, "The Executive Branch."

Before that statement could sink in, Flo said, "It will also take extensive community support. That's where I come in."

"That's where—"

"Yes. Me. Son, I was in college when Vietnam was accelerating. Drugs consumed everything and everyone in sight. Don't get me wrong, I enjoyed a good time as much as the next guy—don't tell Mister Executive Branch over here—but there's a time and place for everything. I know what happens when you lose a generation. When every minority group on the planet has a real, legitimate reason to say that they are being ignored and passed over. When all of society arrays against you. I will not let that happen again. Not on my watch."

Paige and I looked at each other in disbelief. "What's our role in all this?" Paige asked.

Now, it was Dean Sumner's turn to smile. "That's the best part."

Chapter 20

THE CAMPUS DID feel different.

For one thing, Sumner and the rest of the administration had clearly learned from their past mistakes. When we came back after Perses, the campus looked neglected. Now? Immaculate. Like it did before an admissions event or parent's weekend. The grass was cut. The trees in the arboretum were in full bloom, firing a rainbow of color into the sky. The buildings were sparkling and spotless, glistening in the sun.

The stained-glass that The Refuge members had shot out had been replaced by ordinary glass. It was temporary, they said.

When I keyed into my dorm, there were fliers. The first was announcing the various ways to call, text, or message campus police, which had recently been augmented by a fresh wave of newly unretired police officers. Rich Augustus donors—led by Flo—had opened their wallets.

The second flier announced the extended hours of the Augustus Counseling Center. They, too, had found a way to expand, and they promised telehealth for students who couldn't get an in-person appointment.

The third flier announced the new and improved Augustus app, complete with mandatory check-ins, and security cameras installed in the dorm hallways. It was a not-so-subtle way of telling us that the party was over.

I sighed. There went sleepovers with Paige.

Speaking of. Paige had flown back home a few days after the attack. I was in a blind panic that she'd fly back to California and I'd never hear from her again—or that her parents would keep her from returning to school—but every worry had been assuaged when I got a selfie of her from the airport, smiling in the bright California sun.

We talked every night. And we kissed deeply when we got together again.

Mo and Mika greeted Paige and me later that day with a mattress. Yes, an actual mattress. I opened my door, and they somehow squeezed in a mattress and rammed me with it. While I was still stumbled, Mo had screamed, "Mattress party tonight."

With a joyful smile, Mika added, "BYOM."

"Does that mean Bring Your Own Mattress?" Paige had asked cautiously.

"BYOM." Mo screamed, smashing me once more with the mattress before running out of the room, mattress in front of him, screaming "Mattress party. Tonight. Fourth Floor. Bring your own mattress!"

I think I laughed for about five straight minutes.

It was nice to have a distraction. Mack was discharged from the hospital a few days after the shooting. I was there, and the pain was engraved on his face. He spent the first few days out of the hospital in a drug-induced haze, barely able to function thanks to the painkillers he was on. Jill told me that he had tried doing some rehabilitation exercises but had screamed in pain the first time he did so. Apparently, she had called him a wuss, and it went better the second time around.

I felt no guilt. Not anymore. This was The Refuge's fault.

Of course, The Refuge had been responsible for the attack on our house. The two men who had lived through the attack admitted they were Refuge members, but said they were acting on their own. It was a statement as believable as tissue paper was thick.

At least one good thing had come from the attack. Per an edict from Augustus, no Refuge member would be allowed on campus.

"Good luck enforcing that one," Paige said, staring at a flier that was on one of the bulletin boards outside of the Student Union.

"Yeah, that might be tough," I agreed.

We linked fingers and turned down Academic Row. That was when we saw it for the first time. Big, white, blocky letters, awkwardly filled in by someone who clearly didn't have any artistic skill. A message in all caps.

THE WORLD IS OUR REFUGE

I craned my neck and looked farther down Academic Row. I couldn't read much in the way of text, but there was no question about it—there was a series of chalky, white text, extending as far as I could see.

I smiled and squeezed Paige's hand. "Nice job with that one."

"I'm glad people are listening."

We were silent for a moment, staring at the various messages in white. They were in different handwriting, with different additional messages written in—"Can we play soccer yet?" was my favorite—but there was no doubt. People wanted something to believe in.

There was one message about theatre that had been blotted out in black paint. The paint was sloppy—it had been sloshed from a bucket—but it was there. Paige and I each found it at the same time, and our eyes found each other.

Speaking of. "Did you get your assignment?"

Paige grimaced. "I did. It's gonna be a hard one. Mountain Top."

I moaned. Mountain Top had lost so many in the Left Behind shootings. Eleven? Twelve? They'd been the hardest hit. "My ride gets here at four. They have me going to a school in the middle of the state. Crimson Hill Boarding School, I think? It's a small school and they've got a couple of Refuge-like groups fighting it out there."

"Ouch," Paige said. "Rural area, right?"

"Yep."

Paige was nodding. "I got one next week and was reading through some of the briefing packet. Rural areas are just getting nuked by mental health stuff."

I nodded. "It's why all these cults are having success there. These guys are having more success picking off areas that are economically depressed."

Paige snorted. "Psychologically depressed too."

The offer from Sumner had been a mind-blowing one. Spend the semester on virtual school, with our tuition *completely* covered. Join a national effort, funded by private donors like Flo and with the formal backing and support of the federal government. We'd be part of a massive communications push to remind people that the world wasn't over, that there was hope in the darkness, and that these cults were absolutely evil. Paige and I would speak about The Refuge and what they had taken from us, what they had done to our school. Augustus's struggles were national now, and the failed effort to kill us had unwittingly made us international celebrities.

Paige and I had looked at each other and said, "No," at the same time.

"Maybe later," I had said. "For now, I kind of want to make sure Augustus is okay."

So, we'd agreed. We'd stay at Augustus for the semester, taking a reduced course load and traveling the region, in addition to working with others at Augustus to make sure that The Refuge didn't make a reappearance. "We can make that work," Kavulich had said. "It's not like there is a shortage of kids who have been impacted by these cults."

We'd all decided to revisit the agreement at the end of the semester and see what we'd do about college.

Our parents had to agree, of course. Thankfully, they'd both said yes, but each had independently made the same demand. It had been happily acquiesced to by Flo—two thick men, one for each of us, wearing polo shirts and sunglasses, with a bulge in their hips that concealed their guns.

Yes, we had armed security now. I was sure we would be fun at parties.

It was necessary. No one had been dumb enough to threaten us, but I'm pretty sure I caught my share of ugly looks when we got back onto campus. To my pleasant surprise, ninety percent of the school had actually come back after the two-week break, and a few who had previously dropped out reenrolled, understanding that they'd have a hell of a lot of catch-up work to do. And yeah, The Refuge was formally banned on campus, but no one thought they'd stopped operating.

There was all sorts of talk on social media. The Refuge was still operating in the shadows, they had fake Instagram profiles and TikTok accounts, they were being funded by the Russians, all that stuff. Some of the rumors that Mo and Mika told us were too outlandish to believe. But the idea that The Refuge was still operating on this campus, still recruiting students, still using the site of their martyrs for propaganda purposes... that, I could absolutely believe.

The Refuge was a virus. I wasn't sure you ever really killed a virus.

And it was a virus that had taken so much from me. Sid was not coming back to campus—Clara in the Dean's office had been kind enough to tell me. Another casualty of The Refuge.

So many of us were still here. And so help me God, I didn't want anyone else to suffer as I had.

Like he had.

Paige squeezed my hand and brought me back to reality. "I wonder what having a normal senior year is like," she whispered. Her voice was buttery soft, originating in a faraway place.

I stopped and brushed a strand of silky red hair away from her face. Her eyes showed doubt and confusion, a rarity from a girl who acted so tough you thought she knew it all. "Who wants to be normal?" My words brought me back to Mack, that day in the hospital. "What we are going to do is important."

That seemed to buck Paige up. "It is," she said solemnly. She leaned up and kissed me on the lips.

Mack had been right. Leadership required sacrifice. I didn't want this. At all. But the moment had called me. Called Paige. And we had a duty to answer it.

Paige and I clasped hands again and walked back to our dorm.

Author's Note

In moments of chaos and turmoil, all of us have different ways of coping. Some find help and healing in productive ways, using tragedy and stress to better themselves and those around you. Others struggle and suffer, turning to alcohol, drugs, or withdrawing from the world.

Almost the End of the World is obviously meant, in part, to warn you against the dangers of cults. But it's more meant to serve as a warning flare against cultic thinking. All I can ask as you read this book is that you keep that in mind.

About the Author

Mike Schlossberg has been a writer since he wrote his first short story in eighth grade, a Star Wars fanfiction. While he claims it was terrible, the creative passion followed him into adulthood.

Serving as a State Representative in Pennsylvania, Mike has had the chance to make a difference. The problem closest to his heart is mental health, where he strives to break the stigma surrounding those who suffer from mental illnesses and give them hope. For Mike, this issue is personal, as he has been treated for depression and anxiety related disorders since he was 18. It was this desire to help which drove him to write Redemption, his first novel, but not his first book. That honor goes to Tweets and Consequences, an anthology about the varied ways elected officials have destroyed their careers via social media.

When not writing, Mike plays way too many video games (both modern and old school), watches anything related to the Muppets (specifically Fraggle Rock!), reads, attempts to get to the gym, and calls his constituents on their birthdays.

Mike lives in South Whitehall, Pennsylvania. He is extremely happily married to his wife Brenna. They have two wonderful children: Auron, born in 2011, and Ayla, born in 2012. Bonus points if you know what video game the kids' names came from.